Sherlock Holmes Never Dies
Collection Seven

Four New Sherlock Holmes Mysteries

Note to Readers:

Your enjoyment of these new Sherlock Holmes mysteries will be enhanced by re-reading the original stories that inspired these new ones –

The Adventure of the Final Problem,
The Adventure of the Empty House,
The Adventure of Charles Augustus Milverton,
The Adventure of the Norwood Builder.

They are available from several sources online for free.

Sherlock Holmes Never Dies

New Sherlock Holmes Mysteries

Collection Seven

The Binomial Asteroid Problem
The Mystery of 222 Baker Street
The Adventure of Charlotte Europa Golderton
The Adventure of the Norwood Rembrandt

Craig Stephen Copland

Copyright © 2018 by Craig Stephen Copland

All rights reserved. No part of this book may be reproduced or transmitted in any form or by any means, electronic or mechanical, including photocopying, recording, or by an information storage and retrieval system – except by a reviewer who may quote brief passages in a review to be printed in a magazine, newspaper, or on the web – without permission in writing from Craig Stephen Copland.

The characters of Sherlock Holmes and Dr. Watson are no longer under copyright, nor is the original stories: *The Adventure of the Final Problem, The Adventure of the Empty House, The Adventure of Charles Augustus Milverton, and The Adventure of the Norwood Builder.*

Published by:

Conservative Growth Inc.

5072 Turtle Pond Place,

Vernon, British, Columbia, V1T 9Y5

Cover design by Rita Toews

ISBN-10: 1720765383

ISBN-13: 978-1720765387

Dedication

To those friends and family who love me and encourage me to continue my quixotic quest of writing sixty new Sherlock Holmes mysteries. Thank you..

Contents

The Binomial Asteroid Problem 1

The Mystery of 222 Baker Street 127

The Adventure of Charlotte Europa Golderton 243

The Adventure of the Norwood Rembrandt 411

About the Author 545

More Historical Mysteries 547

Note to Sherlockians

These four novellas are *pastiche* stories of Sherlock Holmes. The characters of Sherlock Holmes and Dr. Watson are modeled on the characters that we have come to love in the original sixty Sherlock Holmes stories by Sir Arthur Conan Doyle.

The settings in the late Victorian and Edwardian eras are also maintained. Each new mystery is inspired by one of the stories in the original sacred canon. The characters and some of the introductions are respectfully borrowed, and then a new mystery develops.

If you have never read the original story that served as the inspiration of the new one—or if you have but it was a long time ago—then you are encouraged to do so before reading the new story in this book. Your enjoyment of the new mystery will be enhanced.

Some new characters are introduced and the female characters have a significantly stronger role than they did in the original stories. I hope that I have not offended any of my fellow Sherlockians by doing so but, after all, a hundred years have passed and some things have changed.

The historical events that are connected to these new stories are, for the most part, accurately described and dated. Your comments, suggestions, and corrections are welcomed on all aspects of the stories.

I am deeply indebted to The Bootmakers of Toronto (the Sherlock Holmes Society of Canada) not only for their dedication to the adventures of Sherlock Holmes but also to their holding of a contest for the writing of a new Sherlock Holmes mystery. My winning entry into that contest led to the joy of continuing to write more Sherlock Holmes mysteries.

Over the next few years, it is my intention to write a new mystery inspired by each one of the sixty original stories. They will appear in the same chronological order as the original canon appeared in the pages of *The Strand*. Should you wish to subscribe to these new stories and receive them in digital form as they are released, please visit www.SherlockHolmesMystery.com and sign up.

Wishing joyful reading and re-reading to all faithful Sherlockians.

Respecfully,

CSC

The Binomial Asteroid Problem

A New Sherlock Holmes Mystery

Chapter One
Gladstone Is Missing

IT HAS NOW BEEN TEN YEARS since Sherlock Holmes vanquished Professor Moriarty, but even today my hand trembles as I write the name of the most brilliant and most evil of the enemies of my dear friend.

In the years I have known Holmes and worked alongside him, I have seen him face down many dangerous men. Some of them were exceptionally treacherous and ruthless and committed vile deeds beyond the most horrifying of human thought.

Yet one stands out: Moriarty.

He does so not because the crimes committed under his aegis were any more horrendous than those of other criminals but because he had given over his brilliant mind and organizational skills to the ultimate vice of humankind, the criminally ruthless pursuit of power. He was not an insane madman, nor a demented creature who merely took pleasure in inflicting pain and suffering. No, he was the master of using terror and fear as weapons to force the submission of any and all who crossed his evil path if in doing so he could increase the breadth and depth of his authority and control.

By the time Sherlock Holmes, at risk to his own life, destroyed Moriarty and his web of criminal agents, the tentacles of his odious realm pervaded London, crisscrossed all of Great Britain, extended across the Continent and even reached over the great oceans of the world.

I put an account to paper of the mortal struggle between Holmes and Moriarty in the story to which I gave the title *The Final Problem*. At the time I wrote it, I believed that Sherlock Holmes had indeed sacrificed his life on 4 May 1891 at Reichenbach Falls. That story first introduced the world to the mysterious and malevolent professor and recorded the *final* days in the battle between his criminal organization and the forces of justice. What I have not previously disclosed are the events that took place in the *first* days of Holmes's encounters with Moriarty, those initial investigations when the professor was still an unknown entity, shrouded and protected behind layers of minions.

I have refrained from doing so not because the events themselves were lacking in interest — indeed, they were both intriguing and tragic — but because we were assisted by several courageous young people whose roles, had they been exposed, might have imperiled their lives and those of their friends and families. Even after the demise of Moriarty, the remnants of his empire, the scions of Colonel Moran, still lurked in the *demi-monde* of London. Now, however, a full decade after that day at the awesome Swiss cataract, and seven years after the return of Sherlock Holmes from his wanderings, it is safe to do so. Holmes has assured me that any of those dear people who might have been put in danger are now far beyond the reach of Moriarty's ghostly revenge.

This account, which I have called *The Binomial Asteroid Problem* (for reasons that will eventually become clear to the reader), began in a most inauspicious manner. The case as first presented to Holmes seemed almost trivial in comparison to the matters of national and international importance in which he had been recently involved. I confess to having been initially amazed that he agreed to take it on instead of referring our lovely young client to the local bobby on the street corner.

It was on a Friday afternoon in the latter part of June, in the year 1890. My dear wife was visiting with friends in the West, and I had accepted Holmes's invitation to stay with him. We were sitting in the front room of Baker Street enjoying a late afternoon tea and chat about the news of the day. The Press were still oooing an ahhing about the magnificent bridge across the Firth of Forth in Scotland. Great Britain was at loggerheads with both Portugal and Germany over who was to have colonial control over certain parts of Africa. And, to the horror of many English sportsmen, myself included, a new park was about to open in Derby so the most un-English of games could be played ... baseball.

Our meandering banter was interrupted by Mrs. Hudson.

"There is a young lady to see you, Mr. Holmes. She admits that she does not have an appointment and, by her accent, I would say that she is a foreigner. Shall I send her away? Or, if you wish, I can take her name and give her a time to return."

Mrs. Hudson handed Holmes a card. He gave it a cursory glance and then cocked his head and smiled ever so slightly before handing it over to me. It read:

Patricia Carla Rojas

Profesora

Instituto Español de St. Ignatius

Milford Lane, London

"My dear Mrs. Hudson," he said. "Please show the lady in."

"Goodness, Holmes," I said. "You surprise me. She walks in off the pavement so late in the afternoon, and you agree to see her? Are you becoming a sensitive creature as the years go by?"

He smiled. "Not at all Watson. You know perfectly well how I abhor the dull routine of existence and whatever this woman might have to say cannot possibly be more banal than listening to you prattle on about sporting activities and, in particular, American baseball."

I did not have time to be offended before Mrs. Hudson announced our visitor.

"Mrs. Patricia Rojas."

We rose to greet the lady. She was an attractive raven-haired young woman, slender, petite, well-gloved, and dressed in excellent taste. Her skin had just a faint tint of the olive color that is characteristic of those people from Mediterranean climes. I would have put her age in her early thirties. With a firm step and an outward composure of manner, she walked across the room and greeted Holmes.

"Señor Holmes, I trust that you are well. I pray that you will excuse my unscheduled visit. I know about you from the stories in the *Strand* and I admire you greatly. *Gracias.* I thank you for agreeing to see me. I am in need of your help."

"It is a pleasure," said Holmes. "You are, I believe, the wife of Dr. Rojas, the Bolivarian scholar at the University of London, are you not? And the happy mother of a fine young ten-year-old boy, or is he eleven by now? When you married and had a child, you interrupted your own academic research, did you not? Otherwise, you would now also be Dr. Rojas, but you do not appear to be saddened by the loss of that opportunity."

For a moment, the lovely woman looked quite surprised and then burst into a loud peal of laughter.

"Oh, Señor Holmes," she sputtered between chuckles, "I cannot say that I was not warned about coming to see you."

"Warned?" asked Holmes, obviously not expecting that response. "And just who might have warned you about me?"

"I told Señor Diego Alvarez, the registrar of the *instituto*, that I would ask for your help and he cautioned that the private matters of my life would soon become exposed to London's most famous detective. And the inspector at Scotland Yard, Señor Lestrado, told me the same thing, but he sent me here all the same because he said that you were harmless and just liked to show off."

Now it was my turn to laugh. The lady joined me. Holmes did not.

"He also said," she continued, "that you would then require an opportunity to explain to we who are *menor* mortals how it was you discerned what you did. So, *por favor*, Señor Holmes, do explain."

Her entire face was sparkling with humor as she teased Holmes and I could not resist joining in.

"Yes, Holmes," I added, laughing, "do explain. You know you are dying to."

Holmes harrumphed, but there is nothing so difficult to resist as the good humor and laughter of those around you and, with an uncharacteristic look of chagrin, he gestured that we should be seated, leaned back in his chair and smiled.

"Ah, where to begin?" he said. "That you are married was indicated by the ring on your hand. That you are the mother of a son by the smudge of breakfast cereal on the shoulder on an otherwise perfectly white blouse. The height indicated that it had been affectionately left by a child of about ten years of age. Given your short stature, he might be eleven, but he most certainly enjoys warm, loving feelings toward you. Daughters, by that age, have become somewhat more refined and remember to wipe their faces before embracing their mothers. Boys do not.

"Your position at an institute of education would not be possible were you not yourself highly educated, a fact that is further indicated by your excellent command of the English language. It is common knowledge that while men are intimidated by women who are more highly educated than themselves, and almost always prefer the company of and to marry those who are less so, women have no such fears and are generally quite happy to find a man who is their intellectual equal. Thus, it can be deduced that your husband has at least your level of academic qualifications and, given your marriage and motherhood, it would be expected that you and he met whilst you were both studying but that you interrupted your studies for family reasons, allowing him to continue and be awarded a doctoral degree. You live and work in London and not in either of our university towns, so the only appropriate place for a highly learned man, your husband, Dr. Rojas, to continue his work is the University of London.

"It is also common knowledge, that by the time anyone, man or woman, reaches the age of thirty he or she has begun to acquire the face he or she deserves. Yours is already showing those tiny creases that come with a habit of smiling and laughing, an unmistakable sign of a woman who is enjoying her lot in life. I might also add that you are quite likely a native of Columbia in South America. Your family name is a common one there and, whilst I do not have a command of the Spanish tongue, it is not difficult to distinguish a Castilian accent from one coming from the northern portion of the southern continent. The only thing that remains a mystery is the reason for your coming to see me. You do not appear to be in any great distress over matters of the heart, or financial concerns, or threats to yourself or your family."

Here he stopped and smiled, looking somewhat pleased with himself.

"That concludes my explanation," Holmes said. "Now, then, Señora Rojas, please state your case. Whilst it does not appear to have serious consequences, I might find it amusing."

She was still smiling happily as she stifled her laughter and assumed a composed posture.

"I fear, Señor Holmes, that my *problema* which, to me, is very large, will to you be found to be inconsequential and not worthy of your time."

"I cannot judge," said Holmes, "until you tell me what your *problema* is. Pray, get on with it."

"My *maleta* ... how do you call it? My valise, my *Gladstone* has gone missing. For me, this is a tragedy."

"Gladstone is missing?" said Holmes. "Oh, dear, well that is a tragedy. But if I were to paraphrase our former Prime Minister, Disraeli, if Gladstone were to go missing, it would be a tragedy. If he were to be found, it would be a disaster."

Señora Rojas did not appear to have any idea whatsoever about what Holmes was alluding to.

He gave her a condescending smile and continued. "By a 'Gladstone' you are describing your missing valise, not our recently deceased former Prime Minister. Pray, explain. A valise itself has little value. Was your Gladstone full of Columbian gold? Peruvian emeralds? Silver from *Cirro Rico*? Priceless artifacts, perhaps shrunken heads from the jungles of the Amazon? What was *in* it?"

She blushed ever so slightly and gazed briefly at the floor before responding. "Nothing like those at all. For the past eight years, I have worked at our *instituto* helping students from all walks of life learn to speak *Español*. For eight years, I have tried to be as diligent as I can be and have put together many teaching materials for use in my classes. These objects, games, posters and such are a wonderful aid in helping *mi chicos* learn our language. For eight years, I have continued to revise and improve these materials. I keep them in a large Gladstone bag to which I had attached a small set of wheels so that I may trundle it behind me as I go from class to class. These materials have no commercial value but *a mi* they are invaluable, priceless. They disappeared out of my small office at the instituto. When I entered my office this morning, the case was gone. Someone had taken it. I searched all over the building, but it was not to be found. I asked all my colleagues, but no one had seen it. I reported the theft to Scotland Yard, but they told me that they were too busy solving crimes of murder, of banks that were robbed, of anarchists setting off dynamite and the like."

"Or perhaps," interrupted Holmes, "with *not* solving them. Pray, continue."

"One of them, Inspector Lestrado, told me to come to you. I think he thought it would be a joke to play on you. But I assure you, Señor Holmes, to me, it is no joke. To me, it is a terrible loss. There was no reason to steal it. It is useless, completely unimportant to anyone else. But to me, it is not trivial. I assure you, it is of great importance to my teaching, to my livelihood."

Holmes sat quietly for a moment, looking at our visitor with a surprisingly sympathetic and concerned gaze.

"Madam, I assure you, there is nothing trivial in matters of crime. Will you permit me to ask some questions? I will have to be blunt, and you will have to be forthcoming in your answers."

"*Por favor*, Señor Holmes, proceed. I have nothing to hide, and if there is anything you can do to help me, I will be very grateful."

"Excellent. Very well then, has there been any recent animosity between you and any of your fellow professors?"

"Oh, no. None at all. *Más* the opposite. As with any group in a city who are exiles from their home countries and language, we band together and try to take care of each other. We enjoy a glass at the local pub after our working day is over. Our families meet for social occasions. We help each other find gainful employment."

"And," asked Holmes, "are all of your colleagues content with their lot here in London?"

"*Si*, most of us. Some of those who have arrived here recently seem … *desanimado* … discouraged, but that is to be expected. All of us found it difficult at first, and I expect these newcomers will adjust. These things are to be expected."

"Ah, yes," agreed Holmes. "Indeed, they are. Now then, amongst your colleagues, has there been anything that led you to believe that one or more of them was not entirely trustworthy? Were you alone the victim of this theft? Or was anyone else robbed at the same time?"

"I cannot think of anyone who was not honest before God, not for a second. But no, I was not the only one who was robbed. My fellow *profesor*, Matias Moreno, was also robbed. His coat and cap were removed from a rack beside my office."

"Were they now?" said Holmes, now somewhat more curious. "And did he report the theft? Is Scotland Yard going to send him over here so that I can be asked to track down his valuable possessions as well?"

"I think not," she replied. "The thief, whoever he was, did not merely steal Matias's coat and cap. He left his own behind. On the rack where the coat had been hanging there was another one in its place."

"Was there now?" said Holmes. "And was the one taken of high quality and the one left cheap and worn? Perhaps your thief was merely upgrading his wardrobe."

"Señor, Holmes, that would have made sense to me as well. But the coat and hat left behind were of a much higher quality than the ones that were taken. Matias's coat was old and thin, and his hat a mere cap left over from his student days. The ones left in their place were much finer. The coat was a stylish, new summer overcoat. It did not appear to be more than a few weeks since it had been purchased."

Holmes carried on his questioning for several more minutes, asking about the building, the neighborhood, the administrative staff, and the clientele and then fell silent for a full minute.

"Profesora Rojas," he finally said, "I will accept your case. Kindly do not worry about a fee at this time. I will not require any payment unless I am successful in helping you. Now, I expect that you have a husband and son waiting for you, two young men who are both getting hungry. I will commence work on your case tomorrow morning and will report to you through your institute. Will that be acceptable, Señora Rojas?"

"Oh, *maravilloso. Muchas gracias,* Señor Holmes. That would be wonderful. And please, señor, please just address me as *Señora Patricia.* It is how I am known to my colleagues and students."

She pronounced her name in a typical Spanish fashion, with the sound of the second syllable like the word *fleece* rather than the English manner of having it resemble the sound in *fish.*

"I will do so from now on, Señora Patricia," said Holmes. "And allow me to bid you *hasta mañana.*"

Chapter Two
Gladstone Found in Chinatown

"GOOD HEAVENS, HOLMES," I said after his latest client had departed. "You never cease to amaze me. You have turned down cases involving hundreds, even thousands of pounds because you deemed them insignificant. And you take on this one? A used Gladstone bag, even one on a set of wheels, could not be worth more than a few shillings. And the contents are worthless to anyone trying to sell them amongst petty criminals."

He slowly took out his pipe, filled it, lit it, and took several puffs before responding.

"There are two aspects to this case which make it interesting. One, you merely failed to see. The second, in all fairness, you might not be aware of."

He took another slow puff and might have continued had I not interjected.

"You are baiting me, Holmes. Kindly cease to do so and just explain yourself."

"Must I? Oh, very well then. What you may not be aware of is that amongst all of the recent immigrants to London over the past decade, there have been thousands from Germany, as many again from France, and almost as many from Italy, Poland, and other European countries. There have been over one hundred thousand Jews. However, there are no more than five thousand native Spanish speakers in all of London, and that includes those coming from Spain as well as from the continent of South America, and Mexico combined."

"I fail to see your point, Holmes."

"Of course, you fail, Watson. You fail because you do not pay close attention to the details in the crime reports in the press, and you never even glance at the proceedings of the courts. Had you done so, you might have observed that over this past year, there has been a sharp rise in crimes reported in which the man, or sometimes the woman, who has been charged has a distinctly Spanish name."

"What of it?" I said, now feeling somewhat defensive. "Perhaps the Spaniards are merely catching up with the

Italians and the Russians. All sorts of those recent immigrants to England have a tendency to take things that do not belong to them."

"Do you truly think so, Watson?" asked Holmes. "Or does it not strike you as curious that one particular group should suddenly develop a penchant for crime out of all proportion to their population in this city?"

"That is curious, I suppose, if you say so," I answered. "Very well, then, what is the other aspect of her case that so intrigues you?"

"I suspect that the thief was an honest man who is now in great danger and possibly fearing for his life."

"Oh, come, come, Holmes. No one is going to kill a man just because he stole a suitcase and left his coat behind."

"You have it backward, my good doctor. A man who steals an object that has no value, and leaves an expensive coat behind in exchange for a cheap one, would only do so if he has an immediate need to disguise himself and so he grabs the first items he can lay his hands on that will conceal his identity. His recently purchased fine coat says that he is not likely fleeing his creditors. The valise on wheels was merely a prop to further his disguise. He grasped at it impulsively when he saw it sitting there. The police were not previously on his tail else they would have said so and not sent Señora Patricia away so discourteously. There is a man out there, trailing a Gladstone on wheels behind him, who appears to be running away in fear. Therefore, this evening I shall review my files and select all those recent items that deal with the intersection of Spaniards and crime, and tomorrow morning I shall go and find the poor fellow and see what it is that has panicked him."

"And return Gladstone to your client?" I asked.

"And return Gladstone, of course."

Throughout our supper hour and the entire evening, he was a miserable companion, doing nothing other than eating, smoking, and reading file after file. At half-past ten, having despaired of any opportunity for conversation, I went off to bed.

I rose early the following morning and was not surprised to find Holmes already at the table, sipping on his coffee and reading the morning paper.

"Good morning, Watson," he said cheerfully. "Do enjoy your breakfast. My apologies for not being able to join you but I will be departing straightaway on Señora Patricia's case. I trust you will have a good day."

I was about to reply with appropriate good wishes in return when, in my peripheral vision, I caught sight through our bay window of something taking place on the pavement of Baker Street below us.

"It appears," I said, "that your departure may be delayed. A police carriage has pulled up. And ... let me see ... yes, that looks like your good friend Inspector Lestrade getting out."

Holmes sighed. "No doubt he and Gregson and Jones are out of their depths again with some case that a schoolboy could solve ..."

"Oh, dear," I interrupted him. "This does not look good."

"What is it?" Holmes said and quickly stood up and stepped to the window.

Lestrade had come out of the police carriage but had then turned around and held out his hand to a second passenger, a woman, who was now stepping unsteadily down to the pavement. She held on to Lestrade's arm as he walked toward our door. Señora Patricia Rojas was returning to see us, this time accompanied by Scotland Yard.

Mrs. Hudson let them in and they slowly ascended the stairs to our room. There was a shocking change in Patricia. Her hair was unkempt, her clothes looked as if she had pulled them on in a rush, and her face was distraught. Mrs. Hudson immediately offered to bring her some hot tea, which I was sure she would enhance with a generous addition of brandy.

"Good morning, Mr. Holmes," said Lestrade in feigned good humor. "Thought you might like to know that Scotland Yard has done your work for you."

If Lestrade had been expecting a response, he was disappointed. Holmes said nothing and just continued to look at his client.

"Seems this good lady," continued Lestrade, "after dropping in to see us, took our advice and hired you yesterday to find her missing valise, so she tells us. Well, just thought you should know that we've gone and found it before you were even out of bed. Not that we official detectives collect any special fee or reward, seeing as we just have to go about doing our job every day, day in and day out."

"Inspector," said Holmes, "kindly get to the point. What is the meaning of this?"

"The meaning? You want to know the meaning? The meaning is that this lady asked you to find her case and we went and did it for you. Found it three hours ago over in Limehouse, near those blocks that the Press is calling Chinatown on account of all the coolies coming and going off the docks. That's where it was and, for that matter, that is where it still is. The case had the lady's name and address on it, so, being a diligent policeman, upon being told about it, I went straightaway and, apologizing for waking the poor lady up, told her to come with us and claim her valise. On the way, she says that she had hired Mr. Sherlock Holmes to find the case so I thought we may as well stop by your office and get you to come along. That way you can at least pretend to earn part of your fee, right?"

"Inspector, please," said Holmes. "Señora Rojas is clearly distraught. Please refrain from the nonsense. This cannot have anything to do with a missing Gladstone bag."

"Why, of course, it does. Mind you it might also have something to do with the dead body we found beside the bag. A bit of a bloody mess he was, I was told. Still is, for that matter. There's at least four constables guarding him and keeping the crowds of Chinamen back. Since the lady's bag was lying beside a seriously banged up dead body, we felt it might be a useful thing to go and get her and bring her along to retrieve her bag and tell us what she knows about the dead man. Since she's your client, I am thinking that it would be a good thing to have you come along as well. So, if you wouldn't mind doing so and joining us in the carriage, it would be right appreciated. You too, doctor. You can take a look at the body and tell us what you think about how he got done in."

Lestrade left the room with Holmes following close behind. Mrs. Hudson and I immediately sat down beside Patricia.

"There, there, dearie," said Mrs. Hudson, patting the woman's hand. "If you are a client of Sherlock Holmes, he will make certain that no harm will come to you. He is an odd duck, but in his hands you will be quite safe from everyone."

"It is not me," she whispered, "that I am worried about. The police came banging on my door an hour ago and demanded that I come with them immediately. My husband and son were not allowed to join me, and they will be horribly upset. I have to get word to them somehow. *Yo debo!*"

"My dear," I said, "we can look after that. Here, quickly, write them a note and tell them that you are with Sherlock Holmes, and I will have one of the street lads get it to them within fifteen minutes."

"Are you sure?" she asked me. "Can you trust a street urchin to deliver a message across London?"

"For a shilling, they will do whatever you ask."

Señora Patricia wrote out a note in Spanish and put an address on the backside. By the time she had done so, Lestrade was standing back in the doorway shouting at us to stop delaying his police work. Mrs. Hudson shouted a few choice words back at him, and the young woman and I came down the stairs and climbed into the carriage.

As it was a Saturday morning, there were few crowds on the streets, and we galloped rather quickly all the way across London. It took a full three-quarters of an hour to get from upper Baker Street to Limehouse. As we traveled, both Holmes and Lestrade attempted to question Patricia, but there was nothing that she could tell them beyond the fact that her case had been taken from the institute where she taught. She knew no more.

The driver slowed down and stopped at the junction of the West India and East India Dock Roads. Lestrade led us back across the intersection to the entrance of St. Anne's Church. Although I had never been in this substantial edifice, I knew something of it. The church had been built several decades ago to accommodate the parishioners in the sprawling new neighborhoods of London. Of late, it had declared a two-fold mission of caring for the material needs of the dock workers and of bringing the gospel to the thousands of Chinese immigrants with the intent of seeing them convert to the faith of the English. They had seen great success in their first mission and almost none in their second.

A crowd of the curious, seeming to have come from all nations on earth, had gathered around the steps of the church and were being kept back by a phalanx of police officers. We were let through the police line and to the open pavement area just in front of the doors of the church. There on the ground, in a pool of now-dried blood, was the body of a man, lying face down. His right arm and leg were in unnatural positions. Beside him was a Gladstone bag.

"Hello, Inspector," said one of the constables. "Another sad scene here in the docklands. Folks say they heard a terrible scream round about three o'clock in the morning, sir. A couple of them come looking, and they found this poor chap just as he was, lying here. They say they knew right well not to move him, so as you see him is as he was."

"Thank you, constable," said Lestrade. "Good work. Please continue to keep the citizens well back."

"Now, Mrs. Rojas," said Lestrade turning to Patricia. "Can you identify that valise? Is it yours? Is that the one that was stolen?"

"Si, it is, señor," she replied.

"And is that the coat that was stolen?"

"It was not my coat, so I cannot say for sure, but I believe that it is."

"Right," said Lestrade. "Now Mrs. Rojas, this might be very difficult, but I am going to have to ask that the body be rolled over and for you to tell us if you know who this man is. Are you prepared to do that, madam?"

"Si, go ahead."

I held my arm out to Patricia in case she might wish to hold on to something. She did not take it.

On instructions from Lestrade, two of the policemen carefully rolled the body over until it was lying face-up. In my days as an army surgeon in Afghanistan, I had seen many mangled corpses and was not overly shocked, but I had to admit that the damage to this body was as awful as anything I had witnessed since coming back to London. The left arm and leg were shattered and flopped like large noodles as the body rolled. The face, however, was gruesome. The right side of the visage and skull had been utterly smashed in, so much so that the skull had been cracked open and some brain matter was exposed. The hair, face, and neck were thick with matted blood, and the jaw was askew, with teeth protruding through the lower lip.

I now felt Patricia's hand on my arm, squeezing quite tightly.

"Crikey," I heard one of the officers gasp. "He's been beaten to a pulp. Whoever done this, must have kept on smashing him long after he were dead."

That had been my conclusion as well. The injuries to the man's body and head would have been fatal after the first few blows. But his injuries went beyond anything required to put out his lights. What had been done to him was horrible and vicious beyond belief.

"Sorry to have to do this to you, madam," said Lestrade. "But I have to ask you if you know this man."

We all looked at her, and she nodded. "I do."

"Can you tell me his name, Mrs. Rojas?"

She took a breath and then spoke slowly to the inspector.

"His name, Señor Inspector, is Tomas Herrera. He lives in Oxford. He is from Quito, and he was awarded a fellowship to study and do research at the university. His family may be contacted through the Embassy of Ecuador."

"Right, well now that is helpful, Mrs. Rojas. Now, would you mind telling me how it is that you know him?"

"He is the *prometido* ... the fiancé of one of my colleagues, Antonia Garcia. She is also a profesora at the instituto."

Here she stopped, and I could feel her hand trembling as she struggled to compose herself.

"They were to be married in September. She will be ... she will be devastated. If you wish, I will go with you to inform her. She is my friend."

"Thank you, miss. That is a very kind and courageous offer," replied Lestrade in a tone bordering on compassionate. "I will have one of our women go with you. They have great experience in having to be the bearers of tragic news to families." Then, as if speaking to himself, he added, "Frankly, I do not know how they do it. I could not."

Then the inspector turned to me.

"Doctor, as you are here, I may as well make you of some use. For our recorded account, would you please examine this body, declare him dead and state the probable cause? Not that I cannot tell myself, but we prefer to have a medical man on record."

I knelt down beside the body and looked briefly at the crushed skull.

"He has suffered a massive blow to the cranium," I said. "There does not appear to have been more than one hit, but that one was more than enough to kill him."

Here I paused and let my eye run down to the man's right shoulder. It appeared to be dislocated. I undid his shirt and felt the joint. It was not merely dislocated.

"His right shoulder also has been crushed," I said. "The bones have been shattered."

I then felt his chest cavity and noted that all of the upper ribs on his right side had been broken.

"The right side of his pelvis has also been shattered," I added.

His right sacrum, femur, patella, fibula and the bones of his ankle and foot were also broken in several places. There had been widespread internal bleeding throughout the entire right side of his body.

But by comparison, the left side of his head and body were unharmed, and I stated the same to Lestrade.

"Thank you, doctor," he responded. "It would appear that his attacker gave him a hard blow to the head with some sort of club, which knocked him down, and then beat him up and down his body. That's what it looks like."

Something about that did not seem quite right. One of the constables who had been assisting also had some doubts and queried Lestrade.

"Begging your pardon, Inspector, sir," said the officer. "But that don't seem like what a murderer does, sir."

"Is that so?" replied Lestrade.

"Well, sir. Yes, sir," the officer continued. "If a chap is lying down with his head bashed in and his brains falling out, then what a killer does next is run. I'n'it, sir? And he don't start at either the top or bottom and whack his way up or down whilst the fellow is standing still and letting him wail away, sir. This just don't seem right, sir, if you don't mind my saying, sir."

"Well then, officer," said Lestrade. "Just how did he end up like this? Any explanation?"

"No, Inspector, sir. But this just don't seem like any murder victim I ever seen, sir."

"Right. Very well, then. How about you, Holmes? Any explanation? He's been beaten to death on his right side and untouched on his left. What happened?"

Holmes waited for several seconds before answering.

"He was not beaten with a club. In truth, he was not beaten with any weapon at all."

"Come, come, Holmes," said Lestrade. "You cannot bust a man's head open with your bare knuckles."

"The murder weapon," said Holmes, "is about one hundred feet above your head."

We all looked up. We were standing directly in front of the high steeple of St. Anne's Church.

Yes, I thought. That makes sense. The body sustained those mortal injuries after falling from the tower.

"Ah, ha!" said Lestrade. "Then it's not a murder at all. He jumped. Sad all the same, of course. But if he took his own life then this is a problem for his priest, not for Scotland Yard. Right. Thank you, Holmes. You just saved the Yard a great waste of time. Just one more suicide. Of course, we'll have one of our women officers go with Mrs. Rojas all the same, but I will not have to assign any of my men to a case of one more jumper."

"Please permit me, Inspector," said Holmes, "to advise you not to jump to conclusions. This man was murdered."

Lestrade gave Holmes a hard look.

"Come now, Holmes. You cannot have it both ways. Either he was beaten to death, or he jumped from the steeple. Let me enlighten you about murderers in London. They kill their victims by shooting them in the head or the heart or they stab them in the heart or cut their throats or they strangle them or garrote them about the neck or they beat their brains out with a Penang lawyer or they drown them in the Thames or they poison them — actually that's the method most preferred by women who want to do in their husbands — but I assure you, dragging your intended victim to the top of a church steeple and then throwing him off is just not done here in London. Maybe they do that in Paris or wherever else you have been working lately. But not here."

"If I may, Inspector," said Holmes. "Allow me to explain."

"Fine. Then get on with it, Holmes. You have two minutes to prove to me that what is obvious is wrong, and what is nonsense is true."

"One minute will suffice, Inspector. A man must have a reason for taking his own life. Was this man under great financial duress? No. He has recently purchased a set of boots that are worth more than yours and mine put together. His trousers are also of a select quality. So, he was not lacking in funds. Was he heartbroken by a shattered love affair? No. We have been informed that he was to be married in three months. A man may very well contemplate taking his own life three months *after* he has been married, but three months before, he is invariably looking forward to wedded bliss. Was he *non compos mentis* and so disturbed by brain fever that he could not bear to go on living? No. We have been informed that he is capably carrying on research and teaching in one of our finest universities. Was he a political or religious zealot wishing to make a grand statement to bring attention to his cause, whatever it may have been? Highly unlikely. The man is of Spanish descent and therefore almost assuredly a Roman Catholic. Had he wished to make a proclamation he most likely would have chosen the steeple of the Roman Catholic Church a block away, and not the Church of England.

"On the other side of the question are the reasons for supporting my deduction that he was murdered. A man contemplating taking his own life does not usually exchange his expensive overcoat and hat for shabby ones. Nor does he steal a cart that has no value and run off from the City to the Chinese streets of the Docklands. The most probable conclusion is that he was fleeing in fear of his life, had disguised his appearance, and was hoping to board a ship to anywhere that would get him out of England quickly. He was followed and caught and forced up the steps of the steeple and thrown off. His murder was not an act of passion but coldly calculated so as to lead the police to conclude that he had taken his own life."

Here Holmes stopped his recitation. Lestrade was still glaring at him.

"Right. Very well then, Mr. Holmes, and can you tell me why anybody would want to do that to this fellow?"

"No, Inspector, I cannot. Not yet. But if you will allow me a few days to investigate this crime, I shall endeavor to find out. In the meantime, might I suggest that your report to the Press be of a tragic suicide. Best not to let the perpetrators of this murder know that Scotland Yard was not fooled by them."

"Right. A good idea, Holmes. Very well, then. Get to work. And you will report to me whatever it is you discover. Do we understand each other, Holmes?"

"Have I ever failed to understand you, Inspector?"

Lestrade said nothing. He nodded to the constables standing by, and they prepared to remove the body and cleanse the site. Holmes, Patricia and I hailed a cab and made our way back out of the Docklands.

Chapter Three
A Mathematics Scholar at Oxford

"SEÑORA ROJAS," SAID HOLMES to his client. "When you meet with the fiancée of Mr. Herrera, would you mind obtaining his address in Oxford? I believe that I shall have to pay a visit to his residence to see what clues may present themselves to me."

"Si, señor. I will do that this afternoon when I go to see her. And tomorrow I will accompany you to Oxford."

"Madam," said Holmes, "that is kind of you to offer. However, I must decline. Whoever has done this deed may already be aware that I have become involved in the case. If you were to be seen accompanying me, there might be dangerous threats made against you and your family. Dr. Watson and I shall have to go alone."

Patricia said nothing for a moment and then turned directly to Holmes.

"Señor Holmes," she said. "*¿Habla español? ¿Lee español?*"

Holmes looked quite puzzled.

"I regret, madam, that I do not understand you as I do not speak Spanish. We will have to converse in English."

"That, sir, is what I thought," she said, smiling. "If you investigate the residence of Tomas, most of what you find that is written will be in Spanish, not English. You will need me to help you."

Holmes smiled back at her. "You make an excellent point, madam. However, as I am concerned for your well-being, may I suggest that we not travel together. Would you be able to meet with us tomorrow morning at ten o'clock at the Randolph Hotel?"

"*Estaré allí mañana.* I will see you there."

The Randolph Hotel in Oxford is a favorite of Holmes as well as of the parents of students attending the university. It being late June, the students had departed, and both the streets and the hotel were devoid of people. Thus, we had the front room of the Randolph to ourselves and the entire attention of the gracious staff who provided us with tea and scones.

"Did you make contact with the police here in Oxford?" I asked Holmes.

"I did. There is quite a capable inspector here, a chap named Morse. However, I was informed that he is on holiday in Italy. His colleague said something about a tour of Italian opera houses. So, we shall be on our own."

Our lovely client and translator arrived on the spot of ten o'clock. I admit to being somewhat surprised as it is a well-known fact that the Latin temperament considers appointment times highly flexible and that a time of ten o'clock usually means that there is no possibility whatsoever of arriving *before* ten o'clock, but any time after is quite acceptable.

Señora Patricia had entered the room from the door that leads to the hotel kitchen. She was dressed in the modest manner that a hotel maid might wear before changing into her uniform. She had a dark scarf covering her head and was wearing eye glasses. It took me a moment to realize that it was indeed her.

I complimented her on her diligent disguise, and after a brief exchange of greetings and pleasantries over tea, Holmes asked her to impart whatever information she had gleaned.

"I met with Antonia, Tomas's *prometida*. Whatever I can report is only what she has told me."

"That is an excellent place to start," said Holmes. "Pray, proceed and do not leave out any detail."

"Si, señor. Tomas is from Quito and attended the Universidad San Francisco, where he excelled in mathematics. Even as an undergraduate, he published a paper in which he recounted the accomplishments of many mathematicians from Mexico and South America. He was awarded the Gunter Fellowship in Mathematics at Christ Church, He has been here in Oxford for the past three years and was considered a very promising young scholar. His work under the elderly Professor Dodgson involved advances in geometry, algebra and mathematical logic. He lectured twice a week to the first-year students and was much loved by them. His rooms were in a private home on Pembroke Street, not far from the Cathedral and it is there, according to Antonia, that he kept all of his notes and papers and his library."

She continued at some length describing the many things that his fiancée had loved about him and her recollections of their cherished times together. Holmes listened, sitting in his habitual pose, holding his hands, fingertips touching each other, in front of him. I took careful notes, reminding myself that items that would to all others seem inconsequential were often the trail of bread crumbs that led Holmes to his unique insights.

"There is one more thing," our client said, "that I must report although I cannot attach any details to it."

"Is there now?" said Holmes. "And what is that?"

"When the woman police officer and I entered Antonia's room, we must have looked very sad. She immediately looked at our faces and said, 'It is about Tomas, isn't it?' I nodded. 'Is he dead?' and again we nodded. She just slowly shook her head and whispered, 'I told him. I begged him. I knew in my heart that he was in trouble. He was acting so fearfully. But he would not listen. He is a revolutionary in his heart and thought he had to be a leader and a hero.' Both I and the woman police officer tried to get her to speak about her premonitions, but she could say no more. Tomas had told her very little, but she knew in her spirit that there was reason to be greatly afraid. She was not at all surprised by our visit and the dreadful news we carried."

Holmes remained silent with his eyes closed for a full minute before responding.

"Excellent. Excellent, Señora Patricia. Well done. Now then, let us away from here and pay a visit to Tomas's rooms. Allow me to suggest that Doctor Watson and I proceed directly south on Cornmarket Street, but that you wait for five minutes and then come by way of St. Ebbes Street. It is a good thing for whoever murdered Mr. Herrera to know that I am in pursuit of them. The same cannot be said for them to know, señora, that you are assisting me. Can you carry out those directions?"

"Si, señor. They are not difficult. Gracias for your concern for my safety."

Our address for Tomas Herrera led us to a rather plain-looking row house on Pembroke Street, one of the many that let rooms to students and younger faculty. The elderly landlady was horrified when we informed her of the purpose of our visit.

"Oh dear, that's horrible," she said, several times. "He was such a friendly young man, with such fine manners. He was kind and considerate to everyone in this house. Just a gracious young man. I cannot imagine why anyone ..."

But she stopped part way through her sentence.

"I was going to say that I could not imagine anyone ever wanting to hurt Tomas, but I must confess that part of me is not surprised. No, not surprised at all, I'm not."

"Would you mind telling us why you say that?" asked Holmes.

"Well, sir, you see, he was a fine young gentleman and all, but it was well-known that he was a revolutionary Spaniard. And he associated far too often with others of the same ilk. Not only were they Spaniards, they were the South American variety, and, well sir, as we all know, those types would as soon cut your throat as look at you. At least twice a week several of them would gather in my front room here, and they would argue well into the night. I could not understand what they were saying, but they were very excitable, as all Spaniards are, of course. And from time to time there would be young men here from other places on the Continent, and then they would be shouting in English. And it would be all about changing the government and giving power to the people. You know, all that radical anarchy talk, the whole lot of them. And they all fight among themselves. So, I am not at all surprised that someone has done him in, the poor boy."

I could see that Señora Patricia was biting her tongue and fighting off the urge to correct this woman's political persuasions, but Holmes quickly interceded and requested permission to visit Tomas's rooms and make arrangements to have his earthly possessions returned to his family.

Tomas Herrera had rented the entire third floor of the house, a further indication that he was far from having pecuniary concerns. The rooms were neat and clean, as would be expected of a scholar who specialized in the study of mathematics. Holmes gave directions to us, and I began to rifle through all the papers on and in his desk whilst Patricia opened and leafed through the numerous books in his bookcase. Holmes concentrated his search on the fellow's personal effects.

"I suppose." I said, having been engaged by Holmes in similar tasks in the past, "that you want us to look for anything unusual, no matter how trivial, that might suggest a connection to a murderer a clue as to who and why. Right?""

"No, you are not looking for any connection to *a* murderer," he replied.

I was puzzled. "But you said that he was murdered, did you not."

"Yes, but not by *a* murderer. He was forced to his death by murder*ers*. There must have been more than one. Master

Herrera was a young man of average size and strength, and somewhat athletic. It is impossible that he could have been dragged up one hundred and forty steps by one man acting alone. Even two men could not force a man who was kicking and flailing and struggling all the way up a narrow staircase. There must have been at least three and, quite likely, four men to have so completely overpowered him."

"Ah," said I, "then you believe that there is a gang of murderers on the loose. Is that it?"

Holmes paused before answering. "That is a possibility. A man acting alone can do as he pleases. Two men can cooperate together. And it is possible that three might as well. But once you reach four, someone has to be in command."

"But Holmes," I protested. "Why would you dispatch four men to drag their struggling victim up a church steeple when one villain could have easily shot him. That makes no sense."

He did not immediately answer. Then he said, rather tentatively, "You are quite correct, my dear doctor. It would have been far more reasonable to do as you have said. If there is a reason to be deduced over and above misleading the police, it may lie in the effect that such a method of execution has on other possible victims. Except for the terror of being buried alive, I cannot think of anything that would more fill a soul with utter dread than the prospect of spending the last few seconds of your mortal existence falling to your death. If the villains behind Tomas's death wished to send a message to his colleagues, I can think of few better ways."

He said no more, and we continued our search. By the end of an hour, each of us had amassed a small collection of items we thought might, due mainly to their being curious or out-of-place, have significance.

"Señora Patricia," said Holmes, "anything to report?"

"There was nothing, Señor Holmes, hidden in any of the books. The books themselves are all about mathematics, or they are copies of some of the great classics of literature. They are mostly written in Spanish."

"As would be expected," said Holmes. "Anything else?"

"It to me seems," she said, "that there is something about this entire shelf of books that is unusual." She gestured to the lowest shelf in the bookcase.

"Yes. Go on," said Holmes.

"These books are all copies of Spanish journals of mathematics. Some are quite *antiguo*. They were published more than thirty years ago. Tomas was fascinated by the history of mathematics but his research, from what little I know about it, was very progressive and modern. So, I do not see why he should have so many copies of older books and journals. And they are not complete sets of books. There is a single copy of one journal, two of another and so on. They do not all come from the same year. There is no organization to them, no order."

"That is indeed curious," said Holmes. "Anything else?"

"Si, señor. In the front of many of these older books, there was a letter or a shipping document from whoever sent the book acknowledging that Tomas had purchased the book in the past year. He has been here at Oxford for three years, but all of these older publications arrived recently. Not one of them arrived here before the past summer."

"An interesting observation," said Holmes. "Quite interesting indeed. Thank you. And you, Doctor Watson, anything of note to report?"

I had set aside several items that I thought might be of some consequence and displayed them to Holmes. He nodded at each one but made no comment. Finally, I placed in front of him a piece of paper.

"The fellow had a file on many of the great mathematicians," I said. "He seems to have made notes both in Spanish and in mathematical symbols of the work of many of them. But this page was at the back of his file on Kepler's *Tabulae Rudolphinae.*"

The page was no more than a list of names. I had counted twenty-four individuals. The first eight had a check mark beside them. All of the names were Spanish.

Holmes perused the page carefully and then showed it to Patricia.

"Do you recognize any of these names?"

She glanced at the list, and her eyes immediately widened.

"Si, I know several of these people. Others are names I have heard. I believe that all of these names are of people from Spain or South America who are now living in London."

"And might any of them have any connection to Johannes Kepler?" asked Holmes.

"No, señor. *Ninguno en absolute.*"

Holmes looked again at the list, this time making small marks beside several of the names whilst ignoring the rest of them.

"I also recognize some of these names. The ones I have marked have either been charged by the police or named in the proceedings of the courts over the past two years. At least a portion of this list appears to be engaged in criminal activity."

"What of those that have the check mark beside them," I asked.

"For that, I have no explanation," said Holmes. "However, I agreed to keep our good Inspector Lestrade up-to-date, and I shall show this list to him and see if he can add any more data to it."

He stopped speaking and again he and Patricia looked at the list for some time.

"*Por favor*," said Patricia. "Allow me two minutes to make a copy of these names. I will ask my *marido* and some of our friends if they can assist in identifying them."

She immediately took a blank sheet of paper from the desk and hurriedly copied the names.

"Thank you," said Holmes. "That would be very useful. But now, please, both of you, forgive me. But I am going to return to London straightaway. Might I indulge your patience with me and allow me to leave the two of you behind so that you might pack up Mr. Herrera's possessions and have them sent to the Embassy of Ecuador. It is on Hans Crescent, a block behind Harrod's in Knightsbridge. At the moment, the Ecuadorians are on good terms with the British, so I expect that they will be cooperative. And now, permit me to bid you good-day."

He exited the room, and I could hear him descending the stairs with considerable alacrity. Patricia and I spent the rest of the day chatting amiably whilst securing cases and steamer trunks and packing up the goods and chattel of the recently departed young mathematics scholar. Try as she might, having discounted the landlady's comment on Latin American revolutionaries, she could not imagine any reason why the fiancé of her colleague had been thrown off a steeple in Chinatown.

Chapter Four
A List and Saint Ignatius

I RETURNED LATER that same day to London, as did Patricia, but by a different train. The following morning, being Sunday, I was moved to rise early and attend morning mass at the Marylebone Parish Church. I am far from faithful in my religious observances, but I felt that a prayer for those young people whose lives had become intertwined with murder might be appropriate. Holmes, knowing that my wife was still away from London, had asked me to join him for a Sunday lunch that Mrs. Hudson would be pleased and proud to prepare for the two of us. I accepted the invitation.

"Do tell, Holmes." I said as we enjoyed a delectable Sunday dinner, "What came of your meeting with Inspector Lestrade?"

"Yes. It was quite enlightening, also rather disturbing."

"In what way?"

"I had noted that several of the names on the list were familiar to me as having appeared in recent records from the courts and the police reports. Lestrade augmented my knowledge with the result that two-thirds of the list could be associated with some sort of criminal activity. There had been several cases of robbery, four of forgeries, five of houses having been broken into and rifled, two of critical papers having been secretly copied, and two in which the names had been listed as accomplices to murder."

"That," I said, "is very peculiar."

"And that was only the men named on the list. There were also six women. Four of them had been named for engaging in prostitution, three for fraud, two for assaulting and wounding, and one for attempted murder."

"Holmes," I said, "that adds up to more than six."

"Then you should have deduced that some of the six were named in more than one case."

"Oh, yes. Of course."

"That a list of immigrants," continued Holmes, "who were associated with crimes should be found in the study of a graduate student of mathematics is peculiar enough. But that was not the most curious aspect."

"Indeed? Then what was?"

"Not a single one of them had been convicted."

I was highly perplexed by that information.

"How is that possible?" I asked. "Surely Lestrade and his men and our prosecutors are not *that* incompetent."

"It should not be possible," acknowledged Holmes. "But it seems that somehow money appeared for their bail, or charges were inexplicitly dropped, or a witness conveniently either disappeared or changed his story. Evidence vanished, or, Lestrade suspects, a judge may have been bribed, and he rendered a verdict of 'not guilty' against all logic and evidence. He even suspects that some of his own constables and inspectors have been compromised."

"Holmes, you horrify me. That is madness. How could that happen? How did such a group of criminal Spaniards come to London?"

"Ah, that is also a curious aspect," replied Holmes. "Lestrade informed me that it was not just among the Spaniards. He has also noted a similar trend amongst recent immigrants from Russia, Italy, and France. And, he has discerned that all of them appear to have been connected in some way to anarchists, labor enthusiasts, and revolutionaries in their home countries."

"Merciful heavens!" said I. "Surely the Home Office knows of this. Why have they not stopped these undesirable types from entering and staying in Great Britain? Cannot they be rounded up and sent back?"

"Had they been convicted, they would have been. But we are not in the practice of sending those who have come seeking a safe haven from persecution back to face torture or imprisonment when they have been declared innocent."

I was in a fog. We appeared to have been led by a purloined Gladstone bag into an inexplicable web of crime and corruption. For several minutes, I said nothing and neither did Holmes. Then a thought occurred to me.

"What of the eight names that had check marks beside them?" I asked. "Was there anything peculiar concerning them?"

"Nothing. Six of them had become known to Scotland Yard for similar reasons. The remaining two were unknown."

Again, the two of us sat in silence for several minutes. Holmes had closed his eyes and brought his hands and fingertips together in front of his chin. I watched as he repeatedly moved his lips and then shook his head. He was as perplexed as I was.

"Very well, Holmes," I said, breaking the silence. "What is next?"

"Our only route of entry so far to this web of crime is Señora Patricia and the Instituto Español de St. Ignatius. I shall have to pay them a visit and ask for their assistance. I will send a note to them now, but as it is Sunday, they will not receive it until tomorrow. Might you arrange to be free to accompany me on Tuesday morning down to Milford Lane?"

Eight o'clock on Tuesday morning found Holmes and me enjoying a full English breakfast at The George on the Strand. This fine public house had been providing excellent ale and victuals to Englishmen for over a century, and it boasted that it was the favorite retreat of the writer Horace Walpole. Fortunately, no ghosts visiting from the Castle of Otranto had been seen.

The establishment was populated with barristers and solicitors from the nearby courts and Temples. It seemed a suitable place to meet.

"Señora Patricia," said Holmes, "has kindly arranged for us to meet with a Señor Diego Alvarez, the registrar of the Institute. She says that he is the one who is most familiar with all of the Spanish-speaking inhabitants of London. That seems reasonable, and I trust that he will be able to provide us with sufficient data concerning the names on our list. She will meet us here shortly so that we may chat before the meeting."

At fifteen minutes before nine o'clock, Patricia entered and made her way past the array of powdered wigs to join us. She smiled at us as she approached our table and Holmes and I stood to greet her. But as she seated herself, her smile disappeared, and a cloud covered her attractive face.

"I see that you have something to tell us," said Holmes. "Please. We are all attention."

"Buenos dias, señors. I trust that you are both in good health and si, there is something that I must tell you. Yesterday, I taught *mi chicos*, my students, here at the instituto. When I had finished my classes at five o'clock, I stopped in at the small restaurant that is a favorite of the teachers so that I might purchase some supper to take home to *mi hijo y esposo*. Whilst I was waiting for my package of food I noticed that at one of the tables there was seated nine people; six men and three women. They were sitting close together and were speaking quietly. I could only hear a few words of what they were saying, but they were speaking Spanish and had accents from South America, not Castilians."

"Yes," said Holmes. "Is there something strange about that? Would that be unusual in a restaurant so close to your institute?"

"No, señor, it would not be, except that I recognized four of them. I did not know the others. But the ones I knew were all names on the list we found in Tomas's room."

That fact caught Holmes's interest.

"An excellent observation. Please, continue."

"Not only were they on the list, but all four bore the names of those who had check marks beside them. Maybe I am imagining, but something in my spirit told me that amongst the five I did not know were also those whose names had been marked. Forgive me, Señor Holmes, if I have been too fanciful in my imaginings."

"An imagination, my dear profesora, is an invaluable asset when investigating criminal activity. I only wish that my friends at Scotland Yard had more than their meager supply of same. Given what you observed, it is entirely likely that those nine names all have something in common and are somehow associated with each other. Well done, señora."

The Centro Español de St. Ignatius was housed in a three-story building just around the corner from the pub. The edifice had a Mediterranean design, with an entryway leading to an interior courtyard with an elegant garden. A cloistered walk surrounded the garden and, on the walls, I could see numerous paintings of saints and scenes from Spain and South America. The centerpiece was a large canvas of a bald-headed cleric staring upwards into the sky at what appeared to me to me some sort of divine lightning flash.

"Is that St. Ignatius?" I asked.

"Si," said Patricia. "He is very revered in Spain and throughout South America. He was the founder of the Jesuits."

"Oh, was he?" I said. I had always thought that the Jesuits started off as Italians. Mind you, to the average Englishman, there is little or no difference between the Spanish and the Italians.

We entered the building and were greeted by a life-size statue of Don Quixote on top of a scrawny horse. At least I knew that *he* was not Italian.

"Buenos dias!" came the greeting from a gentleman who had emerged from an office adjacent to the entry door. "It is *muy bien* to have such a famous visitor grace us his presence. *Bienvenido*, Señor Sherlock Holmes, and Doctor Watson. Welcome to our center. *Por favor*, come in."

He was on the small and slender side, but quite stylishly dressed. His hair and eyebrows were dark, and his complexion was what might be expected of someone from the Mediterranean region. The most striking aspect of his face, however, was his odd mustache. The ends of it were waxed and pointed upwards, somewhat like the hands of a clock at ten minutes past ten.

"I will excuse myself," said Patricia, "whilst you gentlemen meet together. I have some work to do in preparation for my lessons." She smiled at us and made her exit down the corridor.

Holmes and I took a chair in the office of the registrar. Its walls were adorned with paintings of all those marvelous places in South America that I had heard of but could only dream of visiting someday. On the wall behind his desk was a large painting of the magnificent Iguazu waterfall that borders Brazil, Paraguay, and the Argentine. In other places were images of towering mountains that I assumed must be the Andes, and one of the strange phenomenon of the enormous mirror lake that sat on top of the great salt flats in Bolivia. The furnishings were made of heavy wood, with an excess of red upholstery.

When necessary, Holmes is perfectly capable of engaging in meaningless social conversation, and he did so for several minutes, asking about the fellow's health, complimenting the architecture and so forth. Then he came to the point

"I have been told, sir, that you are by far and away the most knowledgeable man in London regarding all those in our fair city whose mother tongue is Spanish."

"And I, señor, have been told that you are the finest detective in all of England," replied Mr. Alvarez, with a smile and a shallow nod of his head.

"Ah, we flatter each other, my friend," said Holmes and the two of them forced friendly laughs. "But I have come because I am in need of your knowledge, sir."

"Si. Such as I have, I will happily share with you. But if it is regarding the theft of Señora Patricia's cart, *perdónami*, but I fear that I have no knowledge with which to enlighten you. We are very embarrassed that such a theft took place here at our Centro. We are reviewing our measures to prevent such thefts in the future. It was a topic of our conversations just this morning."

"No, Señor Alvarez," said Holmes. "It is not concerning the theft. It is concerning the death of the young man who Scotland Yard believes to have been the thief. You are aware, no doubt, of the tragic end to which he came, are you not?"

"Si, señor," replied the registrar, with a very grave face. "This is a very sad event. His prometido, Señorita Antonia, is a dear member of our staff. I have sent my secretary over to her home to see if there is any comfort we can bring to her. Our Centro has offered to pay for the funeral and to have a mass said for him even though the young man was not one of our employees. We felt it was as our saint, the revered Ignatius would have us do. But, por favor, Señor Holmes, how is it that you are curious about him? The report from the police said that this poor young soul had taken his own life? Why is our famous detective asking after him?"

"It was because of the theft of the cart," said Holmes. "When a suicide and a crime are somehow connected to each other, the police always conduct an investigation. Because I had already been asked to look into the theft of the cart, Scotland Yard asked me to continue and complete the inquiries. That is all."

"Ah, si, of course. *Muy bien*, is there anything with which I can assist you in that regard?"

"Yes, sir," said Holmes, as he removed the list of names from his suit pocket. "We found a list of names, all Spanish names for that matter, in the rooms of Tomas Herrera. We have no idea who these people are, and I was hoping that you might have some information concerning them."

He laid the paper on the desk in front of the director. The gentleman looked at it briefly with a puzzled scowl and then broke into a wide smile.

"Of course, of course," he said. "I do not know all of the names. Maybe only two-thirds of them. But I can tell you immediately the purpose of this list."

"Then please do," said Holmes.

"This young man, Señor Tomas, was what you would call ... what is the word? ... ah si, a *sportsman*. I had heard that he was organizing a football team. All members were to be from Spanish-speaking countries. Our young men are in love with the sport of football, as I am sure you know. All these on the list, at least all those whose names I know, are also sportsmen and they were very eager to come together and to take on the English. I must warn you, señor   our boys are very skilled at this sport. They will be *muy formidable,* when they play other teams. Perhaps a team of solicitors from the Temple will agree to a match. It will be great fun to watch. Do you not agree? Ah, but now we must find another of the members on the list to be the one who organizes the team. Please, a moment."

He hastily took out a piece of paper and copied the names at the top of the list.

"These will be enough," he said. "Is there anything else, Señor Holmes?"

For a moment, Holmes made no reply. He was looking intently at the list of names.

"A football team, you say?" he said. "But sir, at least one-quarter of these names are women, are they not?"

"Ah, señor, señor," said Mr. Alvarez. He was smiling with that smile that one man gives to another when he is about to discuss matters that are not spoken of in front of a lady. "Señor, you must be a bachelor. But me? Not only am I married, I have spent many years working with young men and women. I assure you, whenever a group of *hombres* come together to form a football team or any sport, there will always be *señoritas* who will be found in their company. They become... what is your word for it? ... the *auxiliary.* They look after sewing the jerseys, bring *tortillas,* serving the beer ... all those things that young women do when their true attraction is to the lean young torsos of the players. It is the same for English girls, si?"

"I assume you must be right," said Holmes, and turned to me. "Would you agree, doctor? The fair sex is your department."

"Most certainly, 'twas ever thus," I said.

Holmes looked again at the list.

"In addition to being members of a football team," he said, "had you heard of any of these people having been arrested or having any trouble with the city police or Scotland Yard."

The fellow looked quite shocked.

"These young men and women? *Nunca!* I am sure that they were no angels and it is possible that one or two of them may have committed indiscretions, but no, none has ever been charged with a crime."

He appeared to read the doubt on the faces of both Holmes and me.

"I assure you, gentlemen. All of the men and women on this list—those that I know—are all of excellent character. On that, I give you my word as a Spaniard."

No good, I thought to myself. I've known too many Spaniards.

Holmes, however, appeared to accept his assurance and, after a few more minutes of conversation, we parted and bade good day to both Mr. Alvarez and Saint Ignatius Loyola.

Chapter Five
Arson and Old Canvas

AS HOLMES AND I walked back to the Strand to find a cab we observed Miss Patricia waiting for us on the corner.

"Señors, *por favor,* may I have a word with you?" she said.

We returned to The George and took a table in the back corner.

"Señors, whilst you were meeting with Señor Alvarez, I went to speak to his secretary and ask for her assistance. She was not in the office, so I took the liberty of looking at the card files of the Instituto. We keep a card for anyone who has ever worked at the Instituto, or taken classes, or attended an event ... anything. I took my copy of the list we found at Tomas's and began to look to see if any of the names on the list were registered in the files."

"Excellent," said Holmes, smiling warmly. "And do tell, what did you discover?"

"They were all there. Every one of them. I copied the addresses of their residences onto my list. I thought you might be interested."

"My dear señora," said Holmes, "you are brilliant. That is exceptionally helpful. Now, I must ask you a question."

"Si?"

"Your registrar, Mr. Alvarez, told us that all of the names on the list were there because they planned to form a football club. The men would be the players, and the women would form the auxiliary. Tell me. What do you think of that explanation?"

Patricia looked very puzzled for a moment and then broke out laughing.

"Oh, Señor Holmes, that would be a very amusing team to watch."

"Would it now? Please explain."

"Some of the boys on the list are indeed quite athletic and could be good players. But several of them are ... how did your Shakespeare describe them? ... 'fat and scant of breath.' They are as round as the football itself and could roll faster than they could run. I do not know all of the women on the list, but two of them find sports of all sorts to be intolerable. I cannot imagine them ever attending a game, let alone offering to help a football team."

Holmes smiled at her. "An interesting observation." Then he returned his gaze to the list before asking Patricia another question.

"Are the men and women on this list all gainfully employed?"

"Si, those I know are. I cannot say for the others."

Here, I felt compelled to interject.

"Goodness, Holmes. Why do you ask that?"

"Because, my dear Watson, you and I are going to pay calls on them. It would be pointless to do so during the daytime working hours as they will not be present. Therefore, I suggest that you return to your surgery and meet me at Waterloo at six o'clock this evening. Several of the addresses of those in the eight who have been marked off are just across the river in Southwark. I think that might be a logical place to begin. What say you?"

At six thirty that evening Holmes and I knocked on the door of a rooming house just off Great Suffolk Street. The fellow we were seeking, a Ceferino Namuncurá, unfortunately, was not at home. We moved on to the next closest address and asked for a Miss Luisana Lopilato. She had moved to another address her landlady informed us and that whilst she had been living there she seldom returned to her rooms before midnight.

"The next two on the list," said Holmes, "share rooms over near Guy's Hospital. We shall give them a try."

We pressed Shank's pony into service and walked briskly across Southwark to a small street bearing the charming name of Mermaid Court, entering from Borough High Street. No sooner than we had taken a few steps along the Court but we stopped in our tracks. Just ahead of us a crowd had gathered. Several wagons from the Metropolitan Fire Brigade were blocking the street and flames and smoke were pouring out of a set of windows on the third floor of a row house. Holmes moved quickly into the crowd and pushed his way as close to the door of the building as was permitted by a local policeman.

"Watson," he said, "this is our address and the rooms that these two chaps have rented are on the third floor. I fear something untoward may have happened."

The courageous firemen had stormed into the building, dragging their hoses behind them. As we and a large crowd of spectators and residents of the house stood and watched, the flames soon vanished from the windows and, within twenty minutes, the smoke ceased to emerge. A burly fellow, clad in his protective coat and boots, exited the building and walked over to the bobby. I could not tell what he said to the officer, but the grave faces and the somber nods indicated that he was imparting bad news.

"Come," said Holmes to me as he walked toward the two men.

"Gentlemen," he said to them. "My name is Sherlock Holmes. I have reason to suspect that this fire may have been caused by arson and that foul play might be involved."

Both of them looked quite startled. The policeman sputtered and replied.

"I 'ave 'eard of you, of course, Mr. 'olmes. An' our fireman 'ere says for sure it were arson. An' makin' it worse is that there are two chaps up there who are quite dead from the fire. An' you showin' up right like this says to me that foul play must 'ave took place. I'm about to send to the Yard for an inspector straightaway."

"An excellent idea," said Holmes. "I strongly concur. As an inspector will soon arrive, might I, with your permission, take a look at the site? I may be able to be of some assistance to you."

The police officer shrugged his broad shoulders and waved his beefy hand to gesture us inside the building. The fireman followed us.

"The fire was only in these rooms," said the fireman when we had climbed to the third floor. "The other residents of the floor sounded an alarm, and everyone in the building got out safely. We arrived within a few minutes, and we were able to keep it from spreading. All we had to do was send some water through the windows and break down the door and send more through into the room, and we soon had it out."

"Most commendable," said Holmes. "You are your men are to be praised for your excellent actions."

"If you say so, sir. But there are two fellows dead inside the rooms and that don't seem to us like something to be praised. We were in a bit of a funk when we found them and thought we had failed to get here in time, but if you're sayin' that they might have been done in, well, that is a different kettle of fish, sir."

"Indeed, it is, my good man," said Holmes. "It is premature yet for me to make any pronouncement, but I strongly suspect that no matter how quickly your men had come and extinguished the fire, there would still have been two corpses behind these doors."

Holmes now entered the rooms, and I followed. The stench was nauseating. Scorch marks from the fire were all over the walls and door jambs, and the furniture was still steaming from the combination of flames and water.

On the floor of the main room were the prone bodies of two men. Their clothing had been burned away, leaving no more than a few charred fibers. The exposed and darkened flesh of their limbs was openly exposed. The portion of their faces that could be seen had been burned beyond all possible recognition. What was odd, I thought, was the position of their hands and feet. Their arms were extended downward and their hands were lying close to their bodies, just beside their hips. Their feet, on both men, were almost touching each other. If they had been overcome by smoke, as happens when caught in a fire, it is highly unlikely that the two men would have fallen as if they had been standing at attention.

Holmes dropped to his hands and knees and examined the bodies closely. He took out his glass and looked for some time at the wrists and ankles of the corpses.

"Watson," he said. "Would you mind taking a close look at these. You may have to scrape away some of the charred skin, but please tell me what you observe."

As an army surgeon, I had seen more than my fair share of horribly burned limbs on the battlefield, and I expected that these would be similar.

They were not.

I knelt down over the bodies, took out my pocket knife, and slowly and methodically began to scrape back the charred skin from the ankles and wrists, as Holmes had requested. After some twenty minutes or so, I had completed one arm and one leg on each body. Holmes had busied himself with an examination of the rest of the room and the bedrooms.

"Holmes," I called to him. "You really must take a look at this."

"What is it?" he said as he returned to my side.

"This is most strange," I said. "When limbs are burned, the flesh underneath the burned area is normally uniform in its condition. Not so here. There is a clear line, above which the flesh is in stable condition and below which it is highly distressed. It is as if some sort of ligature, a rope or a wire, perhaps, had tied them in place and these fellows struggled violently to free themselves. Yet there is no fragment of a rope or wire in sight. What do you make of that?"

Holmes descended to his hands and knees and, with his glass, examined the wrists and ankles that I had exposed.

"Burned fibers," he said, "every bit as much as burned tobacco ash, leaves its own signature. Wool, cotton, silk and linen are all distinctly different, as are the various types of those cloths. Worsted appears subtly different from flannel, as does felt from gabardine. Both of these men were wearing woolen trousers, as might be expected. The fibers you have scraped away from the chafed areas are cotton. More specifically, they are canvas. These men were bound with twisted swatches of strong canvas, which subsequently were consumed in the fire. It is an ingenious attempt to remove the evidence of their murders."

Holmes stood and poked his head outside the door into the hallway and summoned the fireman who had been posted there. A tall, somewhat stooped fellow entered, removing his helmet from his head as he did so. His grizzled hair said that he was no longer a callow youth.

"I say there sir," he said. "You look as if this was not your first fire. How long have you been with the Brigade?"

"Goin' on fifteen year, sir," the chap replied.

"Excellent, then you have witnessed many and sundry different fires throughout London, have you not?"

"That I 'ave. Maybe three or four a week. Some of 'em was nothin' more than a flamin' pot on a stove, and some was ragin' infernos. Mind if I ask why you're askin'?"

"I have nowhere near your experience in your trade," said Holmes. "In fact, very little. So, please permit me to draw on your wisdom. Does this fire strike you as odd or peculiar in any way?"

The fireman gave Holmes a sideward glance and tilted his head back ever so slightly. "Blimey, there, sir. Course it's odd. Any fool can see that this 'ere fire were started by some devils throwin' several gallons of kerosene all over the edges of the floors, and on the furniture, and then on the bodies of these poor chaps on the floor. You can smell it, can you not? Clear as day. Look. These lads are burnt to cinders, but the carpet two foot away is 'ardly touched. There's scorch marks up and down the walls, but none under the sofa. The upholstery on some of the furniture is gone, but on that chair over there it's all still there. They must 'ave missed that one. No sir, you don't need to be no bleedin' Sherlock 'olmes to know what's gone on 'ere. When all the other residents escape, even the elderly, and two young men are roasted, then it's bleedin' clear. It were murder and arson, plain as the nose on your face."

"Ah, thank you, sir," he said. "That has been very helpful."

Any further comment was cut short by the sound of footsteps rapidly ascending the stairs. Inspector Lestrade walked quickly into the room.

"I was going to send Forrester to look into this," he announced. "But then the bobby told me that Sherlock Holmes himself was here. So, I knew that something more than a run-of-the-mill arson was up. What in the name of all that is holy is going on here, Holmes?"

Holmes patiently explained the evidence that we and the fireman had observed and then he added, "Inspector, do you recall the list of names I showed you yesterday?"

"Of course, I do."

"In front of you are Camilo Tenorio and Mariano Rodríguez."

Lestrade slowly sat down in the unburned chair and folded his arms across his chest.

"Let me see. If I recall, correctly they were on your list. Near the top. Right?"

"The third and fourth names," said Holmes.

"Right. Now, if I tax my memory, these two were apprehended a year ago and charged with some sort of fraud. Something about selling shares in a mining company in South America. I remember it because just before the trial, the men who had come forward to say they had been swindled suddenly changed their stories and the charges were dropped. Yes, I think that was what happened. And now these fraudsters are dead. Right? With murder dressed up to look like an accident. And the fellow who wrote their names on the list got himself tossed off a church steeple and made to look like a suicide. Right?"

"Precisely," said Holmes.

"Right. And now I suppose that you are going to tell me that Scotland Yard and the City Police had better send out officers to everyone else whose name is on that list so as they don't end up cooked or smashed. That is what you're about to tell me, isn't it?"

"Precisely."

"And it does seem a bit odd that we should be using our men to protect those foreigners, most of whom have already faced some kind of criminal charge and gotten away with it."

"Indeed, highly irregular. But then so are bodies tossed from steeples or burned to death."

Lestrade unfolded and refolded his arms across his chest and nodded. "Right. I agree. Lend me your list, and I'll have a bobby copy the names. It may take us a week or two to track down addresses. Not easy with these foreigners."

Holmes took the list from his pocket and handed it to Lestrade.

"All of the names," said Holmes, "have addresses below them."

Lestrade looked at the list and then at Holmes.

"And just how, Mr. Holmes, did you accomplish that so quickly?"

"As you have said many times, my dear Inspector, you have your methods, and I have mine."

Lestrade stood and left the room, returning some ten minutes later to give the list back to Holmes.

"Right. We'll get on this. By tomorrow evening we should have the ones at the top covered. Another few days for all the rest. But you could be a bit more useful to Scotland Yard,

Holmes if you can tell me why these two men and the steeple jumper got themselves murdered and by whom."

"Inspector, I regret that I do not know. At present, I am entirely in the dark, but I do intend to find out. As soon as I do, I will inform you."

Lestrade said no more and departed from the building. Holmes took one long last look around the room, and then he and I also walked out.

Chapter Six
Don't Cry for Me, Colombia

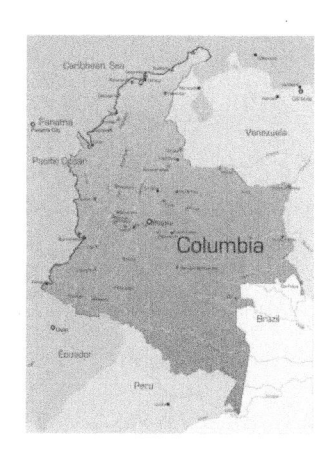

THE FOLLOWING DAY, I heard nothing from Holmes, but the next morning a note was delivered to my door before I had finished my breakfast. It was from Holmes and ran:

```
See attached note from Lestrade.
Patricia has arranged a meeting with a
Luisana Lopilato from the list. Kindly
join me at 9:00 pm this evening at Ten
Bells in Spitalfields.
          S.H
```

The note from Inspector Lestrade was rather puzzling. It ran:

> Holmes: This evening, S.Y. men called on the six names still alive at top of your list. The four men and two women were not to be found. Inquiries informed us that they had departed earlier this afternoon of a "nature outing" to the North. Act accordingly.
> G. L.

Even in a cab with a determined driver and with the traffic having departed for the day, a journey across London from my home near Paddington all the way to the Spitalfields Market area takes over an hour. I left in adequate time to make sure I arrived punctually. Holmes was waiting for me at a back table in the Ten Bells when I entered.

The East End of London is not a well-to-do part of our great metropolis. It is populated by thousands of recent immigrants, sailors, petty thieves, and unfortunate ladies of the evening. The clients of the pub were obviously drawn from the less reputable parts of the surrounding populace.

"Ah, Watson," said Holmes, standing and smiling as I joined him. "Thank you for arriving somewhat early. It gives us an opportunity to prepare ourselves for this interview."

I nodded in agreement. "And is Miss Patricia joining us?" I asked.

"No. Brave young woman that she is, she offered to, but I thought it unwise. I now strongly suspect that our actions are being observed."

"By whom?"

"That, my dear Watson, I wish I knew."

We chatted for a few minutes until the hour drew close.

"Do you know what this woman looks like?" I asked. "How will we identify her?"

"I suspect," replied Holmes, "that she is reasonably attractive and somewhat exotic looking, as she is from one of the warmer climes. Beyond that, I am in the dark. However, I rather expect that she will be fully capable of finding us."

He had no sooner spoken those words when I noticed a young woman walking toward our table. She was of average height and body contours, and although she was not smiling, her face was singularly beautiful. Her skin tone was faintly olive and her eyes as dark as coal. Her hair matched her eyes and swayed in long curving splendor as she walked. What was even more remarkable was the way she was, shall I say, *provocatively* dressed and adorned. Her full lips were bright red, her cheeks glowing, and her décolletage more than somewhat distracting, making it an arduous task for a gentleman not to lower his gaze.

When we both looked at her, she averted her gaze and fixed it on the floor. Before we could rise to greet her, she drew out a chair and sat down.

"Señorita Luisana Lopilato?" said Holmes.

"Si. *Perdóname,* Señor Holmes y Doctor Watson, for having you meet me here. It is the only place possible for me to do so."

"I assure you, miss," replied Holmes, "that we are honored to meet you anywhere in London. I thank you for agreeing to do so. By your words, I assume that you perceive yourself to be in some danger. Is that correct, Miss?"

"Si. You must buy me *una bebida,* something to drink. It must be *caro,* a brandy perhaps, not just a glass of ale. After we talk here for ten minutes, the three of us must rise and leave and retire to one of the rooms upstairs, and you must leave a tuppence at the bar as you pass. *Por favor,* tell me now if this is acceptable to you. Otherwise, I cannot continue to meet with you."

She spoke these words quietly and kept looking down at the table as she did so. It seemed to me to be a very odd set of requests, but Holmes immediately agreed to them.

He waved at the barkeep, who came immediately to our table.

"My good man," said Holmes, "three glasses of your finest cognac if you would be so kind."

"Aye, aye, captain," came the reply from a stout fellow whose arms were covered with tattoos. "Only the best for two gentlemen who are enjoying the company of the loveliest señorita in London. Right away, gentlemen."

Holmes then turned to Miss Luisana, smiling warmly. "Miss, your good friend Miss Patricia speaks very highly of you. She told me that you are one of the most talented poets and singers in all of Colombia."

The young woman raised her head and smiled back at Holmes. "*Mi amiga* is very kind to me. It is *mejor*, better, to say that I once wanted to be a poet and a musician." She paused and gave a furtive glance around the patrons of the pub and then lowered her voice to a whisper. "Por favor, señors, you must try to look joyful and laugh often as we speak. You must pretend that you are enjoying my company even if you are not."

It was an unusual request, but I complied and took a swallow from the snifter in front of me and let out a loud laugh. That brought a laugh in return from Miss Luisana.

"Oh, doctor," she said. "You are a very good man and a terrible actor. It is quite acceptable if you just ... *cómo se dice*? ... *chuckle* from time to time."

That comment elicited a genuine laugh from Holmes. I did not see the humor in the situation.

"Pray tell," he said to Miss Luisana. "Why do you not speak for several minutes telling us about yourself? That would be most enjoyable for us. Please, tell us your story."

She smiled again, and I confess to being stunned by her radiant beauty.

"*Ciertamente*, señor. I am *colombiana*, from Bogata. My family has been respected in my city for over a century. I am the daughter and only child of Profesor Lopilato of the Universidad Nacional de Colombia. He is capable, as is my mother, of speaking not only Spanish but also French, English, and German. My parents and my tutors made sure that I also learned to speak these languages. My father is very esteemed and admired for his years of fighting on behalf of the workers and the poor of our country. He also spoke out against the injustices of some of the leaders of our military. Three years ago, he wrote a long article in one of the newspapers read by the workers of our country in which he exposed the crimes of two of our generals and three cabinet ministers. The people of Colombia loved him for saying these things, but the police came and arrested him. He is still in jail in Bogata.

"My *madre* and I were very disturbed by what took place, and together we tried to make his situation known and to raise the people to demand justice. But one night a cousin of ours who is an officer in the military came to our house with a warning. He said that to silence us and to make an example of my father, I was about to be abducted and forced to work as a maid in the household of one of the generals my father had accused. My cousin made it clear to us that I would not just be a maid. I would be the *concubina*, the *puta* of the general and that I must flee unless I wished to be violated every night for years to come.

"Our cousin also told us that he had heard of a man who provided services to those like me who needed to escape quickly. He said he could contact this man and ask him to help. Of course, my mother said to contact him immediately. The very next night, after midnight, a knock came to our door and a man, *un hombre bien vestido*, entered. He was very confident and spoke as if he was a diplomat. He said that for a fee he could provide all the papers and tickets I would need to escape first to Caracas and then to London. Political refugees were safe in London he said, and he could arrange for me to have employment immediately so that I could support myself. We believed him, but the cost was extraordinary. It was far more than my mother could pay without selling our home. He said this was not something that should worry us because after I arrived in London and began to work, I could repay the amount with a small installment at the end of each month. Within five years it would all be paid back.

"We knew nothing of who this man was and not even his name, but we were desperate, and so we trusted him. My mother gave him all the cash she could provide and the very next day a package was delivered to us. It contained complete official papers and travel documents as well as reservation notices for hotels and tickets for the trains and ships that would bring me to London. That night a carriage came to our gate, and I departed from my home. All of the travel arrangements were well-ordered. All connections were made and, when necessary, other men, also very polished gentlemen, appeared and escorted me to my next train or carriage. I fled my country. I have not returned.

"When I arrived in London, I was met by yet another gentleman, an Englishman this time, who took me to my lodgings, where my rent had been paid in advance. My rooms were clean and spacious. For the first time since my father was arrested, I believed I was safe. The neighborhood was friendly. People were kind to me, especially my landlady.

"Somehow, the Instituto heard that I was in London and they invited me to pay them a visit. Soon I had employment with them and was earning a good wage. I made many friends amongst the other teachers and the students. I was able to send some gifts back to my mother. Life was very good."

Here she stopped speaking and took a large swallow of the cognac.

"Do you, miss," asked Holmes, "need some time to reflect before going on? There is no rush."

"No sir," she replied, quietly. "What I need, if I am to continue to tell my story is for the three of us to leave this room and go to one of the rooms upstairs. There we will have privacy. Here we do not. Please follow me and leave a tuppence at the bar, and please try to look happy and lecherous. Or, it would be better if you left sixpence as there are three of us."

She rose, and we followed her. The floor above the Ten Bells consisted of one long corridor with doors to rooms on each side. In the hallway were several tables, all with clean bedding and cleaning products sitting on top of them. Slowly, it dawned on me as to what sort of establishment I had entered.

The room we were led into had black velvet draperies on two of the walls but no windows behind them. On the remaining walls were cheap copies of some classical paintings, all of which depicted men and women in amorous contortions *sans vêtements*. The only piece of furniture was a large bed covered in a scarlet velvet bedspread and adorned with a cluster of puffy white pillows.

"*Lo siento*," said the young woman. "We will all have to sit on the bed."

"I am sure," replied Holmes as we arranged ourselves, "that it is exceptionally comfortable and sturdily built. But please, my dear, continue with your story."

At this point, she ceased looking directly at either Holmes or me. Her gaze was cast downwards, and she spoke to the floor.

"Six months after I arrived in London, I returned one evening to my rooms. I unlocked my door and was shocked and terrified to find the lamps turned on and a man sitting on my sofa. I turned to flee for help, but he loudly called my name and, speaking in Spanish told me to come in and sit down, for he had very important information concerning my father, whom he named, and my mother. I did as he had instructed me and he proceeded to tell me many details about my family, including my grandparents and cousins and he said that unless I could provide enough money to bribe to police and the government officials who gave orders to the police, my entire family was in danger of being harassed, or tortured, or thrown into prison, or even murdered. He knew so many things that I thought he could not be lying.

"I was beside myself with horror and cried for him to tell me what had to be done. He said that I would have to provide one hundred pounds every month to be used for the bribes. That was an amount far beyond what I could ever dream to earn as a teacher at the Instituto, and I despaired of my ability to ever save my family. He then told me that there was a way for me to earn not only that much but indeed twice that much and that I had only to pay half of what I earned every month and I could keep the rest."

Here she stopped speaking, paused, and took a slow deep breath.

"And so, Señor Holmes, Doctor Watson, I became a *puta*. Please do not ask me to describe my current life in details. It is humiliating, and I am certain that I have condemned my eternal soul to hell, but I had no choice. I began my work here at Ten Bells, and the other *chicas* and the barkeeps were kind to me. They became my friends. But I was blessed with an attractive face and a healthy body. I am highly educated and speak several languages. So, it did not take long for my customers to change and I began to attract gentlemen, and eventually, some very wealthy men—aristocrats, members of parliament, rich businessmen—and I moved my work from the East End to Pall Mall and St. James. I keep a suite at Brown's. Gentlemen pay me a visit whilst pretending to be attending their clubs. I have become a wealthy woman. Please forgive me for asking you to meet me here. Were I to meet you at Brown's, it is certain that within an hour all of London would know that Sherlock Holmes had acquired a courtesan. Here, they do not recognize you, and even if they did, they would not say anything."

She paused and looked up at Holmes.

"I beg your pardon, miss," said Holmes. "But there is nothing in what you have told me that constitutes a crime here in England. Pray tell, why did you agree to meet with me?"

"Señor, Holmes," she said, now looking directly at him. "I am not the only one who is has been forced to work in a way not of our choosing. Most of my colleagues at the Instituto have a story similar to mine. They fled their countries in fear of their lives, but with the assistance of men who had the ways and means of transporting them to London. They were offered employment in a reputable business, only to be later required to engage in crime and turn over a portion of their earnings. Some of them have become expert thieves. Some engage in fraud. Some are agents for passing on bribery money to politicians, judges, and policemen. Some assist in the illegal transport of arms to South America, where people are rising up against oppression and where armies are shooting them. Both sides are buying rifles and ammunition from England. Whilst I have not been myself a criminal, I am required to encourage my customers to speak far too freely about their affairs, which all men are wont to do foolishly during their phase of recovery. I am required to pass on what they tell me to the man who first appeared in my room. Every fortnight he meets me, takes my money and demands information. All of us are required to perform in the same way. We have heard that there are also young men and women from France, Russia, and Germany who likewise came to England for refuge and who have also been pressed into criminal service. Telling you this is my reason for agreeing to meet with you. Patricia says that you can be trusted. She thinks very highly of you."

Holmes slowly withdrew a piece of folded paper from his pocket and spread it out in front of Miss Luisana. It was the list of names we had discovered in the room in Oxford.

"Are these the names of your friends who have been brought to England and forced to commit crimes?"

The beautiful young woman looked the list over and nodded her head several times before looking up.

"Si, this is an old list, and some of these people are no longer in England, but most of them are still here."

"And these names, miss, at the top of the list, the ones with the marks beside them. Yours is amongst them. Why are they so designated?"

Again, she looked closely before answering. A puzzled look overtook her countenance.

"These were the members of what we called the *Consejo de la Resistencia*, the Council of the Resistance. The Council's members today are not all the same as are listed here but these were all members in the past. We came together because we wanted to fight against the evil men who had brought us here and forced us into crime. We have been gathering evidence that we can give to your Scotland Yard."

"You were one of them. Are you still?" asked Holmes.

"Si, I am. But *por favor*, may I ask how it is you have come to have this list, señor?"

"It was found in the room of Tomas Herrera in Oxford. You knew him?"

"Si, but he was not one of the refugees on this list," she said. "He and Antonia and Patricia and her husband came to England as scholars, not as refugees so they could not be recruited into crime. They are our friends, but we do not speak to them of what we have been forced to do. I am surprised that Tomas would have this list. It is not something he should have known."

Holmes paused briefly, and it was as if I could hear the wheels of his mind turning and he absorbed this latest piece of data.

"All of the other names at the top are no longer in London. Do you know where they have gone?"

"Si. Yesterday, I received a visit from Señor Alvarez of the Instituto. He came to warn me that I and the other members of the Council were in danger. He said that he had received a visit from the famous detective Sherlock Holmes and that there was a list with our names on it. He had made arrangements, he said, to have all the members, nine of us now, removed from London to some place in the North where we would be safe. They departed this morning."

"And do you know where they were taken?" asked Holmes.

"No, señor, I do not."

"But you did not go. Why was that?"

"I was told later that I did not have to, that I would be safe here in London."

"Mr. Alvarez told you that?"

"No, it was someone else."

"And may I ask who?" said Holmes.

"One of my customers—he is my most important customer—told me to remain here. He is the man who arranged my suite at Brown's. He is a very strange man. I do not even know his name, but he is very generous to me, although he demands that I confide in him and tell him all about my life and my friends and the Council. But I trust him, and he takes care of me."

"You say you do not know his name," said Holmes, "but can you describe him to me?"

She seemed uneasy about answering that question and then, in a whispering voice, replied.

"He is an older man, about your age, señor. He is tall and thin. His skin is pale. His eyes are set deep in his face. He is rich and dresses well. He does not reveal much at all about himself, but once he said something about his former students, so I think he might have a been a professor. I do not know for sure."

Holmes continued to ask her questions for several more minutes before rising to depart.

"My dear young lady," he said. "Thank you for agreeing to meet with us. It was very courageous of you. It would be wise if you spoke to no one about our meeting and what we discussed together."

"Si señor. I will do my best."

"Now Watson," he said, turning to me. "Could you please give this fine young woman several pound notes and then be seen putting your wallet back into your pocket as we exit the room?".

Chapter Seven
North to Darlington

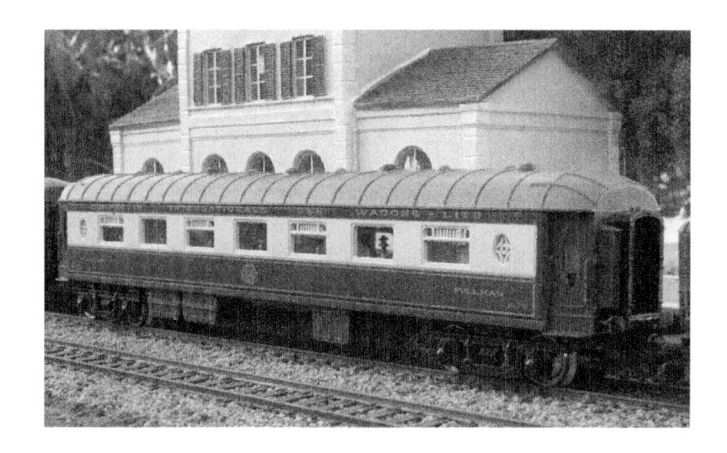

WE DEPARTED THE TEN BELLS pub and hailed a cab for the long ride back across London. Holmes sat in silence all the way. My only attempt to engage him in conversation was met with a wave of his hand indicating that he was not to be bothered. Finally, as we turned off of Oxford Street, he spoke.

"I fear that our brave young members of the Council of the Resistance might still be in danger."

"Why? That registrar chap acted quite quickly to get them out of London, out of harm's way, did he not?"

"He did. But it was not necessary for him to concoct a lie about a football team. He clearly knew the names on the list and why they were there."

He said no more. The cab stopped at 221B Baker Street, and he stepped out and bade me goodnight. I continued on the several blocks to my home between Paddington and Little Venice, all the while trying to make some sense of the events of the evening.

I spent the following day at my medical practice and by five o'clock had returned to my home to enjoy tea with my beloved Mary, who had now come back to London. Whilst sitting in our front room, I saw through the window a cab hurtling down our street at breakneck speed. It halted immediately in front of my house and out of it leapt Sherlock Holmes. He ran up the pavement and pounded on my door.

"Good heavens, Holmes," I sputtered as I threw the door open. "What is it?"

"Immediately, Watson. You must come immediately," he shouted. "Pack an overnight bag at once. We're traveling north. And fetch your service revolver. Now!"

I was at a loss and gave a helpless glance toward my wife.

"Away you go, darling," she said merrily. "You know you live for these moments. I will contact Anstruther and have him do your work for you. Come. I'll help you pack."

Within seven minutes I was out of the house and into the waiting cab. Holmes shouted at the driver to get us to King's Cross.

"A sovereign, driver if you can get us there before the last train to the North!"

The fine fellow laid his whip to the horse, and the hansom was soon bouncing and rattling along Marylebone Road.

"Are you," I asked, "going to tell me what we are doing or do I have to guess?"

"I should have seen it immediately," he replied.

"Seen what?"

"The registrar. That Alvarez blackguard."

"A blackguard? He seemed quite decent. Rounded up all those young Spaniards and hustled them out of London, did he not?"

"Yes. That is exactly what he did. The football club was an obvious lie. But do you recall how many people Miss Luisana said were taken away?"

I thought for a moment. "She said there were nine now but she did not go, so that would make eight."

"Precisely. But there were only eight names on the list to begin with. Two others were murdered in the fire. That only leaves six."

"Very well, they must have had some new recruits. She did say it was an old list."

"Think! Watson, think!" he shouted at me. "How did he know? How could he have possibly known that more had joined the Council?"

I pondered that one for a moment. "He could not have, unless…"

"Exactly, Watson. Unless they were betrayed. And, unless he is in league with the masters of the network who direct their criminal activities."

"Very well then the man is a blackguard. But why King's Cross?"

"I spent the day making inquiries. A man matching his description—the mustache is a memorable feature of his face—boarded a train to the North yesterday afternoon. Eight young people were with him. All had several pieces of luggage each. I have reason to fear for their safety."

"Where were they going?"

"The ticket booth issued them passage to Darlington."

"Darlington?" I said. "Why that's hours north of here. With all the stops, they could not have made it there before this morning."

"Correct. Those stops and delays may have postponed their fate. We can only hope and pray."

As it was the end of the day, the traffic on Marylebone Road was heavy and try and shout as he might, the driver was constantly having to stop for yet another slow carriage or strolling pedestrian. Shopkeepers bringing in their goods off the pavement shouted and cursed back at us. Holmes kept looking at his watch every second minute.

At King's Cross, he tossed the driver a sovereign and started running toward the platform.

"Pray that the train was delayed," he shouted back to me as he shouldered his way through the crowd of travelers.

My prayer was not effective. The train, the last of the evening to the North, had departed on time, three minutes before we reached the platform.

"There should be one at six in the morning," I said.

"Too late. That could be too late," he said as he stared at the empty track where our train must have stood only minutes ago.

He continued for several minutes to gaze to the north and the open side of King's Cross station. Then he turned to me.

"We shall have to engage a special."

"To Darlington? Why, that will cost a king's ransom," I protested. "Holmes, I do not have the money to pay for that. Neither do you."

"There is a way," he said. "Come, the station master's office is this way." He started walking briskly, pushing his way through the crowd but this time at least offering apologies to those he elbowed aside.

"Let me understand you," said the station master. "You want a special all the way to Darlington, and you want me to telegraph every stop on the route and have them pull all the regular trains onto a siding so you can run express. Is that what you are asking me, sir?"

"It is indeed," replied Holmes as if he undertook such arrangements every other day.

"Very well, sir. The cost is one hundred and ten pounds."

I was about to cry out loud at what I heard, but I felt the sharp pain of Holmes's heel kicking me in my shin.

"As I expected," said Holmes. "You may charge it to the account of Mr. Mycroft Holmes and send the bill to the Diogenes Club on Pall Mall. I believe he has an account with your railway."

"Right, sir. That he does, sir. That he does. And he is known to engage a special even to travel to Reading. Very well, sir. I will order it up. If we offer to pay the engineer, his brakeman, and a fireman double their usual wage, we should be ready to go within three hours."

"Faster, if possible," said Holmes.

"Very well, sir. I will do my utmost."

At twenty minutes to nine, a railway page boy fetched us from the passenger waiting room and led us out the west door of King's Cross to a siding, half way between King's and St. P. There sat a small, sleek engine, attached only to a coal car and a short, gleaming Pullman. We boarded and were greeted by a uniformed steward.

"Welcome aboard, gentlemen. I trust you will enjoy your voyage. If there is anything I can do to make it more comfortable, please do not hesitate to ask."

The interior of the coach was utterly opulent. I have not seen such fine quality anywhere, not even in London's most select hotels.

"Good lord," I exclaimed. "Do people truly travel in this fashion?"

The steward laughed pleasantly. "The gods were smiling on you tonight, sir. Prince Authur came in from Kings Lynn just a few hours ago in this car. That is why it was available when you engaged a special. Enjoy your journey, sir."

I enjoyed a small late dinner whilst watching through the train window as the lights of our great metropolis slowly diminished and vanished while the train rolled northwards into Hertfordshire and beyond. Then I stretched out on one of the plush couches to try to catch a few hours of sleep. Holmes did not sleep. He smoked and paced. Several times during the night I woke up only to catch a glimpse of him, still smoking and still pacing.

"Watson, wake up. We're pulling into the station."

I felt a hand gently shaking my shoulder. I turned up the small lamp beside the couch and looked at my watch. Four fifteen in the morning. We stepped out of our luxurious carriage and onto the train platform.

There are few places on earth that feel more lonely and desolate than a deserted railway platform in the small hours of the morning. As the chugging of our special engine faded into the distance, a complete stillness enveloped us. The temperature had dropped at least twenty degrees since we departed from London and I grumbled inwardly at not having dressed more warmly. The lobby and waiting room were in total darkness as we worked our way through the small station, but we noticed a glimmer of light at the end of a hallway.

"Hello there!" shouted Holmes, as he rapped on the window of a small office. "Hello!"

A man in a railway uniform leaned over a desk, sound asleep. His head and shoulders rested on his crossed arms, and it took several loud knocks and shouts to rouse him.

"Oh, good morning," said the sleepy-eyed fellow. "Are you the chaps that came on the special?"

"That we are," said Holmes. "Sorry to disturb you but might we bother you with a request for some information."

"By all means, sir," Mr. Sleepy replied. "What is it?"

"Were you on duty early yesterday morning as well, sir?" asked Holmes.

"I was."

"Did a group of travelers get off the early train, the overnight from London?"

"Aye, they did. Lots of travelers. 'Twas a big morning for travelers, yesterday was."

"About ten of them, perhaps?" asked Holmes.

"Foreigners? Young ones?"

"Yes. That must have been them," said Holmes

"Aye, there was a group of ten or so foreigners. There was one small chap with them, a leprechaun-looking fellow with a silly mustache."

"And do you know where they might have gone. We have some terribly important news from the family of one of them, and it is essential that we find them."

"They disembarked right smart from their coach, they did, and then they took carriages over to King's Hotel. But I had the impression that they were all going trekking after that."

"Trekking?"

"Aye, sir. It's a right popular thing around here in the summer. The Pennines are an area of outstanding natural beauty, they say, and we get quite a few foreigners coming through here in the summer. Sorry that I cannot help you any more than that, sir. You might ask at King's. They should open up for early breakfast not long after six o'clock."

"That is what we shall do," said Holmes. "We thank you, sir, and terribly sorry to have disturbed your sleep."

"Not to worry, sir. I plan to go right back to it. But was it only those travelers you needed to know about? The foreigners?"

"Yes, why do you ask?"

"Well, sir, there was another group of fellows got off the same train."

A very tiny change in Holmes's facial expression told me that he was more than somewhat interested.

"Was there now? Dear me, that is a bit confusing. Were they foreigners as well or Englishmen?"

"Oh, they were English all right, as English as they get. Looked like a rugby team from the East End of London if you ask me. They were right slow about getting off the train. I had to reprimand them several times. They held up the departure, and we don't like any of that around here."

"No, that was terribly inconsiderate of them. Is there a match taking place against your local boys?"

"Not that I've heard of, sir. Mind you I don't hear everything, seeing as I work through the night and have to sleep during the day. So, maybe there is, I can't say for sure.""

"Did you happen to hear where they were headed?"

"Can't say, but I would guess the nearest pub. They didn't look to me like the trekking types. Most likely the Greyhound, just up the road. But as I said, I can't say for sure. But neither did they look the type that would have two gentlemen coming after them in a special. More like what a London bobby might come chasing after, if you know what I mean, sir."

We thanked the fellow again and departed from the station into the dark and deserted streets of Darlington.

"Where to now, Holmes?" I asked.

He did not answer quickly.

Finally, "I am debating whether to follow our young Spaniards or to find out who this rugby team was and what they are doing here."

"I thought the chap at the station said he wasn't sure, but they might have come for a match with the locals."

Holmes positively glared at me with undisguised scorn.

"Good Lord, Watson, I know it is not yet daybreak, but surely you cannot be so dull as to think that a possibility."

"And why not?" I demanded, feeling rather indignant. "Teams from London travel all over to country to play matches against the locals. Happens all the time."

"And when, and in what town, have you ever heard of a match taking place of which the station officer had no knowledge? They are privy to all news and gossip even before the local press have heard a whisper. No, Watson. Those men, mere ruffians most likely, did not come here for a rugby match."

I had to admit that he had me on that one.

"I suppose you are right. So, where to then?"

"We do not have any firm data on the whereabouts of the ruffians. We do know that our young Spaniards were taken to the King's Hotel, so that is where we go next."

"But nobody there will be awake yet."

"They will be five minutes after we arrive."

Chapter Eight
One Thing Alvin
Will Not Do

HOLMES SEEMED TO KNOW exactly where the hotel was located. This did not surprise me as it was his common practice to review a map of a town or village he was about to visit and commit every detail into his prodigious memory. The hotel was a few blocks from the station, on the other side of the River Skerne. As we arrived there, I heard the hour of five o'clock sounding from the town clock nearby. The front door was unlocked, and we entered the dark and silent lobby.

There was a bell on the front desk, and Holmes picked it up and rang it loudly and without ceasing until a groggy chap emerged, still tucking his shirttails into his trousers.

"All right, man. Quit your ringin'. I've not gone doylem. What's it you two gadgies want at this hour?""

"Very sorry to disturb you, sir," said Holmes. "However, we are in need of urgent assistance."

"Well then say wat you wants so I can gan back to me scratcha."

"What we wants," said Holmes, "is to confirm that a group of young foreigners came by yesterday morning, and might they still be here?"

"Ah, and you would be another nebby chap from London, would you? Well all I can tell you is aye, they came, and they gang. Fine group of lads and hinnies they were. They were clammin' so the missus gave them their full English and sent them on their ways."

"And, my good man, can you tell me where they went after they departed from your fine establishment?"

"Wot's it to you?"

"It is a tragic family matter concerning one of them. Pray understand and assist us, sir."

"Very well, sir. I can tell ya. Come noon hour they booked two carriages, from Jimmy Purvis and Hector Carr they did.

And they took them up into the Pennines. Where to I dinna ken. You can ask Jimmy and Heck when they come around at breakfast. Starts at half six for the trekkers. Now, if'n you no mind, I'm plum paggered and goin' back to sleep. You can wait yourselves here in the lobby seein' as no one in the town will be up until after six."

He turned and departed back into his quarters.

Holmes looked thoroughly vexed. He did not take kindly to being forced to wait. I began to walk over to one of the large chairs with the hope of a short nap before being conscripted for breakfast at an ungodly, uncivilized hour.

"Come, Watson. Let us redeem the time," he said, and I felt that sinking feeling one has when a much longed-for nap vanishes.

"The Durham Police have a small station just three blocks away. They will have a night officer on duty, and we shall recruit him for our mission."

He did not wait for my reply and was already out the door and on the pavement when I caught up with him.

"Really, Holmes. Do you honestly believe that we need reinforcements from the police? For all we know, these young folks may be off on nothing more than a pleasant walk in the park."

"If that is the case, I shall apologize to the constable for wasting his time. It is, however, a risk that I am not willing to take."

The small police station was, as Holmes had said, only a few blocks away and through the street window we could see a policeman sitting at a desk, apparently reading a magazine.

The door was open, and Holmes walked inside. I followed.

"Good morning, officer," said Holmes cheerily. "Might I have a word with you?"

The fellow put down his magazine and gave a questioning look up at Holmes.

"And just who might you be?" he said.

"My name is Sherlock Holmes."

"You don't say. Well, then I'm the King of Siam. Now it so happens that I was just reading about Mr. Sherlock Holmes in this here magazine, but it don't say anything about him living up here in the North or ever having visited. At the moment, you're supposed to be wondering around the Dartmoor Moors."

Holmes walked over to the desk and looked at the copy of the *Strand* that the constable had been reading.

"May I?" he asked as he picked up the magazine. He quickly flipped the pages until he came to one on which I could see an sketch of himself created for me by my illustrator, Sidney Paget. He spread the magazine wide open and held the illustration up beside his face.

"I believe, officer, that you will discern a distinct similarity." He put the magazine back on the table. "Now sir, might I request your assistance?"

The dear chap was utterly flabbergasted.

"I don't ... I don't ... I don't believe it. Sherlock Holmes walks into my police station at five o'clock in the bleedin' morning. And you, sir? Are you Doctor Watson?"

"Indeed, I am," I answered, extending my hand, which he took and shook rather uncertainly. "And who do I have the honor of addressing?"

"Who? You mean me? Name's Rutherford, doctor. Constable Third Class Timothy Rutherford, doctor, sir."

"A pleasure to meet you," I said, "and do excuse our barging in on you at this ungodly hour but, I assure you, my friend, Mr. Sherlock Holmes believes that some heinous crime is about to take place here in Darlington. Is that not correct, Holmes?"

"Possibly. It is not yet certain, but there is a distinct possibility."

The two of us seated ourselves on the far side of Constable Rutherford's desk, and Holmes patiently explained the events that had culminated with our being in a police station in the North before dawn. The dear fellow's eyes went wide and stayed that way. He asked numerous questions that demanded that Holmes merely repeat what he had already told the fellow but, to his credit, Holmes displayed not a jot of his notorious impatience with police officers and clearly answered the man's questions.

"What then sir, do we do now?" the fellow muttered once he had become convinced of the peril that might descend on his jurisdiction.

"We now," said Holmes, "return to the King's Hotel, enjoy a decent breakfast, enquire as to where our possible unfortunates have been taken, and engage a means of livery to follow them. Shall we go?"

By the time we returned to the hotel, the staff were laying out the tables in the basement breakfast room. The three of us took our seats, and within ten minutes a score of other hotel guests had entered. They were all dressed in the somewhat theatrical manner of those who pretend to alpine accomplishments, and the conversation seemed to be a constant round of one-upmanship regarding which mountain peak, or which splendid sea-side view, or which rare species of migrating bird had been seen. But one of the guests sat by himself at a small table in the back of the room and was clearly not interested in engaging in the exaggerated tales of these latter-day Audubons.

"Watson," Holmes said. "Would you mind going over to that fellow who is sitting by himself and insist that he join us for breakfast? And do not take 'no' for an answer."

I gave Homes an odd look, but I had learned time and again that he would have his reasons that mortal reason knew not of.

The fellow was a large man, carrying a considerable amount of body fat, but underneath it, I could discern a powerful young body.

"My good man," I said "we see that you are here all alone and that just won't do. Please, come over and join us for breakfast."

He looked up at me, his face betraying his surprise and he managed to mutter a reply.

"Oh, oh, well thank you, sir. But it's no matter. I am fine here, sir. But thank you kindly."

"My dear fellow," I said in my most doctorly voice, "I am a doctor, and I can see by looking at you that you are enduring a great amount of stress. Sitting and having a friendly chat with two gentlemen and a police officer about rugby or football or the racetrack will not make whatever it is disappear, but it will make your breakfast far more enjoyable and digestible. What say? Do come and join us. We insist."

He looked at me and then over at Holmes and Constable Rutherford, who were smiling at him and making beckoning gestures. He rose, rather awkwardly and came over and joined us. He dropped his large body into the vacant chair at our table and nodded to my colleagues.

"Delighted to have you join us," said Holmes, raising his cup of coffee toward the fellow. "My friend and I are also visitors to this lovely part of the country, and the local constable is telling us all about its wonders. And who might we have the pleasure of having join us?"

"Uh...right...name's Alvin Benson. Just Al is what I'm called."

"An honor to meet you, Mr. Benson," said Holmes. "This here is Constable Rutherford of the Durham Police. My colleague is Doctor Watson, and I am Sherlock Holmes."

Holmes handed the young chap his calling card. The fellow stared at it, saying nothing. The blood vanished from the lad's face, and his eyes began to look furtively around the room as if seeking a means of immediate escape.

"Please, sir," said Holmes, "do try to compose yourself. We have no interest whatsoever in apprehending you. All we need is for you to be somewhat forthright with us as to why you find yourself in Darlington at half six on a summer morning."

"I...I don't know," he stuttered. "I'm...I'm just here, that's all. Can't a fellow come and enjoy the North? No crime in that is there?"

"None whatsoever. None in the least," said Holmes. "And if I am not mistaken, you have already paid your debt to society, have you not? You are the Alvin Benson who was recently released from Newgate after serving two years for a robbery on Saville Row? That is who you are, is it not?"

Again, a look of near panic overtook his face and Holmes continued.

"If I recall correctly, you were rather rough on one of the clerks at a very select tailor's shop, and you walked away with a dozen fine suits over your arm. I must say, you have excellent taste in men's garments. A shame you were not allowed to keep them. You would look quite splendid now if you were wearing one of them."

Rutherford and I laughed heartily at this comment, and the beefy fellow relaxed and smiled.

"It were not my finest hour, sir."

"No, Alvin," said Holmes, suddenly in a quiet grave voice. "You finest hour is about to begin now. And you are going to tell us why it is you are here in Darlington and what has happened to the group of young foreigners who you followed here."

The poor fellow said nothing and merely stared at the full plate of breakfast that had just been placed in front of him. He raised his head and gave a firm look back at Holmes.

"I will tell you what I know, but there must be one condition."

"I assure you, Alvin, and I am sure that Constable Rutherford will agree, that should you be forthcoming and tell us what we need to know, no charges will ever be pursued against you. You will agree to that, Constable?"

"Fine with me," answered Rutherford.

The big fellow smirked in reply. "Do you truly believe I fear being sent back to prison? Hells bells, I would be safe there. No, the condition is that it must never become known that I was the one that informed on the rest of my team. If they knew, if *he* knew, then my life would not last longer than a fart in a hurricane. That's my condition. Will you agree to that?"

"We shall indeed," said Holmes. "I have been trusted with the secrets of the lowliest pickpocket up to the noblest of swindlers and have never betrayed a confidence. You have my word as you do the word of these two men."

Rutherford and I both nodded our assent.

"You already seem to know, Mr. Holmes, that I have had a few encounters with the law."

"I am aware of that."

"Mostly I got away with what I done. I would come by a fine shop first thing in the morning when there was no other customers. I would enter real quiet and come up behind the clerk, grab him and punch his lights out before he knew who it was or what hit him."

"Ah, the shops along Old Bond Street? That was you?"

"Right, sir. That is was. I should have stuck to jewels and plate but I got foolish and went for fine suits and boots."

"And you were apprehended," said Holmes, "were you not, because the suit you were wearing at the time was obviously several sizes too small for you and even a junior inspector from Scotland Yard spotted you?"

"Right, sir. That was me,"

"But you are not here to rob a shop," said Holmes. "Not to disparage the shopkeepers of the North but it would be hardly worth your time. So why are you here and why are you no longer with the rest of your team, as you called them?"

"Sir, I am not a good man, and I confess to having robbed and assaulted my share of blokes, but I don't do murder."

All three of us looked hard at the fellow before Holmes spoke quietly.

"Explain yourself, please."

"What I'm saying is that I can face prison. But I don't fancy swinging from a gallows, and I am not fond of spending my eternal life in hell. Is that explanation enough?"

"I was not asking you to explain your objection to murder, Alvin. Kindly explain who is about to be murdered and where and how."

"We were recruited over the past two days by some men who we knew to be right up there in the ranks of London's criminals. They said that they were having a rebellion amongst some in the lower ranks and that they had to be taught a lesson. They were going to bring the lot of them out here to the hills and have us lie in wait for them, and then give them the thrashing of their lives and frighten the livers out of them and then go home again. We were offered five pounds each if we would carry out the job. That was the best money anyone could make for two days work and so we all accepted. But then last night as we were drinking in the pub, one of the chaps who was a bit of a leader starts to talk and, like they say, *in vino veritas,* and he whispers to me that the real job is to take them far into the forest and murder all but one of them and send that one back with the story of what happens to those who do not do what they've been told. That's the true job, and I lay awake all that night thinking about it and decided that I wanted no part of it. So, yesterday afternoon when they all got up and drove away I was nowhere to be found. The first train back to London leaves in an hour. So, as soon as I have something to eat, I am running back to the station and going home. There, sir. Is that enough of an explanation for you?"

"No, Alvin, it is not," said Holmes. "Where are those young foreigners and where are the other members of your group now? Kindly be precise."

"I don't know."

"I don't believe you."

"Honest. I swear. I swear on the soul of my gran who raised me. I don't know. We were told something about trekking in the Pennines, but that was all. You'll have to ask the livery men who took them away."

What followed was a short staring contest between Holmes and Alvin. Then Alvin rose and gave a nod to the three of us.

"Good day, gentlemen. I think I can live with my conscience now, having given it all over to you. If you need me again, I am sure you can find me in London."

He deposited portions of his breakfast in his pockets and quickly departed the room.

Holmes glanced at his watch and turned to the constable.

"Do you know the residence of the livery drivers? Can you take us there?"

"That I do, Mr. Holmes. But it will save us no time. They come by the hotel at a quarter past seven every morning to pick up the trekkers. That's only fifteen minutes."

Holmes said nothing as he left the breakfast room. I assumed that he would spend the next quarter hour pacing and smoking on the pavement outside the hotel.

Chapter Nine
Oh! Dear God, ... NO!

ON SCHEDULE, TWO CARRIAGES, outfitted as small omnibuses, approached the hotel. The constable strode up to them before the drivers could climb down.

"Hector, Jimmy, here, please. Yesterday afternoon, which of you drove some trekkers up into the hills?"

"We both did," replied one of them.

"Right, well which of you took a group of young foreigners?"

"That would have been me," answered one of them. "What of it?"

"Where did you take them?"

"All the way to the High Force Hotel."

"Did you now?" said the constable. "Fine. Well, you now have to take the three of us there too, and as fast as you can make it."

"Aw, Timmy. You can no do that to me. I've a contract to take the hotel's guests every morning."

"Not this morning, you don't, Hector."

Here, I interrupted. "I assure you, sir, that you will be compensated the same or better. The guests will still be here waiting for you when you return. You will double your wage for the day."

The driver smiled and shrugged. "As you wish, gentlemen. Climb aboard."

The constable and I moved toward the carriage. Holmes hesitated and turned to the other driver.

"Sir, do I understand that yesterday afternoon you also drove a group up into the hills."

"That I did, sir."

"And who were they?"

"Don't rightly know, sir. They looked like they could be a rugby team but they were a bit of a sullen lot. No singin' or laughin' and they just sat quiet all the way."

"And where did you take them? To the same hotel?"

"A few blocks away, sir. There are some roomin' houses nearby that are available cheap to trekkers who have less to spend. I dropped them off there, sir."

Holmes now stepped quickly into Hector's carriage.

"Driver," he shouted. "As fast as you can go. An extra sovereign if you run the horses the whole distance."

"Will do, sir. I can fast trot my darlings all the way to the Castle but we'll still have to stop there to give them some water and some nourishment otherwise they'll never make it up the hills."

He laid his whip across the haunches of his two horses, and we took off at a quick pace out of Darlington and into the rolling hills of County Durham.

A pleasant carriage ride through the country on a beautiful sunny day does much to lift one's spirits and the constable and I relaxed and enjoyed the brisk morning air and glorious sunshine, occasionally chatting to each other about the places we were passing.

Holmes said nothing. His face was set as flint. His hands, which he would often place in front of his chest with his fingertips touching, now rested on his thighs. His fists were clenched.

After ninety minutes of travel, we stopped at a small livery station within sight of the magnificent Bernard Castle. The constable and I stood and admired it whilst Holmes did nothing but glare at his watch.

"Can't be helped," said the driver to Holmes. "It's uphill all the way from here. They need the rest and water if you are going to make it all the way there."

For Holmes, I am sure those twenty minutes seemed an eternity. But we were soon on our way, leaving the open farmlands behind and entering the great valley of the River Tees. It led us into the towering hills and rock outcrops of the North Pennines.

Holmes broke his silence only once and spoke to me.

"You did bring your service revolver, did you not?"

"No."

"No!? Watson ..."

From the medical doctor's bag that I and all doctors never travel without, I took out my revolver of choice when traveling into the countryside.

"A short-barreled Webley is useless at distance," I said. "I brought my Colt. The Americans do know something about shooting across wide open spaces."

"Ah, excellent."

That was all he said until ten o'clock when we alighted at the High Force Hotel in the middle of the River Tees Valley. Holmes quickly entered the building and accosted the proprietor.

"Are the visitors from Spain still here?" he demanded.

"No, sir. They've gone hiking for the day. Mind you they let me know in no uncertain terms that they were not all from Spain. Most of them were from South America, Ecuador and the Argentine and the like. They are quite proud…"

"Where did they go?" interrupted Holmes. "It is urgent that we know."

The constable chimed in, "You heard him, Stanley. Urgent. Where did they go? What trail?"

The fellow looked rather ill at ease and sputtered his reply.

"They're gone all day on the trail to the great fells and back. We packed them lunches and sent them off about an hour ago. If you run, you should be able to overtake them in a mile or two."

"Come," said the constable. "I know the trail. A bit of a climb but it is well marked."

Holmes threw a furtive glance toward my leg. I could read his thoughts.

"I cannot change it for a better one, Holmes," I said. "It will keep up. I'll have to make it do so."

The three of us flew out of the hotel and began a steady run up the trail to the north-west. There was an immediate climb as we ascended to the top of the escarpment that lay just beyond the hotel. In the distance, I could see, and I could soon hear the roar of the High Force Waterfall, one of the highest in all of England. The rains of the past few weeks had increased the flow of the River Tees so that the great cataract was in full flood. At any other time, it would have been an inspiring sight to stop and gaze upon. Soon, we had reached the pool below and were getting drenched in the mist that was flying from the nearly hundred feet of falling water.

Suddenly, Constable Rutherford raised his hand, halting our run. He pointed to the ridge of open rock that must have been another fifty feet above the falls.

"There they are!" he shouted above the thunderous cascade.

"Why would they stop there?" I shouted back to him.

Holmes swiftly pulled out his small pocket telescope and raised it to his eye.

"Our thugs are up there as well. They are standing in a group, but it looks as if the young visitors are kneeling. Yes, it looks as if they have been bound hand and foot. And ... oh, dear God ... NO!...NO!"

In horror, we watched at one of the young women was grabbed from the group. As two burly men held her fast, another cut away her bonds and then, holding her two arms to the side they ran toward the edge of the precipice and hurled her over. Even above the roar, we could hear her screams of terror as she plunged into the racing waters above the brim and then was swept over the falls to her death.

The men had already moved back to the prisoners and were lifting another one of them, a young man, to his feet and forcing him to toward the edge.

"Watson!" Holmes shouted at me. "Shoot them! Now! By the time we get up there, it will be too late. Shoot them!"

I pulled out my Colt and took aim. The killers had already cut the bonds of their next victim. He was struggling violently, but five men were on him and had him completely overpowered. I raised the revolver and aimed into the cluster of thugs. It was a very long shot even for a powerful gun with a long barrel. I took an account of the drop in the flight of the bullet, the wind blowing back off the falls, and then I said a prayer and pulled the trigger.

One of them fell to the ground, clutching at his leg.

"Good. You got him. Now, another," screamed Holmes.

I took aim, prayed again, and fired. Another one of them fell to the ground, holding his shoulder. Now the rest of them let go of the intended victim and took cover. They obviously knew that they were under fire. Quickly they threw the arms of their two wounded comrades around the shoulders of those who had not been struck and hobbled them away over the far side of the crest and out of sight.

"Fast, up the hill!" cried Holmes.

"Follow me," shouted Constable Rutherford and he led the led the way. I scrambled behind him and Holmes, cursing the Jezail bullet of so many years go with every step up the rocky incline. By the time we reached the top my leg was in agony, but there was no choice but to keep running.

The killers had vanished and the young folks, led by the fellow who had so narrowly escaped being hurled into the abyss, were already untying each other. Several of them, both men and women, were sobbing hysterically.

Holmes's gaze was fixed along the path that the killers must have taken in their escape as if he were about to give chase after them.

"Never mind," said the constable. "I'll put the word out. We'll have a troop of officers and dogs up here by late this afternoon. If there's one thing we know how to do, it's track fellows who are running into the forests and dales. We'll have them all by daybreak. Noon at the latest."

Holmes nodded and turned to the solace of the now free prisoners. One of them, a small short man, threw his arms around Holmes and started shouting words in Spanish that I assumed, hearing 'gracias' over and over again, appeared to be words of thanks. It was the registrar of the Institute, Mr. Alvarez.

Holmes abruptly loosed himself from the embrace and threw the fellow to the ground.

"You despicable monster," he said. "How could you have been so vile? What were you paid? Thirty pieces of silver?"

"Oh, señor, señor," Alvarez, cried. "You have saved my life. They would have killed me too."

"No, they would not," snapped Holmes. "You were in league with them, and you would have been the sole person spared so you could be sent back with the story to instill terror into the others.

"Constable Rutherford," Holmes now said to the policeman. "Arrest this man. He is to be charged with being an accessory to murder, and with conspiracy to commit murder."

He then turned and leaned over the kneeling registrar.

"If you want to escape the gallows you had better reveal everything you know about the organization behind all of these crimes. Start talking. Now!"

Instead of responding, the man, still on his knees, buried his head in his hands and began to shake his head.

"No, señor. Por favor, no. I cannot do that. Please do not ask me. I have a wife and children. If I say anything, he will kill them. He will torture them. Send me to the gallows but do not force me to inform. Shoot me. Shoot me now. It would be better."

He went silent for a minute, still shaking his head. Then he lifted his eyes and looked toward the edge of the gorge. Suddenly, he jumped to his feet and pushed Holmes away. Holmes made a futile effort to grab him as he began to sprint toward the abyss.

"No!" I screamed. "Don't!"

Constable Rutherford reacted like a startled jack rabbit and ran after him, tackling him around the knees just inches from the edge. He quickly overpowered the much smaller man and soon had a set of cuffs around his wrists and another around his ankles.

Mr. Alvarez continued to cry and sob. "Let me die, just let me die. *Te lo ruego*, it is better if I die. He cannot punish me if I am dead."

Chapter Ten
Why the Mathematician?

$$(a+b)^n = \sum_{k=0}^{n} \binom{n}{k} a^{n-k} b^k$$

WE STAYED ON IN DARLINGTON for three full days. True to his word, Constable Rutherford and his colleagues on the County Durham Police Force tracked down and arrested all of the band of killers. Those who bore the bullets from my revolver were found before morning less than a mile from the waterfall, shivering and suffering from exposure. The hounds and their keepers ferreted out the others before they could get close to a railway station.

The body of a young woman, identified as a Miss Sofia Roccuzzo of Cordoba in the Argentine, had been pulled from the River Tees as it flowed through Middleton-in-Teesdale. A delegate from the British Legation in Buenos Aires had been wired and dispatched to inform her family.

Lestrade appeared the following afternoon, along with two of his men. They interviewed all of the culprits, but to a man, not one of them would reveal anything about who had recruited them to the deadly task.

The young people from Spain and South America were likewise fearful to speak, but Lestrade's efforts with them were far more successful.

"They all had similar stories," Lestrade reported to Holmes and me as we sat over a late dinner. "Every one of them was facing some sort of persecution back home. Some in Spain, most in South America. Poor idealistic young revolutionaries and labor organizers, that's what they were. Or their parents were. They were all approached with an offer of safe travel to London and refuge and shortly after they arrived they were forced into crime to pay off their debts. And these were just the Spaniards. They say there are also Russians and Italians, French and Germans…all in the same boat. They gave us good information about who all is behind this web of crime."

"Did they not," I asked, "fear for their safety if they spoke to you?"

"We made them a promise. Told them that they would be guaranteed safe passage out of England and to the overseas country of their choice. Made to same offer to that Alvarez fellow for his family."

"Where will they all go?" I asked. "The Cape? Canada? Australia?"

"They're no fools. They all chose New York."

On the fourth day, we were back in London and had been asked to meet Lestrade down at his office on The Embankment.

"A few things I thought you might like to know," he said to Holmes and me as we sat in his barren office.

"And what might those be?" said Holmes.

"Right. All the rest of the names on that list you gave me? We brought them all in and made them the same offer of transport and protection. They all spilled the beans as far as they could, although none seem to know who is behind it all, pulling the strings, if you know what I mean. Within a week all of them will be escorted to Southampton and then on to America. They'll be fine. But that's not all."

"I am sure there is more you just cannot wait to tell us," said Holmes.

"Right. What else? Well, last night the bobbies pulled a body out of the Thames. No papers on him, but in his hip pocket he had a card that bore the name of Mr. Sherlock Holmes of 221B Baker Street."

Holmes quietly sighed. "A big lad?"

"Could have been a fine prop in a scrum. You might leave the poor fellow's name at the desk when you go, Holmes."

"I shall do that. Is that all?"

"Yes. Well…no…not quite."

"Yes, Inspector?"

"One question, right from the start."

"Yes, Inspector?"

"The first fellow, the one what was tossed off the steeple," said Lestrade.

"Yes, and what about him?"

"He doesn't fit with all the rest of them. He was a bleedin' mathematics scholar, not a petty criminal. He came on a scholarship to Oxford, not by way of some secret recruiting scheme. Where does he fit in?"

"That, Inspector, I do not know."

"Well, would you bloody well mind finding out, Holmes?"

"I shall do forthwith," answered Holmes. "And may I assume that I have your permission to use my methods and not be confined to yours?"

"I didn't hear that, Holmes. Now get out of here and get to work."

We hailed a cab outside of Scotland Yard.

"Brown's Hotel!" Holmes called to the driver.

"Do you think," I asked Holmes, "that Miss Luisana will know any more than she has already told us?"

"Possibly. It is also possible that she is in grave danger herself and must be warned. She may also need to get herself to Southampton as quickly as she can."

I had not thought of that likelihood and once again quietly admired Holmes's thoughtful consideration. Although he claimed he eschewed any emotional attraction to women, he was invariably paternal in his protection of them.

"Awfully sorry to disappoint you, gentlemen," said the man at the desk of Brown's, giving us a sly wink and a smile. "You will have to find another way to enjoy your evening. Miss Luisana checked out of here this afternoon. Took her bags, paid her bill and departed. We'll miss her. She was jolly good for business." He winked again.

"And do you know," asked Holmes, "where she is going?"

"Wanting to follow her, are you? Cannot blame you in the least, sir. But awfully sorry. We have no forwarding address. All she said was that she was off to a country estate somewhere. I would hazard a guess that another one of her gentlemen friends has decided he alone will be looking after her from now on."

Holmes was crestfallen as bade the fellow a good evening and we left. Immediately upon setting foot on the pavement, he called for one of the waiting cabs. I followed him into it.

"And now where?" I asked.

"The George Pub on the Strand," he called out to the driver. Then he turned to me.

"We are meeting Señora Patricia. She is going to assist us one more time."

"To do what?"

"Burgle the Institute of St. Ignatius and look for data in Mr. Alvarez's office."

"Oh, is that all?" said I. "And did you bring your lock picking tools along?"

"Not necessary."

"How is that, Holmes? It is now getting on to dark, and they do lock the doors at the end of the day. How are you going to get in without picking the lock?"

"Señora Patricia has a key."

We met Patricia at the pub and walked around the corner to the Institute. She seemed to me to have become an admirer of Holmes and rather in awe of his character and intellect. She eagerly opened the door and turned up the lamps.

"Is that wise," I asked. "Anybody can tell that people are inside."

"We teach classes in the evenings," she said. "They do not start for another hour. We will have to move quickly."

The registrar's office door was closed, but it opened in a few seconds with the application of a small nail file that Holmes kept for such occasions.

"We are searching," he said to the two of us, "for anything that might have a possible connection to this web of criminal enterprise. Miss Patricia, if you could direct your efforts to documents written in Spanish, the doctor and I shall do the same for materials in English."

We started our search immediately. It seemed all for naught. The file drawers and cases were stuffed with bills of lading, purchase orders and invoices, registration cards for students going back the past ten years, copies of tests and examinations, blank certificates of accomplishment, and all sorts of similar records as would be expected in the office of a registrar.

I was working my way through a drawer of general correspondence when I came upon an unmarked file immediately behind one that was labeled for 'Morgan.'

There was a score or more of letters and documents in the file, but my eye was immediately attracted to the one on the top. It was a list of names in Spanish of some thirty people, mostly males but with several females as well. As I looked it over, I recognized the majority of them as also having been on the list we had found in Oxford. The date at the top read only five days ago. There was a small note pinned to the page. On it, in small but neat handwriting were the words "Good work," and signed "M."

"Holmes," I said. "You might want a look at this."

He came over, looked at the list and nodded several times. Then he picked it up and set it aside and looked at the page below it. It was a letter with an envelope attached. The date read a fortnight ago. There was no address, but the Royal Mail stamp read 'Oxford.' It was typed, and it ran:

Dear Sir:

I am writing to give you the opportunity do the right thing and confess your grievous fraud to the community of scholars.

You have a reputation as a learned mathematician and a lucrative practice as a mathematics coach. Your reputation has been established by the brilliant works that you claim to have written, viz. "A Treatise on the Binomial Theorem" and "The Dynamics of an Asteroid."

I am a scholar of the history of mathematics and have made my area of expertise the study and recognition of the many accomplished but unhonored mathematicians of South America. I have discovered in our small journals, written in the Spanish language, two articles that are almost identical to what you claim to have written yourself. One was written by Profesor Rafael de La Fuente of the Universidad de Los Andes, the other by Profesor Oswaldo Calero, a brilliant scholar from the Universidad Católica de Santiago de Guayaquil.

You have stolen the work of these scholars and passed it off as your own. I cannot allow this sin to remain uncovered.

I will give you ten days to announce your falsehoods and resign your coaching positions.

You are advised to govern yourself accordingly.

It was not signed. Attached to it, in the same small neat script was a note that read: "Find out who wrote this and report back immediately." Again, it was signed "M."

Holmes looked the letter over for several minutes before putting it into his pocket.

"This is significant," he said. "It may open the path for me to whoever is behind this vast web of crime in London and beyond. Whoever it is, he is a monster beyond belief. A man who throws a scholar from a tower, who burns others alive and who murders a young woman by pitching her into a raging waterfall must not be allowed to continue to live."

He paused again and closed his eyes. He spread his long arms out and rested his hands on the desk, his head bowed.

"Watson," he said, still with his head still down. "I fear I have no choice. I must devote such intellect and skills as I have to unearthing and destroying this evil genius, and I will do so. I swear to you and to Providence that I will not stop until he is hoist on his own petard. I will do it, if it is the last thing I do."

Epilogue

READERS OF MY ACCOUNTS of the adventures of Sherlock Holmes already know what took place in the months and years following the events I have put to account in this story. Shortly after our return to London from the North, Holmes discerned the identity of Professor Moriarty, although he did not share that knowledge with me until a year had passed. That following year, 1891, was the time when the two of us raced away from England and over to Switzerland and where Holmes and the Napoleon of crime engaged in their deadly encounter at Reichenbach Falls.

As readers also know, the web of crime that Holmes discovered as a result of the seemingly inconsequential theft of a wheeled Gladstone bag exposed only the tip of the iceberg. Eventually, an enormous layered organization of criminals engaged in both their own pursuits and for hire, was exposed and destroyed. The small group of Spanish-speaking young men and women turned out to be only a tiny strand of the vast web.

With the help of Scotland Yard, all of "the Spaniards" were safely transported to America, and I have been informed that were soon engaged in supporting revolutionary changes that would advance the cause of downtrodden workers, from fishermen in Maine to farm laborers in California. Holmes wished them well, although he advised them that their struggle might take decades.

To this day, I am not aware of what became of the beautiful Señorita Luisana, although a woman who looked remarkably like her could be seen in a recent photograph in the *Times*. She was standing in a group of people just behind the Prince of Wales.

Señora Patricia, without whose initial request to Holmes for help and subsequent invaluable assistance we could not have succeeded, informed us that she and her husband would be departing London for Canada. Her doing so was delayed by the joy of learning that, after a decade's hiatus, she was expecting a second child. I was pleased and honored beyond words when she asked if I would be her doctor and assist in the delivery. I, of course, gladly accepted, but with one inviolable condition. In no uncertain terms, I insisted, no matter how great her admiration, should the baby be a boy, was she to name him *Sherlock*. One of those in my life was more than enough.

Historical and Other Notes

Sherlockian scholarship has determined that the final battle between Sherlock Holmes and Professor James Moriarty took place at Reichenbach Falls in Switzerland on the fourth of May, 1891. The events recorded in this new mystery therefore occurred one year prior to that.

During the late 1890s and early 1900s, the city of London became the safe destination for thousands of political refugees from many countries in Europe as well as for labor activists and revolutionaries from South America.

Darlington, in County Durham is located about thirty miles / fifty kilometers southeast of the High Force Waterfall. Those falls are among the highest in the United Kingdom and are a favorite of hikers and tourists still today. The North Pennines are designated as an Area of Outstanding Natural Beauty.

For those with sufficient money and in a great hurry, it was possible to "engage a special" railway engine and private car. In the Canonical story, *The Final Problem*, this was the tactic Professor Moriarty used in his pursuit of Sherlock Holmes.

There is no Instituto Español de St. Ignatius in London, but there is today an Instituto Cervantes near the same address which provides excellent services to those seeking to learn the Spanish language and enjoy Spanish culture.

The George on the Strand still serves food and drink to barristers and solicitors. The Ten Bells Pub adjacent to the Spitalfields Market is still in operation. It is famous for having played a role in the murders committed by Jack the Ripper.

The Mystery of 222 Baker Street

A New Sherlock Holmes Mystery

Chapter One
The Old Order Changeth

QUEEN VICTORIA DIED the day before this mystery began. Her passing at her residence on the Isle of Wight was not unexpected. We all knew that our dear Old Girl was not only getting on but had been in failing health for some time. And yet there was not a living soul in the entire British Empire who did not, like me, feel a profound sense not just of loss but of having become unmoored, adrift upon the sea of history.

Except for the elderly, all of us, male and female, young and old, light-skinned or dark, had never lived a day of our lives under any other monarch. She was always there. She was the constant North Star around which events great and small revolved.

The following morning, the newsboys were screaming out the news, and I bought a paper on my way to my medical practice. My immediate reaction was to ache for the company of my beloved wife, Mary, who had departed our home at the same time that morning as I had and was on her way to visit friends in Wimbledon. It was, I knew, a common human response when suddenly faced with sad news to feel a need to be with those who are close to you, and I sorely missed her company. Somehow, I carried on and fulfilled my duty to my patients through the remainder of the day, but as soon as my schedule would permit, I departed from my office and walked slowly over to Baker Street to be with my closest friend, Sherlock Holmes.

As I ambled my way through Paddington and Marylebone, I was inundated with the shouts of the newsboys announcing the latest. Condolence messages had been received from across the globe, and the papers were already trying to outdo each other with the news and retrospective summaries of all the events and changes that had taken place during the six decades and more of Her reign.

And, oh my, but how the world had changed. When I was a schoolboy in short pants, the great schooners and magnificent sailing ships gracefully bobbed over the waves and cut through the seven seas. Now they were long gone, replaced by steamships belching coal's black smoke and racing across the oceans at speeds that were previously unimaginable. If my father had wanted to send a letter to a relative in Australia, he could count on its arriving there two months later and wait another two months for a return. Now, a telegram could be fired off and a return received in less than an hour. The owner of a tea garden in Darjeeling could take his tea in the Windermere Hotel and read in the local paper the news of his home football team's win or loss on the previous day.

As I strolled along the wide boulevard of Marylebone Road, I pondered the sights and smells of London that had been part of my life since returning from Afghanistan. When, over twenty years ago, I first moved into to the rooms I shared with Holmes, the streets of London were packed with horse-drawn cabs, omnibuses, and carriages. The smell of horses and horse manure was omnipresent. Today, there were far fewer. They were being steadily replaced by the trains of the ever-expanding Underground, and, more recently, by motor cars, powered by internal combustion engines. Already there were several hundred of these vehicles in the great metropolis adding the distinct odor of their exhaust fumes to the air, and it was predicted that in a few more years, there would be thousands.

On reaching the corner of Marylebone and Baker Streets, I stopped and gazed north toward 221B. This familiar avenue was also changing. The Underground station had been installed and expanded several times and now served two lines. In the mornings and again in the afternoons, the doors of the station would open and both disgorge and swallow thousands of busy working men and women. Adjacent to the pavement, shops and tradesmen's stalls had come and gone.

Across the street from 221B was another rooming house managed by Mrs. Hudson's friend, Mrs. Turner. The occupants of that establishment were constantly changing and, having moved away from the neighborhood, I could never keep track of them. The house immediately opposite my former abode, in which Holmes and I had overpowered the devilish Colonel Moran, was once again empty and advertised to let. Immediately below my old rooms, an enterprising couple had opened a sandwich shop and offered lunches delivered in under five minutes.

221B itself, thankfully, had not changed. Sherlock Holmes still lived there and carried on his now-famous investigations, dutifully attended to and fussed over by the long-suffering Mrs. Hudson. He still devoted himself to the relentless pursuit of justice and the undoing of an endless succession of criminals. For the greater part, he continued to act alone, keeping Scotland Yard at arm's length and complaining about their disappointing lack of imagination. Holmes and Inspector Lestrade, as always, tolerated each other but something there had changed as well. Now, when they found themselves in the same ring, they looked on each other in the way that aging pugilists do when facing their all-too-familiar opponent one more time. It was not what anyone would call a friendship, but Holmes and Lestrade had developed a grudging respect for each other, born of observing the dogged determination, the zeal, the unswerving integrity, and selfless passion for justice by which both of them were marked.

They also shared another trait of character: the refusal ever to give up. Criminals might have appeared to have escaped their clutches at the time of the crime, but time and again both Holmes and the Yard continued their relentless pursuit. Often they succeeded, months or even years later, in dragging villains to the bar. I have not put many of these accomplishments to account as they were not particularly dramatic and appealing to readers, but they were a passionate, if quiet, recurrence in the lives of both Holmes and Lestrade.

Inspector Lestrade, when he wanted to appear officious and assertive, would summon Holmes to the offices of Scotland Yard and assign him a case that he admitted was baffling to his dedicated assistant inspectors. Yet he would also, with increasing frequency, drop in to 221B to discuss some arcane matter or just to visit and pass the time with a man who, though unlike him in so many ways, was, in his heart, a kindred spirit.

It was just such a visit on 5 January 1901 that gave rise to a most puzzling and tragic case.

I had completed my walk to 221B Baker Street, and as I still had a key, I opened the door and entered. Before I closed the door, I heard a shout from the street.

"Doctor Watson! Hold the door for me, please."

I turned around and saw Inspector Lestrade walking toward me from the other side of the street. I gave him a wave and entered, leaving the door ajar. I ascended the stairs, and Lestrade followed me a few steps behind. On reaching the landing at the top, I turned to greet him, but my words were caught in my mouth. The man looked awful. His entire countenance was utterly distraught. I had known Lestrade now for over twenty years, and he had always been the picture of cool, detached competence. Never had I seen him like this.

"Good heavens, man," I said. "What is wrong? You look as if you just lost your best friend."

He gave me a look, walked past and proceeded into the front room and dropped his body into a chair without removing his coat.

"No, Doctor Watson. Not my best friend. One of my best men."

Holmes was sitting opposite him and immediately dropped the file he had been reading.

"One of your best men?" asked Holmes. "Inspector, please explain."

"My man   Inspector Forbes   has been murdered."

"Merciful heavens," I exclaimed. "I just saw him yesterday. That's dreadful."

Lestrade hung his head and slowly shook it. "Yes   it is. And he had a family, a wife and three children. I shall have to go soon and tell them."

Then he looked at my friend.

"I need your help, Holmes."

"Of course," came the reply.

"Thank you. If you could come straight away with me, I will take you to where it happened. Please, Dr. Watson, if you are free, come with us. Your medical opinion would be very useful."

"Most certainly," I said. "Let me hail a cab." I turned to leave and started back down the stairs.

"That will not be necessary," said Lestrade. "Forbes is lying dead right across the street."

Baker Street is a somewhat usual street in the residential area of London and comprised mainly of two- or three-story row houses. Some of the buildings are inhabited by the owners and their families, and others are let out to tenants who are of much the same class as Holmes and I were when we first agreed to share rooms. The house across the street at 222 Baker Street bore the pretentious name of Camden House but suffered from a lack of care and attention by its owner. For that reason, it was often, as it was now, devoid of tenants. Although I had observed the exterior of the house countless times, the only time I had ever been inside was on that fateful night immediately following Holmes's return from the dead, when we watched and waited for Colonel Sebastian Moran.

As Holmes, Lestrade, and I crossed the road, I noticed that two police carriages had pulled up and stopped, and a half-dozen constables had gathered on the pavement in front of the door. They nodded respectfully to Inspector Lestrade and then, recognizing Holmes and me, gave another nod to each of us, but no words were spoken.

"He's back here," said Lestrade as he led us from the vestibule and into the central hallway.

The house was entirely empty. There were a few decrepit pieces of furniture that needed to be put out for the dustman and some cheap paintings on the wall that no thief could be bothered to steal. The air was heavy with the smell of mildew and mold, and the paint on some of the walls was peeling.

Lestrade kept walking all the way to the back of the ground floor. The lamps had been lit and turned up, and we passed police officers standing at the doorway of every room. At the back of the house, we entered the kitchen and crossed over through a short rough door that led into a small windowless back room. I assumed it had served as the abode of a cook or maid but was now empty. There was not a stick of furniture to be seen. On the floor, lying prone in front of the hearth, was the body of a man. He was wearing a heavy winter trench coat, woolen trousers, and the type of boots that were commonly issued to police officers.

Waiting for us in the room was Inspector Peter Jones, also of Scotland Yard, who had worked closely with Holmes in the case of the Red-Headed League. The four of us instinctively stood for several moments in respectful silence. Then Holmes, in a manner that was most uncharacteristic of him, put his hands on the shoulders of Lestrade and Jones and spoke in a quiet and gentle way.

"Inspectors," he said. "Would you be able to tell me what you know so far?"

Lestrade nodded. His body heaved up and down again as he took in a deep breath.

"There's not much I can say. The estate agent came by just over an hour ago to check on the premises and found Forbes in this room. He immediately ran out and called for the local police. They came, did a quick look, saw who it was, and then sent for me."

"The house was locked, I assume," said Holmes "prior to the arrival of the estate agent?"

"Not only the house," replied Lestrade, "both front door and back, but this room too. The agent has a set of keys, of course, and he told us that the owner has the only other set. No one else."

I looked around at the barren little room. It was no more than twelve-foot square, with only one door, no closets or windows, and a small hearth on the back wall. Two cheap imitation Dutch paintings hung askew on the walls. The floor was dusty except in the central portion where numerous people had walked in the past hour.

In the only time I had entered this house in the past, I had not been aware of this room. Holmes and I had approached the back of Camden House by way of the alley that runs north off Blanding Street and moved immediately up the stairs to the second floor and the window that provided such a clear view of our rooms across the street. I assumed that the room in which we now stood had been closed off to ventilation for much of the past few months whilst the house stood vacant. It certainly had an odd odor to it that would have been disbursed by the application of fresh air.

If Holmes had remembered that night with Colonel Moran — and I am sure he did — he gave no sign of it's having any relevance to our present situation. He already had his glass in hand and was plodding around the room, examining the walls and tapping against them. Then he used his stick to tap against all parts of the small ceiling and then the floor.

"There appears to be no other access to this room than through the kitchen and the door of the room," he said. Then he turned to me.

"Watson," he said. "Please examine the body and give the inspector and me your learned opinion as to the time and cause of death."

I got down on my knees and began my examination of the corpse. Rigor mortis had started to set in and was quite apparent in the eyelids, jaw, and neck, and just starting to appear in the limbs and torso. His face was still rosy, and his cheeks somewhat flushed.

"He has not been dead long," I observed. "No more than eight hours and possibly as few as five. It's going on six o'clock now, so that would place his time of death sometime between nine o'clock this morning and one this afternoon."

'You are quite sure of that, Doctor?" asked Lestrade. "The first constables to arrive here asked everyone they could find on Baker Street or in the alley behind if they had seen anything earlier today. No one had seen a thing."

"I have no explanation for how he ended up here," I said. "But there is no doubt that he has not been dead for more than eight hours. The rate of the onset of rigor mortis is well-known. He definitely died sometime between morning and early afternoon."

Neither Holmes nor Lestrade made any reply, so I continued with my post-mortem. There was no evidence of damage to any of the bones in the feet, knees, or legs. The same was true of the pelvic region, the spine and the shoulders. The back of his neck and his hands had not been harmed. With the assistance of a couple of the police officers, I gently rolled the body over. There were no wounds on the body and no evidence of bleeding that was of sufficient volume to have soaked through the clothing, which indicated that he had not died from a gunshot, or stabbing, or a garrote. His forehead and cranium were generally smooth, with every hair still held in place by a light treatment of Macassar. There was a small bump on the back of the skull, but no blow hard enough to kill him had struck his head.

I loosened some of his clothing and gave a cursory glance to his powerful torso. Again, there was nothing, and the skin was still faintly pinkish with occasional batches of pale blue. There was not a single bruise on his abdomen.

"He does not appear," I said, "to have been in any sort of a fight—no signs of a struggle at all. And no marks of any ligature or bruises on his neck. He was not strangled."

"Very well, then," said Holmes. "That eliminates a physical attack. The remaining possibilities are heart failure or poison." He turned then to Lestrade. "I presume that

Forbes was not suffering from any fatal disease or a weak heart?"

"None," said Lestrade. "He was as healthy as a horse."

"Could he have been suffocated?" Holmes asked me.

I shook my head. "No. No man lies still and allows himself to be suffocated. He struggles violently. But there is not a bruise anywhere."

"Your conclusion, doctor?" asked Inspector Jones. "Poison perhaps?"

"Quite possibly," I said. "But as to what type of poison, I cannot tell. There is no sign of vomit or excess saliva. He has not soiled himself. So that rules out curare or some venom from the tropics. Arsenic takes far too long. Cyanide is a possibility."

Holmes dropped to his knees beside me and moved his body so that he could lower his nose to the mouth of the deceased and he sniffed several times.

"Cyanide," he said, "has a telltale scent of almonds. There is none."

I stood up and turned to Inspector Lestrade. His face had a vacant, dazed look and it was clear that his thoughts were elsewhere.

"Inspector?" I said

"Yes oh yes. What?"

"You will send the body to the police morgue, will you not?" I asked.

"Oh, yes. Of course. I will have a couple of the constables look after that."

"You might," I said, "ask them to tell the chaps at the morgue to look for any signs of a skin puncture. I did not see any, but I could easily have missed one. He may have been injected with a syringe."

"Yes. Right. Sorry not to have been paying attention. I'm afraid my mind has been on what I am going to say to his wife and children."

I wished that I could have offered some magic words of comfort to pass along. But there are none. As a doctor, I had learned years ago that the best course was to speak in as kind and gentle manner as possible and give the bereaved a factual account of what had taken place. I knew that Lestrade would do the same, as duty required him to.

I looked again at the lifeless body of Inspector Forbes. Except for the faint but growing tinge of blue, he looked the picture of robust good health. His complexion was as if he had just stepped in from an hour of standing out in the cold, had entered the room, laid down on the floor, and given up the ghost.

"How did he get in here," I asked, "if both exterior doors and the one to this room were locked?"

Both Holmes and Lestrade gave me a condescending look.

"I suppose," I hastened to add, "that someone could have picked the locks."

"I could name twenty men," said Lestrade, "who could have opened both doors in minutes."

"How true," agreed Holmes. "But please tell me, Inspector, did he have his notebook on his person?"

"He did. I have it here. I'll leave it with you. But there was nothing in it that was helpful. Last entry was yesterday afternoon when he sorted out some minor squabble between fishmongers."

"He did, I presume, leave a note at the dispatch desk as to his expected destination?"

"I expect he did," said Lestrade. "Perhaps Inspector Jones can ask about it when he gets back to the Yard. Now, if you will excuse me, I have to go and speak to his family."

Inspector Lestrade walked slowly out of the room and back down the hall. He did not look well.

Holmes turned to Inspector Jones. "Now then, sir, do you know when Forbes was last seen? Did he stop in at the Yard this morning? Was he out and about on any other assignment earlier this morning?"

"Well now, that is a peculiar matter," said Jones. "He was not seen anywhere this morning as far as I know. Last time he was seen anywhere was last night at the Langham Hotel."

"Why!" I sputtered. "That was with me. We walked back together after the reception. I said goodnight to him on the corner of Marylebone and Baker Street."

"Yes, Doctor," said Jones. "You were the last person to see him alive that we can account for. Would you mind telling me why you were with him?"

Chapter Two

Attacked in the Press

THE PREVIOUS EVENING had been a splendid affair, not just because it was a posh reception at one of London's finest hotels, but because I, Dr. John H. Watson, had been the guest of honor.

The delightful event was the annual dinner of the British Medical Association. Being doctors, they are always looking for some fresh ways to remind the populace that the profession of medicine is to be revered and respected beyond all others. Thus, they are constantly on the lookout for yet another member of our club who could be feted for selfless rushing out on a snowy night to deliver a baby, or a handsome, heroic young army medic fresh from the battlefield, or the latest brilliant researcher who had discovered a miraculous cure for a dreaded disease. They had, in some desperation I expected, decided that my humble exploits in accompanying the famous detective, Sherlock Holmes, and in helping him in some small ways to solve no end of heinous crimes, merited a citation of sorts. The Strand magazine had made a sizeable contribution to the evening and had several of their staff present so that they could take the names and addresses of all who attended and subscribe them free for three monthly issues, after which they would have to pay the full fare.

And so, I had been honored and toasted and given a small plaque as "a token of our esteem." To me, it seemed rather a bit much, but Mary was thrilled. Holmes, as would be expected, did not attend, but several officers of Scotland Yard had been invited to add a touch of drama for the benefit of the Press.

At the end of the evening, my wife and I left the hotel and, it being a perfectly still, deep winter night with the stars shining in their vast heavenly display, we decided to walk back to our home near Paddington. Inspector Forbes bumped into us as we departed the hotel and joined us for the stroll. When we reached the corner of Baker Street, he bade us goodnight and, saying that he had some police business to attend to, turned and proceeded along Baker Street. Whatever happened between that time and the discovery of his body was entirely unknown.

"Why were we with him?" I said to Jones. "There was no particular reason. We met by happenstance as we were leaving and we chatted and agreed that it was a jolly good night for a stroll and the three of us walked together."

"Indeed," said the inspector. "And what did you talk about? It is a good twenty minutes from the Langham to the corner of Baker Street. Did Forbes want to know something? Did he ask you anything? What was discussed?"

I wracked my memory.

"Nothing."

"Nothing?" persisted Jones. "You do not chat for twenty minutes about nothing. There must have been something."

"Good Lord," I exclaimed. "Of course, we talked about something, but nothing of any significance."

"Well, such as?"

"Oh goodness. We chatted about the lovely starry night, and about how we had spent Christmas, and all that. And yes, he did ask how Holmes was getting along. He thinks quite highly of him."

"And that was all? All friendly like? No harsh words?"

"Of course not. I did not know the man well, but there was never so much as a hint of animosity between us."

"No, perhaps not. But you did make him look bad in that story you wrote about a case he was involved in."

"Oh, come now," I said. "That was years ago."

It was true that in my account of the missing naval treaty I might have presented the police officer as a bit of a numbskull, but there was no malice intended.

"So, you did not have any words at all between you."

"No. None at all. Besides, I was with my wife, and Inspector Forbes is, or at least was, enough of a gentleman that even if he did hold a grudge against me all these years later, he would never voice it in front of my wife."

"Hmm. Yes. Well, if you say so."

"Good heavens! You are not suggesting that I had anything to do with his death, are you?"

"Oh, no. No. Not at all. Just trying to gather up all the pieces and put them together. That is what we professional detectives have to do even after all these years of watching Holmes do otherwise. It was necessary to confirm that you were the last man to see him alive."

"Other than whoever killed him," I said, in a manner more forceful than I am accustomed to using.

"Right. Yes. Of course. Other than person or persons unknown, who appear to be clever enough to kill a strong, healthy policeman without leaving a mark."

I did not like the tone of this conversation and was about to give Inspector Jones a piece of my mind when Holmes graciously intervened.

"Was there anything, Inspector, that connected Forbes to me? He was, after all, found on Baker Street directly across the road from my home."

"Right. Well, that is a good question, Mr. Holmes. I do not know of anything at the moment, but I shall be looking into it. Now if you will excuse me, I have to return to the Yard and continue my investigation into this case."

He turned and departed, leaving Holmes and me in the small back room along with the corpse of Inspector Forbes and a constable who had been posted there.

"Are you," I asked Holmes, "going to inspect the rest of the house?"

"No. The site has been quite disturbed, but the marks on the floor indicate that he was dragged by one man through the back door and deposited in the place he now rests. The scuffs from his heels and the marks of one man walking backward are still discernible. Had items been disturbed in the other rooms of the house, Lestrade's men would have informed him."

"Anything else?" I asked.

"Only one thing, and I cannot make any sense of it. If you look at the floor in the doorway to this room, it appears to have been wiped or dusted. I am sure that it has some significance, but as of yet, I cannot decide what."

I looked at the spot he had referred to but could make no sense of it either. As there was nothing more to discuss, Holmes and I returned to 221B across the street.

"I found," I said after we had left the empty house, "Jones highly annoying."

"He was just doing his duty," answered Holmes. "And I am aware that he and Forbes were quite close and worked together on many cases. Rather like you and me, my friend. He was doing a good job of keeping the stiff upper lip, but I suspect that inwardly, he was in great turmoil. And when men are in that disposition, they tend to forget their social graces. It is nothing to worry about. But come now, let me offer you a brandy by the fire so you can still your soul before returning to your home. If I am not mistaken, your good wife should have returned by now and will be waiting for you."

He was right, so I quaffed my brandy quickly and made my way out into the dark, winter night. I left Holmes to ponder over the reasons that a murder of a Scotland Yard inspector had happened immediately across the road from 221B Baker Street. Somewhere along Marylebone Road, it dawned on me that I had forgotten completely about our dear departed Queen.

By the time I returned home, my dinner was cold, and my dear wife was none too pleased with me.

I hastened to explain my tardiness, and she graciously sat and had a cup of tea with me whilst I struggled through a plate of now dried out lamb chops, during which time I recounted to my wife the events of the past several hours.

"And so," she mused, "you and Sherlock both believe that it was some unknown poison?"

"That is the best hypothesis so far," I said.

"That is rather curious, you know."

"Really, darling? In what way?"

"Sherlock Holmes solved another case that started out at the Langham Hotel and ended with murder by strange poison."

He did?" I queried and searched my memory. "Which case was that?"

"Mine, dear husband. Mine"

"Oh yes of course."

I heard nothing from Holmes for the next two days, and I busied myself with attending to my patients and catching up on reading the medical journals. Then, early on the third morning, before we had even gotten out of bed, my wife awakened me with a friendly kick to my lower leg.

"Darling, there is something going on outside our door. Listen."

I shook the slumber from my brain and became aware of voices coming through our front door. I got up and peeked through the curtains and observed in the early morning light a score of men gathered on the pavement in front of our home. They were all dressed somewhat carelessly in trench coats that did not appear to be keeping them warm on a cold January morning. Most were puffing on cigarettes, and all were clutching either notebooks or cameras.

"The Press," I said. "What in heaven's name are they doing here?"

"Well darling," answered my wife, "they must be waiting for either you and me to emerge, and I suspect that it is not me."

"Should I go out and see what they want?"

"No darling, you should bathe, dress and have your breakfast and then depart at your usual time."

"They won't be very happy having to wait there in the cold," I said.

"Good. And if half of them caught pneumonia and died, would the world be any the worse?"

"Quite so. Let us enjoy a leisurely breakfast."

Throughout our breakfast there came several knocks on our door and persistent ringing of our bell. We ignored all of them, but I must admit that my curiosity was getting the better of me. I gulped down my last swallow of tea and went to the front hall closet to pull on my coat.

"Not that coat," said my wife. "It is cold outside. You need your warm winter coat. You do not want to appear to be shivering whilst they are taking your picture."

Warmly clad in my heavy woolen coat, scarf, gloves, and hat, I ventured out into the late January morning. I had no sooner opened the door than a young reporter bounded up my stairs.

"Good morning, Dr. Watson. Mind if we ask you a few questions, and how about being a friendly chap and letting us come inside to do so?"

I ignored the impertinence, pulled the door closed behind me and descended into the gaggle. Several flashes of powder from cameras exploded in front of me, followed immediately by a cacophony of shouted questions.

"Dr. Watson! Is it true that you were the last person to see Inspector Forbes alive?"

"What? No, that is not true."

"Do you deny seeing him after your reception at the Langham?" came from another reporter.

"No. I did not say that?"

"Why did he demand to have a word with you?" Now a third man had chimed in.

"He did no such thing."

"So, you deny talking to him."

"I did not say that," I said, now shouting in return.

"You just said that he did not talk to you."

"I said no such thing," I replied, now more than somewhat annoyed.

"Did he inform you that you were being investigated? Maybe sued for slander?"

"Good heavens, no. What possible reason would he have for doing that?"

"Did he tell you that he had evidence that your citation was fraudulent?"

"That is nonsense. He said nothing of the kind."

"So, you now admit that he did demand to speak to you. What did he accuse you of?"

"Nothing," I shouted, now quite angry.

"Nobody talks about nothing. What did he have on you? Did it make you angry? Angry enough for you to want to get rid of him?"

I could not believe what I was hearing from this pack of unruly hyenas and walked briskly along the pavement in search of a cab. The swarm of reporters dogged my footsteps, keeping up their highly offensive questions. Finally, I hailed a cab and reflexively gave them Holmes's address.

I was upset beyond words as I raced up the steps at 221B and barged into the front room. Holmes was dressed in his blue dressing gown, pacing the floor and puffing on a cigarette. I blurted my outrage. He said nothing in response and merely gestured for me to take a seat across from him.

"Well!" I demanded. "Are you not going to tell me how to make this vile nonsense cease and desist? It was unbearable. I have never been so egregiously insulted in my life!"

He puffed several more times.

"My dear friend," he said. "I am terribly sorry for what you had to endure, and, quite possibly, you have not seen the end of it. However, the fact that it happened is of singular interest."

"What can you possibly mean by that?"

"What I mean is that someone obviously slipped the information to the Press, else how could they have known?

Prior to this moment, the only people who were aware that you chatted with Forbes late that evening are yourself, your good wife, myself, and Inspectors Lestrade and Jones. I am quite certain that none of the above said anything to any member of the Press. There must have been someone else who not only attended the reception but followed you to Baker Street. Whoever it was is may be involved in the murder of Forbes."

"But why send lies about me to the Press?"

Holmes paused and puffed some more. "Whoever it was knows the Press well enough to assume that they will print anything regardless if it is true or false as long as it makes a sensational headline and promotes sales. If they did that, it is quite possible that their motive was not merely the death of Forbes. They may be angry at all of Scotland Yard and, given the location of the crime, at me as well. He may be seeking to wreak revenge not merely by murder but by raining humiliation on all of us. Ah, yes. It was very instructive of them to invoke the scandal mongers of the Press."

"But why me?"

"It was not about you. It was about me. You are my dear friend and my Boswell. Mark my words, Watson. Whatever they say about you, false and distorted though it may be, will be sure to include a reminder of our splendid friendship. And the murder of a Scotland Yard inspector almost on my doorstep will cast aspersions not only on me but on Scotland Yard. Yes   yes   whoever it is, is starting to show his hand. How terribly foolish of him. But I should not worry, Watson, within a few days I suspect that you shall be all but forgotten and that I shall become the target. That is quite useful. An angry man seeking revenge makes for a very poor criminal."

I had half expected that he would begin rubbing his hands together in expectation as he often did. Instead, his fists were clenched, and his knuckles had whitened.

Chapter Three
A Rothschild
in 220 Baker Street

I TOOK A CAB back to my medical practice and managed, with great efforts of concentration, to give my attention to my patients. At the end of the day, I departed my office and picked up an afternoon copy of *The Evening Star* on the way home. As expected, I was on the front page. There was a picture of me appearing to be running away from the reporters. The headline read 'Famous Doctor Friend of Sherlock Holmes Refuses to Answer Questions.' The story began with the self-serving words 'On a freezing cold morning, our reporter waited outside a lavish home in the posh neighborhood of Little Venice for Dr. John H. Watson, the 'partner-in-crime' of Sherlock Holmes, to appear.' It went on to quote 'reliable sources' who had revealed that I was 'the last known person to see Inspector Forbes alive' and therefore might be a suspect in his murder. The paper ever went so far as to print a photo of the inspector's wife and children in distress on receiving the awful news of the death of their 'dear Daddy.' And, as Holmes had predicted, the location of the crime 'on the doorstep of Sherlock Holmes, possibly whilst he was napping' was repeated in various ways throughout the story.

I was furious at the duplicity of the Press, and even the kind ministrations of my wife failed to soothe my righteous indignation. I slept little and got up the next morning ready to give the gang of blighters a piece of my mind, but when I opened the door, there was not a single reporter in sight. As Holmes had also predicted, they had moved on. I was yesterday's news.

My day passed uneventfully, and I was happy that my waiting room had emptied by just after three o'clock. For reasons that I cannot truly explain, but that were no doubt tied to the disconcerting happenings of the previous day, I was anxious to speak again with Holmes. I caught a cab and directed the driver to Baker Street, but as soon as we turned off Marylebone, I looked up the road and could see the pack of pests from the Press now gathered on the pavement outside of

221B. Holmes was right. They were now out to sell more papers by disgracing his good name.

I told the driver to pass by the address and come back up the alley that lay behind that stretch of Baker Street. Once we reached the back door of 221, I stepped out of the cab and knocked on the back door. A very distraught Mrs. Hudson greeted me. She was holding a rolling pin in her hand.

"Oh, Doctor," she gasped when she saw me. "I am so glad it is you. If one more of those vermin had pounded on my door, I was ready to let him have it."

I had never before suspected the good woman of contemplating violence, but she looked ready to do battle. I tried to calm her with assurances that, just as in my case, the hounds would depart once they were attracted to a new scent.

Holmes was sitting again at the table, again smoking a cigarette, but this time poring over a stack of papers that, from a distance, appeared to be a list of names and addresses.

"Watson, good to see you," he said in a manner that betrayed his calm state, entirely untouched by the raving rabble outside the door. "I could have used your help earlier today. It would have made matters much more efficient, but I did somehow manage to get by eventually on my own."

That piqued my curiosity. "What were you up to?"

"I dropped in at Number 12 Burleigh Street. They are very fond of you there."

"The office of the *Strand*? Whatever for?"

The Strand had been publishing my stories about the adventures of Sherlock Holmes for over fifteen years and was wonderfully grateful to me for the way their sales and subscriptions soared every time a new story about Holmes appeared. Although modesty forbade me to boast about it, I had to admit that I was one of their favorite people in all of London. I was always greeted as next of kin to royalty every time I entered their premises.

"You had a fine reception a few days back to which they made a generous donation."

"Yes, Holmes. I am aware of that. I was there, and you did not attend. Remember?"

"Quite so. But you did happen to mention that they offered free subscriptions to all those who attended, and paid the exorbitant entrance fee that was tantamount to robbery."

"It all went to a good cause, The British Medical Association," I said.

"Ah yes, of course, to give aid and succor to all the underfed, underpaid, and terribly put-upon doctors. The rents those poor dears are charged for their suites on Harley Street are miserably unfair. But questioning the righteousness of the cause was not my purpose. I wanted a copy of the list of all those who signed up for the free subscription. At first, they were not willing to give it to me, citing proprietary assets, privacy and the like. I had to suggest that their failure to cooperate might result in my refusing to have you accompany me on any more of our adventures, thus bringing to a halt yet again their glorious and highly profitable publishing of your sensational accounts of my investigations. It was a bit heavy-handed of me, but time was of the essence, and the threat worked wonderfully."

I was about to express my outrage at the gall of Holmes's threatening my publisher, but he called me over to look at the lists.

"You attracted quite that interesting audience I must say," he said. "Look here. There is a fine assortment of blue-bloods, captains of industry, bankers, writers, publishers, actors even a clergyman or two. Well done."

"Thank you, Holmes. But what is the purpose of your wanting the list."

"Elementary, my dear Watson. It is highly probable that whoever murdered Inspector Forbes and subsequently slipped the details of your walk home with him to the Press must have been present at your reception and followed you."

"Fine. I agree. But there was over a hundred people there. You cannot investigate every one of them."

"An excellent conclusion, Watson. But I can quickly remove all those who I know to be upright citizens and beyond reproach. And then I can look for names and addresses that seem incongruous with such an event."

"Very well. Did you find any?"

"Oh, there were at least twenty that I either had never heard of or that I recognized and knew to run rather close to the law. But take a look at the name I have circled. Do you recognize it?"

He handed me the sheets of paper. On the fourth page, I read the name he had circled:

Lionel Walter Rothschild

"Good heavens!" I exclaimed. "I had no idea I had attracted one of the wealthiest men in the Empire."

"My dear Watson," said Holmes, condescension dripping from his voice. "You had no idea because he most certainly did not attend. Kindly look at the address given for the complimentary subscription to the Strand magazine."

I looked again, and again I was startled.

"Why, he gives an address of 220 Baker Street. That is just across the street from here."

"Precisely, and I assure you that the Baron Rothschild does not live in Mrs. Turner's boarding house and nor is he likely to need to take advantage of a free magazine subscription regardless of where he lives."

"That does appear to be very odd," I said.

"Precisely, now Watson, does that not also strike you as suspicious?"

"Most assuredly. We should send a note off to Inspector Lestrade this instant and have the whole lot of people living there brought in."

"Not so quickly, my dear doctor. I am inclined to suspect that one of them may be a murderer or at least connected to the crime, but if we reveal our hand too soon, we have nothing with which to charge and hold him, and he would be back on the streets in minutes. If I am correct in my suspicions, he or, we must bear in mind, possibly *she*, would disappear from London before morning. I think it best that we continue our investigation and come up with more evidence before making our move."

"And just how are you going to do that?"

"With the help of our dear landlady."

He stood up quickly and walked to the door and called for Mrs. Hudson. She appeared in less than a minute.

"Yes, Mr. Holmes. Is there something you need?" she said.

"I need you to help me solve a case."

She smiled involuntarily. "Oh, well, if you think there is some little thing I could do, I would be happy to oblige."

"Not a little thing, Mrs. Hudson. Possibly a very big thing. It has to do with the murder of Inspector Forbes."

Her eyes widened, and she gasped. "Oh, my. Why, that was awful, and to think it happened right across the road from our home here. Let me tell you, Mr. Holmes, the whole neighborhood has been talking about nothing since."

"Have they now? Asked Holmes. "And what have they been saying."

"Oh, you know, Mr. Holmes. All about how terrible it was and how we all thought our street was safe, and how everyone needs to lock their doors all the time now because you never know who is out there. Just the things that you would expect."

"Of course, but allow me to be more specific. What have they been saying about me?"

"About you, Mr. Holmes?"

"Yes, Mrs. Hudson, about me? And please, the truth and the whole truth."

The poor woman blushed and looked very uncomfortable.

"Well, Mr. Holmes, if you must know "

"Yes, Mrs. Hudson, I must."

"Very well, Mr. Holmes. Before the terrible murder of the police inspector, all of the neighbors were quite proud to share the street with London's most famous detective. But now, and I am not sure how to say this, now they would rather you found somewhere else to live. What with the murder, and the nasty things in the paper about Dr. Watson, and the swarm of reporters on the street all morning. It has made them all quite distressed."

"They have my sympathies. I cannot blame them. But what about your friend across the street, Mrs. Turner. Does she feel that way as well?

Mrs. Hudson gave Holmes a bit of a look.

"It is odd that you ask about her, but I suppose I might have expected it, coming from you. I did have a chat with Mrs. Turner just an hour ago. She was quite strong in her condemnation of all the gossip and sang your praises, saying how fortunate we all were in times of trial to have a famous detective as a neighbor looking out for us. As far as she was concerned, it made the entire street safer."

"That was very kind of her," said Holmes. "Please remember to pass along my appreciation for her thoughts."

"Well, if you must know, Mr. Holmes. Those thoughts were not truly hers. She said that, at first, she was inclined to agree with the rest of the neighbors and, being my friend and all, she had a duty to let me know how she felt about you living here and all. But then she said something about it to the boarders living in her house and didn't they give her something to think about. They must be quite your fans Mr. Holmes. They would not hear any talk about telling you to move. No, they were the ones that made it clear to Mrs. Turner that they did not want you to leave Baker Street. No, not one bit. As a matter of fact, if you must know, they said that you're being here was one of the reasons they chose this street to live on. They feel good and safe knowing that you are right across the road from them and had members of Scotland Yard always coming and going."

"Ah, well, they must be quite the fine lot of boarders, wouldn't you say, Mrs. Hudson?"

Again, she gave Holmes a bit of a look before answering.

"Well now Mr. Holmes, I do not know that I would quite say that."

"Indeed? And why not?"

"Well, if you must know, Mr. Holmes, they are the oddest lot of boarders I ever laid my eyes on. Odd indeed, that's what they are."

"You don't say. Please, Mrs. Hudson, I am intrigued. Why would you say that?"

The good woman hesitated before answering. "Mr. Holmes, it is not a good Christian thing to speak ill of anyone behind his back."

"Of course not, Mrs. Hudson. It is not at all. But as part of the investigation into the tragic death of Inspector Forbes, it is simply a matter of course that we learn everything we can about everyone in the neighborhood where the crime occurred. I do believe that the Holy Scriptures instruct us to obey the laws and give honor and obedience to those in authority over us."

"Oh, yes, well, if you say so. I suppose it would not be improper then if I were just to say that they were odd. Being odd is no sin. The way they all came to Mrs. Turner in the past four months was the first odd thing. She keeps a fine house and has always had her rooms full, but starting four months ago the toff, the aristocrat chap, came to her door and said he wanted to rent a room, and she said that she had none to let and he said that he would pay her twice the rate she was receiving and pay it all up front for a full year. Well, that is a situation that a landlady cannot afford to say no to and I will have to be honest, Mr. Holmes, if he had come here and made the same offer, I would be hard-pressed not to send you packing and take him in instead. No offense intended, Mr. Holmes."

"And none taken. It would be a practical business decision. Pray continue."

"Well, if you must know, she gave notice to one of her boarders and sent him off even though he had done nothing amiss. But, and here's where it gets very odd, Mr. Holmes, over the next month don't two of her boarders suddenly up and leave, and another two show up. And then two more all come to her door and make her the same offer and say they are willing to pay much more than what she has been receiving. They're all saying that they want to live on Baker Street not just because of the Underground nearby but because it is a famous street on account of Mr. Sherlock Holmes living here, and it is something they can brag about to their families wherever they might be as they have all heard of Baker Street from the stories written by Dr. Watson. So, Mrs. Turner gave notice to all the last two of her old boarders and has a whole new lot of them, and near twice the income she had expected for the year. As far as she is concerned, and I cannot blame her one little bit, the lot of them can be as odd as they want seeing as their money is not only good but twice as good as what she was getting before. Now that is quite all I know, Mr. Holmes. If you must know anything more, you'll have to ask her yourself."

Holmes nodded and smiled warmly at the dear lady. "You have been exceptionally helpful, Mrs. Hudson. I do not know what I would do without you. But I need to beg your indulgence and ask you to help me with one more thing."

"If it is something I can do, then it is something I will do, Mr. Holmes."

"Would you be so kind as to ask your friend, Mrs. Turner, over for early tea tomorrow? And try to do it on very short notice, and do not mention that Dr. Watson and I will be present. Now, I am not asking you to lie to her, just not to voluntarily reveal anything about our interest in her and her boarders. Would you mind doing that for me, Mrs. Hudson?"

The lady looked quite puzzled but gave her assent. However, she did give Holmes a long, queer look as she departed from our room.

I bade Holmes goodbye, promised to return the following day at the same time and made my way home in time for supper.

Chapter Four
Quite the Rum Lot

I RETURNED THE NEXT DAY as I had agreed and found Holmes pacing back and forth with a cigarette in hand. His appearance and manner betrayed a soul seething with barely controlled anger. He ignored me and kept pacing and appeared to be rehearsing his lines for a performance on stage. After observing him for several minutes, I took advantage of a short pause when he reached the far wall and had to turn around.

"Would you mind terribly, Holmes," I said, "stopping whatever it is you are doing long enough to say 'hello' and tell me what is about to happen, seeing as I have come over to try to assist you?"

"Oh, yes, of course, Watson," said, coming back to his usual congenial self. "Mrs. Hudson, bless her, has gone over to invite Mrs. Turner to tea. Both of them should be back here in five minutes. I have to find a way to have Mrs. Turner tell me all she knows about her current boarders without alarming her or rushing back to tell the lot of them that I am making inquiries."

"Very well, do you have to ask about every one of them? Do you believe they all murdered Forbes?"

"No, of course not. But it is highly likely that at least one of them is tied to the crime. However, as I do not have near sufficient data to lead me to know which one that might be, I have no choice but to ask about all of them."

I thought for a moment and then offered the advice given to all men in the medical profession.

"Then just tell her the truth. Be completely candid. No varnishing or sugar-coating allowed. Tell her that one or more of her boarders might possibly be connected to the murder that took place next door to her and that you need her help to identify that person. Or, if you are mistaken, clear all of their names so that Scotland Yard will not be investigating her entire house, and possibly herself."

"I cannot see how that would encourage her to want to assist me. She is thrilled to have lodgers who have paid twice the going rent and given it a year in advance."

"Then point out to her that if any one, or two, or even three are taken into custody and sent away, she can just go right ahead and rent out the rooms one more time. She will end up with thrice the income."

Holmes glared at me as if I had just landed from an unknown planet.

"Watson that is brilliant. Forgive me for underestimating your business acumen."

"Must I remind you, Holmes, that I am by heritage a Scotsman. Some matters concerning money are in the blood."

For the next few minutes, Holmes and I rehearsed our lines and plotted how we would gently coerce Mrs. Turner into giving up all she knew about her boarders. Holmes insisted that I should take the lead, reminding me that the fair sex was my department.

The two ladies arrived with Mrs. Hudson leading the way. Her friend, Mrs. Turner, was well-known to both Holmes and me as she had on numerous occasions over the years stood in for Mrs. Hudson when family matters took our landlady away for a spell. I had first met her years ago at the time Holmes had been engaged by the King of Bohemia and she had prepared our dinner in Mrs. Hudson's absence. We stood and greeted the two of them when they entered.

"Oh. Why it's Mr. Holmes and Dr. Watson," exclaimed Mrs. Turner as she entered. "Martha did not tell me that both of you were in. Oh, I am so glad that you are here. I have been praying that God would help me out of the terrible quandary I am in, and He has sent you."

I was not prepared to have divine provision accorded to us, but I smiled and extended a friendly greeting in return.

"My dear Mrs. Turner," I said. "Please, relax yourself, have a cup of tea and tell us all about your quandary."

I fully expected that she was about to launch into her latest scrap with the gas man and I hoped that we could dispose of it before enticing her to reveal all we needed to know about her boarders.

"It's my boarders," she said. "I do not know what to do about them and, frankly, I have become quite fearful."

My surprise was overtaken by my amusement, concealed of course, at seeing Holmes react as if someone had sent a jolt of electricity through the chair he was sitting on.

"Is that so?" he said. "Why then, by all means, let us hear about it. As your friends and neighbors, we have an obligation to do whatever we can to help."

"Oh, thank you, Mr. Holmes, but I was worried that your fee would be far beyond my means seeing as you have become so famous and in demand by all the nobility and royals and what not."

"My dear Mrs. Turner," Holmes replied. "There will be no fee whatsoever charged. The good Lord commanded us to love our neighbor as ourselves, and you are our closest neighbor. So, consider any assistance I can provide to be a labor of love and moral obligation. All other cases will be put aside, and yours will have precedence. Please, tell us about your situation and hold nothing back. You have my complete attention."

I took out my notebook and pencil and prepared to record a wonderfully uncoerced account.

"Well, Mr. Holmes. I do not know if Martha, Mrs. Hudson I mean, has told you, but over the past four months I have taken in an entire new set of boarders."

"I had," said Holmes, "noticed that myself. There has been a new set of faces coming and going from 220 Baker Street this season. Are they freeloading and refusing to pay their rents?"

"Oh no, not at all. Every one of them, all five of them that is, has paid an entire year in advance at a higher rate than I had been receiving last year. Oh no, the matter has nothing to do with money, Mr. Holmes."

"Ah, well that is good news," said Holmes. "Then what is the issue? Are they engaging in illegal activities? Gambling? Immoral liaisons? Wild debauched parties?"

"Oh no, nothing like that. They are quite clean living, every one of them. Mind you, none of them, not one, appears to be gainfully employed. They come and go at all hours during the day, but they do not appear to be short of funds. No, not at all. Oh, I am going to sound like a foolish old woman saying this, but I have become afraid of them. They insisted on paying all that rent and handed me envelopes filled with notes. Not one offered a check on their bank accounts. I usually demand a letter from a tenant's previous landlord but they all claimed that they had either been abroad, or had owned property themselves, or some such excuse and as they paid a year in advance, I wasn't concerned about their probity."

"Yes. That is unusual. Pray, keep going," said Holmes.

"I began to suspect that perhaps one or two of them might be using a false name, an alias, and maybe on the run from the law or creditors. Several times I heard them address each other by names other than the ones they had given me."

"Ah, did you now? That is a good cause for suspicion."

"Well, I did something that I fear I might regret for the rest of my life. Three weeks ago, I told my doctor about my fears. I believe you know Dr. Trevelyan down on Brook Street. Well, he was very kind — he always is — and he suggested that I come and speak to you, especially as you are my neighbor here on Baker Street. I told him that I was in no position to pay for such services and he then suggested that I have a chat with Inspector Forbes at Scotland Yard, who he knew as well, and he offered to arrange a meeting with the inspector. Well, I did have that chat and, at first, I thought the inspector considered me a silly old widow but as I told him about my suspicions he became very interested. He took down notes and asked me all sorts of questions, and two days later he paid a visit to my house on the pretense of being concerned about vagrants in the empty house next door, Camden House they call it, but of course you know that. He wanted to have a chat with each of the tenants to see if they had heard of anything untoward happening and make sure that the neighborhood was safe. So, he did that — quite clever he was at chatting with them — and in doing so he asked for their names and some questions about their identity. And he took down everything they said. Now, I was not in his presence whilst he was doing that, so I did not hear what all they said. Well, I might have overheard one or two things, but that was all."

"Ah, but you remember those things that you did hear, do you not?" asked Holmes.

"Oh yes, mind you they are not of much use to anyone for it seems that everything they said was made up."

"Indeed? And how do you know that?"

"Well, a week later, Inspector Forbes comes by again and first he takes me aside and tells me to be very careful. It seems he had checked out all the stories he had been given by my boarders and not one of them was true. He said, and he was quite sharp on this, that I should take precautions because he suspected that the lot of them were up to no good. And I should be careful to lock my bedroom door at night, and not go out into the back alley behind the house alone, and especially not at night. And then after he talks to me he takes each of the boarders into the parlor alone and has a chat with them."

"Yes, and did you happen to overhear any of those conversations?" asked Holmes.

"No. Not a word. But each of them, all five of the boarders that is, comes out of the meeting and has quite the dark look on his face, or her face when it was one of the two women. I could tell that after their meeting the four who were not having a chat with the inspector were gathered in one of the bedrooms and having quite the chin-wag amongst themselves."

"An excellent observation," said Holmes. "That is quite significant. Now, what can you tell me about the boarders themselves?"

"Oh, they are quite the motley crew, they are. The second chap who came by says that he is a doctor, Dr. Govinda Roulston he says he is. He's from India all right. No arguing that. Brown skin, black hair and all. Mind you he is awfully big for an Indian. Most of those chaps are scrawny, the runt of the litter if you know what I mean, but not the doctor. No, he's a big one he is. As tall as you, Mr. Holmes and as thick as Dr. Watson here. I would not be surprised if his father were not an Indian at all, but one of our big soldiers who served under the Raj. So many of those boys went native, as they say, which is to be expected, boys being boys as they will be."

"And is he," I asked, "treating patients? Or associated with any hospital?"

"No. Not yet, he says. Just recently come from Calcutta and waiting to get his papers, he says. After that, he will be a right legal doctor."

"Interesting," acknowledged Holmes. "And the next one to register with you? Who was that?"

"That was Miss Alwyn Owen. As you can guess from her name, she's as Welsh as the day is long. She says she is a 'Miss,' but she is no spring chicken. She's about your age, Mr. Holmes. She says that she has spent her life in service but when her last master died she was left a bit in his will, and now she wants to live in London. Nice enough, lass. Friendly and talkative as you might expect from the Welsh and seems a bit overfond of the gentlemen folk. A bit of a temper too, mind you, but again that is to be expected from those who grew up in those wild hills. Now the very first fellow to come by, well, he is a conundrum if ever there was one."

"Is he now? In what way?"

"He says his name is John Clarke, which is about as common a name as you can imagine. But heavens, if he does not strut around like he is Prince Bertie. All manners and posh he is. Dressed to the nines all the time. I overheard him once remind the others that he had royal blood in his veins and didn't the lot of them start calling him Little Lord Fauntleroy. Not to his face, mind you. And what surprises me is why he would want to live in a boarding house. The man is not without means. He drinks fine claret and sends his clothing out once a week to the laundry service. And he even owns a motor car. He keeps it parked behind the house and every Saturday he takes it out for a jolly run through the country. Not so much now that the winter has set in, but come spring, he will be off and running again I would wager."

"A curious fellow, I must say," mused Holmes. "There are two more. Yes?"

"Oh, yes. The German girl. Fräulein Gretta; Greta Schmidt. Now she is quite the piece of work, she is. Young and beautiful. Takes a man's breath away she does. As tall as you, Mr. Holmes. Blonde hair, blue eyes. Walks as if she had a ramrod for a spine. If you ever wondered what Princess Brunhilde looked like, well, that's her. Not friendly though.

Not in the least. Just about as aloof and arrogant as they come, and again I cannot imagine why she is living in a boarding house on Baker Street. She should be married to some kraut Count or mistress to the Kaiser she should."

Holmes was clearly fascinated by the accounts of the boarders across the street. He kept nodding and had begun to rub his hands together.

"And the last one, Mrs. Hudson. Tell me about the final fellow."

"Mr. Tarker, yes. Well, he is the smallest of the lot. Smaller even than the Welsh woman. But bless me if he is not the most frightening of the bunch. He has those dark eyes that are always darting back and forth. He walks without making a sound. Hardly ever says a word. But I swear if he had it in for you, he would cut your throat as soon as look at you. I do not know anything more about him, so I cannot say any more. So, that's the whole of them, Mr. Holmes. Is there anything else I can tell you? I really cannot think of anything else, but if there is, sir, just let me know."

Holmes smiled and nodded and then closed his eyes. For the next minute, his lips moved almost imperceptibly and his head alternated between small nods and shakes. Poor Mrs. Turner looked at him as if gazing at some alien being. Mrs. Hudson reached her hand over and patted the wrist of her friend and mouthed some words of reassurance, then held up her hand to signal 'just be patient.'

Having observed Holmes in this type of behavior before, I was fully expecting that in a few seconds he would open his eyes, smile, and pronounce his verdict.

I was wrong.

Suddenly we were interrupted by a terrific pounding on the door to Baker Street, accompanied by a non-ceasing ringing of the bell. Mrs. Hudson leapt to her feet and scampered down the stairs. I heard the door open and then a familiar voice, louder than I had ever heard it before.

"HOLMES! HOLMES!" Inspector Lestrade was screaming. "Holmes get down here! Now! NOW!"

I jumped up and rushed down the stairs with Holmes on my heels.

"What is it?" I shouted.

Lestrade was already out of the door and part way across Baker Street by the time we were on the pavement.

"This way!" he shouted. He ran across the street and around a police wagon that was parked on the far side.

We followed him into the open door of Camden House. There were several constables standing in the entryway, all with grave faces.

"Back here," called Lestrade. "Same room."

We hustled our way through the kitchen and into the room we had first seen a week earlier. On the floor, in the same position as Inspector Forbes had been before, was the body of a man. He was clad in a similar heavy trench coat, woolen trousers, and police boots as Forbes had been.

"It's — it's Jones. It's Jones," said Lestrade, his voice almost inaudible and trembling.

Holmes and I, stunned, stood speechless for a respectful moment before Holmes quietly spoke to Lestrade.

"Everything the same as last week?"

Lestrade nodded took in a deep breath and answered. "Everything. The estate agent checked in an hour ago. The doors were all locked. Nothing else disturbed. No one, neither in the back or on Baker Street, reported seeing anyone enter the house all day."

Holmes was silent.

Lestrade turned to me, his face white as chalk. "Doctor, would you please pronounce again?"

I got down on my hands and knees and began again to examine the body. Once again there were no signs of any struggle — no cuts — no swellings. His face was flushed and healthy looking. Rigor mortis was beginning to set in, and there was a bluish tinge to the eyelids, lips and neck, and just the beginning of discoloring and stiffening to the limbs.

"The exact same as before," I said. "He has been dead anywhere from five to eight hours. Again, I suspect some sort of poison, but all the usual concoctions are ruled out."

I stood up slowly, and the three of us remained still for another minute without speaking before Lestrade broke the silence.

"There was one peculiar thing this time around."

"Yes," said Holmes. "And what was that?"

"His notebook. It was all quite the usual, except that there was a folded page that he had inserted into it."

"All it had on it was 'Sherlock Holmes. 220 Baker Street.'"

"220?" I said. "Surely he knew where Holmes lived."

"I was not Jones's handwriting," said Lestrade. "It was Forbes's. And I am quite certain he knew where you lived as well. Thanks to you, Dr. Watson, your address has become the most famous in London outside of Buckingham Palace."

"I suspect it was no mistake," said Holmes. "And, I beg your forgiveness, my dear Inspector. I should have seen this coming. I shall take steps tomorrow morning and, Lord willing, this will all come to a stop."

"Please, Holmes, do whatever you have to do, and I do not care how you do it, lawful or otherwise. And now, if you will excuse me, I have to go and take the news to Mrs. Jones and her children."

He walked slowly out of the room and down the hall. He demeanor was like that of a man who wished he were dead.

I followed Holmes out of Camden House and onto the pavement of Baker Street. He stopped and lit a cigarette. Neither of us had taken the time to pull on our overcoats before answering Lestrade's call, and I knew that we would both soon be shivering in the deep winter cold. Holmes took two more slow draughts on his cigarette, his head still dropped and his gazed fixed on the ground. Then he raised his head and looked up into the sky and at the light flakes of snow that were falling on us. I could see his entire countenance change, as I had seen it so many times in the past. His lips narrowed, and his face hardened. His eyes took on that intense burning sheen that accompanied the fixing of his mind. I knew that the game was on.

"Watson," he said without looking at me. "Please send a note off to your wife and tell her that you will not be home for dinner this evening. You will be staying over with me. I will require your assistance first thing in the morning and for the next several days. Thank you. Now, we must have a word with Mrs. Hudson."

I hastened to scribble a note and, putting my cold fingers inside my mouth, gave a sharp whistle. No one appeared. I whistled again, and I heard the door of a go-down open and close, and one of Holmes's faithful Irregulars appeared. I felt terrible looking at him. His overcoat was threadbare, and he had only thin socks and shoes on his feet. The poor child would catch his death of cold.

"Son," I said, "here is a shilling if you can deliver this note to the address on it. And there will be another shilling waiting for you in our rooms when you return, but only if you run all the way there and back. You will stay warm if you keep running. Can you do that?"

"Yes, Doctor."

He grinned and took the note I had written for my wife and began running off in the direction of Paddington. As soon as he was out of sight, I entered 221B and climbed the stairs into our front room. Holmes was sitting there, puffing on his pipe. He gestured me to be seated.

"I have asked," he said, "Mrs. Hudson to join us."

"Mrs. Hudson?"

"Yes, our landlady."

"Holmes, I know who Mrs. Hudson is. But what could she possibly have to do with the murders of two Scotland Yard inspectors?"

He declined to answer and took another long draft on his pipe. Mrs. Hudson entered the room before I could repeat my question and demand an answer. Holmes gestured for her to be seated as well.

"What is it, Mr. Holmes?" she asked.

"You are aware," he replied, "of the dreadful murders that have taken place across the street?"

"Well, I have just heard about the second one a few minutes ago. It is horrible. Just horrible. It is terribly upsetting, it is. If something like that had happened in Whitechapel, I should not be surprised. But here, on Baker Street. Why, it is just horrible."

"Yes, Mrs. Hudson, it is," said Holmes. "You have no doubt observed that I have been asked by Scotland Yard to assist in the investigation?"

"Well, I had noticed the short chap, Inspector Lestrade, coming and chatting with you and I am not at all surprised that he needs your help."

"Nor am I," said Holmes. "However, we also need your help."

"Mine?"

"Yes, Mrs. Hudson, yours. It is imperative that three days from today, first thing in the morning, that you leave and go somewhere for several days. You have a cousin, I believe, in Southampton. The weather is bound to be a few degrees warmer there. I am quite sure that you will enjoy the break and I will look after all your expenses."

The poor woman looked utterly devastated. I expected tears to form in her eyes any second.

"Mr. Holmes," she said in a trembling voice, "what have I done wrong? I have tried. Honestly, I have, never to interfere in your work. Never. I can see that you have been frightfully angry these past few days. Was it something I did? I swear, I have always kept in confidence anything I heard going on. I have never gossiped with the neighbors, not once in over twenty years, about who I saw coming and going. What have I done wrong? Why are you sending me away?"

"Oh no. No, not at all," Holmes quickly replied. "I am not sending you away. I need you to be absent for strategic reasons that will help me investigate. And I also need for you to ask Mrs. Turner across the street to look after meals for Dr. Watson and me whilst you are away."

Now the dear woman looked awfully confused.

"Has there been something wrong with the meals I have prepared, Mr. Holmes? I have tried to make them to your liking. Do you wish me to wish me to change the dishes I prepare? I do not believe, Mr. Holmes, that Mrs. Turner, would make anything better for you. But if you insist, I will ask her to come over and prepare your meals, but you might have to wait for them a while as she has five boarders of her own to look after first."

"No, no, no," said Holmes. "I do not want you to ask her to come over and serve meals here. I need for you to ask her to add Dr. Watson and me to her table and have us eat our meals there for the next two days. That is all."

For several moments, Mrs. Hudson looked at Holmes and said nothing. Then, slowly, a faint smile crept across her face.

"If that is your wish, Mr. Holmes. I shall arrange for your meals to be taken across the street And, if I might say, it is about time you took a good look at that lot of boarders. Mrs. Turner has been telling me for several weeks that there is something rotten in the state of Denmark over there. Yes, it is about time. And having me go away is a very clever excuse for you to look into the lot of them. Quite the rum lot they are, if you ask me. So, yes, Mr. Holmes, I will make those arrangements as you request, but there is one condition."

"A condition, Mrs. Hudson?"

"Yes. I have watched you work now for over twenty years, Mr. Sherlock Holmes, and I can tell when you are about to make your move. It is written all over your face. And I will have you know that there is no way on God's good earth that

I wish to be miles away from London when all hades is breaking loose on Baker Street. I do not mind going away, Mr. Holmes. But I am not about to leave London."

Holmes smiled warmly at her. "An excellent condition to set, Mrs. Hudson. Would you agree to be a guest at a select hotel for two nights instead?"

"That will do just fine, Mr. Holmes."

After the good woman had departed, I turned to Holmes.

"And kindly tell me just what it is you are planning for the next two days?"

"My plan, my dear Watson, is that you could, should you so choose, return to your medical practice. Alternatively, you could join me in closely observing, indeed dogging the very footsteps of the boarders of 220 Baker Street, one of whom, I suspect, might be a wickedly clever murderer. What would be your preference, my friend?"

"You are asking me if I would prefer to poke and prod the bodies of the English citizenry or join you in the pursuit of the villain who has murdered two fine police inspectors and set the rabid Press on me?"

Holmes smiled back at me. "I will take that as a 'yes' and will assume that you will join me. Together we shall breathe down the necks of this odd lot without their knowing that we are anywhere within a mile of them."

"We will be in disguise, I assume."

"Precisely. I imagine that I will become an aged, stooped seller of used books. Do you think that would be appropriate?"

I glared at Holmes before answering. "You know, I still have not forgiven you for using that on me."

"Ah, but only because it fooled you so completely. Therefore, I am sure you would recommend its use on others. And you, my dear doctor, would you mind if I were to dress you up as a common laborer?"

"As long as your dress me warmly. It is winter, you know."

Chapter Five
Following Our Suspects

AT SUNRISE the following morning, Holmes and I were huddled on the street corner immediately south of 221B. He had procured for me, from whence I do not know, a battered but perfectly serviceable British Army greatcoat, similar to the one I wore years ago in the mountains of Afghanistan, and a warm woolen cap. I was quite comfortable. He was clad in a shabby trench coat, and I feared for his well-being, but he assured me that he had several layers of loose-fitting garments underneath. His head was kept warm by the ridiculous wig that I have described in numerous of my accounts of his previous adventures.

We had not been sitting there long before the door of Mrs. Turner's house opened, and a man emerged and began walking in the direction of Marylebone. He was a tall chap and was walking quickly. His hat was pulled down, and his collar turned up to keep out the cold, and it was difficult to see his face. At the corner, he turned west on Marylebone and started off towards Paddington, but shortly after crossing Edgeware Road, he left the main thoroughfare and turned right on to one of the side streets. After another two turns, I grabbed Holmes by the forearm.

"This is the street that I live on," I whispered.

"I am certain," he said, "that it is not a coincidence."

The fellow appeared to be looking at the numbers on the houses and to my horror, he stopped directly in front of my home. He stood and gazed at it for several minutes. Whilst he was doing so, it was possible to get a good look at his face. He had a somewhat dark complexion and jet-black hair.

Holmes had his spyglass out and was watching the man intently.

"He is the Indian fellow, all right. Quite tall and athletic. However, he is not particularly dark in color. Many shades lighter than the Tamils. I suspect that Mrs. Turner was correct in deducing that he is Anglo-Indian."

"But what is he doing looking at my home? My wife is there now and except for the maid, all alone."

"He will not do anything hostile this morning," said Holmes. "He is obviously on his way to some place for some purpose, and whatever it is, it is important to him. I suspect that he realized that he has time to spare before his appointment and finding himself very near to your residence, he decided to take a look. Ah, but now he moves on. Come."

I was utterly unnerved by what I had just observed, but Holmes seemed to take it as of no account, so I followed along as we rounded the corner and came to the front entrance of St. Mary's Hospital on the north side of Paddington. A family of Gypsies was seated on the ground by the gate, begging. To my surprise, the Indian stopped, squatted down and chatted with them for several minutes before taking out some coins and giving them to the father. The look on the Gypsy's face indicated that it was a generous almsgiving. The doctor then stood and uncertainly checked his watch before entering the hospital.

"What is he doing?" I wondered out loud.

"Most likely applying for a position at the hospital," said Holmes. "And most likely, he will not be successful."

"Why do you say that?"

"This fine hospital is administered by a very competent order of Catholic sisters who graciously provide care to people of all faiths, colors, and creeds. However, they are also shrewd businesswomen who know that their patients demand to be treated by an English Catholic doctor and have an aversion to removing their clothing in front of a man they would consider a snake-charmer, regardless of his medical pedigree."

"Holmes, you horrify me. That is a terrible thing to say about common English people."

"I horrify myself, but please observe. Our man will reappear in short order and will not be happy."

He was right. We sat amongst the waiting patients for no more than twenty minutes before seeing the Indian doctor emerge, his face clouded and his head down. He walked quickly out of the building, pushing the door open with a hard jab. Upon reaching the pavement, he turned and looked back at the hospital and then spat on the ground before walking to the cab stand.

We clambered into the cab immediately behind his and Holmes told the driver to follow the one that had just departed. Soon we were rattling through the morning traffic, traveling east along Marylebone. The cab we were following passed Baker Street, and then the Marylebone High Street before turning south on Harley Street. If the fellow was looking for a medical practice in which to seek employment, he had certainly come to the right neighborhood.

His cab stopped in front of one of the quite well-to-do surgeries. I knew the place. It was the medical practice of Dr. Richard St. John Long, the distinguished physician, and pillar of the BMA who treated many of the wealthiest men and women of London. He had kindly attended the reception that was held for me at the Langham and had passed along encouraging words, although I suspected they were more intended to keep me writing stories than healing the sick.

Holmes and I sat in our cab watching and waiting. Holmes had his spyglass at the ready, but it was almost an hour before the young doctor emerged. The difference in his posture and gait from what we saw at St. Mary's could not have been more obvious.

"The fellow," said Holmes, "appears to be smiling. There is a decided bounce in his steps. Either he has just been cured of some terrible disease, or he has secured a position."

"I would be surprised," I said, "if it were either."

"As you know this medical chap, St. John Long, would you mind dropping in and having a chat with him and seeing if there is anything that can be gleaned about his recent visitor?"

All doctors are bound by strict confidentiality when discussing the affairs and symptoms of their patients, unless, of course, they are speaking to other doctors in which case they are irrepressible gossips. I assured Holmes that I would do my best. I doffed my coat and hat in the cab and entered the tastefully furnished office. I could not help noticing a collection of Strand magazines strewn across the coffee and end tables of his waiting room, some dating back a decade or more.

"Why, John Watson," came the ebullient greeting as I poked my head inside his office. "What a surprise. Do come in. To what do I owe this honor?"

We chatted briefly about the recent reception, and I answered his many questions about Sherlock Holmes. Then I casually posed a question about the Indian fellow I had seen exiting the office as I was approaching.

"Oh, that fellow. Yes, quite a well-qualified young man. Exactly who I need on my staff."

"Indeed? I would not have thought that an Indian fellow would have many prospects in this neighborhood," I said.

"Oh, quite the opposite," he said. "Over the past few years, we have had no end of very well-off Hindus, Mohammedans, and Sikhs, and who knows who else depart the Raj and move to London. And they all need doctors and are much more at ease, especially the women folk, with one of their own than a white man. We may be their colonial masters, but when they are paying the piper, they call the tune. It is just the way they are. I have been looking for a fellow like that Dr. Roulston for some time now. Being from Calcutta, he is quite the expert on all those nasty, awful ailments that those poor folks acquire from insects, bad water, snake bites, damp air and the like, about which I know so very little. He is almost a perfect addition to my staff."

"Almost, you say? What does he lack?"

"A wife."

"Oh, come, come."

"No, I am in earnest. All those Indian women are much happier if they have an Indian doctor and they know he has a wife."

"But why?"

"Because, if they do not like how he treats them, they will go and complain to his wife and then she will make life miserable for her husband until he behaves. It is just the way they are, my good man."

We chatted a bit longer and then I excused myself and reported back to Holmes. He made no comment on my observations and merely nodded sagaciously. When I had finished, he smiled.

"Excellent, Watson. I have a contact in Calcutta to whom I shall send off a wire asking for confirmation on the story given by the young doctor. Now, however, as we have lost our Indian, I suggest that we return to Baker Street and see if another one of Mrs. Turner's boarders goes anywhere this afternoon."

We did so, and upon arriving there, I rushed into the sandwich shop that had recently opened beneath 221B. Whilst Holmes and I were unceremoniously eating a quick lunch by the bay window, another one of Mrs. Turner's boarders emerged, a woman this time. We hurriedly bounced down our stairs and followed her. She walked to the Underground station and boarded the recently opened Bakerloo line. We did the same and followed her for three stops to Piccadilly Circus. Once there, she exited the station and, walking quite proudly, entered the Criterion Bar and Restaurant, the very same establishment in which I had encountered young Stamford so many years ago. The place had moved decidedly up the ladder of taste and cost from the days it catered to the needs and wants of impoverished returning soldiers from Afghanistan.

"We can join her," said Holmes as he handed the fare to our driver and dismissed him.

"We are not exactly dressed, "I said, "like the customers they are now accustomed to serving. I dare say, we might get the bum's rush."

"I think not," said Holmes and we sauntered in and found a table that allowed us a clear view of the woman we had followed in. One of the waiters immediately approached our table and was, I am certain, about to suggest that we seek some other bar in which to relax ourselves. Holmes, with a flourish, laid five sovereigns on the table and the waiter's demeanor changed abruptly.

"Ah, yes, gentlemen. And how might I be of service to you?"

We were soon sipping two generous snifters of excellent brandy whilst surreptitiously regarding the lady.

"Very well, Watson," said Holmes. "Tell me what you observe and what you might deduce from your observations."

Holmes loved playing this game with me as I still, even after so many years, failed to either see or reason when looking at someone intently. However, I played along.

"She must be the Welsh woman," I said. "She certainly has that look about her. No longer young. About our age, but still quite handsome. No longer thin either. Ample around both bosom and buttocks. Well-dressed, I must say. Her clothes are made from quite fine fabrics. The hat is excessively large but quite stylish. She ordered a decent glass of claret. That, and her attire say that she is not lacking in money. I do not see a ring on her finger, but I suspect that she has been married in the past. Her face is pleasant, perhaps bordering on florid more than is caused by the cold weather. She seems quite the jovial type, very confident. What else should I have noticed, Holmes?"

"Not bad, Watson. Not bad at all. You might have added that when she entered the *maître d'* greeted her by name. When she approached her table, the barman gave a warm smile. She has exchanged familiar glances with three of the gentleman who are sitting at the bar or other tables. The Criterion caters now to the upper classes and the chaps who are its customers, with the exception of you and me, are a well-heeled lot. She appears to know the clientele rather well and is exceptionally comfortable in the company of men. Now, did you happen to get a close look at her smile?"

"Not particularly. It seemed pleasant and attractive enough."

"Indeed, it was. However, between her two front teeth, there is a distinct gap. Does that remind you of a character from your lessons as a schoolboy?"

I searched the recess of my memory and replied. "The Wife of Bath?"

"Precisely. And what were you told that such a dental feature signified?"

"For Chaucer," I said, "it was a mark of sensuality a tendency to indulge in the pleasures of the flesh. But come now, Holmes, that is mere folklore and superstition."

"Quite so, but such longstanding beliefs invariably find their origins in the shared experience of the people who believe them. I suspect that in the case of our lady from Wales, there may be some truth."

I harrumphed. "I fear you impugn the woman's character. All we know is that she is friendly towards gentlemen and nothing more."

"Perhaps. Let us relax and keep our eyes on her."

Within another five minutes, one of the finely attired chaps who had been sitting at the bar, rose and came over to the table where Mrs. Owen was seated. After a brief exchange of conversation that engendered smiles from both parties, he seated himself at the same table and ordered another round of drinks.

"Isn't that Lord Downash of Horton-sub-Namdon?" I asked.

"The same. He has a reputation for being overly fond of the ladies, but that is to be expected of a liberal."

Mrs. Owen and his lordship chatted amiably for another ten minutes, interrupted by outbursts of joyful laughter. They quite clearly enjoyed each other's company. I then saw him lean in quite close to here and whisper in her ear. Then he paid the bill, and the two of them rose and began to walk towards the door.

"We shall follow them discreetly," said Holmes and the two of us shuffled our way out of the Criterion and back on to the pavement in front of Piccadilly Circus. The lord and Mrs. Owen had crossed west over Lower Regent Street and entered the posh new Piccadilly Hotel.

"Dear me," I said, "is she a courtesan? Is he about to engage in an unlawful dalliance with her?"

"Quite possibly," said Holmes. "I shall have to observe. Perhaps you should wait here on the pavement in case either one of them makes a hurried exit."

"Holmes, you cannot just walk into a select hotel looking as you do."

"I am delivering a book to the good lady."

He stumbled toward the door of the hotel, and I waited. Five minutes later he reappeared.

"Quite the interesting woman," he said.

"Explain, please."

"When she, not his lordship, approached the front desk, the reception clerk immediately handed the room key to her without asking her name or room number. Then the two of them walked over to the staircase. I approached the desk and noted the empty pigeonhole from which the key had been extracted. Room 341. If my memory serves me correctly, it is a corner suite of rooms and as fine an accommodation as is offered in London. It would seem that she is a longstanding guest. I told the clerk that I was delivering some books that Mrs. Owen had purchased and would he mind if I took them up to her room. His reply was mildly surprising."

"Yes?"

"He said 'Who?'"

"I repeated her name and added that I had just seen her walk into the hotel with her husband. He gave me a very puzzled look and then replied, 'Oh, yes, of course, Mrs. Owen. Yes, she just came in, but she asked that she not be disturbed. and as she is one of our long-term guests, I must respect her requests. If you wish, you may leave the books here, and I will look after that matter for you.'

"I thanked him, claimed that the books had to be signed for personally, and promised to return later when the dear lady was not occupied. We chatted for a few minutes. It turns out that he is quite the bibliophile and delighted to find another one. A friendship with the chap will prove useful in the future."

"Well," I said, "books or no, the Welsh woman most certainly does seem to have some very unusual moral standards."

"Perhaps," said Holmes. "Perhaps she is merely a very astute woman, or perhaps utterly ruthless. I will need to make further inquiries."

That ended my surveillance adventures for the day, and I retired to a supper at 221B. Holmes ate little and spoke less. On several occasions, I noticed him gripping his knife and fork tightly and his eyes blazing in anger. I was most certain that he would not rest until he had struck down those who murdered police officers that he respected and sought to humiliate him by doing so.

Chapter Six
Bless Me, Father

THE NEXT MORNING found Holmes and me again on the street and in disguise. At shortly after eight o'clock the door of Mrs. Turner's boarding house opened, and the Indian doctor fellow emerged.

"We shall ignore him today," said Holmes. "I hope to hear back from Calcutta by the end of the day."

We waited another half an hour before the German woman stepped out onto the pavement.

"Excellent timing," said Holmes. "Let us see what our fräulein does with her time whilst in London."

Like the Welsh woman, the German also strode toward the Underground station, howbeit in a much more stately manner than the older woman the day before. We followed her on to the Bakerloo Line and exited behind her at Charring cross. From there she rounded the south end of Trafalgar Square and crossed through the Admiralty Arch. She then turned right and walked through a narrow alley between buildings and emerged on to Carlton House Terrace.

"She is walking toward Prussia House," said Holmes, "The German Legation."

At the gate of the building, she stopped and handed a note to the guard. Then she turned and walked back along Carlton Terrace until she came to a small café whose signboard advertised that it specialized in German food. She sat at a table near the door, ordered a coffee and waited. Holmes and I had found a bench across the street and, like two undesirables, sat and watched her. The contrast to the Welsh woman could not have been more telling. She did not even look at the waiter who brought her a demitasse, and her posture radiated haughtiness to all around. After some ten minutes, she turned her head and looked down the street, continuing to look for several more minutes. Then she rose quickly to her feet and stepped away from her table. The object of her intentions was a young man walking toward her. He was tall, blond, and dressed in a military style of overcoat. We could see her face break into a smile as he approached and the two of them threw their arms around each other and held the embrace for a rather long period of time. Then they sat down and began to chat. At first, both were clearly enjoying each other's company and then their faces clouded over, and they drew their heads together.

"A singularly revealing encounter," mused Holmes as he continued to regard the couple through his spyglass.

"In what way?" I asked.

"The two are known to each other, have not seen each other for some time, and share a strong, affectionate attraction."

"Wife and husband?" I said. "Lovers?"

"Goodness no, Watson. Come now, what did you notice about their embrace? Was it the type of embrace you would expect to receive from your loving wife if you had not seen her for some time?"

I hesitated and reflected on that one. "No. I suppose not. It was quite loving and warm and enthusiastic, but no more than their shoulders touched each other. It was completely devoid of any sensual contact."

"Precisely. Now, use the glass and look at both of the faces. What do you observe?"

I looked, and then smiled, and handed the glass back. "A distinct family resemblance," I said. "They are brother and sister."

"Exactly. And although they are thrilled to see each other, they are also involved together in some sort of secret and possibly nefarious activities. As the brother appears to have emerged from the German Legation building, we can consider the possibility that some subterfuge and intrigue may be in play. I will have to make further inquiries concerning her."

"Her name," I said, "is Schmidt. It is the most common name in Germany. How will you trace her?"

"I would wager, Watson, if you were willing, that her name is not Schmidt and that Schmidt is only her alias. She has assumed it to protect her true identity. But I will also wager that her brother, who is apparently an officer in the German Legation, is listed under his true family name, as the Germans are highly regimented in such matters. We merely learn his name, and we shall have hers."

I did not accept his wager. We sat and continued to observe the couple as they whispered to each other. At one point in the conversation, the young man took out a notebook and began to scribble somewhat furiously. I could not imagine what they were up to.

After a full half hour of observing them, Holmes rose from the bench. "Come. There is no more to be seen here. Let us return to Baker Street and see if we can track any more of the motley crew."

Holmes insisted that we wait yet again in the winter cold so that we could follow another boarder if he were to emerge from Mrs. Turner's. I objected and argued that we could sit comfortably by the bay window in 221B, with our overcoats at the ready, and be on the tail of our quarry with only a few seconds sacrificed. He grudgingly agreed, but I suspected that he was not altogether dissatisfied with his acquiescence.

For a full two hours, we sat in silence and watched the door across the street. At just after the noon hour, it opened, and a small, thin man emerged.

"That is the one Mrs. Turner called Tarker," said Holmes. "Come, let us see what he is up to."

Yet again we followed our man into the Baker Street Station but this time boarded a train on the older Metropolitan Line. Our journey was much longer, taking us all the way to Aldgate, the final station on the line, before getting off. The cars were crowded when we started the journey, but by the time we passed Euston, many of the passengers had departed, leaving sufficient seats for everyone. Some read books or the newspaper, some chatted with their neighbor, and some rested their heads on the back of the seats and dozed off. Mr. Tarker remained standing. He constantly shifted his position, and his eyes never ceased furtively darting around the rail car. Several times I felt his gaze rest on Holmes and me.

"That fellow," I whispered to Holmes, "is as skittish as a cat in a dog kennel."

"Yes," said Holmes. "We may face some challenges in following him. He has seen us and will not forget us."

At Aldgate, we departed the Underground and climbed the stairs back to the pavement and the open air. I was not familiar with the section of London in which we had found ourselves. It marked the beginning of the Whitechapel borough of London's East End and had a reputation for all sorts of unpleasant goings-on. Fortunately, we did not have to walk any distance along the streets, as our man made his way straight to an old pub, The Hoop and Grapes. I recalled reading that this establishment had survived the Great Fire of 1666 and prided itself on not having a single window, door frame or step that was still square. It had been noted several times in the Press as the place where the police had apprehended some petty and several not-so-petty criminals

"We cannot follow him there looking as we do," said Holmes, grabbing my forearm and halting our walk. "He will know immediately that we are following him. Please wait here and hold my coat until I return."

He quickly pulled off his overcoat and handed it to me and just as quickly removed his beard and wig. Then he pulled a woolen cap from his pockets and placed it on his head. Finally, he produced a large ornate cross that he hung around his neck.

"Do I look priestly enough?" he asked.

"Remarkably so," I said. "But should a priest be walking into a pub that has a reputation for harboring criminals and prostitutes?"

"Where else does one go if one is looking for lost souls in need of saving?"

I waited a full half hour for Holmes to return, making use of my time by recording the details of the last two days in my notebook. Just as I put my pencil back in my pocket, Father Sherlock came out of the pub.

"Bless me, Father," I said. "Pray impart your teachings to me this afternoon."

For the first time since this case began, Holmes offered back a faint smile.

"Mr. Tarker in consorting with known criminals. Upon entering, he sat at the bar and spoke to the barkeep, who immediately went into one of the back rooms. He returned, followed by a fellow I recognized. You might recall his name, Roger Sneyd-Kynnersley."

I did recall the name. He was a schoolmaster and a scoundrel who had been charged with using his school boys to commit countless robberies. But the evidence against him was thin, as his charges refused to testify or, if they did, lied through their young teeth. He was convicted only with possessing stolen goods and given a light sentence.

"What could he and Tarker have to do with each other."

"The exact nature of their engagement, I do not know. However, when Tarker emerged from the back office he immediately approached the bar and ordered a very select whiskey, which he paid for with a five-pound note. He would appear to have been contracted by Sneyd-Kynnersley to carry out some task, and I would be quite certain that whatever he has done or is about to do is criminal in nature."

"Should you alert Scotland Yard?"

Holmes pondered his answer. "Perhaps I should, but doing so could alert Tarker and the others that someone is spying on them and they would be fools if they could not deduce that it was me. So, we shall wait until we have sprung our trap on them before diverting any involvement by the Yard."

We waited for another half hour before concluding that our man was intent on spending his remuneration in the pub and it would be a waste of our time to sit in the cold until he staggered out. So, we returned to the Aldgate Station and took a train back to Baker Street.

By tea time we were back sitting by the bay window as the late afternoon light faded from the sky. We enjoyed a cup of cocoa that Mrs. Hudson had kindly prepared to take the chill out of our bones. We had just requested that she begin to prepare dinner when Holmes suddenly stood up brought his face to the window.

"Mrs. Hudson," he shouted. "put a hold on dinner until we return! Come, Watson. The fifth boarder has just left Number 220. Quick, we can catch him."

We grabbed out coats and scampered down the stairs. Holmes opened the door to Baker Street and then stepped back inside immediately, pulling the door closed behind him.

"He is not going anywhere. He is standing on the pavement likely waiting for a cab to appear."

He opened the door just a crack and peered out into the twilight.

"There is a cab coming. Yes. He has hailed it. Ah, we are in luck, Watson. There is another one close behind. Come now, quickly. We shall have to grab it before it passes."

Holmes ran out into the road and raised his hand in front of the cab. The driver pulled hard on the reins, causing the poor horse to rear up. In no uncertain terms and several quite certain oaths, the driver let Holmes know of his displeasure.

Holmes apologized and offered the fellow a sovereign. The string of oaths ceased, and we quickly began our pursuit of the other cab. We followed it south on Baker Street, across Oxford and then to Hyde Park Corner. There, the cab we were following stopped. Mr. Clarke got out, immediately hailed another cab and continued into Mayfair. It came to a stop on one of the most exclusive streets in London, a well-lit mews just beyond Grosvenor Square. We pulled in behind it, about half a block back, and Holmes took out his spyglass. The winter sun had set, but there was sufficient light from the street lamps for us to watch as the boarder who Mrs. Turner had identified as John Clarke climbed out of the cab in front of us. He was splendidly dressed in a tailored frock coat and a bowler hat and carried a large valise. He paid the driver and turned and walked up to the door of the nearest row house.

"Whatever is he doing in this neighborhood?" I wondered out loud.

"And why would he be carrying an empty piece of luggage," added Holmes, "to a house that appears to be uninhabited?"

The front of the house had numerous windows, but there was no sign of light coming from any of them. The front door area was easily seen in the light from the street lamp, and I watched as the fellow put down his valise and knocked several times on the brass door knocker. The door did not immediately open, and he waited about half a minute before knocking again.

"Good heavens," said Holmes as he fixed his gaze through his spyglass. "He is knocking with one hand and appears to be picking the lock with the other, without even looking at what he is doing."

A moment later, the door opened, and the fellow entered the house, closing the door behind him.

Holmes lowered his glass. "Watson, did you see that? I have never in all my dealings with criminals watched anyone so brazenly walk up to a door in full view, expertly pick a lock with one hand in less than a minute and walk inside. That was singularly impressive. I do not know who this fellow is, but he is an utterly brilliant thief. Come, let us try to observe through the back windows of the house."

We got out of our cab and ran along the alley behind the row of houses. On reaching the lot of the house that had just been entered, we climbed over a small back garden wall and silently worked our way to the kitchen window. The house was in darkness, but we could see the faint flickering of a light from an electric torch somewhere in the front rooms. The light danced around for some ten minutes before it became much stronger as the fellow holding it walked out into the central hallway. From the movement and dimming of the light, I could see that he was working his way up the stairs. Holmes and I moved back from the kitchen window and could observe a faint glow now coming from the windows on the second floor.

"What is he doing?" I asked.

"It looks as if he is robbing the place," said Holmes. "And I do not believe that in my many years of observing criminal behavior, I have ever witnessed anyone so utterly fearless. I expect that in a few more minutes, he will leave the house with his valise packed full of plate and jewelry. Come, back to the front of the house."

We had not been back on the street long before the door of the house opened, the thief emerged, and he closed the door behind him. Then he turned and faced the door, lowering his right hand to the lock.

"He is locking the door behind him," said Holmes. "The man is inhumanly skilled."

He then left the porch, descended the steps and, now carrying an obviously heavier valise, walked toward the corner.

"Are you not going to apprehend him?" I asked. "I have my service revolver with me. We should be able to hold him until a policeman shows up."

"No," said Holmes. "If he is the murderer of the inspectors, I do want to have him charged and tried for mere house theft before we find the evidence we need to send him to the gallows."

From the shadows, we watched the man hail a cab and head back towards Hyde Park.

"Enough," said Holmes. "It is time now for us to lay our trap. Your breakfast tomorrow morning, Watson, will be served at 220 Baker street."

Chapter Seven
Preparing to be Murdered

BEFORE THE SUN had risen the following morning, Holmes and I were sitting at the table waiting for the return of Mrs. Hudson. At a quarter past seven, we heard the door open, and she ascended the stairs.

"Your breakfast across the street has been arranged, gentlemen. All you have to do is arrive there in fifteen minutes, and Mrs. Turner will show you to the table. She was already busy preparing the food when I told her that I had been called away on an urgent family matter, so she will not have time to let her boarders know they will have company before they appear for breakfast. Now, if you will excuse me, I will be off. If you need me, you may send a note to the Langham. Good day, Mr. Holmes, Dr. Watson. Mind you I expect to hear every last detail of what you will be up to. I do not expect to have to read about it in the newspapers first."

She smiled, picked up her overnight bag and departed.

"Do we," I asked Holmes, "have a plan for this escapade?"

"No. We shall merely chat with them amicably. They will not be expecting us, so nothing untoward is likely to happen. Kindly follow my lead. We shall return at dinner. By then, whoever has been responsible for the murders, if indeed it is one of them and I suspect it is, will be prepared for us."

"Prepared to do what?"

"To murder us, of course. Come now, we would not want breakfast to get cold."

We crossed over Baker Street and knocked on the door of Number 220. Mrs. Turner opened it, looking rather rushed and put upon, but she smiled all the same.

"Please, gentlemen, come it. I had to water down the porridge a little, but the rest of the food will have decent portions. Please, come in to the dining room."

We followed her into the dining room of the house, where five boarders were already seated. They looked up at us, and I struggled to refrain from laughing at the looks on their faces.

"Good morning, all," said Mrs. Turner. "We have two extra for breakfast. Mrs. Hudson across the way had to run off on an urgent family matter, so her boarders are joining us. She does the same for me when I have to be away. All of you likely know these two, as they are somewhat famous. Please say good morning to Mr. Sherlock Holmes and Dr. Watson."

The three men stumbled and tottered as they pushed their chairs back and stood up. As the room was already cramped, Holmes smiled and graciously introduced us.

"Please, gentlemen," he said, "no need to get up. So sorry to have intruded on your mealtime. Please be seated. And ladies, good morning."

We quickly took our seats, and before any of the slackened jaws had closed, Holmes carried on as if such a breakfast event were as common as dirt.

"My colleague and I," he began, "have already been introduced by the good Mrs. Turner. So perhaps each of you could introduce yourselves to us so that we may do you the courtesy of remembering your names. You, sir. Who might you be?"

He looked directly at the large Indian fellow who was, I had to agree, quite the powerful looking chap, for an Indian that is. The man looked more than a little nonplussed for a moment before recovering.

"Who, sir? Me, sir? Ah, very, very good, sir. Yes, Mr. Holmes, sir, I am Govinda Roulston. Dr. Govinda Roulston."

"Delighted to meet you, doctor," said Holmes. "And at which hospital do you practice?"

"Umm none yet, Mr. Holmes. None yet. I have only recently arrived in London from Calcutta and am applying for a position at several hospitals. I expect that I will be accepted soon."

"Excellent. We wish you great success. And you, madam," he said addressing the Welsh lady. "What brings you to this corner of our great city. I suspect that you are not a native Londoner. What is your name and where might you be from?"

"I am from Caerdydd, sir. My enw, my name I should say, is Alwyn Owen. *Mrs.* Alwyn Owen."

"And now from London. Well done. And what was it that brought you to the great metropolis?"

"My meistr died. I was left a bit of arian, so I moved to Llundain, sir."

"I cannot blame you, madam. I would have done the same."

"And you, sir? By what name are you known?"

He was looking at a man of average height and weight who was exceptionally well-dressed. His head was bald, and he sported a beard and a pince-nez, which he adjusted with his fine, manicured, pale hand. He was unmistakably the thief we had observed the night before.

"You may address me, Mr. Holmes, as Sir John Clarke."

"A pleasure to do so, Sir John. Is the 'Clarke' with an 'e' or without."

"With. And is it Holmes with an 'l' or without?"

"With, sir. We both bear the burden of unnecessary letters in our names."

I laughed, and a couple of the boarders joined me. Sir John did not.

To the striking, tall blonde woman, Holmes now smiled.

"And you, miss. Your bearing and countenance suggest that you are also a visitor to London. From Germany, perhaps?"

"Ja. I am from Deutschland."

"And your business in England, Fräulein?"

"What business is that of yours?"

"None at all, except that in my line of work I have met countless people and might be able to refer you to those who could assist in your endeavors."

The woman gave a haughty shrug. "*Ich bezweifle das.* But if you must know, research into military history, I am doing."

"And do you need any introductions at Sandhurst, perhaps?"

"Nein."

"Very well, then. You, my good man. Who might you be?" He spoke to the small, wiry fellow on the far side of the table. The man did not look up but continued to look and speak to the English breakfast that had recently been deposited in front of him.

"Name's Tarker."

"A pleasure to meet you, Mr. Tarker. And what is your line of work, sir?"

"A laborer."

"Ah, a man who works with his hands and earns an honest day's wages."

The fellow made no response. He looked up for a moment and nodded and then picked up his knife and fork and gave his full attention to his meal.

Holmes made a few more pleasant comments, and the entire group of us stopped speaking and began to devour our breakfast until Sir John put down his fork and glared at Holmes.

"The chap beside you is a doctor," he said. "You did not tell us what it is that you do, Mr. Holmes."

"Oh, dear. How thoughtless of me. I am a detective."

"I am not familiar with that profession," said Sir John. "Do they teach that at Oxford or Cambridge?"

"No, sir. I am afraid that my reasoning mind was formed in the school of facts. I stick to the facts, sir." said Holmes.

"Hmm. Pity," was the reply.

"Indeed, it is," agreed Holmes. "Ah, Fräulein, would you mind passing the pitcher of water? Water and fresh fruit-juice are all I drink these days. My studies, such as they were, informed me that alcohol and caffeine such as are found in tea and coffee are poisonous to the body, and I have sworn off all such substances, unless, of course, someone is proposing a toast, in which case I might imbibe."

That was news to me, and if it were true, such a decision must have been taken sometime following last evening's late dinner, which Holmes had washed down with several glasses of claret.

Within a few minutes, the Tarker chap had wolfed down his meal and rose from his chair and departed without a word. By five minutes after that, the other four members lay down their cutlery and rose and, after a few polite words, departed. Holmes and I were left alone finishing our breakfast.

"Really, Holmes," I said. "Since when "

"Shush! ask me later. Now please, Watson. Enjoy this fine meal that Mrs. Turner has prepared. It will fortify you for your medical services throughout the day. And then please meet me back at 221B at six this evening, so that we may return to this friendly establishment for our evening meal."

He rose and left me alone. However, it was a fine English breakfast, and I was determined not to let it go to waste, so I relaxed and enjoyed it, alone.

Six o'clock found me back at Baker Street and prepared to cross over to 220 for supper. Holmes was stretched out on the sofa, clad in his dressing gown, smoking a cigarette and reading a journal.

"You asked me here for six," I said.

"Ah, yes. My apologies. But I received a note to say that dinner had been postponed until nine."

"Nine? Why?"

"Apparently two of our neighbors had obligations in the City. That was what it said in the note."

"What do any of them do in the City?"

"Nothing."

"Holmes, please."

"I am certain it was merely a ruse to postpone our time together this evening."

"But why?"

"So they could murder us at a more appropriate hour."

"Oh, is that so? Well then, if I am going to be murdered, Holmes, then the least you could do is explain how and when it is going to happen and by whom."

Holmes put down his journal and smiled at me.

"I do wish I knew and that is what we are about to find out."

"Holmes."

"Really, Watson. It has become rather obvious, has it not? Two healthy police inspectors made visits to Mrs. Turner's. They then appear dead next door, having died, as you have borne witness, somewhere between morning and mid-day. Yet not one them entered Camden House anywhere near those times. Therefore, they must have been drugged

217

earlier, quite heavily sedated in fact. They were then taken at night to the empty room next door whilst unconscious and then killed by means unknown a few hours later. I do not know how they were drugged, or who did that and moved their bodies, or how they were killed. Therefore, we shall present ourselves to the killer as the next victims and find out. There is no doubt that I am one of the intended targets and you are likely to be as well due to your guilt by association."

"Holmes."

"Oh, come, come, Watson. They will not get away with it. Have you brought your service revolver?"

"Of course."

"Excellent. There on the chair and the coffee table are your armor and weapon of choice for this evening."

I looked and observed a heavy leather long-sleeve shirt lying across the chair, and a small pewter goblet on the table.

"Holmes, what is the meaning of these?"

"You and I shall don the leather shirts prior to going for dinner. They are not terribly comfortable, but they do protect against anyone inserting a hypodermic needle into one's torso. Do you recognize the goblets?"

I picked it up and looked at it.

"Mrs. Turner had a large set of these on her sideboard," I said.

"Yes, she still does. Except that set is now two short. Put one in your pocket."

"What in the world for? If I am to defend myself, a blackjack would be of more use."

"Oh, my dear Watson. You will not be physically assaulted. You will be drugged. At least that is what will be attempted. Either the killer stabbed his victim with a needle or, more likely, he placed a powerful mixture of laudanum in a glass of wine or whiskey and gave it to the inspectors. I have prepared them by telling them that the only liquids I now ingest are water and fruit juices, neither of which is strong enough in taste to cover the taste of laudanum. They have only one choice."

"A toast," I said. "To our dear departed Queen."

"Precisely. I would not be at all surprised if Forbes and Jones were also invited to join in such a toast when they came to visit. Or perhaps it was a toast to her dissolute son, our Prince of Wales and future king."

"But why steal the goblets?"

"I did not steal them, Watson. I merely borrowed them. You shall keep the empty one in your pocket and shall slyly substitute it for the full one that is given to you before raising it to your lips. Then, when no one is observing, you may pour the full one out on the carpet beneath the table, and slip that one into your pocket. Do you think you can pull it off, Watson, even if you know they are trying to kill you?"

"I am your man."

"Capital. I knew you would be."

"Holmes, if someone is about to attempt to murder me, would you mind telling me which one of the odd lot that you suspect above the others."

"As I have told you in the past, Watson, it is always a mistake to theorize "

"Confound it, Holmes. I know what you have said a hundred times. Just answer my question. If someone is about to murder me, who is it likely to be?"

He took a slow, annoying puff on a cigarette.

"Anyone of them could, I suppose. But there were several peculiar things about the thief who calls himself Sir John that I found quite curious. Did you notice anything about him?"

"Other than his brilliant means of robbing a house? No. What did you notice."

"His bald head."

"That is not exactly a trait that distinguishes murderers."

"No," agreed Holmes. "But he is not naturally bald. He shaves his head. Unfortunately, he neglected to before breakfast this morning, with the result that a fine sprouting of stubble could be observed. And did you notice his eyes?"

I thought for a moment. "He was wearing a pince-nez. A fairly strong set. They distorted his eyes when I looked at him."

"Ah, an excellent observation. Watson. However, he was not wearing the pince-nez when we entered the room, and he pulled them from his pocket immediately upon seeing us.

When shaking some salt on to his breakfast, he held them up so he could see clearly. Obviously, he is using them to disguise himself. He was worried that I might recognize him."

"And did you?"

"Of course. He claims that his name is Clarke, but on the register at Mrs. Turner's, he signed without an 'e.' That is quite obviously not his true name."

"What is it?"

"Clay."

"Clay? Not John Clay? That fellow? The 'do not touch me with your filthy hands, I have royal blood in my veins' bank robber?"

"Precisely. I have only looked at him once, and that was in the dark basement of the City and Suburban Bank. After that, Inspector Jones took over the case and put him away for a rather long time. But I did get a good look at his eyes, and they have not changed, even after his years in Newgate."

"And his reason for wanting to murder you and the fellow from Scotland Yard?"

"Revenge. He prides himself on his brilliance and has been seething for years in prison knowing that I easily bested him. Plus, he could never go back to his brilliant criminal ways as long as I am alive. I would have known his telltale signs as soon as he tried."

"But he tried and succeeded last night."

"Ah, yes. But the occupants of that house are away. The theft is not likely to be discovered for another fortnight. I suspect that by that time he expects to have done away with me. You too, quite possibly."

"And you think he is now going to try to kill us both."

"No. I only have deduced that he is the most likely suspect. We shall have to wait until whoever it is makes his, or her, move before I know for sure. Can you play the role until that time?"

"I am sure I can."

"Excellent. I was sure you would be up for the game. Now, please relax yourself until it is time to dress for dinner and depart."

I was not sure what a man did to relax prior to being murdered, but a copy of the *Times* for the day was strewn on the floor, and I amused myself with it.

At a quarter to nine, I pulled the leather shirt on beneath my mine and adjusted my pockets to carry both my service revolver and the small pewter goblet. Holmes did the same, and just before leaving 221B he put a small Webley into his pocket and handed me a blackjack.

"Just in case," he smiled.

We crossed over to 220 and were met with a jubilant Mrs. Turner, who showed us into the dining room. This time the rest of the boarders rose and greeted us as if we were long lost friends. The dinner was a pleasant affair. We dined on an excellent roast of beef, complete with Yorkshire pudding. The conversation was lively and interesting, although I had the strange feeling that I was listening to speeches that had been rehearsed and practiced before being delivered. As Mrs. Turner was clearing away the dishes from the main course, the Welsh woman put her hand on the landlady's forearm.

"Mrs. Turner," she said sweetly. "We've kept you so late. Please, just leave the dishes. We'll look after them. You need to retire for the evening. Several other heads nodded and made murmurs of agreement. Mrs. Turner smiled kindly back to them and departed.

Sir John rose.

"It was just a few days ago," he began, quite sonorously, "that our beloved Queen Victoria passed on to her greater reward."

He continued for several minutes saying all sorts of things about the Old Girl. As he did so, Mr. Tarker placed small pewter goblets in front of every one's place setting. The fräulein followed him with a sherry decanter in each hand and filled the goblets.

Sir John reached the end of his oration with "A toast to the Queen."

We all reached for our goblets. I felt a kick from Holmes under the table and whilst pushing my chair back to stand, quickly slid my hand into my pocket and extracted my empty goblet whilst concealing the full one behind my back. We all raised our glasses and sat down again.

223

No sooner had we done so, but the German woman and Mr. Tarker came around again with more sherry. This time it was the doctor from Calcutta who rose to speak. He was nowhere near as articulate as Sir John but in his heavy Indian accent proposed a toast to our soon-to-be new king, the current Prince of Wales. He said many complimentary things about Prince Bertie which struck me as absurd as we all knew that he was a bounder of a womanizer and a thorough cad.

Whilst he was expounding, I slid my hand well under the table and silently poured my second full glass of sherry onto the carpet. I could sense Holmes doing the same thing.

We all stood when the toast was called for, and this time I raised my now empty glass to my lips and concealed again the full one. I was afraid that they might go on with toasts to all the royal princes, dead and alive, and that I would end up with a rather large puddle under my chair, but they stopped at two. Once we were seated, Holmes began one of his favorite stories about his time in Tibet, posing as Sigerson, and his conversation with the Head Lama.

I had heard the story several times before and thought that he was drawing it out. He started in Bombay and worked his way, slowly up to Delhi and then Kathmandu before trekking all the way to Tibet. He had gone on a bit about the secret words of wisdom that the holy man was going to impart to him and we had just reached Llasa and had Holmes/Sigerson seated at the feet of the lama and the old man about to share his eternal words of wisdom when Holmes suddenly stopped in mid-sentence. He sputtered and coughed and raised his hand to his chest whilst his eyes rolled back. He stood up as if to run for the door and then staggered, dropped to one knee whilst grabbing the back of my chair, then he fell on the ground and convulsed.

"Get help!" I screamed. "One of you call for an ambulance. He has passed out!"

I leapt to my feet and dropped down to my knees beside him. I felt his pulse. It was still strong. I leaned my ear to listen for his breathing. Whilst my ear was within a quarter an inch of his nose and mouth I distinctly heard something I was not expecting.

"For heaven's sake, Watson. Faint. Now."

Ah ha, I thought to myself. I jumped back up to my feet.

"Get help," I shouted. I made as if to walk to the door and staggered, grabbing a chair for support. I staggered another step and grabbed another chair, then I fell onto my shoulder on the floor and rolled over onto my back. Being a doctor, I had seen hundreds of unconscious men over the years. So, I did my best. I rolled my eyes back into their sockets and blinked my eyelids irregularly. With a little effort, I worked up some saliva in my mouth and forced it out like froth. I thought I was quite convincing and apparently the folks at the table did as well.

"Well, tallyho and a-halloa," I heard Sir John saying. "Well done there, chaps. Well done. Do you agree, Gunga Din?"

"No," came the reply from the Indian. "It is very, very bad. He was about to tell us what the secret words were of the Lama. Now I shall never know. This is very, very bad."

"You will just have to get by without them, my boy. Now here, you grab Dr. Watson and I will drag Holmes, and we will get them next door."

I felt a strong pair of hands reach under my arms and start to drag my body across the floor and through the back door of the dining room. I was still rolling my eyes, which allowed me intermittent vision, and I could see that Sir John was doing the same with the limp body of Sherlock Holmes. There was a small flight of stairs leading to the back door and out into the alley. No care was taken to protect my legs and feet, and they bumped and banged rather uncomfortably down each step. Had I not been feigning, I might have shouted something to the effect of, "Do they not teach you how to move a body in medical schools in India?" but, given the circumstances, I refrained.

Next, I felt the fresh, bitter, cold night air of the alley as I was pulled along to the house next door.

"Wait here, *ladaka*," said Sir John. "I will get the lock."

I heard him drop Holmes's head and shoulders to the pavement and marveled at Holmes's resilience in just allowing it to happen. It would not have been pleasant. Not at all surprising, Sir John had the lock open in seconds. I was dragged into Camden House, through the kitchen and into the small room in which the bodies of Inspectors Jones and Forbes had been found. Then, my head and shoulders were unceremoniously dropped to the floor. Holmes endured the same fate and was deposited beside me. I could now account for the bumps on the back of the skulls of the two inspectors.

The door closed and I heard it locked. I was about to move and sit up when I felt the firm hand of Holmes on my forearm.

"Not yet," he whispered.

I lay still for a full ten minutes and then whispered, "Is it all right now?"

"Yes. But keep your voice down."

"What happens now?"

"They kill us."

"Lovely. How?"

"I do not know yet. We will have to wait and see."

"Well, please let me know before it happens," I said.

"I will do my best. I promise."

"I apologize," I said, "for not seeing that your fainting was a pretense. You were a bit dramatic, you know."

The stage had indeed lost a fine actor when Holmes gave up his theatrical aspirations.

"At least I did not start drooling," came the rejoinder.

"That is what men do when they are drugged into unconsciousness."

"If you say so, doctor. I prefer to keep saliva off my collar."

The two of us might have started to laugh at the absurdity of the situation had we not been worried about our ruse being discovered.

"How long do we have to wait?" I asked.

"Assuming that your diagnosis of the time of death of the other two was correct, I suspect it will be until morning. There was enough laudanum in that sherry to put a horse to sleep for an entire day. Somewhere past daybreak, they should murder us."

"How?"

"That is what we are about to find out, Watson. However, I do not recommend falling asleep. And keep your hand close to your revolver. You may need it."

"What if we need help?"

"Lestrade is sitting in the front room with two constables. There are three more in the back alley and three out on Baker Street."

"You truly are expecting something."

"They would not have gone this far just to leave us to wake up."

"They? So, it was not just Clay on his own."

"Correct."

I moved my body so that my back rested against a wall. I had enough foresight to put three small candles in my pocket and a box of Lucifers. In the dim glow, I could write up the events of the last few hours in my notebook before I was murdered.

We sat in the dark for a full eight hours. I managed to record everything I could remember of the events of this case so far and then went back to polish some of the other cases I had written in the recent past. The last candle was burned down to a stub when I looked at my watch and noted that it read six o'clock in the morning.

"Have they forgotten us, Holmes?"

"No, we are still alive. Patience, my friend."

My legs and backside had gone numb, and I stretched and stood up. I began to walk slowly and as quietly as I could around the small room.

"Stay still!" came Holmes's stage whisper.

"What for?"

"Listen!"

I did. At first, I heard nothing and then, very faintly, the sound of air swooshing. The noise appeared to be coming from the hearth.

Holmes crawled over to the hearth and gestured for me to follow him. He was passing his hands over the back bricking when he stopped.

"Here. Feel here."

He grabbed my wrist and moved my hand to a spot just below the flue plate. I could feel a strong current of very warm air. I leaned my head in and sniffed it.

"Good Lord. It is exhaust from a petrol engine."

"Clay's no doubt. They have started it up and attached a hose to the exhaust pipe and are forcing it through a chink in the brickwork. How very ingenious."

"But it has carbon monoxide in it," I said. "We will be dead in fifteen minutes in a small room like this. I am going to shout for Lestrade."

"No!" came the stage whisper command. "We cannot alarm them. If we do, they will be gone in a flash. They only have to clamber into the autocar and they will be long gone before we can apprehend them."

"Well then, let me get into the hearth and force the plate open with my feet and legs."

"No. They will hear us. Get over to the door. I will pick the lock," said Holmes.

On our hands and knees, we both moved silently to the door, and Holmes pulled out his small case of locksmith tools that he always carried. He had just started to work when my candle finally gave up the ghost and burned out.

"For goodness, sake, Holmes. We do not have much time."

"I am aware of that, doctor. We can get a gasp of fresh air by putting our noses to the base of the door. Clean air will be coming in from the other side."

I did as he suggested. There was not a breath of fresh air to be found.

"Ah, yes, of course," said Holmes. "They have laid a towel across the floor on the other side to block it. How very ingenious. That Clay fellow is quite the worthy adversary."

"Holmes, I do not give a tinker's cuss how clever he is. Quite frankly, I would not mind at all if you had his same skills in lock picking. We have only a few minutes left. I can feel myself getting dizzy now."

"Then take your belt off and use the stiff tongue to push the towel back."

I did so, and again dropped my nose to the floor and took a deep breath of the clean air seeping through under the door. Holmes stopped what he was doing and did the same. It took him several more minutes before he silently turned the door handle and opened it in complete silence.

"Come," he said. "We have to find Lestrade and slip back into Mrs. Turner's."

Without making a sound, we tiptoed through the house and alerted the inspector and his men. He, in turn, moved silently to find and alert the constables on Baker Street and in the alley.

Holmes then stealthily led Lestrade and two of his men into the back door of Mrs. Turner's house, and we stood in the kitchen. In the dining room, we could hear the voices of those with whom we had dinner.

"I trust you all slept well," I heard John Clay say cheerily. "Our task here is finished. Holmes, Watson and two of Scotland Yard's finest are dead and gone."

"I could have done it weeks ago if you hadda let me," growled a voice that I assigned to Mr. Tarker.

"Ah, Mr. Parker," said Clay. "Kindly remember that revenge is a dish best served cold. Your special garroting services would have been much too obvious and led Holmes directly to you. Our patience has been rewarded. As it was we ended up being rushed but the job is done. Would you agree, Dr. Roylott?"

"Yes, yes. But I do wish you had waited until Holmes told us what the Holy Lama had said."

"You are now free to go and ask him yourself. All you have to do is leave England and find your way to Tibet. And bon voyage," said Clay with a laugh.

"Now," continued Clay, "let us all be ladies and gentlemen and put the dear Mrs. Turner's dining room back in order, pack our bags and be gone before the poor old saint wakes up."

We could then hear some dishes being cleared and chairs being moved around.

"What the !" came a loud exclamation from Clay.

"Bloody hell!" he was now shouting.

"*Was ist los?*"

"Look. Under their chairs!"

"*Was is es?*"

"On the carpet. On the carpet! Look. Two wet spots."

"So what?" said Mr. Parker. "Perhaps they had an accident, and bloody well pissed themselves."

"No! You fool. It's the sherry. They poured it out on the floor. It's a trap!"

Clay was now shouting.

"All of you. Into my car now. I'm leaving in one minute. If you are not in the vehicle, you can bloody well stay here and fend for yourself."

A second later, he crashed through the dining room door into the kitchen. He was met by five men, all with revolvers pointed at him.

"Good morning, John Clay," said Holmes. "We meet again."

Clay turned and tried to push his way back through the door.

"It is no use," said Holmes. "You have no chance at all. But I must compliment you. You took your revenge on Inspector Jones. Your automobile exhaust idea was very new and effective. And you, doctor," he said to the Indian chap, "a chip off the old block, are you not?"

The big fellow glared at Holmes. "You murdered my father. I have a right to kill you."

"Oh, come, come, doctor. Do I look like a swamp adder? And, my good inspector, allow me to introduce you to two women who also seem to not be very fond of either Scotland Yard or me. The woman who introduced herself to us as Alwyn Owen is actually the sensuous Miss Rachel Howells, at one time of the Musgrave estate. Many years ago, she was wronged by a butler named Brunston and avenged herself by subjecting him to a rather nasty and lonely end. I have been on her trail, relentlessly, now for thirty years.

"And the German lady, Princess Brunhilde, is rather angry at Scotland Yard and at me, and so is seeking her revenge."

"What in heaven's name for?" said Lestrade. "We are not at war with Germany, at least not yet."

"No, but this cold-hearted woman is the brother of Captain Franz Stark, currently employed by the German Legation and they have been continuing their father's plot to destroy Britain's economy by introducing millions of pounds of coined currency into circulation. She inherited her disposition from her father, Colonel Lysander Stark of the Kaiser's Imperial Guard. Your men caught up to him after he escaped from Eyford where he was pressing coinage. I believe that he swung for his crimes a few months back after you ignored the demands from Berlin for his extradition. It is a shame that his daughter has his ruthlessness in her blood and not the compassion of her mother. Would you not agree, Fräulein Stark?"

"*Fahr zur Hölle,*" was all the statuesque blonde woman said.

"And Mr. Parker, the Garrotter," said Holmes, looking at the small, furtive man. "You were here in the house quite recently were you not? Your loyalty to Professor Moriarty and your master, Colonel Moran, is remarkable if misguided. Both of them are now dead thanks to Scotland Yard and yours truly. Last time in this house, you escaped. Not this time though."

"You fiend. You clever fiend," Parker hissed in reply.

"Now, Inspector," said Holmes. "Whilst your men put the derbies on the lot of them, perhaps you will join Dr. Watson and me for a safe glass or two of sherry. Or perhaps brandy. Both are wonderful for the constitution."

Chapter Eight
In the Heart of All Men

OUR BRIEF MOOD of exultation and celebration did not last long. By the time the three of us were seated in 221B Baker Street, a somber cloud had descended. Whilst justice had been served, we were forced to remember that two fine police inspectors had died and two families had been deprived of husbands and fathers.

Inspector Lestrade sat in silence for several minutes, sipping slowly on his sherry, before turning to Holmes.

"Well done, Holmes. Good work. Losing two of my best men is extremely upsetting. Thank you for acting so quickly. Well done. Might I ask when it was you deduced, as you say, that it was not just one killer behind the deaths, but all five of them?"

"That they were all using false identities was clear early on," said Holmes. "Inspector Forbes had discovered that. But that alone does not make a person suspect for murdering a police inspector. As I observed them and suspected the true identities of each of them, it occurred to me that all of them bore strong grudges against either me or Scotland Yard or both. The Indian doctor's true family name was confirmed late this afternoon by my contact in Calcutta. I had suspected that there might be a connection to Grimsby Roylott when Dr. Watson reported that the fellow had expertise in poisons, snake bites, and tropical ailments, and when he exhibited such an easy familiarity with Gypsies. He is his father's son in many ways. It is a shame, as he could have had an excellent medical career on Harley Street had blood not been thicker than water.

"I have been on the trail of Rachel Howells since the days when I was a student and invited down to Hurlstone by Reginald Musgrave thirty-five years ago. Back then, she was a lusty lover of a butler whom she did not hesitate to dispose of when he betrayed her affections. I was aware of the accounts of the deaths of two men who were the former husbands of a woman who now calls herself Mrs. Alwyn Owen."

"Yes," I interjected. "I recall those inquests. It was recorded that both husbands had suffered heart failure while in the throes of conjugal bliss, was it not?"

"It was," said Holmes. "I heard rumors that the coroners suspected that the old chaps may have been suffocated at a most inopportune time, leading to their heart attacks, but there was nothing that could be proved. Watching her confident and sensual familiarity with the men at the Criterion led me to connect her with the long-lost Rachel Howells.

"John Clay gave himself away both by his boasting, as reported by Mrs. Turner, of his royal blood and his uncanny skill as a criminal. I suspect that he would rather have postponed his plan for a while longer, but the ball was set rolling by the suspicions of the good Mrs. Turner and the diligent work of Inspector Forbes.

"The young German was an unknown entity until she greeted her brother. It was a simple task after that to learn the name of the young man working for the German Legation. As soon as I saw the name of Captain Stark on the directory, the connections all fell into place.

"Mr. Parker is simply not the sharpest knife in the drawer. Witness that he could not come up with a more clever disguising of his name than changing the first letter. Seeing that he was a paid criminal under contract to one of London's now most dangerous men suggested to me that he might be a killer for hire. I had seen him in the darkness when we surprised Colonel Moran in 222 Baker Street and even though I did not have a clear look at his face, his furtive and stealthy body movements were sufficiently similar to the garrotter Parker.

"Well now, Holmes, that is interesting, but not a full explanation," said Lestrade. "It only tells me that you had good reason to know that anyone of them might be the murderer."

Holmes gave the inspector a thin, sheepish smile. "I confess, that it was not until they all colluded over the dinner table that it dawned on me that the five of them had come together with the joint goal of murdering all of us. If you question them thoroughly, I expect that four of them will claim that it was John Clay who organized the series of events. He has the mind and the motive to do it."

"How would he have known about the others?" I asked.

"My dear Watson, it was thanks to you. He read all about them in the Strand. All he had to do was track down the appropriate parties and convince them to join his plot. And he almost got away with it."

It had not occurred to me that such might have been the unintended consequences of my setting Holmes's adventures to account. But another question vexed my spirit.

"But why, in heaven's name, would they go along with it and risk imprisonment or even the gallows?"

"Revenge."

"Revenge? Merely revenge?"

"My dear Watson, there is nothing *mere* about revenge. It has been one of the greatest forces for suffering, enmity, and death known to the human race throughout history. There may be the rare saint — our dear and recently departed Queen perhaps — whose heart is free of desires for revenge, but otherwise, it is an omnipresent evil. Over two thousand years ago, Thucydides informed us that under the euphemistic guise of honor, revenge was one of the universal causes of war. Homer reminded us that it launched a thousand ships. Nothing has changed. Revenge has set brother against brother, village against village, and nation against nation. It festered like a cancer in these five people and when tempted with an opportunity to exact revenge, they yielded."

"But that is so utterly irrational."

"Rationality, my friend, has aught to do with it. A man may easily guard against the foolish decisions of his brain. I do so easily several times a day. It is in his heart and soul that a man succumbs to his evil desires. It is not without reason that Sir Francis told us that *a man that studieth revenge keeps his own wounds green.*

"Drake, the pirate, said *that?*" I asked.

"Please, Watson. Sir Francis Bacon."

Historical and Other Notes

On January 22, 1901, Queen Victoria died while staying at Osborne House, her residence on the Isle of Wight. She had ruled over the British Empire for sixty-three years, the longest of any British monarch until surpassed recently by Queen Elizabeth II.

Countless changes took place during the era of her reign, only a few of which I have noted in this story. The first automobiles appeared in England during the years immediately before the turn of the century.

The names and locations of various places in London that are mentioned in this story are accurate, with two exceptions. I stretched the date of the opening of the Piccadilly Hotel (now a Le Meridien) back a few years, as I also did with the opening of the Bakerloo Line of the Underground. The Metropolitan Line had been up and running for several years, and was used by Alexander Holder when he came to see Holmes, as recorded in *The Adventure of the Beryl Coronet.*

The symptoms of asphyxiation by carbon monoxide are as described in the story.

The marriages and wives of Dr. Watson are a matter of longstanding debate among Sherlockians. Some scholars have argued that he was married up to six times. Many agree on three. And there are those of us who stick with one — the only one ever clearly recorded, Mary Morstan. Passing references in the stories to "my recent bereavement" or Watson's having "forsaken me for a wife" can be readily explained away without having to posit the existence of more wives and marriages.

The Adventure of Charlotte Europa Golderton

A New Sherlock Holmes Mystery

Chapter One
Miss Ruth Naomi Lightowlers

THE INCIDENTS that I am about to impart took place in London quite recently. Under normal circumstances, when similar events occurred and would have placed a heavy burden on those involved should the public become informed, I have delayed, sometimes for years, or obscured their identities. In this case, I have done neither. My reasons are simply that most of the principals of the case, other than Sherlock Holmes, myself, and the good men of Scotland Yard, are either dead or in prison. Those still living might object to having their stories made public on the grounds that modesty inhibits their wishing the world to know of their bravery and heroism. But such recognition is their due.

On the other hand, there is a moral imperative that the public be made aware of some of the dangers that became apparent as a result of Holmes's solving of this highly intricate case. I am not suggesting that Sherlock Holmes and I are entering the realm of moral crusaders that was led for so long and so well by the great Charles Dickens. Far from it. But the citizens of Britain and abroad need to be ever vigilant that the fine institutions in which we place our trust—in this case, the Royal Mail—can become the instrument used by the forces of criminality and evil. To adapt a well know phrase, *caveat lector.*

The events began on a Saturday afternoon of the second week of January, in the early years of the new century. My dear wife was on a visit to America to consult with the women in that country who were leading the crusade for universal suffrage and temperance. As I often did whilst she was away from home, I moved back in temporarily to 221B Baker Street. In part, this was because of my affection for my friend, Sherlock Holmes but, I confess, it was as much or more my desire to have my needs attended to by the great-hearted Mrs. Hudson.

"Holmes," I said, as I pushed back after a delectable meal, "the sun is shining, and I have a mind to take myself for a brisk walk whilst you read and smoke the afternoon away."

He looked up at me, quite startled.

"Oh no. Please, Watson, do stay here. I was counting on your presence."

"For what possible reason?"

"This afternoon, I have three appointments. Every one of them is a woman. The fair sex is your department, and I was hoping that you would be present to make sure that I conduct myself appropriately."

His familiar long face and deep-set eyes conveyed such an innocent look of need that I could not say no. I smiled, retired to my familiar chair by the hearth, and after adding another log to the fire, sat back and relaxed.

"When does your first client arrive?" I asked.

"She is scheduled to be here in ten minutes, but that could mean anytime in the next half-hour. She is, after all, a woman."

I gave my friend a bit of a look of disapproval at his attitude toward one-half of the human race. Mind you, I did not disagree with him.

Exactly ten minutes later, the bell on Baker Street rang, and Mrs. Hudson descended the stairs to greet our visitor. She returned to us moments later and handed Holmes a slip of paper.

"The lady does not have a card," she said, "but she gave me this name."

Holmes looked at it and handed it to me. In a refined handwriting it read:

Ruth Naomi Lightowlers (Miss)

"Please, Mrs. Hudson, kindly show her up," said Holmes.

Our dear landlady did not move.

"I shall do that, Mr. Holmes," she said. "But I must warn you that she appears to be terribly distraught as well as highly attractive. Just the type for whom you have a hopeless weakness for waiving your fee."

Holmes feigned a look of mock surprise and smiled. He looked over at me and gave a sheepish shrug as Mrs. Hudson departed.

"Do I truly do that?"

"From time to time."

We stood to welcome our visitor. All I can say is that Mrs. Hudson's appraisal of her was understated. The woman who entered the room was beautiful; stunningly beautiful. She was not particularly young—I would have placed her approaching thirty—but she had a perfect alabaster complexion and a singularly attractive face. Long ringlets of her rich, red hair hung down and bobbed sensuously as she moved. Mrs. Hudson had taken her simple frock coat, but a dark tam hat, of the Parisian style, sat jauntily on her head. Her figure, accentuated by an inexpensive, tightly fitting black dress, would have given Botticelli's Venus cause for envy. The only aspect of her being that marred her perfection were her lovely green eyes. As Mrs. Hudson had noticed, they were somewhat swollen and reddened from a recent bout of tears.

She took a few hesitant steps into the room, stopped, and gave an imploring look at Holmes.

"Mr. Sherlock Holmes?"

"I am indeed, Miss Lightowlers. Please, do come in and be seated. A spot of tea, perhaps, to help you compose yourself?"

"Oh, sir. That would be very nice. The cab ride was quite unsettling."

"Mrs. Hudson," said Holmes. "Would you mind bringing our guest a cup? A little added fortification might be in order."

As Mrs. Hudson turned to depart, she gave me a look that seemed to say, *See what I mean*. I nodded back to her.

"My dear young lady," began Holmes, "you must be chilled from the winter weather. Warm up by the fire and enjoy your tea. There is no rush. Compose yourself, and we shall get to your concerns in due time." He stepped over to the hearth and placed yet another log on the fire.

"Thank you, sir. You are very thoughtful," she replied. Then she waited, saying nothing until the adulterated tea had arrived and she had consumed several sips. Then she dabbed her eyes with her handkerchief, lowered her head, and spoke.

"Thank you, Mr. Holmes, for agreeing to see me. I have nowhere else to turn, and I am horribly worried. In all honesty, Mr. Holmes. I am terrified."

"I can see that you are in great distress. Permit me to suggest that before telling us about what has upset you so deeply, just begin by introducing yourself and imparting to us a few details about who you are and your history. It is always good to get to know a client before plunging into the depths of a case. Relax, a few more sips of tea, and then proceed when you are ready."

I could not recall Holmes's ever having been so solicitous. His standard practice was to dispense with any social graces and brusquely tell the client, "State your case."

She did indeed take several more sips and then, in a dulcet voice, began.

"My name is Ruth Naomi Lightowlers, as you know. My family once came from County Connemara but have been living here in London since I was a young child. My father passed away nearly twenty years ago, and I have lived with my mother in Islington until recently. She has been, of necessity, very strong in spirit although somewhat weak physically and has not been able to earn much of an income. She takes in laundry, sewing, and mending work from time to time, but it pays a pittance. Since I was a young girl, I have earned enough money to support us both. I had to quit my schooling early, but I taught myself to type and take shorthand and have managed to secure a series of secretarial contracts from various firms in the City."

"Forgive me," said Holmes, "for interrupting. But why did you not seek reliable continuing employment? It would have provided far greater security."

"Oh, yes, Mr. Holmes, it would. I am not sure how to express myself in answering you. It is a somewhat embarrassing matter."

"I assure you that Dr. Watson and I are no strangers to matters that are delicate and confidential. We are here to help, not to judge."

The young woman looked up, wiped her eyes again and forced a smile.

"Sir, I have been both blessed and cursed with a physical appearance that men seem to be attracted to. I learned, soon after I entered work in the City, that if I were to stay too long in the same firm, one or more of the men would begin to say impolite words to me. The young ones claimed they wish to marry me, and the older, married ones, hinted at immoral arrangements. Young or old, it was obvious that their intentions were less than honorable and I wanted none of that. All I ever wanted was to have a quiet, peaceful life with enough money to support myself and my mother. I prayed that God would show me a worthy young man with prospects who might want me as his helpmeet for life and mother to his children. I recently met a man who professed his love and commitment to me, but he breached his promise. I am still praying."

"And no doubt Providence will indeed provide in its own time," said Holmes. "However, I am sure that you did not come here for my help in finding a husband, so please take another good swallow of Mrs. Hudson's tea and tell me why you are so upset."

She forced a smile, displaying a gleaming and perfectly aligned set of teeth. Then, after, draining her cup and pouring herself another, she carried on.

"Thank you, Mr. Holmes. Your kindness and understanding have made me feel much better already. My reason for coming concerns my mother."

"Yes. You said you lived together until recently. You have since moved out and live on your own?"

"I have," she said. "That was what led to the current concern. I said that my mother had a strong spirit. I have to confess that I must have inherited her fiery Irish temper. She was not at all pleased when I took my own room in a go-down on Warner Street in Clerkenwell. It was only a few blocks from her, and I continued to visit her twice, sometimes thrice a week. Then, four months ago, I received an offer to do work for a prestigious firm that was setting up an office in Europe. The billet they offered was at a rate of pay several times greater than what I had been earning, and they would provide me a pied-à-terre in Paris and travel on the Continent. It was a dream come true, but my mother would not hear of it. She scolded me, warning that I would be an innocent abroad and taken advantage of and it could ruin my reputation. We exchanged harsh words, and I took the offer and went over to Europe. I dutifully sent a note or card off to her every evening, assuring her that I was safe and living a most circumspect life. She sent several letters back that were quite forceful, which I fully expected. But then … but then, the letters stopped coming. For the entire last two months that I was there, I heard nothing. I could not imagine what had happened. I wrote letters and sent telegrams to her neighbors, and two of them wrote back that they had not seen her recently. One of them even went to her flat and knocked on her door, but there was no answer. As soon as I returned to London, I raced up to Islington. She was gone. Her flat was undisturbed. All of her clothes and belongings were there in place. But she had vanished.

"I asked the neighbors, but they knew nothing. I reported it to the police, and they took down her particulars, but they said to me, 'Frankly, Miss, we have many more serious things to look after than a middle-aged woman who has taken herself on a bit of a holiday.' Well, I continued searching for her for several more days, becoming more and more upset. I shared my worries with one of my closest friends, and she said that I should come and talk to Sherlock Holmes. She had read those stories in the Strand about how you solve so many crimes. I told her that it sounded like a good idea, but that I had nowhere near the means to be hiring a famous detective. Well, she told me to go anyway. No harm in asking, she said.

"So here I am, Mr. Holmes. I have nowhere else to turn. I really do not know what else to do. In my heart, I know that something has happened to my mother and that I was the cause of it. You just have to help me find her."

Again, she was using her handkerchief to dab her eyes as she haltingly spoke these final words. Holmes reached his long arms across to her and placed his hands over the hand of hers that was not holding her handkerchief.

"There, there, my dear'" he said. "I am sure your mother is just fine, and I vouchsafe to you that I shall not rest until she is found." He sat back and continued, again in an unusually soothing voice. "Please give me some facts about your mother. Tell me anything that might be useful in helping me find her. And do not suppose that any detail is too small."

Miss Lightowlers smiled wanly and opened her handbag.

"Here is a small photograph of her. I take it with me wherever I go. Does that help?"

"That is very useful. And her full name?"

"Oh, yes, of course. How foolish of me not to have stated that already. Her name is Charlotte Golderton."

She then went on to describe her missing mother in some detail. Holmes sat and listened most attentively, nodding sagely at each detail.

"Your mother's name is not the same as yours," he observed.

"That is correct, Mr. Holmes. After my father died, my mother remarried. It was … it was a mistake is all I can say. They were not happy. He was not a good man either to my mother or to me. He did things … terrible things that were unforgivable. Fortunately, he deserted us after five years, and we were much happier with him gone. My mother is still legally married to him and has retained her married name. I might also add that of late she had been spending some time with a man named Lloyd Sunday. He is the man who so discourteously made promises to me and then violated them. I suspect that their friendship is not beyond reproach. Please, sir, do not ask me to speak of these matters again. It is painful and humiliating for me to do so."

I suspected that Holmes, true to form, was about to do exactly opposite of what she asked and so I intervened with an altogether unrelated question.

"Pardon me, Miss Lightowlers," I said when she had reached an end of her recitation. "As a doctor, I could not help but notice that the skin on the back of your neck is giving you some problems. Would you like me to take a look at it and suggest some sort of remedy? Or, I can refer you to a colleague of mine, a physician on Harley Street who has particular skill in the care of the skin."

She responded by putting her left hand on the back of her neck and wincing quickly. "Oh, you must mean Dr. Lomaga. Thank you, Dr. Watson. It is just a minor skin affliction. Being of Irish descent, I inherited the complexion. It's nothing really, and I went to see Dr. Lomaga yesterday and gave me an ointment and told me that it would go away in a few days. Brought on by mental distress, he said. All I had to do was to relax, and my skin would clear. But I am afraid that there has not been a chance to do that. But perhaps I could if I knew that you and Sherlock Holmes were helping me find my mother."

"Which," said Holmes, "indeed, we are. You may relax your mind and body."

"Oh, thank you, Mr. Holmes. Thank you. You are too kind. Thank you. And please do not think badly of me if I now have to speak of how I might be able to pay you. You are far too decent a gentleman to bring up the matter but I assure you that I am not here is ask for charity. I have a bit saved from my time in Europe and could pay that as a deposit. And then as soon as I start to work again, I promise to send a bit of my salary every fortnight until everything has been paid. I am proud to say, Mr. Holmes, that I have never asked anyone for charity and never accepted any when offered. I will pay, sir, truly, I will. You will just have to give me time."

She had opened her gorgeous green eyes wide and was gazing at Holmes like an affectionate puppy dog.

"My dear young lady," he said, smiling warmly. "Now is not the time to be worried about that matter. You keep your savings, my dear. You will need them to live on until you secure your next contract. Once you have found another lucrative arrangement, we can discuss the payment of my fee. I am not offering you charity, but until then, there will be no fee and no expenses charged. Is that acceptable to you?"

"Oh, Mr. Holmes, Mr. Holmes. You are an angel. I knew that you were a brilliant detective, but I could not have known that you were also such a kind Christian gentleman. Oh, thank you, sir. Thank you."

She was now beaming radiantly at my friend. The look was so warm that had there been frost on the window, it would have melted in an instant. The three of us continued for several more minutes with inconsequential chat, and then Miss Lightowlers rose to leave. Holmes immediately stood up and faced her.

"It has been a pleasure, Miss Lightowlers," he said, and then in a manner most uncharacteristic of him, he held out his left hand, palm facing up, just above her right hand. She responded in the appropriate manner and placed her hand in his. He raised it up and bowed forward to kiss it. The action exuded old-world manners and charm, and for that reason alone, Holmes had never done anything like it before. Mrs. Hudson returned to the room, bearing the young woman's coat and saw her to the door. I poured myself a generous snifter of brandy, leaned back in my chair and glared at Holmes. He was serenely looking off toward the bay window.

"Do you believe her, Holmes?" I demanded.

"What? Believe her? Not entirely. Some of what she said has most likely been fabricated. Such is standard practice when a new client is fearful and not yet fully trusting me. But she seems fundamentally truthful. Would you not agree?"

"Quite frankly, Holmes, no. Even I could see that she was far from being entirely forthcoming."

"You don't say. How so, Watson?"

I could not believe that Holmes had been such a dullard. "She claimed," I said sharply, "to have come by cab. She did nothing of the sort. She came by the Underground and must have walked from the Metropolitan Station. I could smell the residue of tobacco smoke from a crowded Underground car. And she said she was poor. Her dress and coat look as if she fetched them from a rag and bone shop, but surely you observed her boots?"

"Her boots, you say. Yes, what about them?"

"What about them? They were Church's. Beautiful bespoke. A pair of them must run at least fifty pounds. It is unthinkable that a secretary could ever afford such a pair."

"Oh, come, come, Watson. Good quality shoes are one of the wisest investments any woman, or man for that matter, can make. It is mere proof that she responsibly saved her income and then spent it very sensibly. A certain sign of her judgment and temperament."

"They did not strike me that way," I protested. "But what about her perfume. Surely you noticed that. It was one of the most select brands ..."

"*Mille fleurs,*" interrupted Holmes. "Yes, wasn't it intoxicating?"

"Holmes, a bottle of that costs a month's wage. Three months for a working woman. I gave my wife a very small bottle for Christmas. It ran me over thirty pounds. How could she afford that?"

"My dear doctor, you have answered your own question."

"I beg your pardon."

"Did your good wife save up her pin money and buy the perfume herself? No. It was a gift from a man who adores her, one who has excellent taste and shows his affection by lavishing fine gifts upon her. Of course, I noticed it. Beyond a doubt, it was a gift from one of her many gentlemen admirers. She had the good sense and steel of soul to accept the gift and then send whoever it was packing. Quite the woman, would you not agree?"

No, I thought, I would not. But there was no use arguing with Holmes. All I could do was speak my mind to him.

"Holmes, I do believe that she has bewitched you."

"Oh, my dear chap," he said, with a smile and a low laugh, "of course I am enticed by her. I am not entirely that calculating machine you have accused me of being. If a beautiful young woman comes asking for my help in the depths of winter when interesting cases have ebbed for the season, why would I not be willing to help her? It would be so much more enjoyable than sitting in this stuffy room. Or would you rather I used my old solution to ease my boredom."

"No. Of course not."

I could say no more and picked up a medical journal that I had brought with me. Holmes turned his chair toward the bay window, lit up a cigarette, and gazed off serenely into the winter sky.

Chapter Two
Miss Gertrude Hume-Craw

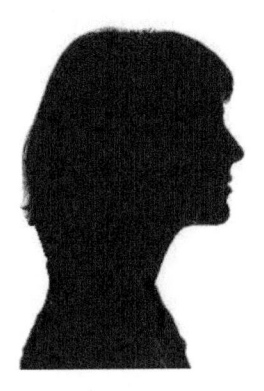

WHEN I FINISHED reading the short article in the medical journal, I put it down and looked over at Holmes. I was somewhat relieved to see that his look of heavenly peace had vanished. Now his eyes were closed, his hands, with fingertips touching, were in front of his chin, and a small scowl creased his forehead.

"When," I asked, "do you expect your next appointment?"

"In four minutes," he replied, without opening his eyes.

In precisely that amount of time, a firm knock came to the door, and Mrs. Hudson descended the steps to welcome the visitor.

"Your next appointment has arrived, Mr. Holmes," she said after climbing back up to the room. "here is her card."

Holmes glanced at it quickly and handed it over to me. It was quite nicely printed and read:

Gertrude Hume-Craw
General Secretary

The Minoan Expedition

British Museum (Department of Antiquities)

"Mrs. Hudson," I said, with a sly grin on my face. "Are you not going to give Mr. Holmes a warning about this one?"

She smiled back at my tease. "Not unless he needs a scrum-half for his rugby team."

A minute later, Mr. Hudson reappeared, carrying what looked like to a military issue overcoat and followed by a rather imposing woman. Miss Gertrude Hume-Craw was not underfed, but then again, not at all fat. The only word that I could use to describe her would be *powerful*. She was as tall as I am, as thick round the neck, and every bit as wide in the shoulders. Her hair was cut like a schoolboy's, and her face was devoid of any cosmetic enhancements. She took two quick steps into the room and barked at us.

"Which of you is Holmes?"

"I am Sherlock Holmes," said my friend. "Welcome, Miss…"

"So, you must be Watson," she interrupted, now looking at me.

"I am he."

"Good. I do not have much time to waste, so shall we begin?"

Without being asked, she strode over to the table, pulled out one of the straight-back chairs with one hand, spun it around, and sat down.

"How much do you charge for your services?" she demanded of Holmes.

"I do not usually…," began Holmes and got no further.

"Well, I usually do. So, let's get that over with."

Holmes looked a little nonplussed, but took a slip of paper and a pencil and wrote a number of it. He stretched out his long arm to hand it to Miss Hume-Craw.

"Sign it first," she said.

Holmes looked at her, and slowly his scowl changed into a bemused smile. He signed the note and handed it to her. She looked at it quickly.

"Right. I accept that," she said.

"There is," said Holmes, "a possibility that it might not apply to your case."

"Why not?"

"It only applies to cases I accept. And I have not yet accepted yours."

She shrugged. "You will. It's altogether too important and too intriguing for you to refuse, assuming that the tales Dr. Watson here writes about you are the truth. They are, aren't they?"

"Ah, yes. Sensationalised, romanticised, and with a regrettable paucity of attention to scientific deduction, but nevertheless true."

"That is what I thought. That is how I know you will accept my case."

"Very well, Madam" said Holmes, looking quite intrigued. "Kindly introduce your good self to us and state your case."

"I will. Are you familiar with my family name?" she asked.

"Yes," replied Holmes. "It is an uncommon portmanteau name, originally from the Borders and now applicable to several hundred families in Great Britain and several hundred more throughout the Empire. I must, however, assume that the question you meant to ask me was whether I know who your father is. And the answer to that is also affirmative. Professor Edgar Hume-Craw of St. Andrews University is a distinguished scholar of ancient history, an archeologist of some note, and currently the director of the Minoan Project, of which you are the General Secretary. Is that correct?"

She smiled a thin smug smile in return. "That is correct. Nice to see that you keep yourself informed."

"I am also informed," Holmes then continued, "that he is generally considered to play second fiddle to the far more renowned Arthur Evans, who has also been conducting archeological excavations in Crete on behalf of the Ashmolean Museum. Is that also correct?"

By the look on the woman's face, I was quite certain that had a paperweight or ink bottle been within her reach, she would have hurled it at Holmes. For a few brief seconds, she gripped the arms of her chair, stifling her anger. Then she replied.

"That is a matter of debate. Some consider Mr. Evans's success to be more the result of his political skills and the ability of his artist to restore ancient frescos so that they look as if they were painted yesterday than to anything approaching scholarship, but that is not what I came here to hire you for."

"I do hope not," replied Holmes, apparently enjoying the verbal jousting. "Why then did you come?"

"I came because my father is dead."

That was shocking news. Professor Hume-Craw was a figure of some reputation, and his death would surely have been reported in the Press.

"My condolences," I said. "We had no idea."

"Thank you, Dr. Watson. News of his death has not yet been released. Once it is, all of England will be aware of it.

But I did not come here for your sympathy. I came primarily to hire Sherlock Holmes to investigate the death."

"You have my attention," said Holmes, "Now, give me the particulars, and I will tell you if I will take on your case."

She leaned back in her chair and folded her arms across her chest and began her account.

"I will not bore you with unnecessary historical details," she said. "You can do your own homework. I will tell you that after many years of scholarly research, my father had discerned the likely existence of an advanced civilization on the Isle of Crete that prospered for many years before the rise of the Athenian and Trojan empires. He, not Arthur Evans, named it the Minoan Era. For several years, using his private resources, he conducted preliminary diggings in Crete and finally, after months of delay, was awarded a substantial grant by the British Museum to carry out a large-scale archeological expedition. I am a very learned historical scholar in my own right, and I agreed to serve as the administrator of the expedition. By the time we arrived in Crete, Arthur Evans, by somewhat devious means, had already secured the site that my father had discovered, and we had no choice but to investigate what everyone considered to be a secondary site. As fate would have it, our site turned out to be to the location of a far greater treasure, of invaluable significance to the study of ancient history.

"Two weeks ago, we closed down our work for the season and boarded a boat that would bring us back to England by way of Athens, Palma, and Gibraltar. On the night we approached Gibraltar, there was a full moon, and the view from the deck was quite striking. My father got up from the table, saying that he was going outside to enjoy the vista. That was the last anyone saw of him. When we pulled into the port and disembarked for a brief time of re-stocking, all of us left the boat, but he did not appear. That was most uncharacteristic of him, and several of us went back on board to see if he was indisposed. We could not find him. We alerted the captain, and a full search was carried out. He was not on board. The captain concluded that he must have fallen overboard and agreed to request a full search of the waters approaching Gibraltar. The entire next day, the local officials, aided by a small fleet of fishermen, scoured the waters. He was nowhere to be found.

"The currents around Gibraltar, as I assume you know, are very powerful, and had he fallen into the sea and drowned, his body could have been swept away for miles. We agreed with the captain that the voyage must be resumed. The expedition's photographer remained in Gibraltar to continue the search, and the rest of us made our way to London, arriving back here just three days ago."

"Clearly," said Holmes, "you suspect foul play, else you would not be here."

"I do. My father had made many sea voyages, often in far heavier seas that we were traveling through. Also, for his age, he was in superb physical condition and could clamber up and down hills and mountains and excavation ladders with the best of them. Such a man does not just walk out onto the deck on a calm night and fall overboard."

"A most reasonable deduction," concurred Holmes. He said nothing for the next minute, and I could almost read the list of queries he was forming in his most unique brain. He gave me a nod as if to say that I should be ready to record the coming interrogation, and then turned to Miss Gertrude.

"Let us be thorough and begin at the start of the expedition. Were there any events that took place prior to your departure that might have given a reasonable person cause for alarm, or at least concern?"

"There were," the woman replied, "the usual inconveniences and delays during the weeks as we prepared to sail, but nothing out of the ordinary, except for one recurring issue."

"Yes, and what was that?"

"Mr. Holmes, how long does it usually take for a telegram to travel from London to St. Andrews?"

"It arrives within seconds. Under a minute," answered Holmes.

"Yes, it does. And it would be very peculiar, would it not, if the time stamped on the sender's copy of the form were a full fifteen minutes ahead of the time stamped on the receiver's?"

Holmes's eyebrows edged up ever so slightly. "Indeed, it would. And this happened more than once?"

"Yes, numerous times. No one noticed at first, as the receiver never sees the sender's copy. But as I was compiling the files and pinning the copies together before placing them in the records, the anomaly of one set of slips caught my eye. That caused me to examine other copies, and there were over twenty of them that had somehow been delayed. At first, I wrote it off to the sloppiness of the Royal Mail and their clerks, but that made no sense. The time stamps are now done mechanically by the postal station clocks. There was no reason for the delay."

Holmes again nodded. "That is of singular interest. Did the delays continue? Have you had time to check since you returned?"

"No, and yes. We received many telegrams whilst we were in Crete, mostly from the Museum. Immediately upon returning to London I went there straight away the first morning after the boat had docked to report my father's death and, giving the reason that I was responsible for the records of the expedition, asked for the copies of their telegram forms. They were supplied, and I examined them, but there had been no delays. Perhaps one or two minutes here and there, but that was normal for messages traveling across Europe and through the underwater cable to the islands."

"Ah, that is significant," said Holmes. "Did you form the suspicion that someone had been intercepting your telegraph messages and delaying them, perhaps whilst making a copy before forwarding them to you?"

"You are the detective, Mr. Holmes, not me. You tell me."

Holmes nodded. "That I am and in good time, I shall. Ad was there any other cause for concern before leaving?"

"None."

"Any animosities during your time in Crete?"

"There were many hard feelings between our people and the Evans expedition, and I would never say for certain that they could not stoop to murder. But whatever animosity was expressed was entirely on our part toward them. The Evans people, whenever we encountered them, were quite civil although I am sure that they gloated mercilessly behind our backs."

"Quite understandable," said Holmes. "A common phenomenon amongst academic types. Very well, let us return to the boat on the night of your father's disappearance. How many passengers were there on board?"

"It was not a large ship. There was a total of only thirty people plus the crew. Our party consisted of seven. Almost all of the other passengers who initially boarded with us in Heraklion disembarked in Athens. The few who remained got off either in Palermo or Palma. Only one man continued all the way to London, and he was an elderly Orthodox priest. He was far too frail to have ever pushed my father overboard."

"Quite so," observed Holmes. "May I assume that you have concluded that the most likely suspects to have done harm to Professor Hume-Craw would be amongst the members of your own party?"

"Were you not listening to me? I repeat: you are the detective, not me. But I can see no reason why a Greek, Sicilian, or Spaniard, who had no idea who we were, would wish my father harm. It is possible that one of them was a hired killer. That vocation is not uncommon amongst those nationalities, but the finger would seem at first to point to one of our party. Yes."

"I assume that the expedition had acquired some valuable artifacts that were to be turned over to the Museum," said Holmes. "The members of your party would have known about these objects, would they not?"

"Not entirely. There were some items that no one except my father knew the value of. And he alone kept the full detailed inventory, which we have not yet succeeded in finding."

Holmes paused his questions and lit a cigarette before continuing his cross-questioning.

"Your case," he said, "does indeed contain some singular aspects. So, pray tell do you trust all of the members of your party?"

She gave Holmes quite the look of annoyance. "Of course not. Would you? Anytime there is a fortune to be had, or a scholarly laurel to be gained, greed and ambition take over. Surely you know that."

Holmes actually smiled at her. "I do indeed. Therefore, I suggest that you provide me with a list of the members of your party and whatever details you have concerning them."

"I thought you would never ask," came the reply, as she opened her satchel, withdrew a file, and handed it to Holmes.

"Excellent," said Holmes, as he, in turn, handed the file to me. "Now, you did say at the outset of our conversation, that the death of your father was your primary concern. By that, I would understand that there must also be a secondary concern. Would you kindly elucidate."

"My mother," she said.

"What about her?"

"She is the principal beneficiary of my father's estate, and there are significant funds, intellectual properties, and royalties that must be transferred to her."

"Do you need me to recommend a trusted solicitor?" asked Holmes.

"No, Mr. Holmes. I already have a solicitor. What I need is a detective."

"Pray tell."

"Because my mother has gone missing. We have not heard from her for the past several months. My inquiries concerning her have come back void. I would like for you to find her so that the matters of the estate can be concluded."

"That can be easily carried out," said Holmes. "Where was the last known address of Mrs. Hume-Craw?"

"I do not know."

"You do not know where your mother lived?"

"That is what I said, Mr. Holmes. My mother and father had been estranged for the past decade. My career kept me in contact with him, not her. They did not divorce, but she, perhaps out of spite, resumed the use of her maiden name."

"Such a practice is not unknown," said Holmes. "And what was her maiden name?"

"Golderton. Charlotte Golderton."

To Holmes's credit, not a flicker passed over his stone face. I had to bite my tongue to keep from sputtering out some expletive, but Holmes merely carried on.

"Duly noted," he said. "And what was your last known contact for Charlotte Golderton?"

"She kept a box at the E.C. post office. Beyond that, I have no idea. I have also been estranged from her for several years. However, I trust that with your contacts in the Royal Mail, you should be able to track her down."

The conversation did not continue long afterward. Miss Gertrude Hume-Craw soon rose, and herself summoned Mrs. Hudson to bring her coat. Then she departed, letting herself out.

"A coincidence, Holmes?" I asked, with a twinkle in my eye.

"Oh ho, Watson. I most certainly hope not. Cases that involve missing people, murder on the high seas, exotic artifacts, and clients who appear to be trying to hire and at the same time mislead me are so much more interesting. We really must find this Mrs. Golderton woman and discover what it is about her that has caused two women, who could not be more different from each other, both to claim her as their mother."

Holmes took out his pipe and slowly filled and lit it. Then he drew his long legs up under his body and took on his Buddha-like posture, his eyes closed. I opened the file that Miss Gertrude had left behind and perused the first page.

"Hell-o!" I involuntarily blurted. "What's this?"

"What?" said Holmes, not bothering to open his eyes.

"The members of the Minoan Expedition Party. You won't believe this one, Holmes."

"Then get on with it and tell me why."

I read off the names as they appeared on the first page.

"Expedition Director, Dr. Edgar Hume-Craw; General Secretary, Miss Gertrude Hume-Craw; Private Secretary to the Director, Miss Bernadette O'Donohue; Head of Excavations, Mr. Allister Baird; Head of Provisions, Mr. Robert Argyle; Head Curator, Mr. Darren Cruickshank; and ..." and here I paused, "Photographer ... Mr. Lloyd Sunday."

On hearing the last name, Holmes's eyes did pop open, and he rose from his chair and came over to look at the list.

"How singularly intriguing," he said. Without asking, he removed the file from my hands and took it back to his chair. He was soon oblivious to all but its contents.

I returned to my reading and, after enduring Holmes's silence for half an hour, interrupted him.

"Did you not say you had three appointments this afternoon? When is the next one due?"

He appeared startled and quickly glanced at his watch.

"Oh, thank you, Watson. I had put it out of my mind. The data already received this afternoon has rather consumed my attention. Now ... confound it. She is due any minute. Had you reminded me earlier, I could have sent a note putting her off for several days. Now we shall have to see her."

"A new client then?"

"Yes, another one of those poor, pathetic young women who claims that her employment situation is intolerable. No doubt some beast of a man, some masher demanding her affection. Please just take down her particulars, and I will try to get rid of her as quickly as possible.

Chapter Three
Miss Rowena Ferguson

THE BELL SOON SOUNDED, and once again Mrs. Hudson answered the door and came back up the stair to report.

"Yes, Mrs. Hudson," said Holmes. "My dear, please do not just stand there. What is this one like?"

"Well, Mr. Holmes, I was about to say that she was the third young woman in the same afternoon, but I hesitated. The first visitor was no longer all that young, and the second was not exactly womanish. This one is both."

"Is she now? And no warning about her?"

"Very well, Mr. Holmes, it would be a very rapid judgement were I to make it, but I must say that if I had a son who was in need of a wife, I would arrange for him to meet Miss Rowena Ferguson before she was snapped up by a dozen other mothers of sons."

That, I thought, was about a generous an introduction as I had ever heard delivered by our dear landlady, and, over the years, she had introduced at least a hundred other women to Holmes in my presence.

"Ah," sighed Holmes, "a veritable priggish Sunday school teacher. Needy, but intolerably dull. Please show her up."

"I will, Mr. Holmes, and I will assure her that in her hour of need, Mr. Sherlock Holmes will give her his full and respectful attention."

She turned abruptly and went back down to the door. Holmes rolled his eyes and sighed.

"Very well, if I must, I must."

Mrs. Hudson soon returned with the young woman in tow and presented her to us. I had stood and glared at Holmes until he did likewise. As he would later admit, Mrs. Hudson's appraisal of this client was right on the mark. She was modestly dressed, bore no cosmetics on her face, kept her hair neatly up on her head and exuded the fragrance of mere soap and water. She was, nevertheless, uncommonly pretty. Had I been father to a son, I might well have agreed with Mrs. Hudson and paraphrased one much wiser than I in saying *behold, a Scot in whom there is no guile.*

"Please, Miss Ferguson, come in and be seated," said Holmes. "We are at the end of a long and busy afternoon, so kindly make yourself comfortable and state your case."

The young woman sat down and, keeping her back straight and her hands in her lap, spoke in a soft Scottish voice.

"Mr. Holmes, I am the victim of a vile blackmailer. As a result, I have stolen scores of valuable documents from my employer and passed them on to this man. Now, it appears that as a result of my actions, an important man may have been murdered." There she stopped and looked directly at Holmes, awaiting his response.

I could not recall any statement of a case being so concise and so quick to grab my friend's undivided attention. He put aside the file he had still been holding and looked intently at this most recent visitor.

"Thank you, Miss Ferguson. Forgive me if I seemed brusque. I assure you that you have my full attention. Could you kindly back up, fully introduce yourself and your situation and present the evidence that has led you to your conclusions?"

"Aye, sir, I can do that. I come from the town of Ayr in the south of Scotland. I am the only child of the Reverend Donald Ferguson, of the Church of Scotland and Mrs. Elizabeth Ferguson. I was raised in a godly home and my father, being a practical Scotsman, insisted that I learn some type of trade so that, should the good Lord not provide me with a husband, I would have an income of my own on which to live. I took up secretarial skills and excelled in my learning, so much so that I was advanced to the class of telegraph operator. I also performed well in those studies. A year ago, a notice came around saying that the Royal Mail was in need of telegraph operators in their large office in Mount Pleasant, which handles all of the mail and telegraphs coming and going from the EC postal district. What with the war in the Cape and so many young men having been sent there, the Royal Mail had decided to hire women to replace them. Even if the wages were less than they had been paying the men, it was still an excellent billet and much beyond what I could ever hope to earn up in Scotland. My mother and father prayed about this opportunity and agreed that it was of such good fortune that it could not be turned down, and so I came to London, found my very own flat in Clerkenwell and began working.

"I did well in my duties and made many wonderful friends with the other young women with whom I was working. I attended some social functions with them and was introduced to a young soldier, a handsome Scottish laddie, Corporal Archibald MacDonald, with whom I fell quite hopelessly in love. For a month we spent every spare minute of our time together and then he was shipped out to the war. He had been gone for only a month when I realized that I was in the family way with his child. I immediately sent a telegram off to my beloved informing him and he, being an honorable man, replied immediately to say that he was thrilled and that we would be married as soon as he returned. I also took some steps that were deceitful, I must confess, but necessary, and went out and bought myself a simple wedding ring and told my employer that I had married a soldier the night before he was sent off to war. The telegraph office is in great need of qualified operators, and I was one of the best, so they announced that they would not dismiss me but would praise me for my patriotic duty and allow me to keep working. They even allowed me to stay on after I began to show. It was out of a need for workers much more than for any enlightened ideal they might have held concerning the employment of women; nevertheless, it sufficed. I lived exceptionally frugally, saved every farthing I could, and then took three months off of my employment and delivered my son. Some of the girls I worked with, of course, knew my true situation but they breathed not a word to anyone. I deceived my parents and told them that what with the war, the demands at the Mount were so great that no one was allowed to take any holidays and so I could not return to visit them. They knew nothing and still know nothing about my situation.

"On the day I returned to my flat from the hospital, a telegram was waiting for me informing me that my fiancée had been killed in action in the Cape. I had leave of one week from my station, most of which I spent in tears, then I took my son to Bernardo's and asked them to find him a loving home. I knew I could not raise him on my own and I trusted them to find a loving Christian family. The next day I returned to my work."

As she spoke these last few sentences, I could hear the faltering of her voice. So must have Holmes for he interrupted her recitation and spoke to her in a kindly way.

"Miss Ferguson, permit me to be candid and forthright. If your parents are, as you say, loving Christian people, then surely they would forgive you and do everything in their power to support you and your child."

Tears appeared in the young woman's eyes. She took a deep breath and carried on.

"Mr. Holmes, I know what you say is right. But I simply could not bring myself to come to them as a fallen woman. Lying to them would just compound my shame. I am their only child and their pride and joy. It would break their hearts. My father is a minister in an austere denomination. Having a fallen daughter would be a cause for scandal in his congregation. I just could not bring myself to do that to them."

Holmes smiled in genuine warmth. "My dear young lady, there is a solution."

She looked up in wonder at Holmes. "What?"

"Arrange for a fortnight of leave from your station. Go to Bernardo's and reclaim your son. They do not send children out for adoption for several months if they arrive as infants. Then take your son and go home to your parents and congratulate them on becoming grandparents. The devastation they will feel at your having been overtaken in a fault will be canceled out by the irresistible joy of holding their grandson. You will face a short time of turmoil, after which your mother will make plans to spend every other week, if not more, in London, helping you care for her grandson. Your father will preach a sermon on the New Commandment Our Lord gave to his people or some other appropriate text, and if there is gossip within the congregation, your mother will remind them that, according to the scriptures, backbiters are to be sentenced to eternal damnation in the lake of fire and brimstone. I implore you to trust me on this advice. I have dealt with an abundance of grandparents in the past. Dr. Watson will wholeheartedly agree with me, will you not, Doctor."

"Entirely," I said. "Could not agree more."

Miss Rowena Ferguson was now trembling and struggled to reply.

"Mr. Holmes, I do not know how I could do that. I am not sure I have the strength to do what you ask."

"It is quite obvious, young lady, that you have more than sufficient strength of character to do what I am telling you, not asking you to do. And furthermore, if you do not agree this instant to do what I have told you to do then I shall refuse to even listen to any more of your case, and you may leave this place forthwith."

I was quite sure that Holmes, in his sincere interest in doing the best for this remarkable young woman, was bluffing. A case involving blackmail and murder was not something he would ever send packing. However, the young woman believed him. For a brief moment, she bowed her head and closed her eyes. Her moment of prayer was accompanied by a set of fiercely clenched fists.

"Very well, Mr. Holmes, I will do what you say. Now, may I please continue to state the rest of my case?"

"Yes, please do. You have my undivided attention."

"Thank you. It happened in this fashion. Several months into my condition, I came to work and to my operator's desk, and I found, hidden under my key, an envelope. It was addressed to me, and the name and address were typed. The contents of the letter were also typed. The contents horrified me. Some vile creature had somehow become aware of many of the facts of my private situation, of my duplicity in lying about my marriage to my employer, and my fear of my family's shame because of me. The letter was very matter-of-fact, and the writer demanded that I either be willing to make copies of certain telegrams and send them to him, or he would inform my employer, my family and the Press of who I was and what I had done. I was sick with fear. For two days, I was frozen in inaction. Then another letter arrived, restating the demands and giving me just one more day to let him know my answer. I was instructed to write my reply and send it to an address in Belgravia, which turned out to be a private postal forwarding service.

"I was physically ill all that night, fearing that were I to stay in that state I would lose the baby I was carrying. So, early the following morning I wrote a letter to this evil man and agreed to his terms."

"Permit me to interrupt," said Holmes. "Was there no indication of who this man was? Any clue at all?"

"He signed his letters with a name, sir, if that is what you are asking."

"Precisely. And what was the name?"

"He signed as Mr. Charles Augustus Milverton."

Holmes was immediately silent and stared at her and then at me in disbelief. The young woman watched both of us and then she smiled.

"Oh, please, gentlemen. I knew it was a false name. Mr. Milverton's murder was reported in the Press some time back. He had been shot by two miscreants who had tried to rob him. I am sure you read that story, as did I. But I have no idea at all what his true name was."

"Thank you, Miss," said Holmes. "Pray, continue."

"I immediately began to receive instructions, coming again as notes that were waiting for me at my desk, explicitly directing me to make copies of telegrams by this noble lord, or that clergyman's wife, or some member of Parliament—all people of some social standing and wealth. I did as I was told, and sometimes I would receive more instructions immediately, and sometimes a week or two would pass without my hearing anything."

"Did anything," asked Holmes, "come of the data you intercepted and passed on? Was any action taken against the people whose secrets you had revealed?"

"With one exception, no. Nothing was ever heard about them. Which leads me to believe that they paid the demands made by the blackmailer."

"A logical deduction," noted Holmes. "And the one exception?"

"Do you recall the recent stories in *The Chronicle* about Bishop Worthington in the Cotswolds?"

The scandal the woman referred to had been in the Press the previous year. Several damning allegations were made concerning the austere bishop, his attraction to the love that dare not speak its name, and his clandestine meetings in the wooded copses of the Cotswolds.

"I do recall that unfortunate series of stories," said Holmes.

"I was the one," said the young woman, "who ruined that man's life."

"In fairness," said Holmes, "the cleric himself may have been solely responsible for his downfall. His punishment was well-deserved."

"What did," I interjected, "happen to that fellow? He just vanished."

"He was transferred to a rural diocese in Manitoba where the forests are either beyond frigid or infested with mosquitos. Any exposed flesh is immediately to mortal danger from one of the two. His parishioners are no longer in danger."

He turned back to Miss Ferguson.

"Pray, continue. You continued to obey the instructions?"

"Yes, and I lived in mortal fear that I would be found out and I was afraid that my fear would harm my baby. I had never been so terrified in my life.

"Then, one day as I was passing the desk of another one of the girls who worked alongside me, I noticed an envelope on her desk. It was addressed to Charles Milverton, at the same address that I sent my stolen information to. At first, I was dumbfounded, but then I realized that I was not the only one who Mr. Milverton had recruited to carry out his vile deeds. So, without saying anything to my colleague—Eleanor was her name—I casually sat down beside her during our tea break and whilst chatting about the weather, I slowly took an addressed enveloped from my purse and displayed it to her, all the while chatting away. The look on her face said it all. She said nothing and just pointed a trembling finger at me, and I silently mouthed back the words *me too* to her. Then, whilst still chatting about the weather, I wrote a note and slipped it to her. On it, I suggested that she meet me after work in the lady's lavatory in the nearest Underground station. We met there, quite sure that no one could overhear us and opened our hearts to each other. I told her about my family, and my son, and my lies to the Royal Mail, and the death of my beloved soldier. She replied in kind and informed me that Mr. Milverton had somehow discovered that she was married with two children, but that her husband was in prison for robbing a post office. Were it to be revealed, she would be terminated immediately. With her husband not able to provide any support, she was the only one who could look after the cost of food and clothing for her children and pay the rent. She knew that should she be forced to leave her employment, the three of them would be in the poorhouse within a week. She had received the same threats I had, and had also succumbed and had sent copies of many highly confidential telegrams to Mr. Milverton.

"I know it is hard to explain, but just knowing that there was one other human being in the same horrible situation as I was, gave me strength, as it did her. We began to meet briefly every day after our shift ended and we shared with each other what we had done that day.

"After a week of meeting, and becoming dear friends, Eleanor said to me that she thought there might be other girls in the same predicament. We came up with a plan to keep an eye on the Royal Mail post box on the pavement just outside the front door of the EC building. It did not take long until we recorded three other girls, making five of us, who were putting envelopes into the box regularly. We quietly approached each of them very privately, using the same actions as I had with Eleanor whereby we chatted about nothing while exposing an envelope with the address of Charles Milverton. Their reaction was the same as Eleanor's had been and we soon were able to set up clandestine meetings for the entire group of us. They alerted us to two more, making a total of seven. Every one of us had some secret that we could not dare to become known. One girl had shaken her baby so hard that it died in her arms. Another's mother worked every night over in Whitechapel as a prostitute. And another was involved in an illicit relationship with a bishop. All of our secrets had been discovered. We were each paying the price and had given in to blackmail.

"But, we were a spirited little team, if I say so myself. We came up with what we thought was a brilliant plan. We would continue to copy and forward all those highly confidential messages that were demanded of us, but we would alter the contents ever so slightly. Not enough to make it appear that we had rebelled, but enough so that the information if ever exposed, could be immediately proven to be false and slanderous, thus saving the reputation of the victim and making the data we were sending useless. We were quite proud of our bold counter-attack as we saw it."

"And did it work?" asked Holmes. "Were you able to implement your ingenious plan?"

"The four of us who continued to work in the Mount carried on for several weeks. Three of our number—Anna, Dorothy, and Bernie—quit their employment and sought greener pastures elsewhere that did not pay so well but that were free of such horrible demands. But then an odd thing happened, Mr. Holmes. We had been kept very busy with all sorts of demands, but then the notes suddenly stopped, for all of us."

"When was that?" asked Holmes.

"Just a bit over four months ago."

"You are quite certain of that?"

"Oh, very, sir. I could give you the exact date for I remember that the last demand I received was on my mother's birthday. The other remaining girls all said the same thing. It was as if a deadly weight had been lifted off our shoulders. We had no idea why the demands had ceased, but we were overjoyed."

"And may I assume," asked Holmes, "that your reason for coming to see me after such an extended period of freedom is because the demands started up again recently."

"Yes," she sighed. "That is exactly what happened. But, during our brief escape from our prison, I had read several dated copies of the Strand magazine in which the stories of your adventures were recounted. I made a pledge in my heart that should the horrid demands ever reappear, I would come immediately to Sherlock Holmes and place myself under your care. And that is why, sir, you find me here speaking to you this afternoon."

Holmes again smiled at her and replied. "I am honored by your confidence, Miss. So, shall we begin with first things first? You said that your actions might be related to a murder. Kindly explain."

"Yes, sir. I can do that, Mr. Holmes. Are you familiar with the name of Professor Edgar Hume-Craw?"

I came close to snapping in two the pencil with which I was taking notes. Holmes, as I expected, did not bat an eyelash.

"You refer to the learned historian from St. Andrew's. The Director of the British Museum's Minoan Expedition?"

"Yes, sir. That is who I mean. He died on his way back home from Crete. He fell overboard in the Mediterranean, and foul play is suspected. He and his expeditions were the subject of the demands for information immediately prior to the four-month lapse, and they were again over the past few days. I cannot prove anything, sir, but I am certain that he was murdered and that it was directly connected to all the data we sent to Mr. Milverton back in the fall."

Holmes nodded sagely and continued. "Was it indeed? Perhaps you could impart to me some of that data."

For the next ten minutes, Miss Ferguson recounted an extensive quantity of detailed information concerning the Minoan Expedition that had been shared by telegraph amongst the members of the party, and back and forth between its principals and the Museum. Her prodigious memory was most impressive and, when I later compared my notes to the information in the file that our previous visitor had left behind, I found that the details matched. I was familiar, from reading of the account of both this expedition and the more renowned one of Arthur Evans, with many of the place names in Crete and those of the various gods and temples. However, she quoted two archeological terms I had never heard of: *Linear A* and *Linear B*. It seemed that both of these were indecipherable ancient languages that had been discovered in Crete. Arthur Evans had claimed the credit for their discovery, but our now departed professor had claimed that he had solved the riddle and could translate them. Such an accomplishment would bring lasting fame and adulation to him and the party.

When she had completed her summary, Holmes then moved to the next stage in the case.

"Excellent, Miss Ferguson," he said. "now, about the telegraphs you perused in the past few days. What all did they speak of?"

"Mostly about the death of the professor. The chaps at the Museum were very distressed by the news, and they kept on asking about 'the priceless treasure' the professor was bringing to them. And there were also several references to two people that the members of the party and the officers of the Museum were very exercised to locate. They had somehow gone missing."

"And who," asked Holmes, "might they have been?"

"Their names were Charlotte Golderton and Lloyd Sunday."

We chatted on for some time before Miss Rowena took her leave. Holmes admonished her to continue in her subterfuge and counter-attack and not breathe a word to anyone about her visit to 221B Baker Street. And, of course, he reminded her of her promise to go as soon as possible back to her parents and disclose to them the entirety of her situation.

"I do believe, Watson," he said after she had departed, "that we have had a singularly intriguing criminal conspiracy dropped into our laps this afternoon."

"It would appear so."

"The intercepting of confidential telegraph messages by an unscrupulous blackmailer offers countless opportunities for crimes that will never be reported to the police. Would you agree?"

Chapter Four

The British Museum

DURING THE FOLLOWING few days, I saw little of Holmes. He departed 221B early in the morning and returned after I had retired for the night. I knew he would be hot on the trail of Lloyd Sunday and the elusive Charlotte Golderton. When he did appear at the breakfast table on the Thursday morning, I began the conversation with the invariable question that every passerby makes to a man standing on a bridge who is holding a fishing rod.

"Any luck?"

Holmes shook his head and gave the equally invariable reply. "Not yet."

After a sip of his morning coffee, he added, "I have picked up the trail of the Lloyd Sunday chap. He returned to London from Gibraltar and has been moving to a new hotel every night. He clearly does not want to be found. But I expect to be able to track him down by the time he wakes up on Saturday morning."

"And Mrs. Charlotte? What about her?" I asked.

"Nothing. Nothing at all. No hotel registrations no postal address, no news from my agents or Irregulars. Whoever she is, she has managed quite brilliantly to elude me."

"Even after your burning the midnight oil for four days straight?" I asked.

"Oh no. It has not been quite that bad, Watson. I only worked through two of the evenings. I spent the other two at the opera and the symphony."

I must admit that this admission left me speechless. Sherlock Holmes and I had been the closest of friends for over twenty years, and we always invited the other to join if we had plans to go to some entertaining event for the evening. My wife and I invariably sent a note asking him along. Usually, he declined, but sending the invitation was simply an unspoken rule of our friendship. I was not only surprised but, quite frankly, my feelings were hurt.

Holmes must have read the expression on my face and smiled at me warmly.

"My dear friend," he said. "Of course, I would have asked you to join me, but it was not I who arranged for the tickets. I was invited as a guest of Miss Lightowlers."

"The redhead? You spent the evening with *her*?"

"Yes, and dinner as well. Both occasions were quite pleasant. She is rather delightful company."

He said no more, and instead picked up the newspaper and began to read it whilst finishing his coffee. I was stunned. In all the years I had known him, he had never done anything like that. He had, I remembered, falsely pretended to court and even propose marriage to the maid at Appledore Towers, but that was no more than a ruse to gain entry to the home of Mr. Milverton. That he would spend an evening with a beautiful woman who was twenty years his junior, was unheard of. I was about to demand an explanation when he looked up over the newspaper and turned the conversation to something utterly unrelated.

"Could you spare me a couple of hours of your time this morning?"

"I suppose so," I replied. "My first appointment is not scheduled until eleven o'clock. What did you have in mind?"

"Splendid. Then please finish your coffee, don your coat, and join me for a visit to the British Museum."

The mysterious disappearance and presumed death of Professor Hume-Craw had become known and was now fodder for the Press. Newsboys across the north end of

London were shouting about it all the way from Baker Street to Bloomsbury. Although there was not a shred of evidence as to who might have disposed of the professor and tossed him into the sea, it did not stop the press from speculating on the Greeks, the Italians, or especially the Cretans. The divinely inspired words of St. Paul, informing Timothy that *all Cretans are liars* was cited as sufficient proof of the culpability of the descendants of the Minoans, regardless of the vast miles of sea that separated them from the Straits of Gibraltar.

The Museum, in Bloomsbury, is not that far from Baker Street and we had soon passed my *alma mater*, the University College of London, and were approaching the great square block in which the complex was located.

"Who are we meeting here?" I asked. "I rather doubt you are bringing me just to gaze one more time at Lord Elgin's trophies or the Portland Vase."

He smiled and replied, "We have an interview with Mr. Edward Thompson, the Director and Principal Librarian, and Fred Kenyon, the Director of Antiquities. I informed them yesterday that I was investigating the death of Professor Hume-Craw and received a reply back at once saying that they wished to meet with me at my earliest convenience."

As we pulled up to the main gate of the Museum on Great Russell Street, Holmes suddenly stuck his head out the window and instructed the driver to continue to the corner, then turn left and proceed once more around the block before returning to the gate to let us out.

"Forgive my being nostalgic, Watson," he said as we turned onto Montague Street. "Just up ahead on the right is the house that I first lived in before we met each other. I could only afford a small single room but it was my first home in London, and I have some pleasant memories of it and the neighborhood."

I did not bother to look at the house as we passed it. Instead, I sat and looked at Holmes, wondering what had come over him. In all the years I had known him, he had not once wallowed in pleasant memories of the past. Nor had he voluntarily spent an evening with a single woman. Suddenly, a side of his character was on display that he had kept hidden very well for a very long time.

As we completed our run around the circumference of the Museum block, Holmes sat with his eyes closed and a serene smile on his face. I was relieved when the cab finished its circumnavigation and stopped again at the gate. This time we got out and walked through the gate, past the rows of Ionic columns, and into the far reaches of the museum.

"Mr. Sherlock Holmes and Dr. Watson. Good of you to come on such short notice."

The well-dressed gentleman who stood stiffly at the door of a small conference room on the top floor welcomed us. We were ushered to chairs at an elegant table in an ornate room. On the walls and in small alcoves were numerous pieces that I assumed were priceless treasures of art that the Empire had purchased, bartered for, and outright stolen and smuggled from the four corners of the earth.

"Permit me to introduce myself," said the fellow who had greeted us. "I am Dr. Frederick Kenyon, the Director of the Antiquities Department. Please, be seated, and I will let Dr. Thompson know that you have arrived."

He departed and returned a few moments later with another finely attired but considerably older gentleman.

"Dr. Watson and Mr. Holmes," said Kenyon, "allow me to introduce Dr. Edward Thompson, our esteemed overall head of the Museum."

The older man smiled congenially and sat down.

"Gentlemen," he began, "I normally begin any meeting held in this room with a few boastful paragraphs about the largest and finest museum in the world. I will dispense with my customary braggadocio and get straight to the purpose of our meeting. I have been given to understand, Mr. Holmes, that you have been contacted by Miss Gertrude Hume-Craw and contracted to investigate the death of her father."

"Yes," said Holmes. "I have."

"Brilliant. Then kindly report to us on what you have discovered to date."

Holmes gave the old boy a cool stare.

"I was not aware that the British Museum had contracted for my services."

"Dash it all, Mr. Holmes," said Thompson, "Miss Hume-Craw is our employee, and it was our expedition. We paid for it. If you are worried about collecting your fee, let me assure you that this Museum has more money than God and is prepared to cover any and all of your costs. What we need is information, and we need it now." He banged his walking stick on the floor for emphasis.

"If you say so," acknowledged Holmes. "I appreciate your strong concern over the loss of one of your expedition's leaders."

That comment brought the walking stick down on the floor one more time.

"Good Lord. We are not here to bemoan the fact that Hume-Craw fell overboard. He was probably drunk, or one of his Greek peons gave him the heave-ho. It matters not. We have an entire long shelf full of reports of expeditions that lost a member, or a director, or an entire expedition. Every other year some damned fool sails off again to find John Franklin. We have expeditions that got lost looking for lost expeditions, and then a few more who got lost looking for those ones. No, Mr. Holmes. We are quite used to losing men in the pursuit of discovery. And why? Look up there, Mr. Holmes."

He pointed to the top of the far wall. An inscription in Latin read: *Dulce et Decorum Est Pro Scientia Mori.*

"You do remember your Latin, do you not, Mr. Holmes?"

"As a detective, I am accustomed to repeating *'cui bono?'* several times a day," said Holmes.

"Ah, well put," the old fellow said, again with a solid tap on the floor. "Who benefits, you ask? All of mankind. We exist here for the pursuit of knowledge, for the discovery of previously unknown facts, for lifting the scales from the eyes of mankind, and for the revealing of truth. It is the truth that makes you free. The entire earth is the beneficiary of our expeditions."

"And this museum benefits as well, no doubt," added Holmes.

"Bloody right, we do. And we do not flinch from admitting it. You are sitting in the leading museum of the British Empire, and blast it, we are not going to be bested by the French, or the Russians, and certainly not by the Americans."

"Or," added Holmes, "by the Ashmolean?"

"Those upstarts? No, especially not by them. They had the good luck to have that Evans fellow as one of their former directors, and now they have been beating the pants off of us in unearthing the wonders of the ancient world. Hume-Craw's find would have put paid to that nonsense."

"I fear I do not understand," said Holmes. "What precisely was it that he discovered that you are so concerned to have brought here?"

Dr. Thompson looked over at the Director of Antiquities and nodded. "Dr. Kenyon, if you would, please."

The younger man rose and from a bookshelf retrieved four large volumes. These he placed on the table as the four corners of a square that was about a yard along each side.

Then, from another shelf, he brought a long cardboard tube. From it he extracted a roll of paper and then spread it out on the table, anchoring the four corners of it with the books.

"Gentlemen," said Dr. Kenyon. "Please, come a take a close look. This is what Professor Hume-Craw discovered. The drawing was prepared by the expedition's photographer. The professor insisted that it was quite an accurate representation on a one-to-one scale. The actual piece is made of solid gold and in pristine condition."

Holmes and I rose and walked around to the other side of the table and took a close look. Suddenly, I felt an unexpected and uncontrolled blush coming to my face.

"Do you remember the story that it represents?" asked Dr. Kenyon.

"How could I forget?" replied Holmes. "It was every schoolboy's favorite. We giggled about it in the refectory for days on end. There was a contest amongst us to see who could find the most detailed and explicit account of it in the library."

The picture was of a small statue. The base was about a foot square, and two inches thick. The two figures on top of the base rose another foot. One was of a large bull, standing on his hind legs. The other was a beast that had the back end of a cow and the front of the face and naked torso of a female human. They were copulating.

"Yes. Isn't it exquisite," said Dr. Kenyon as he looked upon the drawing, his face aglow. "The ancient story of Poseidon's bull, so beautiful a bull that Parsiphaë fell in love with him. She had Daedalus construct a wooden cow that she climbed inside so that she could consummate her love."

"If I remember correctly," I said. "That story did not end well. Wasn't there a Minotaur that came along nine months later."

"Ah, yes. What an exciting story, is it not?" said Dr. Kenyon. "So beautifully depicted by an ancient craftsman whose name we shall never know."

"You say," said Holmes, "that this statue is made of solid gold."

"Yes," snapped Dr. Thompson, again with a tap on the stick. "But that is not why we want it here so urgently. This museum is overflowing with carved gold. A few more pounds, even a hundredweight, would not make much difference. What we want it for is what is written on the base. You cannot see that in the drawing."

On the drawing, there were a series of lines with squiggles and random scratches. They were meaningless.

"What do you know," demanded Dr. Thompson, "of what that Arthur Evans rascal has brought back to the Ashmolean?"

By now, I had read several accounts of the Evans expedition to Crete. He had uncovered the great temple of Knossos near Heraklion. Underneath the temple was a maze of walls that Evans had claimed was the ancient Minoan structure in which the Minotaur had been imprisoned. He had named the intricate cellar The Labyrinth. On the site, he had discovered several hundred clay tablets on which were the two distinct sets of markings that Miss Gertrude Hume-Craw had spoken of.

"He brought," I said, "all those clay tablets. But nobody knows how to read them."

"Exactly," said Dr. Kenyon. "He named the two languages Linear A and Linear B. They appear to be one of the first written phonetic languages known to man. Professor Hume-Craw wrote to us to say that one side of the base of this lovely work of art is a record of the story of Parsiphaë, written in Linear A. One another side is the same story, written in Linear B."

"If those languages," said Holmes, "are undeciphered, how can he say for sure what story it is they tell?"

"An excellent question, Mr. Holmes," said Dr. Kenyon. "The answer, unknown beyond a very few scholars, and will now be expanded to include you, is that the third and fourth sides contain the same story, but written in the oldest version known of ancient Greek. It is a veritable Rosetta Stone of the earliest civilization to have occupied the Mediterranean. It is a priceless find. It opens the door to an entire world of knowledge. And it is the property of the British Museum."

"And may I presume," said Holmes, "that once it arrived here, all the world shall have to bring their clay tablets and statues that contain those two Linear languages if they want to have them translated?"

"More or less," said Dr. Kenyon, smiling. "Of course, we shall eventually publish a dictionary of sorts in which the codes will be revealed. Perhaps we shall do that some twenty years from now. But until then, this museum shall be the center of the entire globe for the scholarly study of the earliest days of Western Civilization."

"And your primary wish," queried Holmes, "is for me to find this statue and get it back to you as soon as possible. Your interest in finding out who murdered your expedition's director is secondary. Is that correct?"

"Precisely, Mr. Holmes. Of course, we all wish to see nasty culprits brought to justice. But that concern falls under the aegis of the fellows in Foreign Affairs and Scotland Yard. We are scholars, sir, not policemen."

"Understandable," said Holmes. "Will you permit me to ask a few more questions before agreeing to take on this case?"

"Go ahead," said the older fellow. "But make it snappy. I do not have all day."

"Nor do I," said Holmes. "Kindly confirm to me the names of the members of the expedition. From the work I have conducted so far, I was informed that in addition to the Director, the members were: Miss Gertrude Hume-Craw, General Secretary   Miss Bernadette O'Donohue, Private Secretary to the Director   Mr. Allister Baird, Head of Excavations   Mr. Robert Argyle, Head of Provisions   Mr. Darren Cruickshank, Head Curator   and Mr. Lloyd Sunday, Photographer. Were there any others?"

"No," answered Dr. Thompson.

"Are you prepared to vouch for the scrupulous probity of the members of the expedition?"

"Those who are known to us, yes," replied Thompson. "We cannot speak for the others."

"And who amongst them is which?" asked Holmes.

"Miss Gertrude is a respected member of the staff of the Museum. The three young men are all from St. Andrews University and came with excellent letters of recommendation from their professors. Miss O'Donohue we only met briefly, and her background and her people are unknown to us, but we have no reason to have less than full confidence in her."

He stopped there.

"And Mr. Sunday?" pressed Holmes. "You did not mention his name."

"Ah, yes, that fellow, the photographer," said Thompson.

"Indeed," said Holmes. "What of him?"

"He has accompanied Professor Hume-Craw on several previous expeditions, and he takes excellent photographs. He and the professor were not fond of each other, but Edgar kept hiring him all the same. That is all I can say about him," said Thompson.

"That is instructive," said Holmes and then gave both of the museum men a hard look.

"Are you aware," continued Holmes, "of any illicit liaisons between members of the expedition? If so, between whom?"

"I beg your pardon!" said Dr. Kenyon. "That is hardly a question that is asked of gentlemen."

"It is," said Holmes, "a question that is asked by a detective. And I shall add to it a corollary. Were either of you or any officers or directors of the museum carrying on an illicit liaison with any members of the expedition?"

"That is enough, Mr. Holmes," came Kenyon's loud response. "If this is how you conduct your investigation, you can get out of the British Museum this instant and never come back."

Holmes merely smiled and turned to face the older fellow.

"Am I to leave, Dr. Thompson?"

The old man smiled back at him. "It appears that it is not without reason that Sherlock Holmes has become England's most famous detective. I have been on this earth long enough to know that *cherchez la femme* is an efficient place to being almost any investigation into matters of illegality. You may continue, Mr. Holmes."

"Very well, then kindly answer my question."

"Mr. Holmes," said Dr. Thompson, "I am seventy-five years of age. I fear that even if I wished to have done so, such a liaison would remain a chimera. I can also vouch for Dr. Kenyon. Even though he is a vigorous man in the prime of life, he is a married man and a faithful member of the Church of England. His reputation is beyond reproach."

"And amongst the members of the expedition? What of them?"

"They are all scholars," said Kenyon. "I would never stoop to indulging in the spreading of rumors behind their backs."

"And you, Dr. Thompson?" asked Holmes.

"Would I stoop to idle gossip, of course not? Would I believe something that appeared to be quite obvious? Unfortunately, yes."

Poor Dr. Kenyon stared at his superior and looked aghast. "Really, sir."

"I am afraid so." Then turning to Holmes, the old fellow continued. "Edgar Hume-Craw and his wife have been estranged for many years. It was well-known, if not openly spoken of, that he was a bit of a bounder when it came to hiring attractive younger women to serve as his assistants. He cared as much for their amorous inclinations as he did for their ability to keep books and write letters."

Holmes now turned to Dr. Kenyon. "Please answer frankly, sir. Are you of the same opinion?"

"Mr. Holmes," protested Kenyon. "There were no reports whatsoever of anything like that taking place on the Minoan Expedition. Furthermore, I govern my tongue by *de mortuis nil nisi bonum*."

"I am not asking about what he is doing now that he is dead. Only what he did whilst living. Please answer frankly."

The chap looked very uncomfortable but raised his head and spoke to the far window.

"If you insist, sir. Although I had no proof whatsoever, I assumed that the Director had a romantic interest in the secretary he hired, Miss O'Donohue. I only met her once, but she was highly attractive."

"And might there have been any other liaisons taking place?" asked Holmes.

"The only other female member of the expedition," replied Kenyon, "was the professor's daughter, Miss Gertrude Hume-Craw. I do not wish to speak unkindly, but suffice it to say that she did not strike me as the type of woman that men would be eager to engage."

"Thank you, sir," said Holmes. "Very well then, with regards to this missing statue, why did the photographer not take a photograph of it? Why make such a complete drawing?"

"Ah, that question," replied Kenyon, "affords an easy answer. They were in Crete, sir. There were no facilities available for the processing of the plates from the camera. All those had to be transported back to England before the photographs could be developed. Therefore, the sketch was drawn instead and sent back through the post."

"Thank you," said Holmes. "A most reasonable thing to do. Now, one final point of inquiry, if I may. What is the connection of Miss, or perhaps Mrs. Charlotte Golderton to this expedition?"

"You mean Madame Charlotte Europa Golderton?" asked Kenyon.

"If that is her full name, then yes. Was she a member of the expedition? Who is she? And where is she?"

"Might I ask, Mr. Holmes, how it is that you know this name?"

"Your telegraph messages back and forth with the expedition were intercepted, copied, and made known to me."

"That is quite alarming, Mr. Holmes," said Kenyon.

"That matter we can address at a later date. Today, I am asking you to tell me about this woman, Miss or Mrs. Golderton."

"Mr. Holmes, she is no one alive today and is nowhere," said Kenyon, smiling smugly. "Charlotte Europa Golderton is the name that Hume-Craw made up and gave to the woman portrayed in the statue."

"I regret that I do not understand," said Holmes

"In the earlier Minoan version of the story," said Kenyon, "it was Europa, the mother of King Minos who engaged with Zeus, in the form of the bull. The bowdlerized version records that he changed back into human form before violating her. The original account does not. A later version of the myth changed the participants to Poseidon's bull and Parsiphaë, who became the unfortunate mother of the Minotaur. It is quite common for antiquarians to give pet names to some of the statues they discover. The professor dubbed this magnificent statue, Charlotte Europa Golderton. Where he came up with the Christian and surnames, I have no idea. We here, on learning that the statue also had Greek wording inscribed on its base, judged it to be of somewhat later origin and so assumed that it was depicting Parsiphaë. We used the name concocted by Professor Hume-Craw when sending telegrams back and forth so as to conceal the matter being inquired after. I am sorry to disappoint you on that score, Mr. Holmes, but no flesh and blood Miss Charlotte exists."

Not long after this exchange, Holmes and I stood on the pavement of Great Russell Street. I continued to scribble notes from our meeting while he stood still, smoking a cigarette.

"I thank you, Watson, for your time this morning. I trust I have not caused you to keep your patients waiting."

"It would not be the first time, nor will it be the last that a doctor keeps people waiting," I replied. "But before I leave, I should like to know what you thought of our meeting. You have not one but two clients who lied to you about looking for their mother when what they wanted from you was to find a missing statue named Charlotte."

"And an exceptionally valuable one at that," said Holmes. "Well worth hiring my services for, would you not agree?"

"Holmes," I protested. "They lied to you."

"I might have done the same were I in their place. The last thing they want known by the Press is that this priceless treasure has gone missing. Quite clever to pretend that it is a missing person."

I was more than somewhat exasperated with him. "I will take a cab now, and shall I see you at supper?"

"No. I shall be otherwise engaged."

"With Miss Lightowlers? Again?"

"Yes, my dear Watson. Again."

He gave me a warm smile and a clap on the shoulder. Then turned and walked towards the Tottenham Court Road station of the Underground. For a full minute, I watched him, all the while shaking my head in disbelief.

Chapter Five
St. Andrews, Scotland

THAT EVENING, Holmes did not return to 221B until well after midnight. The following morning, he shuffled out of his bedroom as I was preparing to depart for my surgery.

"Good morning, Holmes," I said. "And did you have a pleasant evening? What was it this time? Dinner at Simpson's and then the opera? Or the theatre?"

"Oh, no neither," he replied, yawning. "We had some delightful fish and chips and then a rollicking evening at the music hall."

I was stunned. "Did you say *the music hall?*"

"I did indeed."

"Holmes, you despise the music halls. Every one of them. Have you lost your mind?"

"*Au contraire, mon ami.* I prefer to think that I have discovered my soul. I laughed heartily all evening, as did the quite enchanting lady who accompanied me."

I bit my tongue to avoid some unkind exclamatory response, and quickly grabbed my coat and smartly descended the stairs. I pulled the door behind me, perhaps a little more forcefully than was necessary.

Partway through the morning, a note was delivered to my medical office. It ran:

```
Watson: Could you be so kind as to cancel
any appointments you might have over the
weekend and join me on a journey to St.
Andrews? We will meet with some other
members of the Hume-Craw Expedition. Shall
return by late Sunday night. Meet tomorrow
morning at Flying Scotsman platform at
Kings Cross. 7:00 am.  Holmes
```

I was greatly relieved. I had convinced myself that Holmes would spend the entire weekend mooning over the admittedly attractive Miss Lightowlers and neglect his pursuit of what was emerging as a most unusual case. Now it appeared that his common sense had returned.

I did not see Holmes at all that evening, nor early the following morning, and I feared the unspeakable worst. But as I entered the platform at King's Cross, I saw him waiting for me. At the far end, adjacent to the first-class cabins, was the tall, slender figure that had become so much a part of my life for the past twenty years. He was waiving at me merrily and smiled as we clambered into our cabin.

"So good of you, Watson, to join me. The game is afoot, and I do not know what I would do without my Boswell to keep track of it."

"Always a pleasure to do my part," I replied.

"I apologize," he said, "in advance for being a dull traveling companion. Our enjoyable conversation will have to be brief. I have an entire valise of reading material to consume before we get to Edinburgh."

"On one condition," said I.

"Oh, and what, my friend, is that?"

"As your friend, who cares for you very deeply, I demand to know what your intentions are concerning Miss Ruth Lightowlers?"

He looked surprised at my question. "Good heavens, Watson. Why do you concern yourself about that? You must admit that you have had a far greater attraction to the fairer sex that I ever have. I am merely catching up to you." He smiled and brought a friendly fist down on my knee.

"*You* must admit that your sudden interest is highly uncharacteristic of your entire life to date."

"I admit that I have deprived myself of what is regarded by sensible men the world over as one of life's truly great pleasures—the company of a beautiful, intelligent, charming, and witty woman. And to top it off, she seems to find me similarly attractive. It must be my tall, lean figure. Who is to say?"

"Holmes, she is more than twenty years younger than you are."

"My dear Watson, your lovely wife, Mary, is a decade younger than you. What is a few more years? And besides, she has no interest in breeding a litter of little Sherlocks, and I have no intention of siring any. So, what is the issue if there is to be no issue?"

He chuckled at his witticism. I was beyond words and could only sputter, "But Holmes …"

He lifted his hand, palm facing me. "Enough, my kind friend. I have far too much work to do, and I am sure that you can consume yourself with writing for several hours."

He then extracted several bound notebooks from his valise. Two bore the imprint of the Ashmolean Museum, and three the mark of the British Museum.

"By the time we reach St. Andrews," he muttered, "I shall be a minor expert on the Minoan Civilization of ancient Crete."

For the next eight hours, the train sped its way north to Scotland. I had not returned to the land of my birth since taking the high road to England so many years ago and had neither close kith or kin still living here. My view from the train window of my home country and city convinced me that it had changed not at all and most likely would not do so in the near future.

Holmes said nothing as we changed trains at the grand Waverly Station and quickly found the local train up to St. Andrews. It was approaching the supper hour when we checked into the old Rusacks Hotel. During the season, it is a favorite of golfers from around the globe as they come to claim boasting rights for having played The Old Course and genuflected at the eighteenth hole.

"This hotel," said Holmes, "has a fine restaurant, if any establishment that still serves mutton and haggis can ever be described that way. I am told that the finnan haddie is an excellent choice to begin a meal, and the poached salmon and shoulder of lamb are both quite delectable. The three young scholars who were part of Hume-Craw's expedition are joining us for dinner. I expect that they will be very pleased with the short but enjoyable departure from the food they are accustomed to in the university refectory."

Waiting for us at the entrance to the dining room were Messrs. Baird, Argyle, and Cruickshank. They were well-dressed for a dinner meeting although two of the suit jackets subtly announced *borrowed-and-a-size-too-large*.

Nevertheless, they were all fine specimens of young manhood—handsome, average to tall in height, and fit. We introduced ourselves to each other and were seated at a table by the window, affording us an excellent view of the North Sea and the Old Course. After enjoying a few mandatory minutes of idle chat, Holmes reminded the fellows of the purpose of the meeting.

"Would each of you," asked Holmes, "please explain to me the roles and responsibilities you had on the expedition."

They did as requested in a succinct manner. Obviously, they had expected the question and had rehearsed their answers so that they might make a good impression on the most famous detective in Great Britain. While they affected a refined Edinburgh accent, there was no mistaking that their counties of origin lay closer to Glasgow. Their speech betrayed them.

Holmes subsequently asked them to give, in the greatest detail they could muster, an account of the evening when their ship pulled into Gibraltar and the professor disappeared.

"Auch," began Cruickshank, the redhead of the lot. "it haed been a lovely evenin'. We waur sittin' at the table an' chattin.' Then the professor got up and says he's goin' for a wee stroll along the deck. Nobody thought anythin' of it, as the auld fellow liked his walks. An' wasnae'at the lest we saw of him."

"Did the rest of you remain at the table?" asked Holmes.

"Aye, we did, but only fur puckle fare minutes. Then we all departed."

"And where did you go?"

"I can only speak for myself and my two colleagues here. We all went back to Allister's room and played a few rounds of cards. We had become guid friends after four months of trial and tribulation together. It wasna 'til mornin' that any of us knew that the auld bloke haed disappeared."

"And the other members of your party? Did you see where they went?"

"Lloyd went off in the direction of the bar, as he aye did. Didna see where the ladies went."

"Did they depart together?" asked Holmes. "Most women do keep other company after men depart from the table."

"Those tois? Nae on your life. Unless it was tae stand at fife paces and fling knives at each other."

The other two young fellows nodded, and Holmes immediately demanded an explanation.

"Auch, sir. There was nae loove lost atween them, sir."

"And why was that?"

The fellow suddenly appeared hesitant to respond. He glanced over at his friends, and the Baird chap answered.

"You know how it is with the Scots and Irish, Mr. Holmes."

Holmes gave the young man a hard look.

"I know how it is when a man does not speak the truth. Scottish and Irish women have gotten along quite well for years even if their men have been at odds. Now, sir, please answer my question."

"Very well, sir," said Cruickshank. He continued slowly and deliberately, his accent all but gone.

"We do not wish to tell tales out of school, sir. But if you insist, I shall try to be candid. Miss Gertrude, as you know, sir, is Professor Hume-Craw's daughter."

"I am aware of that. Carry on."

"And Miss O'Donohue was his personal secretary, who had been hired only for the expedition. Being gentlemen scholars, we never spoke of it … well, perhaps not more than once, maybe twice … but we all knew that the friendship between the professor and Miss O'Donohue was quite intimate. It is understandable that a daughter might take exception to another woman who is the same age or younger than her sharing her father's bed. And so, the two of them were more than a little frozen in the way they got along."

"Thank you," said Holmes. "Very well, no more on that matter. So, if the ladies did not spend time together, where did each of them go?"

"Well sir, Miss O'Donohue says she would go and chat with the professor and see if he needs anything. And Miss Gertrude made a rather unkind remark in reply."

"Yes. What did she say?"

"She said, sir, something along the line of 'we'll be at the dock in a few hours. I am sure he can find a brothel there.' Or something close to that. Wouldn't you say?" He directed the last question to his friends, who nodded in agreement."

"Ah," said Holmes, "so this Miss O'Donohue was the last person to see the professor alive. Is that correct?"

"Nae. Lloyd, Mr. Sunday that is, told the police that at close to midnight, the professor came into the bar and had a wee dram, bade him good night, and went off. That's what he said."

Holmes asked several more questions, but the three men could offer no new information about the final hours of Professor Hume-Craw. Thus, he turned to another subject.

"I have been told that a priceless treasure was discovered at the temple you were excavating. Would you describe it to me?"

His question was followed by an awkward silence before Mr. Cruickshank replied.

"Aye. We were told that as well, Mr. Holmes. But it was found by one of the diggers late in the evening, and he brought it straight to Dr. Hume-Craw. The doctor cleaned it up by himself and had Lloyd Sunday take a picture of it, before putting it in his safe in his cabin. We never saw it, sir, only the sketch done by Lloyd."

Holmes looked at the other two, and they nodded their agreement. "Nae, sir. We never saw it. That's right," said Baird.

"And what about his secretary, Miss O'Donohue? Did she see the actual artifact?"

"You would have thought she did," said Cruickshank, "seein' as it came late to his cabin. But she was there when Lloyd rolled out his drawing, and she was as amazed as the rest of us. So, it does not seem she did."

"Quite so," said Holmes. "You are, I assume, aware, that the statue has disappeared?"

"Aye, so we have heard. But we have heard neither hide nor hair of where it might have gone. Have you, Mr. Holmes?"

"No. I fear not. But what of the other artifacts you discovered? Anything else of singular value or interest to scholars?"

Again, his question was met by a moment of silence, and the three young fellows glanced at each other. Finally, Cruickshank spoke up.

"You might say, *In mezzo mar siede un paese guasto che s'appella Creta.*"

His colleagues chuckled their approval.

"Perhaps," said Holmes, "instead of showing off your erudition, you might just answer the question."

"Oh, yes, I suppose I could answer in English. As Dante once observed, in the middle of the sea is a wasted island called Crete. That is what we found, Mr. Holmes. You see, the three of us thought the entire expedition was a bust. Arthur Evans and his troop from the Ashmolean had secured the prime location at Knossos and kept pulling up one clay tablet after another. But we were at what must have been a small temple a few miles away. Sure and we found all sorts of shards of pottery and pieces of weapons and the like. The professor kept saying that these were brilliant finds that would unlock volumes of ancient history. But sir, all of us have been studying antiquities for the past six years, and we can tell pretty well if something is a great treasure or a piece of broken trash that had been tossed in the midden. Most of what we found, sir, except for the statue, was not worth a tuppence."

"Oh my," said Holmes. "That must have made the entire time somewhat disappointing."

"Disappointing it was, sir," said Cruickshank. "Bloody frustrating is more like it. You might say we toiled all night and caught nothing."

"I understand," said Holmes, smiling sympathetically. "There have been times when I also worked for weeks on a case and finally had to admit that I had found nothing."

"You don't say, sir," piped up Master Argyle. "In all those stories we have read about you, there wasn't one like that."

"Of course not," said Holmes. "Dr. Watson knows that any account of such a case would disappoint the reader. So those cases are wisely overlooked. Is that not right, Watson?"

I affected a pose of shock and outrage. "Never. I thought all your cases were concluded successfully. As I fully expect this one will be. I am quite sure that one of these fine young chaps has a very good idea of who the culprit was."

"Quite so," agreed Holmes. Then, turning to the three young chaps, he said, "Forgive me if I am being blunt, but I suspect that all of you have thoughts on who may be behind the theft, even if you do not have any idea about the professor's disappearance. Please, speak now."

Again, there was an uncomfortable silence, with none of the fellows willing to speak first. Finally, Cruickshank ventured forth.

"I can say for right sure, Mr. Holmes it was nae one of us."

"I agree. None of you impress me as having the temperament to take such a risk, nor the brains to pull it off without being caught. But you are sufficiently clever to have a reasonably well-founded suspicion."

"If you say so, sir," replied Cruickshank. "Aye, we have a suspicion, sir. For a wee while, not wanting to believe that the professor was dead, we fancied that he might have snuck off the boat and taken Charlotte with him. That was the name he gave to the statue. But that made no sense. We talked it over many times, and now we agree that Lloyd Sunday must have taken the golden cow."

"Thank you, that is helpful. But now you must explain to me why you suspect him."

"Well sir, it was mainly on account of when the baggage was all unloaded off the boat down at the Docklands, there should have been a packing case of the right size to carry the statue of Charlotte, but there was none. The only other place it could have been taken off was when we stopped at Gibraltar. That was where we left Lloyd off as well. So, that's the main reason. And the other part is that we just don't trust him. He was decent to the three of us, but he just seemed to be always hiding something. I cannot say beyond that, Mr.

Holmes. It's just that you get a feelin' about some chap and it sticks with you, and all three of us got it."

Holmes continued for some time to cross-question them about Lloyd Sunday, but there was no new data given beyond what I have recorded. Then he changed tack one more time.

"Professor Hume-Craw lived here in St. Andrews, did he not?"

"Aye, he did," they all said and nodded.

"Are his wife and family still living here?"

Cruickshank again took the lead in answering. "That's another hard question to answer. The professor has lived apart from his wife for as long as any of us can remember. She still lives in the town but has a completely different life. His only child that we know of is Miss Gertrude, and she lives in London. Sorry, we canna be of more help to you on that one, sir."

"It is quite all right. You have been very helpful. And I thank you for joining me for the evening."

"Auch, it is us," said young Argyle, "who should be thankin' you, Mr. Holmes. It is a bit rare for us to have a meal like this. So, thank *you*, sir."

The other two added their murmurs of agreement, and they rose and departed into the snowy winter evening.

"Do you believe them?" I asked Holmes after the three fellows were gone and he and I were ensconced in chairs by the fireplace in the parlor.

"Entirely," he replied. "I am quite sure that had I asked them their opinions on Victory at Samothrace, or Venus De Milo, or Myron's Discobolus, or the Rhodian Laocoon, any one of them could have prattled on *ad infinitum ad nauseam*. But otherwise, they are as thick as planks. There is not a shred of evidence of minds clever enough to have undertaken murder and the kidnapping of a priceless artifact."

"The kidnapping?" I queried.

"Oh, Watson. It is elementary. Even a brilliant thief cannot sell a famous work of art or artifact to even a latter-day Jonathan Wild of devious fences. The only way today to profit from such a scheme is to hold the treasured item for ransom. The owner, usually one of our great museums, willingly pays the ransom and sends the bill to Lloyds. Now, my dear doctor, was there anything about those three earnest scholars that would suggest to you that they were capable of undertaking such a scheme?"

I had to admit, that he had adjudicated the fellows' abilities accurately.

"Well then, I said, "it would appear that it was a rather long journey all the way up here for nothing."

"Not at all. Watson. Not at all. Until this evening, they were still on my list of possible suspects. Now they have been eliminated. That is a useful task to have accomplished."

I shrugged and agreed. "Very well, shall we catch the morning train back to Edinburgh?"

"The eleven o'clock train would be better. We have a visit, perhaps two, to make in the morning."

"We do? Where to?"

"Mrs. Hume-Craw, the estranged wife of the recently departed professor, still lives in St. Andrews. I have sent a message to her requesting an interview but have not received a reply as of yet. Professor Hume-Craw had an office at the university, and we shall pay a visit."

"But Holmes, the man is dead. How can you obtain permission to enter his office?"

"If he is dead, Watson. He cannot object."

Chapter Six
The Dead Professor's Office

WITH THE WINTER SOLSTICE just a few weeks past, the daylight hours in St. Andrews were miserably short. When I met Holmes in the breakfast room the following morning, the sun had not yet risen, and a fresh new layer of snow was covering the ground of the first tee of the Old Course. From the inside of the window, it was a lovely site. I was not, however, eager to venture out. Holmes, as I feared was of a different mind.

"Eat up, Watson," he said, smiling. "There is nothing like Scottish oatmeal to prepare you for the day."

To my way of thinking, there was nothing like Scottish oatmeal—a staple on which I had been raised—to make one appreciate Mrs. Hudson all the more.

"What are you going to say," I asked, "if someone stops us and asks why we are breaking into a professor's office?"

"That is highly unlikely, my friend," said Holmes. "Before eight o'clock on a Sunday morning, the only Scots who are awake are dour Presbyterians off to the kirk. The rest will be still recovering from imbibing in too much of their national beverage last evening. Come, fetch your valise and let us be on our way."

Holmes seemed to know his way through the buildings of the old university. This did not come as a surprise. He had a habit of obtaining and memorizing maps of any destination that he might visit, and his memory of every lane and alley in London never ceased to amaze me.

The snow crunched and squeaked beneath our feet as we left our tracks in the virgin blanket of white. There was not a soul in sight, and so, rather than hurrying, I made of point of stopping for just a few seconds and enjoying the emerging faint morning light that was making silhouettes of the ancient buildings.

"This in Hume-Craw's office," said Holmes, after we wandered our way through several corridors and stairwells of one of the academic edifices. He tried the door handle and, to my surprise, it was not locked.

"A trusting lot, these Scotsmen," I whispered.

"Either that," Holmes replied, "or there is nothing in here worth protecting."

Holmes closed the curtains and turned up the lamps. For the next hour, the two of us rifled through the files of the deceased professor. It gave me a queer feeling, something akin to robbing a grave. I voiced my concerns to Holmes who replied as I should have expected.

"I assure you, he is not going to lodge a complaint."

I moved quickly through old lecture notes, and copies of essays and papers submitted by students over the past two decades. I slowed down when I reached the files covering his various summer expeditions to various places in the ancient world.

"Holmes," I said idly as I perused an expense claim file from a past trip to the Greek isles. "What might you expect to pay for a room in a small hotel on the island of Naxos."

"I have not the foggiest notion," he muttered, as he inspected the pages of the files that were in the professor's desk. "Why do you ask?"

"Would you expect the rate to be twenty-two pounds a night?"

He looked up at me. "Good heavens no. I would be surprised if it were more than a pound a night."

"That's what I would have thought. I am no authority on the cost of traveling to the Mediterranean, but it looks to me as if our professor has had a bit of a history of inflating his expenses."

"Are there chits backing up his claims?"

"Yes, mind you, they are all written on the same stock of paper. Not only that, but he seems to have submitted the same claims to two or three different funds, and been paid by all of them."

"How singularly interesting," said Holmes. "You might remove several of the more egregious examples. They could prove useful."

"And what are you finding?" I asked.

"There are several inches of files of correspondence between our man and this Lloyd Sunday fellow. I do not have time to read all of them, but I will take the entire lot with me and look at them on the train."

He returned to his inspection and I to mine.

"Ah, what have we here?" he exclaimed.

"What is it?"

"A thin file of letters—seven of them, the dates are spread over the past fifteen years—all from the office of the Rector of the Ancient University of St. Andrews, in his capacity as the Chairman of the University Court."

"Yes, go on."

He extracted one of them, held it up, and started to read:

```
"Dear Professor Hume-Craw:
Be assured that the University is
most appreciative of your many
```

> efforts in securing bequests and other invaluable gifts of ancient artifacts. Kindly take the following admonishment in light of our gratitude.
>
> We advise that you should not be unmindful of the persistent rumors and two formal complaints made to my office of your ungentlemanly behavior to several of the young women in the stenographic pool.
>
> We trust that you will henceforth govern yourself accordingly.

"There is another letter, some years later, from the office of the Vice-Chancellor that respectfully reminds Professor Hume-Craw that it is not a wise practice to hold meetings with the mothers of students in his office after eight o'clock in the evening."

"I must say," I said, "that our dear departed doctor appears to have been a bit of a cad."

"Indeed, he was."

"But what we have here is a common academic miscreant," I observed. "That is a long stretch short of stealing a priceless gold statue. Do you think he could have had a hand in that before he went for his midnight swim?"

"Anything is possible. It is also possible that whoever else was party to the crime most likely did away with him."

"That tends to point the finger at this fellow Sunday, does it not?"

"Possibly. We must not forget his stocky daughter or even the secretary."

"One of the women?" I asked. "Surely, that is not possible. Even if the secretary were so vile as murder her employer, she could not lift and toss him overboard."

"No, she could not. Not if she were acting alone. Mind you, the daughter could."

We bundled up a selection of the files and departed from the office. At the hotel, a note was waiting at the desk for Holmes. It was a reply from the widow of Professor Hume-Craw. Holmes handed it to me. It ran:

```
Mr. Sherlock Holmes: I have for
reply your note requesting an
interview this morning. As I have
had nothing whatsoever to do with
the affairs of my husband, Professor
Edgar Hume-Craw, for the past
decade, such a meeting would be a
waste of my time and yours.
```

It was signed 'respectfully' by Mrs. Margaret Hume-Craw.

"As I had expected," said Holmes. "So, come now, Watson. We can begin our reading of files before catching the train."

We took a cab back north to the station in Leuchars and waited inside the station for our train to arrive. Whilst we were waiting, Holmes suddenly stood and looked out the window to the platform. The train from Edinburgh had just pulled in, and the passengers were disembarking.

"Watson, come, please. Do you see that passenger carrying the Gladstone bag?"

I saw to whom he was referring.

"Yes, I do. He is wearing a cassock. Must be a priest. Why?"

"No Watson, *he* is not wearing a cassock. *She* is wearing a dress. Now, does that bring someone to mind?"

I looked again. If it was a woman, then she was far from petite.

"The daughter. Miss Gertrude."

"Precisely. And I suspect that she is on her way to her father's office. Or possibly to visit her lost mother. Perhaps both. It is a good thing that we came and left when we did, else whatever we found might have been long gone."

We both spent the entire journey back to London reading and re-reading the files of the late Professor Hume-Craw. By eleven o'clock in the evening, as we were approaching King's Cross, bleary-eyed, I laid down the last file. Holmes did the same and leaned back and lit a cigarette.

"A penny for your thoughts, Watson," he said.

"Edgar Hume-Craw," I mused, "had an excellent mind, but I had a sense of his playing rather close to the line."

"Ah, how so?"

"He claimed to have made some splendid discoveries throughout the ancient world and published extensively, but on some occasions, the places he claimed to have visited and studied were so remote or in dangerous regions where tribes were battling, that no other scholar has had to opportunity to follow up and continue his work."

"Precisely. And, as a result, no one since has been able to confirm or refute those claims," replied Holmes

"On his Minoan Expedition," I said, "he appears to have finally found the pot of gold at the end of the rainbow. A bit of a shame that he is not alive to enjoy the reward."

"A shame? Yes, I suppose one could say that."

As it was close to midnight when we finally returned to Baker Street, both of us went directly to bed. I fell off to sleep immediately, and I suspect that Holmes did the same.

The next two days passed without incident. On the Tuesday afternoon, I returned to 221B about the same time as did Holmes. Before indulging in something to take away the winter chill, I picked up the small pile of post that had arrived that afternoon.

"Holmes," I said as he poured two snifters of brandy, "You might want to take a look at this one before you attend to our medicinal needs."

I had selected one of the letters. It had the return address of Miss Rowena Ferguson, on Easton Street in Clerkenwell.

"Kindly read it to me whilst I pour," he replied.

I opened the letter and read it aloud.

Dear Mr. Sherlock Holmes.

Words cannot begin to express my gratitude to you, sir. My life has not only been restored to me; it has been blessed beyond all I could ask or imagine. It is all because I followed your advice. In my prayers, I am thanking God every night for a man such as you that Providence led into my life.

After our meeting, I spent an entire night in tears, prayers, anger, and turmoil. The following morning, I rose and realized that my path was set. I would do exactly as you advised. As soon as morning light had come to the streets of London, I went directly to Bernardo's Home and informed the staff that I did not wish my son to be put out for adoption, or shipping off to one of the colonies. I wished to raise him myself, with the help of my family.

I confess that when I made this statement to them, I had not yet secured any response from my family. They knew nothing whatsoever of my fallen condition.

The dear saints at Bernardo's were wonderfully helpful. They not only joyfully returned my son to my care, they

> *gave me an assortment of clothes, blankets and diapers, and even a small basket in which to carry him. I then sent a telegram to my parents telling them that I had earned a bit of a holiday and would be coming to visit. I did not warn them that their grandson would be coming with me.*

"Oh my," I interjected, "the Reverend Ferguson is in for a bit of a surprise." I chucked at the prospect and continued to read aloud.

> *It was a long journey, but the other women on the trains were so very helpful, especially after I told them that I was a widow who had lost her husband in the war in the Cape. They offered to look after all my needs, and then some. I told them that I was taking my son for his first visit to his grandparents and that his name was Donald, after his grandfather.*

"A wise young woman," I commented.

"Yes. Very clever. Keep reading," said Holmes.

> *On arriving at the door of my family home in Ayr, I was overcome with fear and was tempted to turn and run away. But I summoned up my courage, said a prayer and waltzed right into my home without even knocking. My mother and father were sitting in their parlor having a cup of tea and in I walked. I put down the basket with wee Donny in it and cheerfully announced, "Thought you might like to get to know your grandson."*
>
> *They were speechless, which for a clergyman is a very unusual condition. So, I simply told them my story, and when I finished, I waited for their reaction. My mother*

said nothing, but my father burst into a terrible rage. He stood up, paced the floor, and called me every awful name—all from the Bible—that he could think of. I am sure that some of them would be new even to you, Mr. Holmes.

My spirit was broken. Yea, crushed. I broke down into tears, and I went to rush out of the room and up to the bedroom that had been mine for my entire life. I did, however, have the presence of mind to lift my son from his basket and, I confess, pretty well throw him into his grandfather's arms. He had no choice but to catch him. I screamed something to the effect of, "Gey weel then, if ye cannae show Christian love tae me, at least ye kinn show it tae the bairnie who bears your name."

Mr. Holmes, I admit that I then I ran from the room, up the stairs, and cried.

I sobbed for at least a half an hour and then there was a knock come to my door. I bade my mother and father enter. My father was still holding his grandson, and wee Donny was fixing his eyes on his grandfather's face, the way infants do. The two of them sat down, and my father quietly said, "It appears that the good Lord in his wisdom has blessed us with a grandson. It has not happened in the manner I might have expected, but it has happened all the same. And sae the Lord be thankit. We shall have to make a few changes but the good Lord gave the Scots the gift of practicality, and so changes we shall make."

I looked at my mother and could see that her heart had softened. My only fear was that my son might have his limbs stretched as the two of them wrestled over who would hold him.

My home became a loving refuge from all the worries of my life in London. Father moved his books and desk out of his study and set it up as a nursery. Mother began straight away to knit and sew clothes for wee Donny. That Sunday, he preached his homily to the congregation, and he gave it the title 'Four Hundred and Ninety-One is an Infinite Number.' That may mean nothing to you, Mr. Holmes, but it is a reference to the story in the Bible when Jesus told Peter that he had to keep forgiving his brother. Without so much as saying it directly, he let the saints in the pews know that if they did not also forgive me, then they were transgressing the Word of God. It sufficed. Mind you, I think it was more as result of their learning that my fiancée had been a soldier and a fine son of Scotland, but that mattered not.

Then on Sunday afternoon, my father told me that there was a young man in the congregation, a Mr. Alexander McTavish, who had asked if he could meet me. He came to the house later that day and told me his story. His brother, Robert, had been in the same regiment as my Archie and had also given his life in the war in the Cape. Not only that, but he himself was a recent widower. His wife, Vera, had died giving birth to a baby girl just two months ago.

To my surprise, he looked at me and suggested that the two of us should consider getting married as it would be good for his daughter and my son to have both a mother and a father. I was stunned, but, as my father had said, the Lord in his wisdom gave we Scots the divine gift of practicality and so Mr. McTavish, and I had a frank, practical discussion and agreed that we should indeed become man and wife.

Andrew is far from the handsome, dashing soldier that Archie was, and I do not have to tell you, Mr. Holmes, that I do not feel the strength of love that I had for Archie. But that will come, I hope and pray, in time. Andrew is an accountant and has a solid income and excellent prospects. He already owns a small house in Ayr, and it is no more than twenty minutes away from the home of my family. I will soon be blessed with a beautiful daughter, and I did not even have to suffer the awful pain of giving birth to her.

So, you see, Mr. Holmes, my life has been completely turned around, and it could not have happened if I had not come to you. If God blesses me in the future with another child and it is a boy, I have determined to name him 'Sherlock.' I hope you will accept my doing so as a small token of my gratitude to you.

"Ah," I sighed. "Can you imagine a happier ending, Holmes?"

"Is that the end?"

"No, there is another paragraph."

"Then keep reading."

I left my son in the care of his grandmother and returned to London yesterday to take care of my affairs here and give fair notice to the Royal Mail of the change in my situation. They have been an honorable employer, and I owe that to them. Before I wrote this letter to you, I wrote out my notice to them, and I wrote one more letter. That was to the vile man who calls himself Charles Augustus Milverton — whoever he may be. I no longer have anything to fear from him. I not only told him in no uncertain words that he could jolly well go to the devil, but that he should find himself a good barrister because I had kept every one of his notes to me and would be taking them straight away to Scotland Yard...

"She *what!!*" shouted Holmes. He jumped out of his chair.

"That naïve young fool," he said. He was pacing the floor, and his eyes were glowing with fear. "She is threatening a murderer."

"How can you say that?" I asked.

"The blackmail scheme at the telegraph office is clearly connected in some way to the disappearance of Professor Hume-Craw. Do not ask me how. I do not yet know. But we are dealing with someone, or some group of people, who were willing to throw a man overboard for the sake of an ancient artifact. They will not think twice of doing harm to Miss Rowena if she has threatened them."

He paced for a few more seconds and then turned to me.

"Her address is on the envelope, is it not?"

"It is. Did you want to ask the police to post a guard?"

"No. There is not time. Grab your coat and your service revolver. We have to get over to her flat at once before they do."

He was already pulling on his winter coat and hat. I ran to my room, grabbed my revolver and a handful of bullets, then my coat, and rushed down the stairs after him.

Chapter Seven
Too Late

HOLMES RAN INTO THE STREET and shouted for a cab. He gave the driver the address and added, "And a sovereign if you will gallop all the way."

The driver nodded and laid his whip to the haunches of his horse. He did his best to move as quickly as possible, but it was already dark, and Marylebone and Euston Streets were still busy with pedestrians and carriages. In the recurring light from the street lamps, I caught flashing looks at the face of my friend. He was as distraught as I had ever seen him.

"That innocent naïf," he said, shaking his head. "I warned her not to breathe a word about her blackmailers to anyone, least of all the villain himself. What was she thinking?"

"The pure in heart," I said, "of this world, can be oblivious to the evil in the souls of men that you encounter daily. I am sure she must have thought that since the good Lord brought her such joy with her family in Ayr, He would watch over her in London as well. We shall just have to hope that her faith was well placed."

At the corner of King's Cross, the cab turned right and sped down toward Clerkenwell. After several blocks at full gallop, we took a sharp corner to the left, and then another one. For another few seconds, we raced forward and then came to a full stop.

"Your address," shouted the driver, "is straight ahead. This is as close as I can come."

Holmes leapt out of the cab and tossed a coin up to the driver. I jumped out behind him and then almost ran into his body. He had stopped and was standing still, looking ahead. Two police carriages blocked the street in front of the house where Miss Rowena Ferguson lived.

"Dear God, no," muttered Holmes. Then he began to walk toward the front door. Two constables were standing on the small porch, and one of them nodded and greeted Holmes by name. In the entryway, a smaller man turned to us as we entered.

"Hello Holmes," said Inspector Lestrade. "I just sent a man to fetch you. Not surprised to see you here, though. Come in. Was she a client of yours?"

I could feel my heart sink as we entered a tiny flat on the far side of the ground floor. Once inside, my worst fears were realized. In the bedroom, in a chair in front of a small dressing table and mirror, was the lifeless body of a young woman. She was clad in only her undergarments with her head drooping down on her chest. Her corset and the floor beneath her was covered in dark blood that had gushed from her throat. I knew immediately that a few hours earlier, someone had cut the throat of Miss Rowena Ferguson.

I felt Holmes's hand on my forearm. For several seconds he gripped me like an iron vice. I brought my other hand across my body and placed it on top of his. Slowly the grip relaxed, and he let go.

"Inspector," he said, "could you please impart to me such information as you have so far?"

"Right. On her table, you can see a packet of postage stamps. Beside it was a note bearing the name and address of Mr. Sherlock Holmes. Other than that, nothing else has been disturbed. The poor lass is in exactly the position she was when she was found. Her landlady knocked on her door an hour or so ago. Seems the young lady had invited her out for dinner as some sort of celebration. When Miss Ferguson, who she said was always as punctual as Big Ben, did not come by her door after a half hour had past the agreed time, she came and knocked. The door was open, and she came in and found her here just as she is. She ran out and called for the police.

First, the local constable came in and then he sent for me. I arrived some twenty minutes back. Soon as I saw your name, I sent for you.

"As far as we can tell," continued Lestrade, "some villain must have gained entry through the kitchen window. It was sitting open and still is. And he must had snuck up behind her and killed her and then ran out the door, leaving it open. That's all we can put together so far."

"That appears to be reasonable," said Holmes. His voice was quiet, and his face was pale. "Might I, with your permission Inspector, examine the rooms?"

"Please do, Holmes. And then let us know your thoughts. We know that you sometimes have insights that we might not, so, do proceed."

For the next half hour, Holmes inspected the small flat that Miss Rowena Ferguson had called her home for the past two years. He slowly looked through her closets and wardrobes, her small kitchen, the cluster of bottles on her dressing table, the hairbrush on the coffee table, her wooden case of writing paper, pens and inks, and her single shelf of books. In so many previous instances when Holmes conducted his close examination of the site of a murder, he moved with energy and determination. On that day, he was listless, moving slowly as if in pain. His heart was not in it.

"I agree with your analysis, Inspector," he said after completing the task. "Your conclusion, for quite obvious reasons, that her killer most likely entered through the window and approached unseen from behind her has some merit. My suggestion is that you immediately send a notice to all available inspectors and constables to look for a man by the name of Lloyd Sunday. On Friday evening, he resided at the Alpha Inn in Bloomsbury. It had been my intention to accost him there on Saturday morning. However, I changed my plans, most unfortunately it now appears. I am certain that your men can track him down from there."

"You believe," asked Lestrade, "that he is the killer?"

"Of that, I am not yet certain. I do have reason to believe that he is connected in some way both to this dreadful crime and to the disappearance of Professor Hume-Craw."

"Very well, Holmes. I will put out the notice straight away, but you best sit down and explain to me what this is all about."

The three of us found a small pub back out on Farringdon Road and Holmes methodically expounded to Inspector Lestrade the elements of the case to date and whatever evidence he had already discovered and deduced.

"Right, so you are telling me, Holmes, that there has been an organized cabal of spies inside the Royal Mail telegraph center, that whoever is behind that ring discovered that there is some priceless gold statue found in Crete, that the statue was stolen and could perhaps be somewhere between London and Gibraltar, and that people are being murdered because of it, and that some chap named Sunday is our best lead. Is that correct, Holmes?"

"That is a reasonable summary," said Holmes.

"Right, so who are these spies reporting to?" asked Lestrade. "You and I both know that when a gang of small fry are working together, there is always a puppet master somewhere in the wings."

Holmes was silent for a moment before answering. "It is highly likely, Inspector, that you are correct. However, at present, I do not know. An answer will have to wait for the morrow when far more data has been acquired. The Good Lord Himself admonished us that sufficient unto the day is the evil thereof."

We hailed a cab and began the journey back to Baker Street. The look I had observed so many times in the past, the keenness of Holmes's eyes, and the determined set of his jaw, were nowhere to be seen. On three occasions he dropped his face into his hands and slowly shook his head. Twice, I heard the barely audible words, "I should have known."

Holmes said nothing to me after we returned to 221B. He poured himself a snifter of brandy and went straight into his room. For the next two nights, he was gone. I could tell that he had been back to our rooms when I returned from my medical practice, but there was no note and no explanation. Mrs. Hudson reported that she had heard him arrive and then leave again a half hour later.

It was not until the evening of the following day that I returned to Baker Street and found Holmes sitting by the fire in his dressing gown and puffing on his beloved pipe. Without speaking, he gestured first to the decanter of brandy on the mantle, and then to my familiar chair across from him. I poured myself a glass and sat down.

He took several more languorous drafts on his pipe before saying anything.

"The past few days," he said, "have been a bit of a tough go on my spirits."

"I can see that, my friend. However, your excellent mind cannot possibly predict the unforeseeable."

"You are quite right, my friend. And I am sure that there have been days in your medical career that one of your patients died who could, in hindsight, have been saved had you acted differently."

I sighed. "Yes. There have been several. It is part of the life of every doctor. We do the best we can with the knowledge we have at the time. I fear it has been the same for you."

He took another slow draft. "I fear it has."

This comment was followed by yet several more puffs. I had seldom before Holmes before in such a melancholy mood, and I merely sat and attentively waited for his next words.

"On those sad days, my friend," he asked, "do you unburden yourself to your dear wife as soon as you return home?"

"Of course. I cannot imagine how I could survive otherwise. Her loving attentiveness and embrace revive my soul and spirit and make it so much easier to carry on."

"Quite so. I have perceived that you, like the poet, after becoming married were surprised by joy."

"Indeed, I was."

"However, you would not call me a marrying man, Watson?"

"No, indeed."

"You will be interested to know that I am contemplating it."

For a moment, I was speechless, and then I became fearful.

"Holmes," I asked, "are you contemplating marriage with the person I think you are?"

"If you are referring to Miss Lightowlers, then yes."

I could not restrain myself. "Holmes," I gasped, "I can see that you are distraught, but have you also taken complete leave of your senses?"

"Not at all, my friend. Over the past few days, you know how deeply my spirit has been vexed. After a full day of fruitless investigating, attempting in vain to atone for my dreadful mistake that allowed the death of that poor young woman, I have enjoyed the revival of my life force that spending time in the company of a highly intelligent, informed, and caring woman brings."

"And beautiful."

"Of course. You yourself could not help but notice how just gazing at her brings a certain pleasure to the soul."

"I am well acquainted with the malady, Holmes. I have had it recounted to me more times than I can remember from starry-eyed men sitting in my office. There is no known cure, but fortunately, the fever does not last long. I expect that yours will break soon and a full recovery will be had."

"Do you truly believe that, my dear doctor," asked Holmes.

"Indeed, I do," I said, with feigned confidence.

Chapter Eight
Un Excellent Déjeuner Français

I SLEPT LITTLE that night. As I tossed and turned and mentally wrestled with what Holmes had said, a growing conviction slowly came over me. Holmes needed my care. I was his personal physician, and he needed my protection. I had no choice but to take action and first thing in the morning, I entered the fray.

Before Holmes had arisen, I had penned a note, descended to Baker Street, and summoned one of the Irregulars. A sleepy-eyed lad appeared in response to my whistle, and I gave him a letter addressed to Miss Ruth Lightowlers. I insisted on meeting her for lunch and informed her that I would be waiting for her at noon at a small café near the delta of Islington Green and Upper Street. I was quite determined to give the young woman a piece of my mind, and, for her own good, make it abundantly clear that marrying Sherlock Holmes was not at all in her best interests. Furthermore, it would be a great loss to the safety of the citizens of London if his extraordinary talents were to be diverted away from the singular attention to the pursuit of justice.

I had chosen a select restaurant that had a reputation for being discriminating in its clientele and offering an excellent if pompously expensive menu. I admit that I hoped my guest would find it somewhat intimidating. At eleven o'clock, I postponed all my appointments until later in the afternoon and took a cab to Islington. By twenty minutes to noon, I was seated at a table. My stomach was in knots as I rehearsed the remarks I was about to deliver, and as I attempted to predict every possible reply that Miss Lightowlers might make and my response in turn.

One of the advantages that years of medical practice bestows upon a man, unwelcomed though it may be, is the immunity to the bewitching effect that a woman's physical beauty has on the rest of the male half of the human race. A female body may be as perfect as Aphrodite's but when it's various leaky orifices are routinely poked and prodded, it loses it magical charms. Listening to a recitation of the problems of bowel movements is not known to lead to a pleasant hormonal response from the attendant male. And there is absolutely nothing on earth so *un*likely to move a man to swoon at a woman's beauty than delivering a baby from her womb. I was, therefore, not worried in the least of being charmed into irrationality by the lovely Miss Lightowlers.

At precisely twelve noon, I saw her come through the door. Were I not a medical man, I might have responded in the same way the maitre d' and the waiters did as this remarkably beautiful woman walked toward my table, smiling at every man she passed and, no doubt, turning their knees to putty.

"Why Dr. Watson," she said, as she approached my table and confidently held out her hand to me, "this is such a splendid surprise. Did Mr. Holmes suggest this lovely restaurant? It is my favorite in all of north London. Why he and I had a splendid dinner together here two nights ago. And now a delightful lunch with another famous and accomplished man. I am honored and thrilled beyond words, sir."

A part of my plan had immediately vanished, but I smiled, lifted her hand a modest direction toward me, and bade her be seated.

From her handbag, she immediately withdrew a copy of my most recently published book, a collection of the adventures of Sherlock Holmes that had appeared in the Strand over the past year.

"Oh, Dr. Watson, you must think me a foolish girl, but I could not resist the opportunity. I have read all of your stories over and over again, and I beg you, sir, do me the honor of signing my copy of this book."

I fumbled to retrieve my pen and asked one of the waiters to bring over a bottle of ink. He did so, arriving with a choice bottle of claret in his hand. He made a shallow bow toward my guest.

"May I presume that the lady would enjoy a glass of her favorite?"

"Oh, Sebastian," she replied, beaming at him, "you do such a brilliant job of looking after me. I do not know how I would get through a meal without you."

Before I could introduce any topic for conversation, she, with a coy smile, began a series of highly informed questions about the books and stories I had published. Although whatever reputation I had acquired was entirely the result of my accounts of the adventures of Sherlock Holmes, I had also published several other stories and books, none of which had sold many copies. Miss Lightowlers, however, had read them all. Not only so, but her knowledge seemed remarkably thorough and her questions quite brilliantly insightful. When the maitre d' approached the table she immediately made sure he knew who I was.

"My dear Jean-Paul," she said, "did you know that the most successful writer in all of London is here today? This is the famous Dr. John Watson. His books have sold literally thousands of copies all over the Empire, and even in America."

She went on with such fulsome praise that I felt a blush coming to my face.

Effortlessly, she took control of the conversation, and ever so subtly making certain that I felt very good about myself in her company. I was beginning to see how even Sherlock Holmes might have fallen for her charms.

Finally, after the excellent main course had been cleared away, I took advantage of her pausing to take a swallow of claret, and turned the conversation to my reason for meeting with her. Patiently, but forcefully I expressed to her my concerns over the obvious infatuation that my friend, Sherlock Holmes had developed for her. When I paused, hoping that a moment of silence would enhance the serious tenor of my remarks, she smiled at me in a most loving howbeit condescending manner.

"Oh, my dear doctor. You are so very kind and thoughtful to take time away from all the important things you are doing to think of my best interests, and those of your dear, dear friend. But I assure you that I am completely certain that whatever interest Mr. Sherlock Holmes has in me is no more than as a plaything for his amusement. I enjoy his attention and am in awe of his brilliant mind, but I expect that he will soon tire of me and move on. I am sure you have seen this all before with any number of eligible unmarried women."

"No, Miss, I have not. Sherlock Holmes has, for the more than twenty years I have known him, shown no interest whatsoever in any romantic attraction to any woman. You are most assuredly the first."

I went on at some length to repeat the point I had just made, and even went so far as to list off, without giving full names, several of the exceptional women whom Holmes had encountered over the years. Not one of them, I pronounced, had had any effect on him at all. Then I dropped the cannonball onto the table.

"He has confided in me that he is planning on asking you to marry him."

My statement had its desired effect. Her eyes went wide and her mouth opened in shock. An involuntary blush appeared in her uniquely beautiful face.

I then carried on with the remainder of my prepared speech, carefully and sensitively listing off all the irrefutable reasons why such a course of action would be disastrous both for her and for Holmes. When I came to the end of my discourse, it occurred to me that for the past few minutes she had not been listening to me at all. Her gaze had gone to some indeterminate spot partway between my left ear and the ceiling. Her entire countenance looked unmistakably rapturous.

"Sherlock Holmes wants to marry me?" she said, in dreamlike tones.

"Yes, Miss Lightowlers, that is what I said." I was about to repeat my most salient point when she merely repeated.

"Sherlock Holmes ... wants to marry ... me?"

She brought her gaze back down out of the clouds.

"Forgive me, Dr. Watson. It is just that I find that difficult to comprehend."

I bit my tongue to avoid blurting out something to the effect of *well you bloody well should. It is utter madness.* Instead, I tactfully replied, "I find it that way myself, Miss. However, I assure you ... I would swear an oath in court were we in one ... that what I have told you is God's truth."

She dropped her gaze down to her left hand and opened up the fingers and smiled. In not much above a whisper, she muttered. "Mrs. Sherlock Holmes." Then a slow smile began to creep across her face. There was a fleeting second when I thought it was developing into a wicked grin, but then her lovely face took on a glowing radiance.

"My dear, dear Dr. Watson. How can I ever thank you? Had you come to warn me that Sherlock Holmes was doing no more than teasing me with his attention, and warned me against believing his protestations, I would not have been surprised, and I would have shared a pleasant laugh with you over the absurdity of the entire episode. But you are telling me, and I can see that you are doing so in utmost sincerity, that this most incredible of men deems me worthy to fall in love with and wishes to marry. What can I say, doctor? I am left speechless."

Now I was speechless. This was not the reaction I had hoped and carefully planned to engender. Before I could recover my wits the stunningly beautiful young woman rose, came over to where I was sitting, leaned down and planted a light kiss on my cheek. She thanked me yet again and floated out of the restaurant. She smiled at the men and thanked the maitre d' on the way.

"You are always welcome, Mademoiselle B," he said in reply.

For several seconds, I sat in dumb amazement. Then, rather suddenly, something hit me like a jolt of lightning.

What did he just call her? Mademoiselle B?

I quickly paid the outrageous bill and sauntered, as nonchalantly as I could, up to the maitre d'.

"Quite the lovely woman, is she not?" I said.

"Mais oui, monsieur. She is très *gor-guuuzzz*."

"Does Mademoiselle B come here often?" I asked casually.

I saw a quick flicker in his eyes, and he turned to me and offered a Gallic shrug.

"Qui, monsieur? Ah, you mean Mademoiselle Ruth. Oui, de temps en temps. But always it is a pleasure to have her grace our table. But of course, it is also a grand honneur to have with us the famous writer, Dr. Watson. You must come again, monsieur."

I assured him I would though I considered it highly unlikely. A spark had been lit in my brain by his careless parting remark to my guest. Something that had made me uneasy from the very moment she waltzed into 221B Baker Street was now crystallizing. This woman who had so bewitched even Sherlock Holmes could not fool me. No. She was an imposter, and if even Holmes could not see through her, I was determined to unmask her, expose her trickery, and bring my friend back to his senses.

But how?

I began to walk south on Upper Street, pondering my next course of action. Then suddenly, the solution presented itself to me. I hailed a cab.

"Harley Street," I shouted to the driver. "Corner of New Cavendish."

Chapter Nine
Dead Men Tell No Tales

AMONGST THE GENTLEMEN of the medical profession, it is an inviolable rule that confidences entrusted to us by our patients must never be discussed outside of the walls of the our offices and hospitals. I had never, in over two decades of being a close friend of Sherlock Holmes, disclosed to him any information about one of my patients, not even in those rare situations when doing so might have been useful to him in the solving of a case. I was highly circumspect even in my conversations with my dear wife. I might talk about some unusual or amusing exchange I had had during the day, but I had never disclosed the name of the person whose health and well-being had been confidentially entrusted to me.

However, when medical men came together, knowing that the outside world had been excluded, we were as chatty as a parish sewing circle. Complaints were shared. Tales of woe were commiserated over. Outrageously funny events were recounted and greeted with guffaws and tears of laughter. Knowing this, I proceeded directly to the office of Dr. Lomaga, the highly respected expert in the care of the skin. Miss Ruth, or whatever her name was, had disclosed that she had been to see him. I was reasonably sure that he would know far more about her than had been disclosed to me or to Sherlock Holmes.

The highly-regarded doctor had built up a prosperous practice amongst the upper classes of London who could pay to have the onset of wrinkles and sagging epidermis postponed. His waiting room was full of women of a certain age, all finely dressed and several accompanied by pet dogs. I gave a note to his nurse and waited for him to dispose of his current patient before being ushered into his office.

"John Watson!" he exclaimed. "What a treat. Welcome, my dear chap. To what do I owe this honor?"

He shook my hand vigorously and bade me be seated.

"I am in need of your help, doctor," I said. "However, I fear I cannot completely disclose the reasons."

I knew that would grab his attention.

"A case for Sherlock Holmes?" he asked, eagerly.

"Quite so."

I confess that I had become something of an object of envy amongst the doctors of London. Whilst they toiled endlessly in their surgeries and hospital visits, I had the splendid opportunity from time to time to race all over creation with Sherlock Holmes as we pursued and apprehended one dangerous criminal after another. I dare say that some of my medical brethren engaged in vicarious adventures through me. Without fail, whenever I suggested to any one of them that he might assist in some small way, they were eager to help. I could be counted on to include their names in my acknowledgments, which ensured that they bought multiple copies of the story for distribution to their family and friends and for the reading tables in their waiting rooms.

"I am in need," I said, with a sincere, imploring look on my face, "of some information about one of your recent patients."

"By all means. Which one?"

"I am not entirely sure of her name. She has been using the name of Ruth Lightowlers of late, but I suspect that it is to hide her true identity."

"No one by that name has come by recently. Searching my memory, I cannot recall a patient by that name ever coming to see me. Can you describe her?"

"She would have been here in the past two to three weeks and possibly presented as a case of eczema on the back and sides of her neck."

"There have been three such cases come through here recently. Pray, describe her appearance. Young, old? Slender, well-fed?" What did she look like?"

"Red hair. Irish complexion. Stunningly beautiful."

"Ha. That would be Miss Bernadette O'Donohue," he said. "Yes, quite the beauty, isn't she? But it was not eczema. She had a common sunburn. I am always telling those with red hair and pale skin that they must keep the sun off of their skin. They are terribly susceptible to the ultra-violet rays. Yes, that young woman had a bit of a problem, but I gave her some aloe, and it appears to have cleared things up. No lasting damage to such a lovely neck."

"A sunburn? How in heaven's name did she acquire a sunburn in England in winter time?"

"Oh, she was not in England. She had been working out of doors somewhere in the Mediterranean. Some manner of archeological expedition, she said. Quite the adventurous type, she is."

It would have been very rude for me to leap to my feet and rush out of his office and hail the nearest cab. So, I chatted on for a few more minutes and then, apologizing for taking his valuable time away from his patients, I took my leave.

"Anytime, Watson, old chap," he said. "Made my day to think I might help Sherlock Holmes. Anytime."

Having departed his office, I then ran to the nearest cab and barked an order to get me over to Baker Street on the double.

On arriving, I leapt from the cab, bounded across the pavement, and then in seven vigorous steps ascended our stairs. I threw open the door to our rooms and beheld Holmes sitting by the fire in his dressing gown, puffing absently on his pipe.

"Holmes!" I shouted. "You have been played the fool."

He looked at me without any evidence of alarm at what I had just said.

"Ah, my dear Watson. Do take your coat off and sit down. And pray tell me, how was your luncheon at *Chez Henri*. Did you have the house specialty, the *canard a l'orange*? Ah, perhaps that is a bit heavy for a noon meal. The *sole meuniere* perhaps? And I do hope you had a pleasant conversation with the lovely young lady. You will have to become used to seeing her around quite often in the near future as I expect that after the wedding she will be moving in here with me. I had thought of looking for another flat that was in a more desirable neighborhood, but I fear I am just too set in my ways to vacate Baker Street."

"How in heaven's name could you possibly have known where I was?" I demanded.

"My dear friend, if you are going to leave your Kelly's Directory of London open on the side table with a note of the address of a restaurant on top of the page, then knowing such a fact is not particularly difficult. And as it is a favorite of Miss Lightowlers, I assumed that you had enjoyed her company whilst there."

"Very well, then, Holmes. But that woman, Miss Lightowlers, is an imposter."

He smiled and took another puff on his pipe.

"I presume you are referring to Miss Bernadette O'Donohue of the O'Donohues of Donnybrook in Dublin. The one who was the personal secretary to our dear departed professor on the expedition to Crete?"

I was stunned. "You *know* that about her? How could you *possibly* have known that?"

"My dear doctor, what do you think a detective does when in a lady's private flat and she excuses herself to use the lavatory. You very quickly rifle through every possible drawer, file, cupboard, ashtray, and wardrobe available and learn as much as you can as quickly as possible. Please, Watson, it is quite elementary."

"Does she know that you know?"

"Of course not. The young woman is living in fear. Two people who had some connection to the Minoan Expedition are already dead. She is obviously seeking the type of protection that she believes I can afford her, and I am, I confess, quite honored and pleased to provide it for her."

"Holmes, quite frankly, that is madness. If she is in danger, she will remain so even if you marry her."

"Oh no, I think not. I am looking into a property in Sussex to which I might retire. Perhaps I could become a country gentleman and keep bees. The two of us could live together in a bee-loud glade. Does that not strike you as a consummation devoutly to be wished?"

I starred at Holmes for several more seconds, shook my head, turned and descended the stairs. I would spend the remainder of the day attending to my patients and not wasting any more time.

When I returned to 221B in time for dinner, Holmes was not present. I poured myself a small glass of sherry and sat and waited for him. Some fifteen minutes later I heard the door and his familiar steps on the stairs. He entered and slowly removed his winter coat and sat down. He looked thoroughly weary and such a far cry from what I had seen earlier in the day. I rose and poured out another glass of sherry and handed it to him.

"Ah, thank you, my friend'" he said. "Your thoughtfulness and the prospect of an enjoyable dinner help to revive the spirit."

"Care to tell me what you have doing that has left you looking so bone-weary?"

"I have spent the entire afternoon dogging the footsteps of Mr. Lloyd Sunday. It has all been in vain."

"Did you find his lodgings?"

"Yes, he stayed two nights ago in Halliday's Private Hotel in Euston. A few of his belongings are still there, but the desk assured me that he did not sleep in his room last night and has not been seen all day. He has vanished once more."

"And have you concluded," I asked, "that he is the key to unraveling this mystery?"

"Of his exact actions with respect to the deaths of the professor and poor Miss Rowena, I am not entirely clear, but I am certain that he is involved. He also presents a significant danger to Miss Lightowlers, or Miss O'Donohue as we now know her to be."

"Is Lestrade looking for him as well?"

"He has assigned several men to the task."

"Very well then, Holmes, you may as well let them prowl the streets of London whilst you enjoy your dinner."

Holmes did not enjoy his dinner. Mrs. Hudson served up a fine supper of lamb chops, but Holmes picked away at them in a desultory manner. His mind was elsewhere.

Mrs. Hudson had no sooner cleared away the table when a knock came to the door. Then the door opened without anyone going to see who had arrived, and we heard a set of footsteps ascending the stairs.

"Hmm," muttered Holmes. "Inspector Lestrade. I wonder what news he brings."

Lestrade was by now very familiar with the rooms at 221B Baker Street, and he took off his winter coat and walked directly to his usual place on the sofa.

"I heard that Sherlock Holmes was all over London looking for Mr. Lloyd Sunday," said Lestrade.

"Indeed, I was," replied Holmes. "My path crossed more than once with your men."

"Well, you will be pleased to know that we found him. Might you be interested in coming to meet him?"

"Indeed, I would," said Holmes. "Are you holding him at a station or at the offices of the Yard?"

"Neither. We're holding him at the Tower Bridge. In Dead Man's hole."

"The morgue?"

"That is the customary place for holding bodies we fish out of the river, is it not?"

"Indeed, it is," said Holmes.

"Well then, come along. Don't expect to learn much. As they say, dead men tell no tales. And Dr. Watson, please join us. Your medical expertise would be helpful."

Chapter Ten
The Bird Has Flown

THE MAGNIFICENT TOWER BRIDGE, spanning the Thames from the Tower of London across to Potters Fields opened about ten years ago. For reasons known only to those responsible for its design and construction, a mortuary was built into the north tower and was quickly given the name of Dead Man's Hole. On average, two or three bodies a week would be fished out of the water and brought to this dungeon-like setting and dried out. They would be left there until identified and delivered to the next-of-kin or, if unclaimed, buried in a pauper's grave.

The three of us rode in Lestrade's police carriage all the way across London from Marylebone, through the City, and over to the Tower. In the early winter evening, there was little light from the streetlights as we hurried through the streets.

"He arrived here yesterday," said Lestrade as we descended from the roadway to the mortuary. "One of my lads thought to come and look for him here and found his name stitched into his suit jacket. The morticians said that he was in the water less than an hour. Some fishermen heard a shot near the Bar of Gold and found him. He was quite dead."

The rooms of the Hole were adequately lit but poorly ventilated, and the place stank with a mixture of death and preservative chemicals. The officials assigned to this dismal location peeled back the sheet from a body that was lying on one of the several tables. On it was a man of about forty years of age. He was well-dressed and appeared fit and healthy. Lestrade pulled back the heavy overcoat and his suit jacket, exposing his white shirt underneath. There was a pinkish blotch that extended from his sternum to his navel. The blood had been washed away in part by the water of the Thames, but there was no mistaking the fact that he had either been shot or stabbed in the heart.

"Take a look, gentlemen," said Lestrade. "And then give me your thoughts."

Holmes extracted his glass and began a slow, methodical examination of the body, beginning with his shoes and working his way up. I opened the shirt and looked immediately at the mortal wound.

When Holmes had completed his examination, he turned to me.

"Yes, doctor, what are your conclusions?"

"A revolver shot directly to the heart," I said. "Without extracting the bullet, I could not say precisely what caliber of gun was used, but just by the size of the hole, it was in the range used by the army. My guess would be a Webley Bulldog. There are many of them all over London, as they were issued to the fellows fighting in the Cape. One shot was all it took since it plugged him right in the heart. He would have died within a minute. The killer was a crack shot. Either that or only a few inches away."

"The latter," said Holmes. "To be more precise, the gun was held directly against his chest before being fired. You can tell by the residue of the gunpowder. Even though much of it was washed away, enough remains to indicate a point-blank distance. The powder had not spread more than a quarter of an inch from the center of the hole in his shirt."

"Right," said Lestrade. "So, it looks to me as if some bloke surprised him, held a revolver up to his chest, backed him up to the edge of the quay, and let him have it."

"Perhaps," said Holmes. "There is some reddening on his cheek that does not look faded. What of that?"

"Right. The killer gave him a left hook to the face and then stuck the gun in his chest."

"Ah, yes. Of course," said Holmes. "No doubt, that is what must have happened."

"Good. Now that we have found your number one suspect, Holmes, where do you go from here?" demanded Lestrade.

"With your permission," said Holmes. "I will search his pockets and then the last hotel room he was known to have rented and see if, perchance, he left any clues behind. Would that be acceptable to you, Inspector?"

"Right. Go ahead. But let me know if you find anything that indicates anything."

"Of course, Inspector."

I had not been inside Halliday's Private Hotel for many years. Oddly enough, it was also the final hotel used by Joseph Stangerson some two decades ago in the very first story I recorded of the adventures of Sherlock Holmes. Back then the Boots had nearly fainted at the sight of a stream of blood seeping out from under the door. On this occasion, however, there was no blood and no body to be found inside the room. There were two steamer trunks and a closet full of men's clothes. Holmes and I carefully went through every drawer, pocket, envelope, cigarette case, and pair of shoes in search of anything that would help us to identify not only the killer but also his motive. Nothing struck me as of particular interest, but in a plain brass cigarette case, somewhat crushing a cluster of Taddy's Navy Cut, Holmes found a small key.

"Ha," he said. "What have we here? A key to a luggage locker, with the number stamped on it. How very useful, would you not agree, Watson?"

"Useful," I said, "if we knew in which of several score of train and Underground stations the locker was in."

"I will think that one over," said Holmes. "But now, we may as well return to Baker Street and importune Mrs. Hudson for a late dessert which can be augmented by glass or two of claret."

The following morning, I emerged from my room to find Holmes already seated at the table and enjoying his morning cup of tea.

"Good morning, Watson," he said. "I trust you slept well. We have a short journey ahead of us immediately you have finished your breakfast."

"Where to?"

"London Cannon Street."

"You have concluded that the locker for which we have the key is there?"

"I have indeed. It is the closest train station to the spot along the Thames where poor Mr. Sunday met his watery demise. It is also where one boards the boat trains over to Europe. Anyone who disembarked a boat from Crete in Marseilles would have arrived in England at that station. I cannot say with a certainty until we go and visit, but at the moment it appears to be the most likely."

I had no cause to question Holmes's reasoning and, as soon as I had finished my breakfast, we set out across town one more time. The newsboys were already on the streets and shouting about the murder of Mr. Lloyd Sunday and, in colorful language, describing his death from a sharpshooter who had popped one right into his heart.

Cannon Street is not as large as Waterloo or Victoria, but it is a busy little place all the same. Railway cars are shunted from land onto a set of rails inside the ferry and, several hours later, are pushed off and onto a set of rails that run to the docks in Calais. With hundreds of passengers coming and going from the Continent, it was to be expected that there would be an ample supply of luggage lockers. Indeed, there were several hundred.

All we had to do was find the one whose number corresponded to the key we had found in Lloyd Sunday's room and see if it opened. We found the locker within five minutes. It was one of the largest available to travelers, but there was no need to bother inserting the key.

The door of the locker was already open. I could see immediately that it had been pried with a jimmy and forced.

"I fear we are too late," I said, stating the obvious.

Holmes immediately bent down and peered inside the locker.

"It is still full of cases and a valise. Here, kindly take these as I pull them out and lay them on the floor."

He first pulled out a wooden packing case, followed by a small trunk, and finally a valise. All had a baggage tag affixed to them, and they all had the name of Lloyd Sunday inscribed. I set them on the floor beside the bank of lockers and, as they were not locked, opened them.

"Are we looking for a priceless Charlotte?" I asked.

Holmes mumbled something and began to inspect what had been retrieved from the locker. Piece by piece he extracted cameras, tripods, photographic plates, rolls of artists' canvas and craft paper, tubes of paint, colored chalks, and the like.

"As I feared," he said. "Everything here is related to Mr. Sunday's job on the expedition. I will have it all sent over to Scotland Yard for inspection and the developing of any plates that were used on the project. But I suspect that there is nothing here of significant value. There was enough room in the locker for another case containing a small statue. Our Charlotte appears to have trotted off to greener pastures."

We returned to Baker Street in time for a pleasant lunch, again provided by the indomitable Mrs. Hudson. We were just finishing our tea when the afternoon post arrived. I sorted through it and selected one letter that was of obvious interest.

"A personal letter for you, Holmes," I said. "Going by the return address, it might even be a love letter."

The address was written in a feminine hand, and the fine ivory-colored paper had a distinct perfumed scent to it. The return address in the corner indicated that the letter was from Miss Ruth Lightowlers, with a postal box number in the E.C. I announced the sender and handed it over to Holmes, who was trying to appear quite nonchalant about it.

"Another one? Very well, do hand it over. The dear young lady is quite the correspondent, I must say."

He stretched out his long arm and took the letter. In a desultory manner, he slowly opened and read it. As he did so, I observed the smile vanishing from his face and a deep scowl appearing. When he had finished, he threw the letter onto the side table, and I could swear that I hear the words, "damn and blast" escape his lips. For the next few minutes, he said nothing and sat with his hands together below his chin, fingertips touching.

Slowly a smile returned to his face, and he turned to me.

"Watson did not the Bard remind us that 'Frailty, thy name is woman?'"

"He did." I was tempted to remind him that Hamlet said it of his mother and that it might not be applicable to Miss Lightowlers/O'Donohue.

"It appears that the lovely young woman who has captured my heart is subject to the timorous and illogical reactions that are so characteristic of her sex. Here, kindly read this and give me your insights."

He handed the note over to me. It was written in a polished hand, and it ran:

My dearest Sherlock:

It is with the greatest force of my will that I bid my heart be still whilst I write this letter to you. Words cannot express my profound gratitude for the interest and affection you have shown me. Your dear friend, Dr. Watson, has convinced me that your feelings toward me are sincere and unfeigned and I am beyond ecstasy in knowing that I have become the object of your love.

However, a great misfortune has befallen me. I have, yesterday, read in the newspaper of the terrible murder of the man who once had promised me his undying love and who breached his promise. My soul has been wracked with fear for my own life. Whoever killed him might also wish to kill me. I have no choice but to go into hiding until the murderer is apprehended.

While I am comforted by your profession of affection and the offer of your protection, nevertheless—and please forgive my doubting nature—I am tormented by nagging doubts of your intentions. You have yet to bring up the possibility of marriage in our delightful conversations, and I cannot help but wonder if your desire for my companionship is a fleeting amusement.

Therefore, I must take steps for my own well-being and remove myself from the public eye for the foreseeable future. You may, if you should so wish, contact me by way of the mail forwarding service I am using. I will have no fixed address for the time being and will, of necessity, make my whereabouts unknown and unknowable. I do trust that you will understand and forgive my fearful spirit.

Be assured that I will once again reach out to you as soon as my safety has been secured.

Yours very truly,

Ruth

"Well, Holmes," I said. "Your pretty bird appears to have flown the coup."

He did not reply. He was pacing the floor back and forth, obviously agitated. For a minute he stopped and stared out the bay window and slowly and purposefully took out a cigarette and inhaled. As he did so, his body appeared to relax, and the scowl on his face was replaced once again by a serene smile. He turned, came back to where I was sitting and sat down facing me.

"My dear friend," he said. "For twenty years or more you have been my faithful Boswell. Now I am in need of you to play another role."

"Yes?"

"I need you, my friend, to be my Cyrano?"

"Your what?"

"Not my *what*, Watson, my *who*."

"Very well, then ... who?"

"My Cyrano. Surely you recall the story of Cyrano de Bergerac. He was wonderfully gifted with a pen and with his tongue, and he gave to Christian the words needed to woo the beautiful Roxanne."

"Yes, yes. I know the story, Holmes. But what in heaven's name has it to do with me?"

"My dear Watson. I acknowledge that I have many unique talents, but the ability to speak or write words of love to a fair maiden is quite beyond me. I need you to compose a letter to Miss Lightowlers ..."

"You mean Miss O'Donohue."

"If you insist, yes. But as she is not yet aware that both of us have unmasked her hidden identity, we must continue to use her pseudonym. What I am in desperate need of is for you to write her a letter not only affirming my love for her but convincing her that I wish to be married to her at the earliest possible date; before the end of the week. I have decided that I cannot possibly live without her. Will you do that for me? I am beseeching you on the basis of our friendship for so many years. I am in need of your help, Watson. Can I count on you?"

Merciful heavens, I thought to myself. In years gone by, Sherlock Holmes had asked me to help him by engaging in actions that were on the wrong side of the law, to help apprehend desperate thieves and murderers, and to put my very life at risk more than once. But never had he made such an utterly bizarre request.

"Good lord, Holmes," I sputtered and again demanded, "Have you gone stark raving mad?"

"Why of course, I have," he replied, still smiling. "Is not that what falling in love is all about."

For the next several minutes, I argued with him. But he was adamant. He would not budge from his request, indeed his demand, that I not only write a letter to his red-headed vixen but that I write it as coming from me and sign it. He was relentless, and I eventually gave in.

"Ah Watson, how can I thank you? If it succeeds, I assure you I will die a happy man."

I bit my tongue and refrained from the rejoinder that it was debatable he might die happy, but it was certain that he would die poorer. I took out a pen and paper and, with significant dictating from Holmes, wrote a letter from Dr. John H. Watson to the admittedly beautiful Miss Ruth Lightowlers, attempting to convince her that Sherlock Holmes was not only in love with her but wanted to marry her.

"Now then," said Holmes, "conclude by begging her to come to the Corpus Christi Church in Maiden Lane at 11:00 on Friday morning, if she wishes to become Mrs. Sherlock Holmes. You might also note that you will be standing up for me as my best man."

I wrote as he had demanded even though in both my head and my heart, I considered the entire venture utter nonsense. When I had finished the final draft on a crisp, clean piece of notepaper, I handed it to Holmes. He read it in its entirety, smiled, and inserted the note into an envelope.

"And would you mind," he asked, "writing out the address as given in her note to me?" I did, and he quickly sealed the envelope, pulled on his coat and was out the door, envelope in hand.

All I could do was to pray that Providence would intervene and that Holmes would come to his senses. Although, I had to admit that I had never seen him smile so genuinely as when he rhapsodized over his red-head.

Chapter Eleven
A Marriage
Not Made in Heaven

PROVIDENCE DID NOT INTERVENE.

On Friday morning, I reluctantly put on my formal morning suit, polished shoes, spats, and a well-brushed hat and trudged slowly down the steps to Baker Street. Holmes was in front of me, similarly attired, and seemed to be walking with a spring in his step.

"What if she does not appear?" I asked.

"Oh, I think that unlikely. I fully expect that she shall arrive at the appointed hour and that the two of us shall meet the blushing bride at the steps of the church. By noon hour, I shall be a married man."

We reached the church at twenty minutes before eleven o'clock and entered. The organist was seated and practicing his processional, while an older stooped man was busy polishing the brass on the altar.

"Where is the priest?" I asked Holmes.

"Oh, do not worry," Holmes replied. "Father McSweeney assured me that he would be here at just before eleven o'clock. He was quite pleased that I asked him to officiate. It seems that he has been a faithful reader of your sensational stories about me for many years."

I walked back toward the door of the church. A small table had been set up in the narthex, and a marriage register book lay open on it. Seated behind the table was a fellow in a cassock who, I assumed, must be the registrar of births, deaths, marriages, and goodness only knows what all else. We went outside and stood on the steps in the cold, waiting for the bride to appear.

At two minutes before eleven o'clock, a well-polished carriage pulled up and out of it stepped a woman who, I had to admit, was beyond stunning in her beauty. She was not wearing a bridal gown but was attired in a very stylish ivory-colored dress that augmented the translucence of her pale skin and rich auburn hair. Her smile was radiant.

"I was prepared," she said, "to arrive and find no groom, but here you are." She laughed merrily, walked up to Holmes and kissed him on the cheek. Holmes gave her his arm and led her into the church. In the narthex, he stopped and turned back to me.

"My dear Watson, would you mind taking a moment with Father McSweeney about matters related to the signing of the registrar and then meet us at the altar?"

At the registrar's table stood a small man, wearing a priest's vestments, and chatting with the registrar as he leaned over the table. He was not facing me, but I could see that he was somewhat elderly, with long gray hair, and a large set of spectacles propped up on his nose.

"Father McSweeney," I said, "I am Doctor John Watson. I will be serving as witness to the wedding and standing up for Sherlock Holmes."

I felt a hand suddenly grasp my arm near the elbow and forcefully pull me over until my head was almost touching that of the priest.

"Watson, do not make a sound," was whispered in my ear.

I looked at the priest and nearly fainted. Behind the eyeglasses and under the wig of hair, was the sallow, ferret face of Inspector Lestrade.

"Follow me up the aisle," he said in my ear. "Then stand behind Holmes and keep silent."

He turned and began to hobble slowly up the aisle, through the nave, and up to the altar. I was beyond speechless, but somehow pulled my wits together and followed him.

Holmes and the woman who I now seriously doubted was about to become Mrs. Sherlock Holmes were standing in front of the altar, gazing lovingly into each other's eyes. The priest came around and stood in front of them.

"Do you have the ring?" he asked Holmes in a low and shaking voice.

"I do," said Holmes.

"Good. Let me see it. We must take a second to practice. I do so not like it when the groom has bought one that is too small and will have to push it onto a bride's chubby finger. It is quite distressing. So, here now. Let me ascertain that it will fit before we get the service underway. My dear young lady, kindly give me your left hand."

The bride graciously extended her hand to the priest. He quickly grasped it with his left hand and in one sudden move snapped a handcuff onto her extended wrist.

"Miss Bernadette O'Donohue, I am placing you under arrest. You are charged with the aiding and abetting in the murder of Professor Hume-Craw, with the murder of Miss Rowena Ferguson, with the murder of Mr. Lloyd Sunday, and with the theft of archeological treasure that belongs to the British Museum. I advise you that anything you say can and will be used against you at trial."

For a brief moment, nothing happened. Then the woman turned and made as if to run away. Unfortunately for her, the other end of the handcuffs was affixed firmly to the wrist of Inspector Lestrade, and she was yanked back. In one swift move, she thrust her hand into a fold in her dress and out came a small revolver. She pointed it directly at the chest of Lestrade.

"Undo the lock immediately," she said, "or I swear I will kill you and Sherlock Holmes."

"Pardon me, Miss" came a voice from the side of the nave. "But you need to drop that gun or else I will have to fire on you. It would be a crying shame to ruin such a lovely dress."

The chap who had been polishing the altar was now standing a few yards away. He was holding a rifle and had it pointed directly at Bernadette O'Donohue.

"That would go double for me, Miss. Best drop the gun." This command came from the organist, who was likewise pointing a rifle at the bride. The fellow who had been sitting at the registrar table was now walking up the aisle toward us, and also holding a rifle that was pointed directly at her.

Earlier in this story, I noted that the warm gaze of this woman would have melted the frost off the window. Now, the blazing heat from her eyes might have melted the window itself. She turned her face toward Holmes and uttered several words which propriety does not permit me to record here. She dropped the revolver on the floor, took a breath, and in a composed voice spoke.

"I fear you have all made a foolish mistake. I demand to be taken immediately to my solicitor in the Inner Temple. I will not respond to any questions until he is present."

Holmes nodded at her and walked back down the aisle, giving me a tug on the arm as he passed.

"Come, Watson. The game is over. It is time to celebrate victory. Simpson's in the Strand is only a block away. They serve an excellent luncheon."

He was already walking quickly out of the church. I scrambled to keep up with him as we walked a few steps along Maiden Lane and turned on to Southampton Street. He had assumed the posture and carriage that I had seen so often in the past when he was satisfied that he had completed his case.

I, however, was furious.

"Holmes," I snapped as we were seated at a table. "You deceived me. You lied to me. You made a fool of me."

I would have gone on in unrestrained anger had he not interrupted me.

"Oh, Watson, Watson. My dear friend. Of course, I deceived you. I had no choice. I could not have possibly done what I did without your help. You were magnificent."

"What do you mean, magnificent? I was played for a dupe."

"And you played your role perfectly, my dear man. I may have some skills in acting and playing the part of a decrepit bookseller, but I have never before been assigned the role of a man in love. Pretending to be such was far beyond my abilities. Bernadette O'Donohue is one of the wiliest women I have ever met. I was certain that she would see through my pretense, and I dare say she did. It was only when you met with her and so sincerely told her of my hopeless attraction to her and my desire to marry her that she was convinced. Her arrest is mostly to your credit."

I was not in the least appeased and was about to launch into a tirade when Inspector Lestrade joined us at the table. He had managed to lose his vestments and wig.

"Ah, Father McSweeney," said Holmes. "How good of you to join us. Have you sent the villainess off under guard?"

"She has one arm handcuffed to Gregson and the other to Bradstreet. She is not going anywhere."

"An excellent precaution. She is as crafty as Odysseus and as ruthless as Atilla. Do not give her an inch, or she will take a mile before you know it."

Inspector Lestrade now turned to me and reached out his arm and gave me a firm pat on the back.

"Dr. Watson. Well done, sir. Holmes tells me that you were the genius behind trapping this daughter of Jezebel. It was your meeting with her and your letter that did the trick and brought her back. Without you, she would likely be in Vienna by now. Well done, sir."

I feigned a humble reply, and Lestrade turned back to Holmes. He lifted his glass of wine and spoke to Holmes.

"Enough of my thanking the two of you. Now, out with it, Holmes. How is heaven's name did you put all the pieces together."

"Ah, where to begin?" said Holmes as he lit another cigarette.

"Begin at the beginning," I said, very wearily, "and go on till you come to the end: then stop."

Holmes smiled a warm smile and began.

"It began when the woman first walked into 221B Baker Street. Why even you, my dear Watson, spotted the incongruity of her expensive boots and perfume with her deliberately inexpensive dress and coat. However, the first thing you failed to notice was the redness of her eyes."

I objected. "Not true Holmes. I could see that she had recently been crying."

"Oh, my good man. She had been doing nothing of the sort. She used a common theatrical trick and held a lit cigarette under her eyes before entering. It brings redness to the eyes without so much as altering the least little spot of her perfectly applied cosmetics. There was a faint odor of tobacco to her which she had attempted to mask with a fresh application of the perfume. Add to that the evidence of her hands and wrists."

"I looked there as well," I said. "She did not have the lines across her wrists that you have made a point of observing in the past. What was there to see?"

"Please, my friend. Just like the dog that did not bark, it was the absence, not the presence that was of singular interest. She claimed to have been working as a private secretary. Had that been true, the telltale marks of a typist would have been present. Therefore, I took her right hand into mine so that I could observe it more closely. Two things stood out. There was a distinct callous on the pad of her index finger, and the backs of her hands were darker than the skin on her arm in the area normally covered by a sleeve. That informed me that she was a skilled and experienced telegraph operator who had quite recently acquired a suntan. You yourself noticed the skin on the back of her neck, which, when taken into consideration along with her hand and wrist, was a conclusive indication of having returned recently from someplace sunny and warm. France, at this time of year, is neither.

"Her claim of having been raised in poverty with a mother who takes in laundry was a preposterous falsehood brazenly designed to arouse my pity and admiration. Whether we like it or not, class cannot be disguised. A woman who moves and acts with her grace and confidence did not grow up in a poor family from Connemara. Her trace accent was undoubtedly Irish, as was her appearance, but she obviously came from a family that was not without means and had paid for a respectable education."

"But Holmes," I said, "she thoroughly convinced you at first. When did you know that she was attempting to trick you?"

"She did no such thing. When you know immediately that someone is trying to deceive you, the most unproductive response is to the expose the deception straight away. Doing so means that you learn nothing. What you must do is play along and trick that person into believing that he or she has succeeded in tricking you. Obviously, her intent was to have me not only believe her story but to engender my sympathy and indeed my affection. Therefore, I gave her both in spades. Now, I confess, that I knew that I was utterly lacking in the skills of portraying a man falling in love, which is why I would have to depend on you, my dear doctor, to give a rave review of my inadequate performance. And you, being the soul of honesty, could not have done that convincingly if you yourself did not believe it. It was you who turned me into a believable lover."

"Right," interjected Lestrade. "Enough of your playing Romeo. How did you come to know that she was a cold-hearted killer?"

"Ah, that took some time. Even I hesitated to consider the possibility that an attractive young woman could be a cold-blooded murderer. However, I had to start with the question of who could have tossed the professor overboard. Miss O'Donohue is simply not physically capable of doing that on her own. One of the students could have, but we eliminated them as suspects. His daughter, the one who is built like a scrum-half, could have done it with one arm, but that would require a conclusion of patricide, which demands a motive far beyond mere greed for treasure. It was possible that the officials from the Museum, avaricious as they are for glory to their institution, might have hired a local killer and arranged the theft, but there would have been no reason for doing so. The treasure was destined to come to them anyway. Their competition in Crete from the Arthur Evans expedition did not need to find more ancient treasure. They already had enough of their own.

"For a while, all of the fingers appeared to point at Mr. Lloyd Sunday, possibly acting in cooperation with Miss O'Donohue. We knew that the only two people who had directly seen and understood the value of the treasure were the professor and Mr. Sunday. The others had only been told and had seen Sunday's drawing of it. Given that Miss O'Donohue had already revealed her willingness to use her beauty and her wiles to have men do her bidding, I theorized that, at some time after seeing the drawing, she had decided to seduce Sunday, become his paramour, and convince him to join her in getting rid of the professor and stealing the statue. Or perhaps it was Sunday who initiated the scheme. Who played the lead in the deadly duo we will never know, but they appear to have acted in concert up until the time when Sunday was murdered by a ruthless woman who decided to keep the entire treasure for herself."

"Holmes," said Lestrade, "that seems somewhat incongruous. If this woman is as clever as she appears to have been, why would she put herself at such a great risk by murdering her accomplice? And do so in broad daylight where she could have easily been spotted and apprehended?"

"An excellent question," said Holmes. "You are quite correct. It does not appear to be a logical action by an exceptionally conniving woman. All I can offer as an answer at the moment is to note that she is Irish, a redhead, and a female. Consistent logic is not the strong suit of such a group of people, but I admit that such a response is not entirely satisfactory."

"Yes," agreed Lestrade. "And if the order of events you have presented is correct, then this woman was so cold-blooded that she could murder her accomplice, jimmy the locker and steal the statue, and an hour later cheerily prance into her lunch with Dr. Watson as if nothing had happened."

I was beyond horrified. To think that I had sat across from her over an elegant lunch whilst the blood on her hands was only a few hours old. How Holmes had concluded that she did, in fact, shoot Lloyd Sunday was not clear, and I asked him about it.

"Oh, Watson, again, I could not have done it without you. Your sincere protestations to her of my honorable intentions led directly to my being invited into her private chambers in Clerkenwell. She did not live in a rented room in a go-down on Wamer Street but in a quite respectable terrace house. Immediately upon departing from it, I went directly to the city clerk's office to look into the ownership. It was registered to a Bernadette O'Donohue. At that point, her true identity was revealed.

"Whilst I was in her rooms," Holmes continued, "I observed an ashtray in which there was a small pile of residue from a cigarette. I examined it quickly with my glass and determined that it had come from a Tabby's Navy Cut, the same brand that we later found in Sunday's room. Without my assistance, she had managed on her own to track him down. Add to that the evidence of how he was shot. If someone were approaching you with a gun, would you stand still, unbutton your overcoat, and then your suit jacket and allow him to place a gun against your sternum? Of course, you would not. You might struggle, or you might turn and flee, but you would never stand still and allow yourself to be murdered. But that is precisely how Sunday had reacted. It was at point-blank range with a gun held against his chest. The reddish mark on his cheek beside his mouth was the additional clue. It was not a bruise — it was lipstick. A woman had approached him and he, for reasons of sensuality, had opened his coat and suit jacket to enhance the romantic pleasure. She engaged him in an amorous embrace, placed a kiss on his cheek, and pulled the trigger. Had he been shot by a man, the evidence would have been otherwise. It was conclusive that he was shot by a woman at very close range and there was only one woman who could have and would have done that."

"But what about the poor young woman, Miss Rowena?" asked Lestrade. "Did not Sunday murder her? But then you told me to charge O'Donohue with that murder as well."

"Of course, I did. My instincts at first were to draw the same conclusion as you as the true nature of what took place was beyond horrifying. But reason prevailed. It was obvious from the evidence that the unfortunate Miss Rowena, for whose death I cannot entirely absolve myself, was killed by another woman. Even you, my dear Inspector, assumed that such a modest and circumspect woman would never have a man present in her flat whilst she sat in her underwear at her dressing table. Your conclusion that a man must have entered through the window and surprised her had to be ruled out. Why? Because she was sitting in front of a large mirror. She would have seen someone approaching from behind and would not have sat still whilst he cut her throat. There was no sign of any struggle. The items on the table were undisturbed. The hairbrush was sitting on the coffee table. The only explanation that made sense was that another woman, a known friend, had been standing behind her, affectionately brushing her hair and whilst doing so had extracted a knife or razor from her pocket and cut the poor young thing's throat."

"But why?" I demanded. "There was no reason."

"*Au contraire, mon ami,*" said Holmes. "Miss O'Donohue was part of the same clutch of young woman telegraph operators who worked together in the Mount Pleasant Royal Mail center. They were friends. Do you not recall Miss Rowena referring to one of the members of the group as Bernie? She quit her position at the same time as the demands for the contents of telegraphed material that could be used for blackmail ceased. The demands returned after O'Donohue returned to London from Crete."

"No," I objected. "If O'Donohue was one of the victims of the blackguard calling himself Charles Augustus Milverton, then Bernie should have cut his throat, not Rowena's."

"Not at all," replied Holmes. "There was no blackguard calling himself Charles Augustus Milverton. *She* was Charles Augustus Milverton. It was highly unlikely that a man, unknown to any of the women working for the Royal Mail, could amass such closely guarded secrets of seven young women. But, as your wives will confirm to you, it is entirely normal behavior amongst women to divulge their life histories, including their scandalous secrets to other women, even those who are near strangers that they meet in a lavatory. It is one of the greatest strengths and terrible weaknesses of the fair sex. They trust each other. Rowena, Eleanor, and the others had unsuspectingly disclosed their secrets to each other, including Bernadette O'Donohue, and she took advantage of the opportunity."

"Acting alone?" demanded Lestrade. "You know my thoughts on groups of criminals. There is always someone pulling the strings. That's even more likely when the gang are all women."

"I assure you, Inspector that you underestimate the fair sex, but, I confess, you could quite possibly be right. I submit to you that both of us may have more work to do."

"And why did she leave and go off on a scholarly dig?"

"An excellent question," replied Holmes. "As to why she decided to leave her lucrative scheme at the Royal Mail, I can only guess. She would have come across information about the Evans expeditions and the one planned by Professor Hume-Craw. It is possible that she expected some treasure to be unearthed that could bring additional riches to her. Or, it may be that she had tired of the miserable fall weather and elected to spend her days in Mediterranean climes. It is safe to assume that she used her seductive charms on the professor, who had a history of being prone to such temptations, and she joined the expedition."

To this, I added my observation. "The man's tendency to think with his little head when he should have used his big head has had rather unfortunate consequences."

To which Lestrade said, "It always does."

The inspector now pushed his chair back from the table, leaned back and crossed his arms over his chest. "Holmes," he said, "again I must congratulate you. Everything you have said makes complete sense. By all rights, this woman should be hanged for her crimes, but I fear that may present a problem."

"Good lord," I said, "why would you say that? She is as deserving of the gallows as anyone I have ever heard of."

"Right you are, doctor," said Lestrade. "But there are no witnesses. Had Sunday still been alive, I might have been able to have the two of them turn and testify against each other. But that opportunity went down the river with Sunday."

"What of the other women," I asked, "who worked in the telegraph unit with O'Donohue? Could they be of assistance?"

Lestrade pondered that suggestion for a moment. "Not likely. Not one of them appears to have suspected anything, and the only one willing to take a risk ended up with her throat cut. Proving the crime of tampering with the mail would be enough to send her away for several years, but where is the evidence? And would those other young women be willing to now have their secrets exposed when they are no longer being forced to aid blackmail? I fear that would be unlikely."

"Then we must," said Holmes, "leave it to you and the Crown to put together the best case you can. And while you are at it, you might try to locate the golden statue. I fear that our shrewd Miss O'Donohue is the only one left who knows its whereabouts. And I suspect that she is not about to divulge that knowledge."

"Might she have been willing to share it with her husband?" I asked.

Holmes laughed at the suggestions. "I confess that I have no idea and that we shall never know. Regardless of her barrage of compliments concerning my mind, my character, and even my physique, there is no doubt she showed up at the church—thanks to your wonderfully effective missive—because she had concluded that being married to Sherlock Holmes would result in my expending my talents to protect her, as any faithful husband should be expected to do."

"Not a role," said Lestrade, "that I imagine for you anytime in the next fifty years."

Chapter Twelve
Miss Charlotte Europa
Golderton

DURING THE NEXT TWO WEEKS, the Press was full of the story. Having a scandalous account of a merciless killer who was also a stunningly beautiful woman was a gift to them from whatever gods they worshipped. Most of the papers wallowed in the lurid details, augmented by creative speculation as to how this Irish beauty had seduced not only the men she murdered but possibly even the poor Miss

Rowena. Miss O'Donohue's capacities for evil were portrayed as bordering on supernatural, leading several of the more popular papers to speculate that she must be in league with Beelzebub.

The woman herself continued to proclaim her innocence and put the blame directly on the competition from the Ashmolean expedition and even on the person of Arthur Evans.

To my surprise, a few of the papers seemed to be sympathetic to her and endlessly stressed the circumstantial nature of the evidence and the unrelenting competition between not only the leading British museums but also amongst the great institutions all across Europe and America. That the entire affair could have been masterminded by the Russians or, more likely, some American interests, was a plausible alternative, they insisted.

It occurred to me, perhaps unfairly but I suspect not, that some reporters and editors might have been careless in the contents of their telegrams and were now paying the price to avoid their sins becoming known. It was far from impossible that they might have received a message advising them of their perilous position should they not portray Miss Bernadette O'Donohue in a kindly light.

My dear wife had returned to our home, and I was no longer seeing Sherlock Holmes every morning and evening. My curiosity, however, got the better of me and one afternoon in early February, with the hours of sunlight now being somewhat longer than they had been in January, I strolled over to 221B Baker Street after finishing my appointments with my patients.

Holmes was sitting in his usual armchair, puffing on his pipe, and reading a file. He gestured to me to help myself to the brandy on the mantle and be seated. I did both.

"Holmes," I said, "now put down the pipe and whatever it is you are reading and enlighten me. What has become of the beautiful killer that was prepared to marry you?"

He laid down his pipe, and a look of resignation swept over his face.

"One must never," he said, "underestimate the ability of a brilliant woman when she is desperate. She had another card up her sleeve that she has now played."

"Yes, go on."

"The British Museum."

"What of it?"

"They want that statue, and she is the only one who knows where it is. She has let them know that she will never reveal the location if she is sent to the gallows, and will not divulge whilst she remains in prison. As a result, the Museum has hired the best lawyers and is letting it be known amongst their stable of press reporters, that our lady should get off with not much more than a slap on the wrist."

"That would be an unspeakable travesty," I said. "She should hang."

"Indeed, she should, but Lestrade has informed me that given the weak circumstantial evidence for the murders, they are moving ahead only with the charge of threatening a police officer with a firearm. It is expected that she will plead guilty to that charge and serve a year, two at the most, in prison."

"Is there nothing you can do about it?" I asked.

He did not immediately answer, as he sat there pondering. Whatever his answer might have been, I will never know, for we were interrupted by a knock on the door.

Mrs. Hudson soon appeared bearing two cards.

"There are two women to see you, Mr. Holmes. The one you have seen before, the scrum-half. She's carrying a small steamer trunk. The other could be her mother."

The first card was indeed from Miss Gertrude Hume-Craw. The other read:

Margaret Hume-Craw (Mrs.)
27A Thistle Lane
St. Andrews, Scotland

The two women entered the room. The younger one deposited the trunk rather forcefully on our coffee table. The older woman was as tall as the younger, but nowhere near as physically imposing. She was finely attired and had an attractive mature face, topped by neatly arranged gray hair.

"Holmes, Watson, meet my mother," said Gertrude Hume-Craw. "This is not the mother I asked you to find."

"A pleasure to meet you," said Holmes. He was looking at her with one eye and eyeing the trunk with the other.

"And it is an honor to meet you, Mr. Holmes, and you as well Dr. Watson," said the older lady. "I regret I did not agree to meet you when you came to St. Andrews. Please forgive my daughter's lack of manners. Her lack of any social graces is a constant source of embarrassment to me."

"Mother dear, put a sock in it. In case you two gentlemen cannot tell, let me enlighten you. My mother and I do not get along. She despises me, and I return the favor. But the death of dear old daddy has forced us to join forces if we ever want to get anything from the estate. So here we are, working together, at least for now."

"And would you be so kind as to explain the reason for your visit?" asked Holmes.

Miss Gertrude was about to speak, but her mother answered first.

"We apologize for coming without an appointment. I had thought that my daughter would have had the manners to request one in advance, but that did not happen. Our reason for coming is, as she has said, tied to the estate of my recently departed husband. The British Museum has, through its select group of lawyers, put a freeze on the distribution of any of the assets of my husband's estate until the matter of the missing statue is resolved."

"That could take years, "I said. "Unless you can get that injunction lifted, it will be a long time before Miss O'Donohue is willing to reveal its location and have the cloud on your inheritance lifted."

"Fortunately," replied Mrs. Hume-Craw, "that may not be necessary. My reason for optimism lies in this trunk."

"Madam," said Holmes, "kindly explain. Who or what is in the trunk?"

"Charlotte."

"Are you referring to the Minoan statue?"

"No, Mr. Holmes," said the younger woman. "She is referring to the barmaid down at the corner. Of course, she is referring to the missing statue. Do you know any other Charlotte that would bring us to see you?"

"Again, Mr. Holmes," said Mrs. Hume-Craw, "please excuse my daughter's belligerence. Yes, we are speaking of the statue. If you will open the trunk, you will see what I mean."

I stood up and moved to a place where I could open the latches of the trunk. Inside was a layer of packing straw through which I carefully threaded my fingers until they touched something hard and solid. Slowly, I lifted an object about eighteen inches in height and perhaps a foot across. It was wrapped in several layers of cloth and was not particularly heavy.

"Careful, doc," said Gertrude, "She's breakable."

Whatever it was that I was lifting was obviously not a gold statue, as such are not at all breakable but exceptionally heavy.

Whilst I held the mysterious object in the air, Holmes lifted the trunk out of the way, allowing me to set the object on the table. Slowly, I removed the strips of wool blanket that were wrapped around it. What emerged was beyond belief.

"Is this your idea of a joke?" I said. "If it is, then it is in extremely poor taste."

The object in front of me was indeed a statue of sorts. It was made of pottery and painted in gaudy colors. And it was utterly, disgustingly obscene. On top of a base of about a foot square, there was a figure of a white bull, standing on its haunches. The face was painted as a lewd caricature, a bull with his leering eyes bulging and his red tongue sticking out. The other figure was of a buxom woman whose face had been altered to look somewhat bovine, and given a look of demented ecstasy. Her posterior region was impaled on the bull's male appendage. On the base was written an obscene limerick. On one side it was written in English, on the other sides, a crude translation of the limerick in French, Spanish, and Italian.

"Madam," I said sharply. "bringing such a vulgar object into this home and presenting to two gentlemen is highly offensive. What do you think you are doing?"

I admit that I was angry. The thing in front of me was of the sort that could be found for sale in the cheapest East End brothel.

The woman smiled at me and then laughed. "My feelings exactly, Dr. Watson. It is precisely how I reacted when my dear departed and not particularly lamented husband brought it home one day. As you have likely learned by now, he had a weakness for all things related to indulging the pleasures of the flesh, whether they be porcelain souvenir objects, dime novels—he was a subscriber to *The Pearl*—or voluptuous young secretaries. He collected them all, and when tired of his latest acquisition, he would move on to the next. One day he returned to St. Andrews from Blackpool and proudly displayed this god-awful monstrosity you see in front of you. He called it *Charlotte Europa* and insisted on having it in our bedroom. It sat on his dresser for a few weeks until he took his next trip abroad, whereupon I wrapped the horrid thing up, stuck in in this trunk and put it in the basement and out of sight. When he returned, he brought with him another one of his artistic treasures which, not being nearly as vulgar, was placed on his dresser. Charlotte Europa was gone from his mind. It has been in my basement for these past fifteen years, utterly forgotten. That is until recently.

"I read in the papers the story of my husband's disappearance, and then of the arrest of his latest mistress for his murder along with those of Lloyd Sunday and the poor young mother from Ayr. At first, I merely shrugged my shoulders and was not at all surprised. Edgar always played too close to the law and had been challenged on numerous occasions for plagiarism in his published articles and for demanding ungentlemanly favors of the secretaries. But then came the description of the so-called priceless statue that had been stolen. I read it, and I exclaimed, 'Why that's Charlotte.

She's in my basement.' I knew immediately that he had fabricated the entire story of the discovery of the statue. He made it up. There never was any statue. But he could not come back to the Museum empty-handed, so he concocted the story, had Lloyd Sunday draw a picture of it, using his memory of Charlotte Europa as a guide, and then he would, no doubt, have arranged to have the priceless artifact stolen before it could be turned over to the greedy old chaps at the museum."

"But why then would she murder Sunday?" I asked.

"For that, sir," Mrs. Hume-Craw said, "I have no explanation."

"Well I do," said her daughter. "And you do not have to be Sherlock Holmes to figure it out. Want to hear it, doc?"

"Please, but do try to refrain from vulgarity."

"Always," she said. "Well, it happened like this. The whole expedition was a disaster. Evans and his gang had cornered the only site worth digging up, and all we came up with was junk. So, daddy and Lloyd come up with the idea of the greatest find ever and, like mum said, it had to get stolen. Dad and Lloyd are the only ones who know the truth. They tell all the rest of us the story, show us the drawing, and we believe them. But daddy doesn't know that the mistress he hired for the expedition is ruthless. She goes to Lloyd and tries to use her seductive charms on him. She says that the two of them should get rid of the professor, steal the statue, and then hold it for ransom and split the proceeds. She tries to persuade Lloyd by agreeing to become his mistress as well.

She thinks that Lloyd is a dupe, but he's not. He's a cad, and a smart one. He knows that there is no statue, but he has this gorgeous young harlot offering to keep him company late in the evenings. He might be getting sloppy seconds, but it's fun all the same. So, he agrees, and together they toss daddy overboard, and when they get to Marseilles, Lloyd tells her that he has sneaked the statue off the boat and sent it overland to London. She says she'll continue to be his mistress after they get to London but he doesn't show up with the statue. She tracks him down, then Lloyd laughs at Bernadette and tells her that he played her for a fool and thank you very much and good-bye. And that if she tries to do anything about it, he will go to the police and confess and she'll swing. Well, Lloyd thinks the sweet, Irish, redhead is going to have a bit of a temper tantrum and then a little cry and a sulk and go away. He's wrong. Like the man said: hell hath no fury like a woman scorned. She's madder than a hornet and pretends to give him a kiss good-bye and shoots him. Then she pushes his body into the river, but she thinks that maybe he was lying about the statue and it really is in the locker. But she forgets to get the key, and the body is now floating away. So, she finds a jimmy and goes back to the locker and forces it and find nothing.

"So that's my theory, Mr. Sherlock Holmes. If you can come up with a better one, let me know. Otherwise, since you agreed to have me as your client, I'm instructing you to take Charlotte to the blokes at the Museum and let them know they were duped and get them to take off the injunction on the estate, and then you get paid. What do you think of that offer, Mr. Sherlock Holmes."

I could sense that Holmes was seething with anger as he sat and looked at the daughter for a long time without speaking. Finally, he answered.

"I believe it would be good for both of you to depart. I will be in contact with you within two days to advise you of the resolution of your case."

"That will do for me," she said. "Careful you don't drop Charlotte."

The younger woman exited the room, leaving her mother behind.

"Mr. Holmes," she began.

Please," he interrupted. "No further words are necessary. You have put up with enough in your life. For your sake, I will see that the matters are resolved. And permit me to bring to your attention that you are now a widow and free to enjoy such remaining years are you are granted on this earth. I wish you well."

She smiled and departed. Sherlock Holmes sat back in his chair, lit a cigarette, and gazed into the fire.

"Watson," he said. "when you come to write up your account of this case, it would be accurate to note that I, Sherlock Holmes, acknowledge, that it was not one that left me with any sense of satisfaction."

"But you did solve the case. The mystery has been resolved."

"Has it? Or is the puppet master still at large?"

For the next several minutes, Holmes continued with his smoking and gazing into the flames whilst I sipped on a brandy. My admiration for his dedication to his calling was as strong as ever but I had to admit that I was still smarting from his deceiving me. I could not resist one last suggestion.

"Of course," I casually added, "if you really do find yourself feeling lonely and wishing for the comfort of loving female companionship, my wife has several still attractive, highly educated friends of a certain age who would be delighted to become Mrs. Sherlock Holmes."

"Watson, that prospect is utterly horrifying."

A request to all readers:

After reading this story, please help the author and future readers by taking a moment to write a short, constructive review on the site from which you purchased the book. Thank you.   CSC

Historical and Other Notes

The Minoan Civilization took place on the island of Crete from about 2000 to 1500 BC. It was first investigated by the British scholar and archeologist (and former director of the Ashmolean Museum), Arthur Evans between 1901 and 1905. Within the ruins of the great palace of Knossos in present-day Heraklion, he discovered the maze that he claimed was The Labyrinth of the mythical Minotaur, and numerous clay tablets that were inscribed with two unknown languages that he named 'Linear A' and 'Linear B.' Linear B was finally deciphered in the 1950s by Michael Ventris, using code-breaking techniques developed during World War II. Liner A remains undeciphered. The references to the exceptional work of Arthur Evans in the story are generally accurate and the snide comments from his fictional competition, the Hume-Craw Expedition, should be mostly ignored.

The related stories of Zeus's becoming a bull and raping Europa, and of Parsiphaë and her offspring, the Minotaur, can be found in any adult collection of Greek mythology.

The local geography of London is accurate for the time setting. The Rusack Hotel still stands at the edge of The Old Course in St. Andrews and continues to be beloved by the golf aficionados of the world.

The officers of the British Museum named in the story held the positions ascribed to them in 1901 but were, no doubt, far finer gentlemen than I have unfairly portrayed them.

In this story, I have attempted to pay tribute not only to the original Sherlock Holmes story, but also to the great mystery story tradition of the *femme fatale*. Mystery lovers will note the obvious borrowing from Dashiell Hammett's masterpiece, *The Maltese Falcon*.

The Adventure of the Norwood Rembrandt

A New Sherlock Holmes Mystery

Chapter One
Sent to Prison with Holmes

```
WATSON: I MUST GO TO PRISON TOMORROW
and need you along. Please meet me at
221B at 4:00 pm. Sentence could last
two or more days.      Holmes
```

This note arrived in the evening of an enjoyable late April day in 1904. I smiled, shook my head, and called out to my wife.

"Dearest, I am being sent off to prison tomorrow with Holmes."

"It's about time, darling," came the merry reply.

Over twenty years had passed since my first adventure with Sherlock Holmes. Throughout those years, I worked to maintain my medical practice whilst being ready in an instant to run off with him as we chased murderers, swindlers, traitors, and the occasional wild goose. A few years back, as I have related in an earlier account, I sold my medical practice. I now offered my services on an occasional basis to several of London's hospitals and agreed from time to time to fill in for my colleagues who were in need of a well-deserved holiday. As a result, most of my time during this first decade of the new century could now be devoted to assisting Sherlock Holmes and the much more lucrative profession of recording accounts of my adventures with England's famous detective.

The gift of more time for writing meant that stories of Sherlock Holmes continued to appear regularly in *The Strand* as did stories and articles I wrote on other topics. Whilst I did some of my writing from my desk in my home, much of it was carried out in the familiar setting of 221B Baker Street so that I could be close to whatever new case walked through the door and up the stairs.

At just before four o'clock the following afternoon, I ascended those stairs and let myself into the front room. Holmes was sitting at the table enjoying the last drops of his afternoon tea and a cigarette, and he motioned to me to be seated.

"My dear doctor," he said, "how good of you to join me on such short notice."

"I would not miss such an opportunity for the world," I said.

"Splendid. We are off to Wandsworth Prison. It will not take us long to get there, and it should be a pleasant drive through the park and then Chelsea and across the Battersea Bridge. It is a lovely afternoon, and the fresh air will do both of us good."

"I am certain that it will," I replied. "Now, as I do not believe that you are about to be incarcerated, although you have earned the right to be so on more than one occasion, would you mind awfully telling me why we are going to prison?"

He smiled back at me.

"I received a letter yesterday from one of the inmates. He is to be hanged a fortnight from today and seems to think that I can alter his destiny. I shall let you read his letter and tell you all I know whilst in the cab."

The ride was indeed pleasant. It had rained during the morning, but the clouds had cleared and the late afternoon sun was bidding adieu to the day. The dappled light and the aroma from the parks brought to mind the words of the poet about being in England in April. Even Sherlock Holmes appeared to be in a good mood.

"Do you recall," he asked, "the case of Lester McInerney down in Norwood some five years ago?"

I did have some memory of it from the Press at the time.

"Was not that the artist chap who stole all those paintings and murdered the butler?"

"Indeed, that was he."

"Is he still alive?" I queried. "I thought he would have been hanged long ago."

"By all rights, he should have," said Holmes. "That is just one of the singular aspects of the case. I was not asked by either the police or the defendant to assist, but it now appears that I am being drawn in at the last minute. Here, please take a moment and read his letter."

He handed me an envelope. The return address gave the name of Lester McInerney and of Wandsworth Prison in Earlsfield. It ran:

```
Dear Sherlock Holmes:
    I am writing to beg you to help me prove
my innocence before I am wrongfully hanged a
fortnight. I swear, by all that is holy,
that I am innocent of that crime.
    I assume that you are familiar with the
particulars of my case. I was assisted by
several capable barristers and solicitors
who were able to arrange the delay of my
execution several times, but they have now
abandoned me. I have nowhere else to turn,
and you are my last hope.
    I am not in the habit of reading
magazines that cater to the general
populace, but a friendly guard at the prison
took pity upon me and gave me a stack of old
copies of The Strand. In them, I read of
```

your many cases and your success in solving even those that at first appeared hopeless. Mine surely qualifies. The evidence against me was overwhelming, and it took the jury less than an hour to convict me. All I have in my defense are my protestations of innocence, and these are not enough.

    Therefore, I am beseeching you to arrange to come and visit me at Wandsworth as soon as possible. I will lay out my entire situation to you and place my life in your hands.

    Yours in need,

    Lester McInerney

"You must," I said to Holmes, "not be convinced of his guilt. Otherwise, we would not be on our way to prison."

"I read some of the records of the case," said Holmes. "There were aspects of it that struck me as being worthy of further investigation. I shall withhold any further judgment until we have met with this fellow and listened to his side of the story."

Wandsworth Prison is one of the newer houses of correction in England. It was built in response to the movement for prison reform and the horror that enlightened people felt when seeing and smelling the dreadful conditions to which human beings were subjected in the older prisons like Newgate. That miserable black hole is now in its last days and would be closed and demolished, not a day too soon.

We entered the front gate of Wandsworth, signed in, and were escorted to one of the six wings that extended like spokes of the massive institution. Even in the section reserved for men who were awaiting their visit to the gallows, the conditions were clean and relatively spacious. Each man had his own cell, toilet, and chair. Large windows at the end of the hallway and in the roof permitted sunlight to stream into all four storeys of cells.

"Here we are, gentlemen," said the guard who had led us through the hallways and stairwells. "One of us walks by every fifteen minutes. Just let us know when you want to come out, and we will escort you back."

The man in the cell stood as we entered. He was tall, lean, and of fair complexion. His full head of wavy blond hair sat on top of a well-defined face that at one time must have been less gaunt and grey. His blue eyes bulged out somewhat from their sockets and were accented by the dark circles under them. He was clad in standard prison garb and walked forward to greet us.

"Mr. Sherlock Holmes, oh, Mr. Sherlock Holmes, thank you, sir, thank you. And Dr. Watson as well. Thank you, gentlemen. I am not a man given to prayer, but I admit that I have been pestering Providence hoping that you would come and meet with me."

"I assume," said Holmes, "that you must be Mr. Lester McInerney."

"I am, sir. That I am. I am so sorry that I cannot offer you a spot of tea or nourishment. And the only place to sit apart from my one chair is on the cot. Should I ever get out of this hell-hole, I promise I will be a much better host."

"No host," said Holmes, "can be faulted for not offering that which he does not have. Permit me to suggest that Dr. Watson take a seat on the chair so as to enable his taking notes. You and I, sir, can sit on opposite ends of the cot facing each other." As he spoke, he sat down on the cot, pulled off his boots and swung his legs up on to the bed and folded them together. Mr. McInerney watched him for a moment and then did the same.

"Now then, sir," said Holmes. "Time is of the essence. So, kindly convey to me your case, beginning with your personal history—your family and your life before your arrest. Then please account for how you ended up serving as an agent for artistic acquisitions for the wealthy collectors of the land and subsequently convicted of murder. Pray be at one and the same time concise and precise. Leave out no important detail and include none that is not germane to your case. Please proceed."

"Yes, sir. I shall do my best, sir." The prisoner then briefly closed his eyes, took a long slow breath and then exhaled. "Forgive me if at times I am incoherent. My nerves are destroyed after having spent the past five years facing certain death several times only to have it postponed at the last minute."

"Your case of nerves is to be expected," said Holmes. "Now, do get on with your story."

"Quite so, yes. I shall begin with my grandfather. He was born in Belfast, but before he had turned twenty" years of age, he left the sodden green isle and sought his fortune in London. He was skilled with his hands and set himself up as a carpenter. By dint of hard work and being clever, he prospered and built a home for his wife and family in Lower Norwood. In a stroke of good fortune, he was in the right place at the right time when the powers that be decided to move the Crystal Palace from Hyde Park down to Sydenham, just a few blocks from grandfather's home. It was an enormous project costing well in excess of one million pounds. He secured one of the largest contracts and became a wealthy man. He passed away in 1875, and my grandmother followed him up to glory in 1880.

"My father was the eldest of three sons and took over the family business. His brothers assisted him for a few years, and then they left England to seek their fortunes in America. I am the third son of my father. My eldest brother now looks after the family firm. The second brother went off to Australia and established a building business there. I, the third son, had no interest in the construction business. From an early age, I am told, I showed a talent and a passion for the arts. My mother encouraged my pursuit of drawing, music, dance, and the theater. If I do say so myself, I showed exceptional talent as an artist. My mother provided me with an adequate allowance permitting me to spend several years in Paris working as an artist and studying under some of the *avant-garde* painters.

"Upon returning, I borrowed some money from my mother, set up a studio in Lambeth and embarked upon my calling. I quickly learned that success or even earning a living as an artist is a difficult path to take in life and depends as much if not more on who you are able to attract as your patrons than on any talent or diligent effort. I realized that I could never support myself let alone my wife and family by selling my paintings. Fortunately, my artistic studies had been rigorous, and I had acquired an extensive knowledge of the great artists of the past and the world of contemporary artists. I knew all about which paintings were becoming available at auction, which young artists were the toast of the town, and which were charlatans with little talent and large mouths.

"Almost by accident, at a small exhibition in Dulwich, I found myself in conversation with a young nobleman who wished to collect art but freely admitted that he knew nothing at all about it. He suggested that I might serve as his agent. I agreed, and he must have appreciated my work for he recommended me to his peers. Suddenly, I found myself with a business opportunity. My fifth client was Viscount Fitzguilford of my home village of Lower Norwood. He had been collecting some very fine pieces for many years and recently had a new wing added to the house to serve as his gallery. I helped him find some paintings from one of the Impressionist fellows in Paris and the Viscount was pleased with my efforts. I thought I was going to have a long and prosperous patronage, but then the dear fellow died. His widow, Lady Fitzguilford, either had no interest in the collection or perhaps she needed money for the estate. I do not know, but I suspect the latter. All I know for certain is that she instructed me to take several of the paintings up to London to have new frames put on them. She is a right smart woman and knows that a painting with the ideal frame will sell at auction for far more than one with a poor frame.

"She and I chose some ten of the Viscount's paintings, and I hired a box wagon to take them to one of the better framers in Chelsea. I had removed them from the gallery and loaded them into my wagon. And that, Mr. Holmes, was the beginning of the unbearable nightmare that has become my life."

Here he paused, looking at Holmes for some indication of approval of his recitation so far before continuing.

"Before we get to the day of the theft and murder," said Holmes, "I have one or two questions about your family and your good self."

"Certainly, sir. Please, sir, ask me anything. Sorry if I left out something I should have mentioned."

"In the Press that covered your trial, there were several references to your grandfather and the firm he established. Some of the comments on his character struck me as rather harsh. What sort of man was he?"

This question struck *me* as rather odd, but I had learned over the years that Sherlock Holmes always had reason for whatever direction his mind took. The baffled look on the prisoner's face said that he was also perplexed. After a brief pause, he nodded and answered.

"I have few memories of him. He died whilst I was still a child, so much of what I know of him is based on what I heard from my mother or other members of the family, or things I overheard in the village later on. Patrick McInerney was said to be a fair man and scrupulously honest. He was a Scots-Irish Presbyterian and obeyed the letter of the law even if at times he ignored its spirit."

"Elucidate, please," said Holmes.

"I suppose one might say that he was a hard man. He paid good wages, and so there was never a dearth of men who wished to work for him. At one time or another most of the men of the village served as his employees. However, he had a fierce temper and would dress a man down for the least little mistake. And woe betide you if you came to work late more than once or with a whiff of whiskey on your breath. You were terminated on the spot, and that was that. He was, I am told, respected, even feared, but he had few if any friends."

"Thank you," said Holmes. "That is useful to know. Now, about yourself. Kindly describe your marriage and family."

A look of pain flashed across the young man's face. For a moment he winced and then answered.

"As a lad growing up in the village, I was considered passably handsome and I came from an established and respected family. Therefore, I was, you might say, sought after by the eligible young women. Perhaps it would be more accurate to say that I was sought after by their mothers on their behalf, but that amounted to the same thing. The one I chose for my wife, Agnes Smithers, was by far and away the most beautiful and spirited of the lot. We married as soon as we were of age and she accompanied me to Paris. Our time there was glorious. Except for an allowance from my mother, we had no money, but we were young and in love and made many friends. We walked hand in hand along the Seine and went to many cafés and parties. The good Lord blessed us with two beautiful children.

"Upon returning to England, our life became more difficult. My allowance had ended, and Agnes did not enjoy the deprivations that come with being the wife of a poorly paid artist. She was constantly on me to give up my calling and go and work for my father. I could not agree, and we often had words between us. Matters improved when the opportunity to serve as an agent developed, but that lasted only a very short time before I was arrested and put on trial. As soon as I was convicted, Agnes asked for an annulment. I did not object as I considered such a decree to be impossible given that we had already consummated the marriage many times over. But it turned out that if sufficient funds were paid to a soiled priest, such a result could be obtained. She remarried soon after to a wealthy industrialist and moved to Belgravia. I have heard nothing of her or of my children since that time. My letters to her and cards to my son and daughter have all been returned unopened. Is there anything else you wish to know on that matter, Mr. Holmes?"

"That will do for now. Let us return to the day of the crime. Kindly recount everything you remember about that day."

Chapter Two
A Fortnight Until Death

"THAT HORRIBLE DAY," began Mr. McInerney, "was a Tuesday, the twenty-ninth of October. Come this fall it will be six years ago. During the previous week, I had met with Lady Fitzguilford several times, and we decided which paintings to take to the framers. We chose the most valuable ones—ten of them—as they were more likely to fetch the best prices at an auction. That morning, I had removed the paintings from the wall and wrapped them so that they would be protected during the transport up to Chelsea."

"Were you alone?" asked Holmes.

"I was, the entire morning."

"None of the household staff assisted you?"

"No, sir."

"I would have thought that such a task would normally involve assistance from the manservant," said Holmes.

"It would, sir. But I was not assisted."

"And was that because there was bad blood between you and Mr. Herman Carter?"

"Yes, sir. There was. It would be fair to say that we hated each other."

"A fact," said Holmes, "that came out during the trial and contributed to your being convicted of murdering him."

"That is correct, sir."

"Why did you hate each other?"

"That matter, sir, is private and embarrassing so I would rather not go into it."

"Good heavens, man!" Holmes exploded. "you are to be hanged in a month. You do not have the foolish luxury of avoiding embarrassment. Now, you will either answer my questions, or I shall depart. What is it going to be?"

Mr. McInerney was taken aback by Holmes's angry outburst. For a moment he appeared to be gathering his wits about him and then, trembling somewhat, he answered.

"I see your point, sir. Very well, then, I will tell you. I was not the first young gentleman in the village to court my wife. Agnes had several other gentlemen admirers before me. Mr. Carter was one of them. He was quite the hero of the football pitch and the cricket oval and exceptionally fit and handsome. For a brief period of time, they were quite attracted to each other. However, when he completed his schooling, he announced that he had decided to go into service and had secured a prize position at the manor house of Viscount Fitzguilford. It was the best service position one could imagine in Lower Norwood, but it was still in service and would never permit him to rise to the level of a gentleman. Agnes had loftier ambitions, and she threw Herman over and took up with me. Herman never forgave either her or me."

"That story is not at all uncommon," said Holmes. "I have heard it countless time, but amongst sensible adults, it does not usually lead to hatred and murder."

"Yes, sir. I suppose that is correct, sir. And forgive me, this is where it becomes embarrassing. The courtship between Herman and Agnes was quite passionate, and they engaged in the type of intimate exchanges that should only ever take place between a husband and a wife. I did not learn of this matter until after I had married Agnes. When I returned to Lower Norwood from Paris, I would run into Herman on numerous occasions, and he took it upon himself to taunt me with his having had my wife before I got around to it. He was merciless and cruel and horribly vulgar. In anger, I taunted him back and claimed that she had obviously found him inadequate in more ways than one. Looking back, as I have countless times over the past five years, I confess that our behavior was pathetically childish, but it happened, and it continued unabated, and it did not remain a secret. The entire village knew that we were often at each other's throats and had made vile and vicious threats to each other. This matter played heavily against me at the trial."

Holmes sighed. "Very well, you are not the first, and you shall not be the last young male whose animal instincts rendered him fatally stupid. Continue with your account. What happened after you finished preparing the paintings?"

"I loaded them into the box on the wagon and closed it up. When I sat down in the seat, preparing to lay a whip to the horse, I saw a note on the driver's seat. It was from the cook, Mrs. Griffiths, who had taken a bit of a shine to me it is fair to say. The note said that there was a small lunch waiting for me in the kitchen and I should come and enjoy it before departing for the city. It was a kind gesture, and I was hungry, so I laid the whip down and went through the house to the kitchen. Mrs. Griffiths was not there, but there was a plate with a tasty sandwich and some cheese, and a glass of ale. I was not pressed for time, and so I took a good half hour and enjoyed it. Then, at about noon, I returned to my wagon and departed."

"Did you not keep the note?" asked Holmes.

"When I went back later to look for it, it was nowhere to be seen. It had vanished. And Mrs. Griffiths, at the trial, stated that she had never written such a note nor prepared a lunch. In fact, she had been at the market all morning and did not return to the house until after one o'clock."

"How convenient," said Holmes. "And when you told this story to the police and during your trial, what happened?"

"I was not believed. There was nothing to back me up. Even the glass of ale, the sandwich plate and the cutlery had all be cleaned and put away."

"Clever, indeed," said Holmes. "Very well, continue. You departed for Chelsea."

"Yes. It only took an hour to get to the framer's shop. I opened the doors of the wagon, and to my dismay, all of the paintings were gone."

"Did you stop on route?" asked Holmes.

"Not once. They must have been removed whilst I was eating lunch. In addition to being charged with the murder of Herman Carter, I was charged with the theft of an exceptionally valuable group of paintings."

"Which, if you did not steal, must have been removed whilst you were eating lunch. I assume that you gave a list of the stolen paintings to the police so that they could be traced."

"I offered to, sir, but at that time they more interested in the murder than the theft."

"That is understandable. Very well, keep going. What happened after you returned to the house?"

"I entered the driveway and saw two police carriages sitting in front of the house. I went running up to report the theft of the paintings, but the constables were not the least interested in talking to me about that and for good reason. Herman Carter was lying dead on the floor of the gallery. He had a bullet through his skull, and a chisel stuck right into his heart."

"Your chisel, if I remember correctly," said Holmes.

"Yes, sir. It was mine. It was part of a set I kept in my toolbox for those few occasions when I needed to make adjustments to frames or wainscoting. I had used it recently and put it back in the box, but there it was, protruding from Herman's chest."

"And bearing your fingerprints?"

"Yes. My barrister tried to argue that evidence from fingerprints was unreliable, but the police extracted a complete clear set, and there was no doubt that they were mine."

"You must have left them on the last time you used that chisel."

"Yes, sir. It was the chisel with the narrowest blade of the set. I had used it the previous week to make a fine adjustment to a frame."

"Interesting. Continue."

"The constables told me not to leave the house, and I waited in the parlor until later in the afternoon. An inspector from Scotland Yard appeared "

"Lestrade?"

"Yes, sir. He interviewed Lady Fitzguilford, all of the staff and then me. When he had completed his questioning of me, to my shock and dismay he said that he was charging me with the murder of Carter and the theft of the paintings. It was at that point that my life as a free man ended. I have not been out of custody since then. What else is there that I can tell you?"

"We need to return to the paintings."

"Yes, sir. What do you wish to know?"

"Do you recall which paintings were wrapped and loaded onto the wagon?"

"Of course, I do. I have burned that list in my memory."

"Would you mind reciting it for me?" Holmes gave a nod to me as he spoke and I indicated that my pencil and notebook were at the ready.

"In order as I wrapped them, they were:

> Rembrandt's *The Storm on the Sea of Galilee*, and his *Lady and Gentleman in Black*,
>
> Vermeer's *The Concert*,
>
> Govert Flinck's *Landscape with an Obelisk*,
> Manet's *Chez Tortoni*, a fine new painting that I helped the Viscount find and purchase,
> Raphaels *Count Tommaso*,
> Titian's *The Rape of Europa*,
> Fra Angelico's *Death and Assumption of the Virgin*,
> Rembrandt's *Self-Portrait, Aged 23*, and
> the Botticelli *Lucretia*."

"You are quite certain," said Holmes, "that these were the ten paintings you wrapped and loaded."

"As certain as I am that you are sitting in front of me."

"Excellent. Now, just one more item. How is it that you are still alive? In clear-cut cases such as yours, the execution usually takes place within a few weeks after a verdict. Yet you are still here five years later. How do you account for that? Have you had a select team of lawyers working on your behalf?"

"Not on my behalf, Mr. Holmes. There is a team, and they are very sharp indeed. But they work for Lloyd's."

"Lloyd's?"

"Yes, sir. Lloyd's of London, the insurance firm."

"I *know* who Lloyd's is. But what is their role in your case?"

"All of the paintings in Viscount Fitzguilford's new gallery were insured. The old man, or perhaps it was his wife, took out a very expensive policy to cover theft, destruction by flood, fire or vandalism, or any and all ways the paintings could be damaged. The Lloyd's chaps told me that the policy required them to pay out over one hundred thousand pounds for the missing paintings. They had no interest in doing so and so they, not Scotland Yard, have been the most diligent in trying to find the paintings. If they were all returned in good condition, then no payment would be required. At first, they believed that I had taken them and knew where they were. If I were to be put to death, then the only hope they had of finding the paintings would be lost. So, it was in their interest that I be kept alive until I finally agreed to confess to the crime and reveal the location. They used every trick in the legal book to postpone my final date."

"And you," said Holmes, "were unable to make such a confession, so they have finally abandoned you."

"Correct, again, sir."

Holmes asked several more questions, but Mr. McInerney could offer no facts not already been revealed during the investigation and trial that might possibly assist in providing support for his claim of innocence. In the eyes of the jury, he had the motive, the means, and the opportunity to commit the murder. His only defense, that he would have been exceptionally stupid to act in a way that left all evidence pointing solely to himself, was given short shrift. Whilst the public enjoyed the fantasy of brilliant mastermind criminals such as Moriarty and his ilk, the truth was that most of them were not the sharpest knives in the drawer. Acting stupidly on impulse was a common trait of the criminal class.

When he had completed his cross-questioning, Holmes pondered for a minute and then issued his verdict.

"I will accept your case, Mr. McInerney. The data is far from complete at present, but there do appear to be some curious and unanswered questions, the answering of which present a worthy challenge. If I am successful and you are declared not guilty, I shall send you my full fee. If I fail, then I cannot send my bill to a dead man. Do you agree to my terms?"

For the first time that morning, Sherlock Holmes's newest client smiled.

"Of course, sir. All I have to keep my soul from descending into the blackest of hatred and brain fever is the hope that you will succeed. I will trouble deaf heaven with my bootless cries."

We hailed the prison guard as he passed and were led out of Wandsworth Prison. On reaching the pavement, Holmes lit a cigarette and stood in silence for several minutes.

"A penny for your thoughts," Watson.

"The evidence," I said, "is heavy against him. All that exists in his favor is his apparent sincerity. However, you and I both know that such a show can be a pretense by a clever actor, indeed by one who has managed to delude himself into believing that what he says is the truth even if it is nothing of the sort."

"Quite true," agreed Holmes. "Against my better judgment, I shall have to rely on my instincts, which at this time lean in the direction of believing him. If he is guilty, then my efforts will not be worth the candle of my time. However, if he is innocent, then I shall have saved the life of a just man, not to mention the reputation one more time of Inspector Lestrade and the courts."

"So, Holmes, is the game afoot?"

"It is, my friend. It is not all that far from where we are now over to Lower Norwood. I have sent a note to the local public house there and reserved two of their rooms. Shall we go? There is still time to inspect the estate of Viscount Fitzguilford before we retire for the night."

Chapter Three
Attacked in the Cemetery

AN HOUR LATER, the two of us were standing on the pavement outside *The Horns*, the ancient pub and small inn that was less than a block away from the Fitzguilford estate. We had checked in to our rooms and, I admit, I was looking forward to a pleasant dinner. Holmes had other plans.

"We still have well over an hour of daylight," he said. "That should be more than enough time to conduct a cursory inspection of the grounds of the manor house. So, come, my friend, let us do a brief circumnavigation of the property." He had turned and was walking away from me before completing his statement. Reluctantly, I followed.

The manor house in which the theft and murder had occurred stood on the south side of Robson Road. The grounds backed onto the great expanse of the Norwood Cemetery, one of the seven public burying grounds that the government had opened a few years back to look after the needs of the population of the common citizens of London. The grounds were quite impressive, what with a dozen or more mausoleums—some that seemed more like follies than monuments—and innumerable large memorial statues and carved headstones. From most vantage places in the forty acres, one could gaze to the south-west and observe the magnificent Crystal Palace on the high ground just to the south of Sydenham Hill.

"As the grounds of the house are adjacent to the cemetery," said Holmes. "might I suggest that we divide and conquer. Could you please start at the gate and walk around the property in a clockwise direction? I shall walk counter-clockwise, and we shall meet in the cemetery at the spot directly opposite the back of the house."

"And what, pray tell," I asked, "are we looking for? Some clue lying amongst the graves?"

"Ah, yes. We are looking for a secondary means of entrance and egress to the grounds. I shall see you in fifteen minutes or so around the back. Kindly be as observant as possible and do not neglect any possibility regardless of how unlikely it might appear to you."

He began on his trek, leaving me to undertake mine. It was a rather idyllic task. The oaks and elms spread out over the paths. Flower beds had been generously planted and well-tended. Many of the graves were adorned with bouquets of flowers, none of which had been allowed to wilt and decay before being removed by the conscientious grounds staff. I could not help but notice the inscriptions on many of the headstones showing the years of military service that had been given for Queen and country. I was quite taken aback by a name I recognized, a fellow who had served with me in the Fifth Northumberland Fusiliers some thirty years ago in Afghanistan. I stood still for several moments pondering this unexpected reminder of my own mortality.

Whilst stand there, I heard footsteps coming up quickly behind me. Then I felt a forearm lock itself around my neck and saw the flash of a knife in the hand just below my chin.

"Sherlock Holmes is not welcome here," snarled a voice in my ear.

My service in the BEF might have been three decades ago, but there are some drills that a soldier never forgets. During my basic training, I and my fellow recruits had endlessly and mindlessly repeated the basic move that one must make in a fraction of a second if one did not wish to find a knife cutting one's throat or plunged into one's ribs.

Instinctively, I drove my elbow back as hard as I could into the solar plexus of my attacker. I heard him gasp and immediately reached my two hands up to the forearm. With my left hand, I grasped the wrist and pulled down and with my right pushed up on the elbow. I forced the arm over my head and kept forcing it until I had rotated it behind the man's back and then I pushed hard until I could feel the head of the humerus become dislocated from the scapula.

My attacker cried out in pain and dropped the knife. I let go of his arm and with two hands reached for the hair on his head and in one move used all my strength to slam his head down upon my rising knee. The responding crack confirmed that I had broken his jaw. Again, he cried out in shock and pain. My next move was to delve into my pocket for my service revolver.

"Do not move or you will be shot," I shouted.

Even in his pain, he was an agile man and jumped immediately to the side and behind the closest gravestone. I aimed my gun at his legs and pulled the trigger, but he kept moving and took cover behind the row of monuments. In a few more seconds he had vanished from sight amongst the trees and stones.

"Watson!" came the shout from Holmes and he ran toward me. "Watson, good heavens, you are not hurt, are you? Please, say that you are not hurt."

"I am not hurt, but I do not like being mistaken for Sherlock Holmes and having a knife to my throat."

I recovered my wits and related to Holmes what had taken place. In the light of the setting sun, I could see a smile spread across his face and for a fleeting moment thought that it was brought about by his congratulations at my manly self-defense.

"You were attacked," he said, 'because that fellow mistook you for me. Splendid. Utterly splendid. That is the type of good luck I could never have expected."

I was not at all pleased by his comment.

"I beg your pardon, Holmes. I fail to see how my being attacked could be seen as good luck."

"Oh, but yes, my dear man. The word has obviously gone out in the village—most likely from the innkeeper with whom I posted a reservation—that I would be in Lower Norwood. Someone has reason not to want me here. That someone must object to me poking my nose into the only crime of any significance in the past few years that took place here."

"You mean the murder of the butler?"

"And the theft of the paintings," he added. "Which means, that there is something more to be discovered and that our client may, in fact, be innocent. Otherwise, why bother threatening me? Can you not see, Watson? It is a splendid piece of evidence, a veritable gift, is it not?"

I shook my head and began walking quickly back toward the village and my supper. Holmes followed me. He had an annoying spring in his step and a smile on his face.

An hour later we sat at the supper table, and Holmes insisted on ordering a bottle of claret.

"My dear Watson. Look at it this way. Unhappy as you are about what took place, I assure you that there is some man not far away—a hired local ruffian I suspect—who is suffering a dislocated shoulder and broken jaw and much unhappier than you are. So, cheer up, my friend. The game is in play, and the first round has gone to us."

Chapter Four
Five Years Ago

TO ADD INSULT to injury, Holmes insisted that we set out the following day before the breakfast room had been opened. At six o'clock the next morning, as the rosy-fingered dawn was bringing first light to the eastern horizon, I found myself standing once more outside the gates of the Fitzguilford estate.

The gates were closed, and there was no sign of grounds staff so early in the morning. I followed Holmes as he slipped through the hedge and into the garden. The house itself was quite standard for a large villa in south London, although I thought that the gardens and lawns looked a little down at the heel.

"The front side of the house," said Holmes, "is all of a piece. If a new wing was added to accommodate a gallery, it must be around the back."

We walked around the be back of the house and observed a small wing and conservatory that was made from newer, lighter colored stone. At the far end of it was a service door, beside which was a set of half-size doors, slanting downward from the wall of the house. They must have lead into a godown basement. Adjacent to those doors was another door that opened to a coal chute. Holmes stood still and looked intently at the wall and doors.

"If what Lester McInerney has said is reliable, whoever removed the paintings from his wagon must have taken them quickly down the steps into the basement. He moved ten large framed pieces in close to twenty minutes. Had he taken them back into the conservatory through the service door he would most likely have been observed by the household staff. Come, Watson. Let us take a look."

He extracted a small leather case from his coat pocket, opened it and took out a small lock-picking tool. The sloping doors were secured with a common padlock, which yielded to Holmes in less than a minute. He left the doors wide open behind us as we descended.

"Holmes," I said. "Anyone who comes along will see the doors open."

"And who do you expect to do so at this hour in the morning? The kitchen staff will not appear until half seven, and the groundskeepers have not yet worked the property since the winter ended. We need the daylight and we have at least a full hour to carry out our inspection. Come."

The basement was obviously new. The floor was of poured concrete, and the walls were clean and dry. Several metal posts supported the floor joists, all of which were still level and true. In the side of the room closest to the outside entry doors was a new, coal-fired furnace that was attached to a boiler and a maze of pipes which supplied the radiators up in the conservatory and gallery. On the back wall was an open staircase of bare wooden boards that led up to a small landing and door.

"Judging by the location," Holmes said, "those stairs must lead directly to the gallery."

Unwilling to accept the logic of his own deduction without putting it to the test, he climbed the stairs and opened the door. I followed him into the gallery room. It was not particularly large but had high ceilings and excellent natural light. The rays from the rising sun gave it a warm glow. We did not stay there long at all for fear that someone from the household staff or family could enter at any time.

Back in the basement, Holmes moved slowly around the walls, tapping his stick quietly every foot or so and attempting to discern any chambers behind the walls. There was one locked closet that he opened using his tool. I lit a match to bring some light into it, but it was entirely bare.

After our thorough inspection of the basement, we returned to the exterior walls of the new wing. One after the other, Holmes checked the lowest tier of windows. All were new and securely locked. By half-past seven, we had exhausted the nooks and crannies, the paths and gardens, and the openings that led into the expanses of the Norwood Cemetery.

"It is time to return to the inn and enjoy our breakfast," said Holmes. "After which we shall call on the residents. Perhaps they will agree to let us inspect the entire house."

"Why would they permit us to do that?"

"Most likely, they will not. But there is no harm in asking."

"No? And what if one of the servants has his jaw wired shut and his arm in a sling?"

"I assure you that the last thing he will do is risk having his other arm similarly abused. Come now, a full English breakfast will restore your spirits."

"Good morning, sir," said Holmes to the young man-servant who opened the door of the manor house for us. Holmes handed him our cards and spoke in a cheerful tone. "I wonder if I might have a word with the lady of the house?"

The fellow nodded, bade us enter the vestibule, and departed. We waited in silence for at least ten minutes, during which time we saw not a single member of the staff or family. Finally, a young man appeared at the top of the stairs. He was wearing a long dressing gown that reached almost to the floor, but the cuffs of his pajamas could be seen drooping over his slippers. Without descending to meet us, he spoke rather more loudly than was necessary.

"What," he demanded, "does Sherlock Holmes want? Why do you wish to speak to my mother?"

"Good morning, sir," answered Holmes. "May I presume that you are Geoffrey Nicholas, the current Viscount Fitzguilford?"

"Of course, I am. Now answer my question."

"I have been asked," said Holmes, "to make some inquiries into the death of Herman Carter and was hoping that I might speak briefly to your mother and have a look through the house."

"You cannot be serious," came the reply from the stairs. "Good heavens, man, that was over five years ago. The case is settled and done with. It was terribly upsetting to my mother at the time, and I will not permit you to antagonize her by opening it up again. If that is the only reason for your visit, then get out of here this instant. Good day, Mr. Holmes."

But then a woman's voice came from somewhere on the upper floor.

"Geoffrey, is that truly Sherlock Holmes?"

"He says he is, mother. I have told him to leave and not return."

"Tell him to have a seat in the front room. I shall be down in a moment."

"Mother "

"Are you deaf, Geoffrey?"

The young fellow gave a nod in our direction, turned, and disappeared along the upstairs hallway. The butler emerged from a lower hallway and greeted us with a faint smile.

"This way, please gentlemen. It appears that the Lady wishes to meet the famous detective, Sherlock Holmes."

He led us into a pleasant parlor and organized a round of tea. Five minutes later, we stood as a woman who I would have guessed had already passed her biblical limits of three score and ten years entered the room. She had a trim and erect posture and a certainty to her step. Her dress was elegant if not quite stylish and her hair was fixed neatly on her head.

"Good morning, gentlemen. Please sit down. To what do I owe the honor of having Sherlock Holmes and Doctor Watson in my home this fine spring morning?"

Holmes repeated what he had said to her son. She smiled and replied.

"Before I answer that, Mr. Holmes, I have a few questions of my own for you."

"Pray proceed, madam."

"You have been the subject of vigorous debate amongst the members of my reading circle here in Norwood. What we wish to know is whether you fell in love with Irene Adler or not."

Holmes looked uncharacteristically discomfited, and I had to bite my tongue to stifle a laugh.

"I did not," he said.

"Well then, that settles that. I shall report that I have had the answer straight from the horse's mouth. But what about Violet Hunter, the lovely redhead of the Copper Birches? Several members of our circle are quite certain that there was a strong attraction between the two of you."

"On my part, none. I cannot speak for Miss Hunter, and I assure you that I shall remain a confirmed bachelor with no intention of distracting my mental energies by any romantic digressions."

"Oh, what a pity. Our meetings will be so much less lively if we cannot imagine interesting affairs in your private life. But on Tuesday next, when we meet again I shall report, quite triumphally, the results of my investigation. Now then, Mr. Holmes, yes, you may proceed with your questions, and no, you may not inspect the house. The fellows from Lloyd's turned the entire place inside out after the dreadful event five years and five months ago. You may speak with their officers and read their report. Now, what do you wish to know?"

"What I wish to know, my Lady, are your specific recollections of the pertinent events prior to, during, and following the murder of your butler and theft of the paintings. I understand that reviewing them will be painful to you, but would you be so kind as to impart them to me?"

"It all happened over five years ago, Mr. Holmes. Time does heal some wounds, and I shall do my best to tax my failing memory. You may interrupt me with your questions. I will not consider you overly rude or impertinent for doing so. I suppose we could begin on Thursday, the twenty-fourth of October in the year 1898. It was on that day, between the hours of 9:25 am and half-past eleven that I met with Mr. McInerney and selected the paintings to be sent out for improvement to their frames. It had been my intention to send them off to Sotheby's or Christie's to be auctioned off."

"Excuse me, madam," said Holmes. "Might I ask why you chose to sell them? Your husband who had recently passed away had been a passionate collector, and their value would have increased as rapidly as almost any asset you possessed."

"My husband's passion was indeed for masterpieces of art. Mine, however, was for fine horses. He indulged his passion whilst he was alive. I was determined to indulge mine now that he had gone. I assure you, Mr. Holmes, his priceless collection held no sentimental value for me at all."

"I understand. Pray, continue."

"Mr. McInerney made the necessary arrangements over the following four days for framing and transport and on the Tuesday, the twenty-ninth of October, returned to the house again at thirty-five minutes past nine, and began the task of taking down and removing the paintings we had selected, wrapping them, and placing them in his wagon."

"Did you supervise his actions?"

"Goodness no. I have better ways to spend my time than watching a tradesman do his trade. Being able to conduct their tasks without being watched is why we pay them, Mr.

Holmes. However, when he had completed his task, he came to me and reported. I confirmed that he had indeed removed the selected paintings by looking at the empty spaces on the walls of the gallery and sent him on his way."

"At what time was that?"

"At thirty-two minutes before noon."

"And did he then depart?"

"I have no way of confirming that, Mr. Holmes. He departed from my sight then, but according to his testimony at the trial, he re-entered the house looking for his lunch. I assume that you are aware of that."

"I am. I am also aware that he was accused of murdering Mr. Carter, your butler, during those minutes before he departed, when he claims to have been eating his lunch in the kitchen. Mr. Carter was both shot in the head with a revolver and stabbed in the heart with a chisel, yet at the trial, no one on your staff or member of your family could recall having heard a gunshot. Can you account for that?"

"Of course, and that matter was addressed at the trial. The gallery and conservatory are a recent addition to the house. The new wing abuts the back of the house and is affixed to a thick masonry wall. The only doors are a double set with the first placed in front of the second and separated by a small room no more than six feet long. The design was deliberate by the builder to protect the gallery and the paintings from fire should it break out in the older main portion of the home. Both doors are kept closed at all times, meaning that sound did not travel from the new wing of the house to the old. I dare say, you could have let off a canon, and the rest of the house might not have heard it. Did you not read the trial transcripts?"

"I did, my Lady. And I thank you for confirming the record. Please, indulge my seeking confirmation of the facts, but now tell me by whom and when was the murder discovered?"

"By the cook, Mrs. Griffiths. The butler was in the regular habit of taking his lunch at half past twelve every day in the kitchen. The cook returned from the market at one o'clock and saw that he had not eaten. This was highly irregular, and so the cook went looking for him. His body was discovered at twelve minutes past one in the gallery. She raised the alarm immediately. My son, Geoffrey, entered the room first, and I followed at seventeen minutes past one o'clock. One minute later, I ordered the groom to run for the police. They arrived at thirty-five minutes past one. The inspector from Scotland Yard appeared at exactly two o'clock. Mr. McInerney returned from Chelsea at six minutes past two o'clock. I do not know at what precise time he was arrested, but he was placed in the police wagon at three minutes past four o'clock, and it departed immediately thereafter. The undertaker appeared one the stroke of five o'clock and removed my husband's body, departing at eighteen minutes past the hour."

"Thank you," said Holmes. "That was most precise and very helpful. Could you please add on what day you rearranged the paintings that remained on the walls? I am assuming that there are no blank spaces where paintings once hung."

"Of course, Mr. Holmes, we rearranged them. I promoted our head groom to butler and had him make the adjustments a fortnight less a day after the murder. Don't ask me to tell you which paintings he moved to where. That is beyond me to remember."

"Thank you. And would you mind telling me the name of the man who supervised the construction of the new wing your husband added to your house?"

She did not immediately answer and gave Holmes a long sidewards look.

"I suspect Mr. Holmes, that you are asking me a question to which you already know the answer. Just a few months ago, in November to be exact, your story about that miserable so-and-so was published in *The Strand*. Mr. Jonas Oldacre was the name of the builder. He was, as Dr. Watson described him, a crabbed and unpleasant little man, but he did excellent work. I suspect you also know that he is no longer available to speak to as he died four years ago and is buried somewhere in the vast graveyard behind my home. You do know that, do you not, Mr. Holmes?"

She was looking quite cross as she spoke.

"My Lady," said Holmes, smiling, "you may report to your reading circle that Sherlock Holmes told you that you would make an excellent detective."

At that, she laughed merrily.

"Now," said Holmes, "permit me to depart from the agreed upon facts and ask for your insights and opinions."

"Oh, you want me to play the role of a detective. How delightful."

"If you say so, madam. In your opinion, who might have had reason for stealing the paintings and murdering Mr. Carter other than Lester McInerney?"

The woman gave Holmes a queer look.

"Frankly, sir, that strikes me as an odd question. The obvious answer is anybody and his dog. The paintings were valued at over a hundred thousand pounds, and anybody who had a connection to the criminal class could sell them on for a considerable sum. Mr. McInerney was foolish to leave the doors of the house unlocked as well as the door of his wagon. A strong, athletic young thief could have spirited away ten paintings, carrying two or three at a time, and hidden them behind a gravestone until the lot was gone. But since you ask me to pretend to be a detective, then I must invoke Occam's razor and point out that the answer requiring the fewest number of hypotheses is the one reached by the police and the court. Mr. McInerney killed his hated rival, our former butler, stole the paintings, deposited them somewhere between here and Chelsea, drove on to the framer's shop so he would have some sort of alibi, and either still has them or knows where they are. That is my logical deduction, Mr. Holmes."

We chatted on for several more minutes and then rose, thanked our host, and departed. The butler showed us out to the drive.

"Thank you, gentlemen," said the butler. "It is very rare that we hear Lady Fitzguilford laugh these days. On behalf of the staff, I thank you. Please excuse Master Geoffrey's manners. He is highly protective of his mother and is anxious for the long drawn out matter of his father's death and the murder of the former butler to finally be put to rest."

"As a protective and loyal son should," said Holmes. "It is entirely understandable."

Holmes smiled at the butler and, to my surprise, extended his hand. "Allow me to wish you success in what I suspect is a difficult position for you and the other members of the staff."

The butler was quite taken aback but then extended his hand to Holmes and smiled. "Thank you, Mr. Holmes. I can see that you have earned your reputation for being highly perceptive."

"Only," said Holmes, in just above a whisper, "for being sufficiently perceptive to see that the staff of this house might be willing to share some matters, in complete confidence of course, that would allow their hearts and minds to rest easier if they knew that I had been made aware of their concerns."

The butler gave Holmes a long look and then whispered back.

"There is a small pub in the village, *The Horns*, where I take my lunch. If you can manage to wait around until eleven o'clock, I can meet you there."

"We shall see you then."

Chapter Five
According to the Cook
and the Butler

THE GATE to the cemetery is close by on the left," said Holmes as we exited the gate of the manor house. "We have some time before lunch. A stroll amongst the dead is useful for reflection on recently acquired data. We shall stay together this time. It is unlikely that anyone will attempt to attack you again."

We entered the vast grounds of the Norwood Cemetery and walked in silence through the well-kept gardens for several minutes.

"Your thoughts, Watson?" said Holmes.

I had expected this familiar question and had made some notes in my mind in preparation.

"The new wing with the lovely gallery and conservatory and the collection of paintings appears to have been added with no expense spared. The remainder of the house and the grounds shows signs of frugal penny-pinching. I suspect that the former could be the likely cause of the latter."

"Excellent, Watson," said Holmes. "Pray, continue."

"I was not impressed by the son, the current Viscount Fitzguilford."

"Nor was I. He is the perfect example of the spoiled, lazy, arrogant, and obnoxious young noblemen who give a bad name to the aristocracy of England. Continue, please."

"The lady was a bit of an odd duck."

"Indeed, she was. But why do you say so?"

"For a woman of advanced years, her memory for precise dates and times was unusual."

"Indeed, it was," said Holmes. "Possibly also somewhat selective."

"Her reference to being confused about which paintings were moved?"

"Precisely."

"One final thought," I said. "I am no expert whatsoever on the management of the household staff of a stately home. But one does not expect the head groom to be promoted to the head butler. Usually, that task is given to one who has worked his way up through the ranks, is it not?"

"That would be my understanding as well," said Holmes. "We shall have to ask when we meet the fellow for lunch."

He returned to his pipe for several minutes and then resumed the conversation.

"I do not suppose I told you that yesterday afternoon I took a look at the bank records of the Fitzguilford estate."

"But those are ," I was about to note that bank records are supposed to be confidential. I rolled my eyes at my incorrigible friend. "And what did you learn?"

"Your observation concerning the extravagant funds spent on the paintings and the new wing is quite correct. The now-deceased Viscount Fitzguilford apparently had an obsession with masterpieces of fine art. He exhausted the family fortune in acquiring them and then on the folly of a place to keep them. When he was no longer able to run around the world buying them himself, he did indeed hire Lester McInerney to serve as his agent. He paid him rather well."

The was the end of our conversation. We walked on through the serene gardens until we came to a comfortable bench that provided a fine view to the south of the sparkling Chrystal Palace. Holmes took out his pipe and pondered whilst I scribbled notes of our meeting. At twenty minutes to eleven, we rose and made our way around the corner to the old pub on the main street of the village.

We were early for the luncheon hour at *The Horns,* and I instinctively began to walk toward a table in the rear of the pub to allow for conversation that would not be overheard.

"I think not, Watson," said Holmes. He moved to a table that was in full view of the entire room. "Our informant will require the appearance of a coincidence that we met here, not evidence of an agreed upon secretive exchange."

He was right. At five minutes past eleven o'clock, the young butler of the Fitzguilford household entered. He was followed by a woman who was a good twenty years older than he was.

"Why, Mr. Holmes and Dr. Watson," he exclaimed in a voice loud enough to be overheard by the barkeep. "I see you have discovered our favorite pub in Lower Norwood."

Holmes rose and gestured to the unoccupied chairs at the table.

"Indeed, we have, sir. Would you care to join us and advise us on what dishes are the specialty of this fine establishment?"

"Delighted to," said the butler. "We are always happy to extoll the virtues of our local businesses to visitors from London. Permit me, sir, to properly introduce myself and my companion. My name is Richard Tanner, and this fine woman is the head maid of the manor as well as our wonderful cook, Miss Mavis Arnold."

For the next few minutes, we chattered on about the history of the pub and its origins several centuries ago during the era of the Great North Wood. Miss Arnold praised her favorite lunch dishes, which included fish and chips and mushy peas, steak and kidney pie, and liver and onions. Holmes kept up the patter and refrained from his familiar observation that "fine English cuisine" was an oxymoron.

Mr. Tanner fetched the lunch dishes and glasses of ale and cider from the counter and served them to the rest of us. After that, we lowered our voices and continued the conversation.

"As you know," said Holmes, "I have been asked to look into the events of five years ago. I refer to the murder of the former butler, Mr. Herman Carter, and the theft of the paintings. Your insights into those events would be most helpful to me. Where do you suggest I should I start with my questions?"

"Well, Mr. Holmes," said Miss Arnold immediately, "if you ask me, and I will have you know that I have been in service in the Fitzguilford house for the past fifteen years, and if you ask me then I would have to say that you should be looking back more then five years, it has in truth been over six years now, to the death of old Viscount Fitzguilford. That is where you should start, if you ask me, Mr. Holmes."

"Is it now?" asked Holmes. "Very well then, pray tell, Miss Arnold, why should I begin there?"

"As I said, Mr. Holmes, I have served in the Fitzguilford house for over fifteen years. When I began, fifteen years ago now, it was a respected and prosperous house, and it was a privilege to serve there. But now? But now it has been reduced to simply me, working as both cook and maid, and Mr.

Tanner, who is unfairly made to do the work of the butler, as well as the groom, as well as the groundskeeper. There are only the two of us still employed at the house."

"That was apparent during our visit," said Holmes. "Kindly return to your claim that I should begin my questions with the death of the former Viscount Fitzguilford."

"Yes, of course, that it what I was getting to Mr. Holmes. Well, the house continued to be a respected place to work until just before the death of the old Viscount. Just over six years ago, Master Geoffrey returned to the house. He had been wandering in America doing goodness knows what for several years. Sowing his wild oats, I suppose. Well, we all called him the prodigal son, and he comes back home and next thing we know, he is terminating the employment of several of the staff. Trusted staff, they were, with many years of service. And out they went. He gave them all a good letter but out they went all the same. And about that time, our dear old Viscount is no longer himself. He's forgetful, and starts using a cane, and is no longer the spry and vigorous gentleman that we all knew him to be. And then and then if he doesn't up and dies."

"That does," said Holmes, "happen to men past a certain age."

"Not to men like the Viscount, it doesn't. If you ask me, Mr. Holmes, his death was very suspicious. Those of us who were left on the staff all thought that, we did. Healthy men do not just up and die, and they especially do not do that just a few weeks after their sons return home from wandering the earth for several years."

"You suspect foul play?" said Holmes.

"All I can say, Mr. Holmes, is that it was very suspicious."

"It could very well be. Now, please, your thoughts on the death of Mr. Herman Carter."

"Herman? Oh, yes, Herman. Well, he had not been on the staff terribly long. Not near as long as I was, Mr. Holmes. And all I can say is that he was more than somewhat attentive to the needs of Lady Fitzguilford. Positively doted on her. He may even have discovered some of the secrets she would rather he had not."

"Secrets, you say? Such as?" asked Holmes.

"Well, every Saturday night, the night before the Sabbath Day, the Lady goes out to meet with some of the other women of the village. She says that it is a reading circle and that they talk about the books they have been reading. But in all the years I have served in the house, that is fifteen years now, I have seldom seen her reading a book. So, if you ask me, Mr. Holmes, if you ask me there is no such reading circle happening at all. No, not at all."

"You don't say. Then what is happening?"

The woman leaned in toward Holmes and lowered her voice.

"The only explanation I can offer is that the lady is part of a coven. They meet every Saturday night, and she comes back into the house just before midnight   just before the start of the Sabbath Day. Does that not sound like a coven to you, Mr. Holmes?"

"If she were a part of such a gathering, that is indeed when they would meet."

"There!" she exclaimed, now looking at the young butler. "I told you so, didn't I, Richard."

"Yes, Miss Arnold, you did," the young man replied.

"That I did, and now you see that Mr. Sherlock Holmes agrees with me. And no one ever knows what a woman will do who has given herself over to the devil, do they, Mr. Holmes?"

"I suppose they do not. What would they do?"

"They can, when they are in their demonic state, commit whatever crime comes into their minds. Theft, perhaps. Even murder. You need to take a good hard look at what the lady might have done. Maybe even aided and abetted by her son. That is where you need to look, Mr. Holmes."

The woman prattled on for several more minutes. When she finally stopped to finish her meal, Holmes turned to the young man who had been promoted from groom to butler.

"And you, Mr. Tanner? What insights do you have to offer?"

The young man cast a quick glance to Miss Arnold and gave a tiny smirk that was seen by Holmes and me but not by her.

"I cannot say anything about covens and their meetings, but I was a groom for the house for several years. During that time, I met Mr. McInerney many times and chatted with him often. He never struck me as the type who would commit theft, let alone murder. I suspect, sir, that he has been framed and is about to be put to death for a crime he did not commit."

"An interesting insight," said Holmes. "Very well, then. If, in your opinion, Mr. McInerney did not commit the crimes, who did?"

The young butler did not appear to have expected Holmes's question and looked perplexed.

"I would have to say, Mr. Holmes, that anyone could have. Master Geoffrey might have been impatient to claim his inheritance. Lady Fitzguilford might have taken drastic measures to keep the old man from squandering any more of the estate. Mother and son might have colluded. Mrs. Agnes McInerney, the unloving wife, might have done the crime with the intent of framing her husband and thus have grounds for getting out of her marriage, possibly with the cooperation of her new husband. The old builder, Mr. Oldacre, was around that day and there was bad blood between him and Mr. McInerney's family. Why, even I could have with the intent of moving up from groom to butler. We all had the opportunity, the motive, and the means. My saying this is, I fear, not at all helpful to you, but it shows you just how impossible it has been for any of us to come to any firm conclusion about those events five years ago."

"No, you have been quite helpful, young man," said Holmes. "However, you made reference to Mr. Jonas Oldacre and touched on something I was not aware of. What bad blood existed between him and the McInerney family?"

"I can only," said Tanner, "pass on the gossip and tales I have heard growing up the village, sir. McInerney's grandfather had the contract to rebuild much of the Chrystal Palace. He is said to have hired the father of Jonas Oldacre, Nigel Oldacre, as one of his workers. Then, one day, Mr. Nigel came to work drunk, and he was given a very public and humiliating lecture by Mr. McInerney and his employment terminated. The sting to the fellow's pride was never forgotten."

"But that," I interjected, "was decades ago. Surely, it would not be a factor in 1898."

"I cannot say, doctor. I am only passing on what I heard."

"For which I am very grateful," said Holmes. "As I am to you as well, Miss Arnold. Your observations and comments have been most instructive."

Our two luncheon guests soon finished their meal and returned to the manor house to fulfill their afternoon responsibilities.

"I fear," I said, "that we just wasted several hours."

"Oh, no. Not entirely," said Holmes.

"Witches covens? The woman is nuttier than a fruitcake. Even I could see the nonsense in that type of talk. The only useful new data was the possible role of Jonas Oldacre."

"He was," said Holmes, "the only name that cannot be added to the list of suspects."

"Why not?" I asked. "You know he had a mind for wicked revenge."

"Yes, but he is dead and buried in the ground somewhere in the vast cemetery for the past four years. Whoever was responsible for attacking you, or hiring as a local thug to do so, is very much alive."

"I suppose so," I said. "But all you have now is a long list of suspects, none of whom can yet be excluded. What are you going to do? Time is passing, and Mr. McInerney's date with the gallows is coming ever closer."

"Right you are, Watson. Rather than taking up valuable time investigating and eliminating all suspects on our list, I am going to cease looking for the murderer."

"What do you mean, cease looking?"

"Only cease looking for the murderer. Instead, we shall look for the missing paintings and hope that they will give us a shortcut to the killer."

Chapter Six
North Side
Trafalgar Square

GREAT BRITAIN'S National Gallery sits majestically on the north side of Trafalgar Square, looking down over the square, the fountains, and Lord Nelson and his lions. Its collection of famous paintings is not the largest in the world, but it is acclaimed for its excellent and encyclopedic selection. Of late, a public trust has been established to fund the purchase of priceless works of art and to stop their being snapped up by

American plutocrats. The current director, Sir Edward John Poynter, has been praised not only for being a competent painter in his own right but for his vigorous program of acquisitions. Fortunately, he was also a dedicated reader of *The Strand* and of the stories about Sherlock Holmes. Upon receiving an urgent request from Holmes, he altered his busy schedule and agreed to meet us the following morning.

"Gentlemen," said the well-dressed and fully bearded man as he welcomed us into his office. "What an honor it is to meet two such famous fellows."

"Sir Edward," I replied, "it is we who are honored. Thank you for making room in your day on such short notice."

"Not at all, not at all. I cannot wait to go home this evening and tell my grandsons that I had Sherlock Holmes in my office. They shall be green with envy. It will certainly give me a standing in their eyes that the Royal Academy and the National Gallery could never come close to."

"Your nephew," I said, "is also quite a famous writer, is he not?"

"The one my grandsons call Barnyard Kipling? Oh, yes, they enjoy his stories about dark-skinned boys running around with wolves and such, but they are nothing compared to having their young spines tingled with your accounts of murderers and traitors brought to justice by Sherlock Holmes. And if, should such a dream be a remote possibility, that I can lay claim to have assisted England's most famous detective in solving a case, why, I shall be elevated to sainthood, I assure you."

We all had a good chuckle and took a seat around his desk, surrounded by high walls that were either covered with paintings or shelves lined with books and portfolio volumes.

"Now, gentleman," continued the baronet, "how may I be of service to you?"

"I am in need," said Holmes, "of some instructions concerning the fate of paintings that are stolen. What becomes of them?"

"Almost all are recovered. Either Scotland Yard finds them, or the detectives from Lloyd's track them down so that they do not have to pay out an insurance claim. The thieves are tried and sent off to prison. Those are the stories we tell the public so that our police will appear to be heroes and would-be thieves deterred from snatching any more of our collection."

"And the stories you do not tell?" asked Holmes.

"Ah, yes. What we do not tell are the stories where thieves kidnapped a famous painting and held it for ransom. We have had to make some rather large settlements over the years to a few enterprising art thieves. We do not release those stories to the Press. If we did, then every common miscreant and his uncle would be raiding our public galleries and private collections and kidnapping famous works of art. However, permit me to ask, Mr. Holmes, are you here concerning a recent theft of a painting? Do tell."

"You are, sir," said Holmes, "aware of the theft of a number of works five years ago from the private gallery of Viscount Fitzguilford of Norwood?"

"Oh, I am indeed. Why that is the grand-daddy of them all. Ten paintings all gone in a few minutes. Not one of them ever found or even heard of. And the butler murdered to boot. Is that what brings you here, Mr. Holmes? How splendid. The grandsons will be thrilled to hear me tell about this. A fortune in paintings gone and the butler with a bullet to the head and a chisel to the heart. Oh, they will be thrilled indeed. Oh, yes, please. How can I be of any assistance to you?"

"At any time over the past five years, has anyone approached the National Gallery offering to sell the missing paintings to you?"

"No, sir. No once. Not even the faintest hint."

"Would you know if they have tried to sell to any of the other major galleries of Great Britain or abroad?"

"Yes, we do know, and no they have not. No other gallery has been offered any of those paintings."

"And how do you know that, sir?"

"It is not difficult, Mr. Holmes. If a theft occurs at any gallery, or museum, or from a private collection, all of the potential buyers for that work of art are notified. We have a list of the names and addresses of all of the directors, and as soon as a theft takes place, a photograph of the work is put in the mail."

"And what keeps an ambitious gallery from agreeing to purchase the work?"

"We would be fools, any of us, to even think of doing so. Any work presented to us must show its provenance. Those without a verified provenance simply cannot be considered. Galleries and museums do not purchase valuable pieces so that we can keep them in our warehouses. We exhibit them. We show off our latest acquisitions to our patrons and the public. If we were to purchase a stolen piece, even one with a fraudulent provenance, the word would be out in a minute. Either the police, who cooperate with the police forces from all countries, would demand that we surrender the works or Lloyd's or some such insurance firm would be knocking on our doors removing them from us."

"And should someone refuse to hand them over?" asked Holmes.

"Impossible, sir. That institution would never again be able to purchase insurance for their collection. Such a turn of events would be ruinous."

"But what about a private collector? Some American, perhaps, with more money than God?"

"Oh, there are several of them, but the same applies. Unless he is an exceptionally odd duck who wishes to hang the Mona Lisa in his private loo so he can lovingly have her all to himself, he mounts the work in his private gallery and shows it off to all his friends. Why else would he buy it?"

"Yes, that does make sense. Now then, about the ten pieces stolen from Norwood I assume that a notice was sent out to every potential buyer throughout the world. Is that correct?"

"Quite so, Mr. Holmes. Of course, that was five years ago. Since then Lloyd's has sent several follow-on notices. To the best of my memory, nothing has been sent out in the past year. Would you like our office to send one?"

"If you would be so kind."

"More than happy to. I will have my secretary find the list from our files and get that out in the post."

"Thank you, Sir Edward. In the interest of time, I have a copy of the list with me. Please just use it and save your office the effort."

Holmes extracted a folded piece of paper from his suit pocket and handed it to the director. He took a quick look at it and was about to call his secretary when he stopped and took a second look. He continued to stare at the list for some time, and I noticed that his brow had furled and that he was shaking his head ever so gently.

"Is there a problem with the list, Sir Edward?" asked Holmes.

"Yes, there is. My memory may not be quite as sharp as it was forty years ago, but this is not a correct list of the paintings stolen from the Fitzguilford collection."

"Not correct?"

"No. I recall several of these being on the official notices that were sent out by Scotland Yard and Lloyd's. But there are some that are new to me. And where are the Degas pieces? Please, gentlemen, wait here for just a minute."

He stood and walked out of the room. Two minutes later he reappeared holding Holmes's list in one hand and another sheet of paper in another.

"This, gentlemen, is the most recent list circulated by Lloyd's. Only half of the list corresponds to yours."

He laid the two lists side by side in front of us. Five of the works on Holmes's list were on the other sheet. Five others were not. The list from Lloyd's included four works by Degas and a *Self Portrait: Miniature*, by Rembrandt.

"This is interesting," said Holmes. "What of these paintings on my list that are not on yours? Do you have any record of their having been stolen as well?"

"No, and if you want, I can tell you exactly where they all are."

"Please, sir."

"They are hanging in Viscount Fitzguilford's gallery in Norwood," said Sir Edward.

"Are you certain of that, sir?" asked Holmes.

"Completely. We received a notice just recently that they would be put up for auction next month."

"Indeed? And by whom was the notice sent?"

"From Sotheby's, naming the current Viscount Fitzguilford as the owner. Just a moment, I shall have my secretary find it for you."

Again, he stood and exited the room, returning shortly with a large envelope in his hand. From it, he extracted a stack of photographs. Each one had a piece of paper attached to it, giving the name, the dimensions, and the provenance of the work that was to be put up to auction. He laid the lot out on the table and moved five of the photographs to the part of the table immediately in front of us.

"These are the ones on your list, Mr. Holmes the ones by Raphael, Titian, Fra Angelico, and Botticelli and the full-sized self-portrait by Rembrandt. Are you familiar with these works?"

Holmes nodded slowly. I knew that he recognized them as did I. Even though we were only been inside the Fitzguilford gallery for a brief few minutes, we saw these paintings hanging on the walls. It was not as if we could not have noticed. All of them were of substantial size, with heavy frames and prominently displayed.

"And you did say, did you not," said Holmes. "That on the lists sent by Scotland Yard and Lloyd's were five works that are not on my list."

"That is correct, Mr. Holmes. If you can wait for just one more minute, I shall fetch you one of their notices."

Again, he departed and returned with another envelope. In it were photographs of five of the paintings on our lists as well as four that I did not recognize but looked like something recent from Paris, and one small sketch of Rembrandt.

"These four are all by Degas." Said Sir Edward. "His early work from Paris and New Orleans was not particularly interesting, history paintings mostly, but starting about twenty years ago he joined the Impressionists and became somewhat consumed with sketches, oil paintings and even small sculptures of young ballerinas. These four pieces that were taken from Norwood are not amongst his most substantial, but they are growing in value with every passing day. The miniature self-portrait by Rembrandt is nowhere near as valuable as the forty two-foot by three-foot oil paintings he did of himself, but it would fetch several thousand pounds all the same."

"And how might they compare in value to the five on my list that are still in the gallery in Norwood?" asked Holmes.

"A fraction of the value of those ones. The Titian, the Raphael, and the Botticelli are each worth tens of thousands of pounds."

Holmes spent another minute in silence gazing at the photographs in front of him before turning to the director.

"Are you planning to bid on these when they are put up next month?"

"Ah, I so wish we could. But our budget for this year is all spoken for. We already have several Titians and an entire room full of Raphaels. I recently acquired another Botticelli, bringing us to five and we have a score of Rembrandts. Of course, if you could find the other five that were stolen, we would be interested. The Rembrandt of *The Storm on the Sea of Galilee* is the only seascape he ever did. And there are only thirty-four Vermeers extant. His *The Concert* is priceless. So, do let us know, Mr. Holmes, if you have any success in finding them. Now, is there anything else with which we can assist you?"

"No, Sir. You have been most helpful. I will make sure that you are apprised of any success we might have in finding the missing paintings."

"An honor to do so, Mr. Holmes. Might it be useful to you if I were to give you the name of the agent over at Lloyd's who has been working on the theft, quite diligently I am told, for the past five years?"

"That would be very helpful indeed, Sir."

"And were you aware, Mr. Holmes, that Lloyd's has recently increased the reward they are offering from five thousand up to ten thousand pounds?"

"Merciful heavens," I blurted. "Why, that is a fortune."

"That it is," said Sir Edward. "But it is a small fraction of what the paintings are now worth."

We bade the man good day and strolled out of the Gallery. At the top of the great staircase that led down into Trafalgar Square, Holmes stopped, sat down on a bench, and pulled out his pipe. Part way into his second pipe, he turned to me.

"This case has become curiouser and curiouser, Watson. What we just learned makes no sense."

"Could Mr. McInerney have become confused?" I asked. "Could his memory have become muddled during his time in prison?"

"Possibly, but highly unlikely. He was very clear in his memory of selecting the paintings along with Lady Fitzguilford. He did note that all of them were of substantial size. It would be very strange if he were to misremember wrapping and lifting ten large paintings into his wagon when five of them were smaller pieces. And the list he gave us was explicit. During the past five years in prison, he has had very little else to think about, and he has, as he said, burned that list into his memory."

"As you say, Holmes. It makes no sense. Assuming he is innocent and someone else removed the paintings from his wagon, why would the thief put five very valuable works back on the wall and then remove five of lesser value?"

Holmes puffed for another minute before answering.

"I have absolutely no idea. So, I suggest that we make good use of our time and pay a visit to this fellow over at Lloyd's. He may have some insights that we do not."

Chapter Seven
According to Lloyd's

WE CROSSED Trafalgar Square and hailed a cab in front of Nelson's column. A quick trip along The Strand and Fleet Street brought us to the Royal Exchange and the offices of Lloyd's of London. Holmes gave his card to the clerk at the desk and asked if we might speak to Mr. Dirk Savage in the theft recovery unit. After a very short wait a man of some forty years, attired appropriately, walked into the lobby and greeted us.

"Dr. Watson and Mr. Sherlock Holmes. I have long expected that our paths would cross some day. And now here you are. Have you had any lunch? May I suggest that we get away from this gloomy labyrinth and enjoy a pint and a sandwich. There is a charming small pub around the corner on Finch Street that is a favorite of those of us who are assigned to chasing criminals. Will you join me?"

The Cock and Woolpack was certainly small and out of the way. After giving our order to the barkeep, the man from Lloyd's led us to a table in the back corner.

"My spies tell me," he began, "that Sherlock Holmes is looking into the McInerney case in Lower Norwood. Be assured, sir, that Lloyd's of London welcomes that news and will be pleased to assist you in any way we can."

"Assist?" said Holmes. "Are you interested in assisting me merely to find the stolen paintings or does your assistance include stopping the execution of a man who may be innocent?"

Mr. Savage nodded and smiled back at Holmes.

"The fact that he is still alive, sir, is a direct result of our persistent efforts to keep him from the gallows. Our purpose in doing so has not been to avoid a terrible miscarriage of justice. That, sir, is the responsibility of the police, the Crown, his personal lawyers, and now you. The responsibility of Lloyd's is to our mutual policy holders and to avoid the very serious financial liability that would be incurred were we to have to make full payment for the missing paintings. If, Mr. Holmes, we can both accept our separate roles, I expect that we shall be able to work together for the benefit of the several parties whose interests we represent. Would you agree, sir?"

"That is an agreeable basis for cooperation," said Holmes. "Allow me, sir, as time is increasingly of the essence, to begin with a straightforward question. Do you believe my client to be innocent or guilty of the murder and theft for which he has been convicted?"

"Forgive me, Mr. Holmes, if I separate your question. No, sir, I do not believe Lester McInerney murdered Herman Carter. I am quite certain he is innocent of that charge. As to the theft, I have come, over time, to believe that it is likely, although not entirely certain, that he is not guilty of that charge either."

"Thank you," said Holmes. "Would you mind explaining the reasons for your conclusions?"

"Not at all. I have read that you request your clients to be as concise and precise as possible. I shall endeavor to do the same. Beginning with the murder — did you read the coroner's report?"

"I regret that I have not yet had that opportunity. My understanding is that it concluded that death had been brought about by both a bullet to the head and a chisel driven into the heart."

"Correct, sir. It also noted that there was profuse bleeding from the head, as would be expected. However, there was minimal bleeding from the deep wound to the chest."

He stopped for a moment to allow his statement to be absorbed. I responded.

"Then the chisel must have been stabbed into the heart some time after the man was dead from the bullet in his brain."

"Yes, doctor. My expertise, such as it is, is in the recovery of stolen property, not conducting an autopsy, but what you have said makes sense. That is what must have happened. And, Mr. Holmes, please tell me. How many murderers do you know who kill their victims by shooting them in the head and then return several minutes later and drive a chisel into their hearts?"

"I do not recall any criminals doing so recently. Mind you, that does not preclude the possibility."

"I agree. However, if you add the act of selecting a chisel which is known to be one of your possessions and on which your fingerprints are clearly visible, does it seem much less likely."

"It does."

"Now, Mr. Holmes, I understand that you have had only one opportunity to meet with Mr. McInerney. Is that correct?"

"It is."

"Did he strike you as a man intent on ending his own life when he had the opportunity of acting in a way that would save his life?"

"He did not."

"That was my conclusion as well, sir. I have met with Lester McInerney at least ten times over the past five years. I did so because I believed that even if he were not guilty of the murder, he was the most likely suspect in the theft of the paintings. On every occasion, I made it explicitly clear to him that if he were to confess to the murder and theft of the paintings and reveal their whereabouts, it was probable that we could intervene on his behalf and have his death sentence revised to a long prison term. His response to our offer never varied. He consistently denied any knowledge of the theft. So, either he is a demented fool who belongs in Broadmoor, or he was telling us the truth. The latter is the only conclusion we reached. Even with his execution now only days away, he has not altered his position. He has lost any possibility he might have had to enrich his life by the sale of the art work. It makes no sense. Does it to you, Mr. Holmes?"

"No, sir, it does not. Now, kindly state your conclusions with respect to the theft."

"In addition to what I have already said, I must add to it the absence of any news of the possible sale of the ten paintings to any gallery, museum, or private collector. I assume you are aware, sir, that we are a very large firm, and that we retain agents and informers throughout the world who assist us in recovering stolen items."

"I am aware. I have made use of some of your people myself in the recent past."

"You have? Excellent. Then you know that whilst they may not be paragons of virtue, they are all eager to receive their share of one of the largest rewards ever offered should they assist in the recovery of stolen chattel."

"I am."

"The response to our offer has been resounding silence. Not a peep from anyone. Those paintings are not on the market anywhere in the world."

"Ah, but that does not mean that Mr. McInerney could not have secreted them away somewhere and is of such a twisted mind as to imagine that it is worth dying for to have them provide riches in the future for some individual or cause."

"Correct, sir. I assure you that we considered that possibility and searched the fellow's entire private life. He has no history of involvement in any radical political or religious cause and his wife and children, having abandoned him, are already quite financially comfortable, thank you very much."

"Very well, pray continue," said Holmes.

"He claimed that he finished the selection and wrapping of the paintings at half-past eleven—and that was verified by the testimony of Lady Fitzguilford—and that, after taking nearly half an hour for his lunch, he departed from the house gate in Lower Norwood at noon—a fact that was corroborated by the groom. He took an hour to travel into Chelsea, to the shop of the framer—which was verified by the framer, along with confirming that McInerney appeared shocked and horrified by the absence of the pictures in his wagon and departed immediately. The police on the site, who had arrived by the time he returned, agreed that it was a minute or two before two o'clock when he returned with his wagon to the house."

"I am following you so far," said Holmes. "What is your point?"

"My point, sir, is that I subsequently went and rented the same wagon and same horse from the same livery service. And I loaded it with ten wrapped objects of comparable size and weight. At noon hour on the same day of the week, I then timed myself and drove it from the house in Lower Norwood to Chelsea, opened and shut the wagon, said hello to the framer in his shop, and then turned and galloped the horse all the way back to the house. Even running the horse at as fast as I could dare, I could not return to the house in less time than McInerney did. He must have whipped the horse mercilessly all the way back. I did the same experiment the following week but that time stopped at a spot along the way and unloaded the wrapped paintings. It added a full twenty minutes to my time. Even exerting myself and galloping the horse, I could not have made it there and back as quickly as he did."

"Ah," said Holmes, "so you are saying that McInerney's account of his time that day must be truthful and that he could not possibly have disposed of ten paintings in the time allotted to him. Interesting, pray continue."

"Finally, sir, there is the matter of which paintings were stolen."

"You are referring," said Holmes, "to the two different lists and the five paintings that appear to have been exchanged after the initial theft."

"Exactly, sir. Lloyd's was notified the following morning of the theft, and I was on the property by that same afternoon. The paintings that had been taken corresponded with the list supplied later to me by Lester McInerney. Ten paintings, all of significant size and value were gone. A week later, when the formal claim was submitted, five of the ones on the list had reappeared on the gallery walls, and five smaller, less valuable ones had been removed."

"Who filed the claim?"

"Geoffrey Fitzguilford, the new Viscount."

"And your conclusions, sir?"

"It is entirely speculation, Mr. Holmes, but I came to the only explanation possible."

"I am familiar with the process."

"On the day of the murder, the paintings must have never left the manor house. During the period from 11:30 until noon, they must have been taken off the wagon and moved back into the house, most likely through the entrance into the basement. They must have been hidden there at least overnight, possibly longer, after which five of them were exchanged for the ones that were subsequently reported as stolen."

"May I," asked Holmes, "assume that you searched the entire house thoroughly?"

"I assure you, sir, that Lloyd's did not become the largest firm in the world offering insurance on valuable movable property by being incompetent. Of course, we searched the house. I sent five trained and experienced men to go through the place from stem to gudgeon. We went through every corner, every closet, every hiding space under the eaves everywhere. I was fully aware of the wicked scheme of Mr.

Jonas Oldacre as you revealed in the account of your story about him some years earlier. As he was the builder of the new gallery and conservatory, I had my men measure every floor and hallway to see if there might be a secret compartment hiding behind some wall. But, I assure you, there was none to be found. There was a small closet in the basement that was not easily discerned, but it was empty.

"It was argued," continued Mr. Savage, "that McInerney fabricated the story about his lunch and removed the paintings from his wagon and put them in the basement. The prosecution claimed that Mr. Carter, the butler, came upon him whilst he was in the act, and that McInerney shot him."

"Is that possible?" asked Holmes. "You would then have to hypothesize that after shooting him, our boy went back to his wagon and fetched a chisel that was marked with his fingerprints, returned to the body and rammed the chisel into the heart of a man that was already dead. He was immediately taken into custody after he returned to the house from his trip to Chelsea and so could not have exchanged the five paintings at some later date. And, as you noted at the outset, he would have to be *non compos mentis* to go to the gallows to protect the knowledge of the stolen paintings."

"I agree, completely," said Mr. Savage. "For all those reasons, I eliminated McInerney from my list of suspects."

"And who did you leave on the list?"

"I left the young scion of the estate, Geoffrey. It was rumored that he might have hastened the death of his father, only to discover that the estate was near bankrupt. He needed the money, so he might have stolen the paintings thinking that he could get quick cash from Lloyd's and avoid the time it would take to have them sent to Sotheby's. Perhaps he met the butler whilst removing the paintings from the wagon and killed him to avoid being exposed."

"And is he still on your list?"

"No, for several reasons. He had no reason to exchange the paintings. And if he were desperate for the money, he would have tried to sell them or demand a ransom payment. Neither has happened. And have you met the fellow, Mr. Holmes?"

"I have."

"As have I, several times. I know it is only my instinct, but he strikes me as an arrogant, obnoxious twit. He has no spine at all. It takes a certain amount of fortitude to pull out a gun and blow a man's brains out, and he seems to me like the type who would turn and run away from an altercation on the double. Would you agree?"

Holmes turned to me. "Doctor Watson, you have dealt with men on the battlefield. What are your thoughts? Would Geoffrey have had the intestinal fortitude to kill a man?"

It did not take me long to respond. "No, I would not have wanted him in my regiment. He's a soft one."

"My thoughts too, doctor," said Savage.

"Who does that leave?" asked Holmes.

The Lloyd's man shrugged his shoulders. "My only other possible suspect was old Jonas Oldacre. He was around that morning at the house and perhaps it was he. But we shall never know as he is dead and buried."

"I think not," said Holmes. "You are not aware that yesterday, Dr. Watson was attacked in the cemetery by some ruffian thinking that the doctor was I. I do not believe that the ghost of Jonas Oldacre was responsible for ordering the attack and so I must conclude that whoever was behind it is quite alive and was not pleased to have me poking around."

He turned to me and asked me to give an account of what had happened. I did as he requested.

"Hmm, yes, that is interesting," said Savage. "I suppose you must be right on that one. Mind you, sir, I have been poking around the case for over five years, and no one living or dead has held a knife to my throat. Of course, I am not Sherlock Holmes."

On that note, he sat back in his chair and sipped slowly on his ale. Holmes did the same and added a cigarette to his reflection.

"There was one other thing," said Savage, when he had finished his ale.

"I am all attention," said Holmes.

"It was merely a scrap of gossip, but it has nagged at me, and I have no explanation. On one of my many visits to Lower Norwood, I stopped at *The Horns* for a spot of lunch. The place was all but empty, and the barmaid was up for a chat and asked me about why I was visiting. I told her and, of course, asked if she had heard anything. Barmaids, as you know, overhear all sorts of things that are connected to crimes and affairs and what not. No, she says to me that she had never heard anything direct about it, but that her dear friend, another barmaid named Bessie, had been told something by the cook, who had heard it from the barkeep, who had it from one of the regular patrons, who had said that another regular patron, an older woman named Mrs. Lexington who is now deceased, had said once when well into her cups, that the silly fool from Lloyd's—and she must have been referring to me—was wasting his time looking all over the house. If he wanted to know what happened, the answer was back in the cemetery.

"I had no idea what she could have been referring to. I thought of looking about the cemetery and even had my men walk through it, but there are forty acres and several thousand graves. I had no idea what to tell them to look for, and nothing came of it. Unless you have any suggestions, Mr. Holmes, that is all I can tell you. You now know everything I do, and I suspect you are equally befuddled."

"I am, sir, I am. You have been most generous with your time, and I am very grateful. If I should ever come across any morsel of evidence that might lead you to your lost paintings, I will inform you immediately."

"That is all I can ask for, and I thank you, sir," said Savage.

We departed the pub and hailed a cab to take Holmes back to Baker Street and me to my home up past Paddington.

"My dear doctor," said Holmes, as he stepped out of the cab. "Thank you for accompanying me and please accept my apologies for the attack you had to endure when it should have been visited on me."

"I prefer to think," I said, "that the other chap got the worst of it. And Holmes, was not Lexington the name of the woman who served as the housekeeper to Jonas Oldacre?"

"It was. Now, do give my warmest regards to you dear wife and have a pleasant evening."

"And you as well, my friend," I said. "But Holmes, why is there a very expensive private carriage parked in front of your home? Turn around, and you will see what I mean."

Holmes turned and looked at the gleaming carriage, attached to a brace of magnificent black horses, that was standing directly in front of the door of 221B Baker Street.

"Watson, when you do return home to your wife, kindly extend my profuse apologies for keeping you away from your home even longer than had been expected. I appear to have a visitor and must request that you join me in meeting him."

Chapter Eight
According to Husband Two

"YOU HAVE A VISITOR," said Mrs. Hudson as she met us at the door. "I must say, you have *quite* the visitor."

"Do I now?" replied Holmes. "Well then, we mustn't keep him waiting." He gave the long-suffering Mrs. Hudson a mischievous wink to which she responded by rolling her eyes.

We entered the front room to see a very large man standing by the hearth and glaring at us. It would be more accurate if I were to describe him as not merely large, but massive and rotund. I would have put him at eighteen stone and maybe a bit more.

"Mr. Sherlock Holmes," he stated in a voice that reminded me of a fog horn. "I am Sir Humphrey Fallingbrook, and I warn you that I am not a man to be trifled with. I assume you know who I am."

"Ah, yes," said Holmes as he sat down. "You are the fellow who is known in the City and by his employees as Sir Humpty Falstaff-and-a-half. Please have a seat, but do descend gently on the furniture."

A red tinge immediately appeared on the face of our visitor.

"Just who do you think you are?" he shouted. "I have broken many men far more powerful than you, Holmes. And I will not hesitate to break you as well."

Holmes leaned back in his chair, clasping his hands behind his head.

"Did you ask, who do I think I am? I suppose I could say that I am one who treats threats as trifles and finds them highly amusing. So, if you wish to entertain me, continue with your performance. Otherwise, be seated and state your case and we shall both chat as gentlemen. It is your decision, sir."

For a moment, I thought the monstrous fellow was about to tear Holmes limb from limb, and I felt my hand reaching into my pocket and grasping my service revolver. However, the man slowly sat down in the chair behind him and crossed his enormous forearms in front of his chest.

"I have learned that you have taken on the case of Lester McInerney. Is that correct?"

"It is, and how does that concern you, sir?"

"My purpose in coming here is to have you agree to remove yourself from the case and have nothing further to with it. I am prepared to offer you two hundred pounds on the spot if you will agree to do so. Will you accept my offer? Yes or no?"

"Oh, my good man," said Holmes, smiling, "the reward for finding the lost paintings is ten thousand pounds. Why should I accept two hundred? You are a man of business, Sir Humphrey. Explain to me why I should accept your paltry offer."

"Ten thousand pounds? I do not believe you. Who would ever offer that much for a few paintings?"

"Lloyd's of London would. You may ask them yourself. Shall I give you the address of their office?"

"Blast you I know where the Lloyd's office is. I have over a hundred policies with them. Very well, Mr. Holmes. I shall offer you eleven thousand pounds to vacate this case. That is my final offer. Take it or leave it."

Holmes pulled out his pipe and slowly lit it.

"I leave it."

"You what! Are you insane, Holmes?" the fellow bellowed. "I have just given you the chance to become a rich man. What sort of fool are you?"

"Permit me to enlighten you, sir. Had I wished to become a rich man, I would have entered your line of work, not mine. As it is, I consider myself to be rich beyond my wildest imaginings, having had my heart and soul rewarded so many times over during the past twenty years. If I may be so candid, sir, you might want to try my path sometime. You would sleep much more soundly at night and not be required to attend so many horribly boring dinners."

"Holmes, I am warning you. I do not take lightly to being taunted. I also have detectives at my beck and call, and I can have them look into every hidden corner of your existence, expose you, and ruin you."

"I assume that these detectives of yours know that your firm is offering a new tranche of shares to the City next week. Over a million pounds is expected, if I recall correctly. Do your detectives also know that the unions in your mill in Birmingham took a secret vote last week to authorize a strike? Do they know that the government of Mexico is moving to nationalize your plantation there? Shall I continue, sir? I suspect that your stock offering would be in far greater peril than my modest practice."

The great fellow's face had gone from red to white. "How, in the devil's name, do you know about all that?"

"My good man, I *am* Sherlock Holmes, and it is my business to know things. But please, I assure you, I have no interest in taking your money and less in doing battle with you. What I *am* compelled to be interested in is why you are coming to me. Might I guess that it is because of your wife?"

The man's demeanor changed immediately. He leaned back in his chair, took out his handkerchief and wiped his brow.

"Yes, Mr. Holmes, it is."

"Watson," said Holmes to me. "A round of brandies would be in order. Would you mind terribly?"

"Not at all."

"Now, sir," continued Holmes. "Your wife—Agnes is her name is it not? —is the former wife of Mr. Lester McInerney. Is that correct?"

"Yes."

"Then please state your case as to why, for her sake, you wish me to abandon the case of her former husband."

I handed Sir Humphrey a generous brandy, which he swallowed in three gulps and then handed me the empty glass with the unspoken request that it be refilled. His second glass was consumed much more slowly, and he appeared to be rehearsing what he was about to say to Homes as he sipped.

"As a husband, I am deeply concerned for my wife's tender feelings," he began.

"Oh, please, sir," said Holmes. "If we are going to have this conversation could you kindly refrain from wasting both my time and yours? The lady you refer to, Mrs. Agnes, is your second wife. You did not care a fig for the feelings of your first wife who, it is well known, allowed herself to acquire a shape not unlike your own and was not capable of having children. You paid her off handsomely and sent her to live in America. Then you married your current wife, and whatever it is that now concerns you, I am certain it is not her tender feelings. Please, sir. Start over and do try to be candid. Your story, please."

Sir Humphrey pursed his lips and gave a small nod. He smiled at Holmes the smile that a chap gives to another chap to indicate that a man-to-man talk is underway.

"It appears that you already know much of my story, Mr. Holmes. Perhaps you do not know how it began, so allow me to enlighten you. Eight years ago, I was in Paris on matters related to one of my firms. One afternoon, I was invited by my guests to attend what the Parisians call a *salon*. It was a pleasant if silly affair in which the various participants tried to impress each other with their cleverness. I was bored and began to chat with the woman beside me who, I was delighted to learn, was also English. She was stunningly beautiful, exceptionally articulate, and was kind enough to laugh at my poor attempts at humor. By the end of the afternoon, Mrs. Agnes McInerney had captured my heart."

"Your heart, sir?" asked Holmes. "Would it not be more accurate to say she captured the organ in nether region below your heart?"

I had to speak up. "Oh, come, come, Holmes," I said. "you know perfectly well that for the entire male population except for yourself, the is no difference between the two."

Holmes smiled and our visitor chuckled. "I stand corrected. Pray continue, sir."

"For a man in my position, it was imperative that he be accompanied to affairs of state and international commerce by an exceptional woman. My wife was no longer suitable for that role, and I bribed her—it cost me near twenty thousand pounds—to agree to a divorce. She signed a false confession stating that she had committed adultery and moved to America. She now enjoys a splendid existence in Chicago where she presides over an entire army of dowagers. She is much happier."

"That," said Holmes, "I can believe. Continue, sir."

"I had kept in contact with Agnes McInerney, in an entirely honorable manner, of course, and was at first horrified when I read of the arrest of her husband. My horror, however, soon turned to a vision of opportunity. When Lester was convicted of murder and sentenced to death, I came to her side and offered to be her protector."

"By that you mean, her financier," said Holmes.

"Come, come, Holmes," I said. "Again, you know that the two are one and the same."

"Point taken. Please continue."

"She was destitute, and I rescued her. I provided her with monthly funds to pay for a decent life in a respectable neighborhood and good schools for her children. The children, whom I am now thrilled to call my son and daughter, are paragons of beauty and promise. They   "

"Please, sir," interrupted Holmes. "Whatever they may be, they are utterly unimportant to the matters at hand. Kindly get through your story and explain what has brought you to my house."

"I suppose you are right. I will attempt to be more concise. Very well, then. I decided that Agnes should become my wife and I discussed the matter with a bishop whom I had come to know. In return for a very generous donation to his latest eponymous project, Agnes was granted an annulment of her marriage to Lester. She resigned herself to his punishment, appeared to put the matter behind her, and we were married. However, as you know, Lester was not hanged. His execution kept being postponed for months and then years. Each time his execution date approached, she acquired a calm, a sense of serenity. But then with each postponement, she became highly distraught. She was not herself and acted very nervously. She shouted at the children and the help."

"And at you?" asked Holmes.

"Yes, and at me. Then, as time passed, she calmed down again. During the past few months, as Lester's date with the hangman approached, she seemed utterly at peace and a joy to be married to. Then she learned that Lester had engaged the services of Sherlock Holmes and she flew into a terrible state of nerves. She knows your reputation, Mr. Holmes, and she believes that she will spend the rest of her life having to face the emotional turmoil that will come as you secure one postponement after another of his death. She is utterly distraught at that prospect. In truth, she has become completely unmanageable and impossible to live with. That is why I came to see if I could force you to give up the case."

Holmes re-lit his pipe and sat back in his chair. Sir Humphrey sipped on his brandy. For a full two minutes, neither of them spoke.

"You may assure your wife, sir, that there will be no more postponements of any magnitude. Within a month from today, Lester McInerney will either be dead or a free man. That is the best I can tell you. You will have to live with whatever consequences take place. I suspect that you do not need me to remind you that it is a truth, universally acknowledged, that a man with a vast fortune who marries a highly spirited woman brings down no end of turmoil upon himself. In your case, I suspect the situation is made even worse by the realization that your wife once loved another man in a way that she will never love you."

Our visitor swallowed the last of his brandy and stood up.

"I fear you may be right, Mr. Holmes. I apologize for my behavior earlier and wish you good day."

He made his way down the steps. A few seconds later we heard his carriage pull away from the curb.

"Would you," I asked, "put it past him to have had a hand in framing Lester McInerney?"

"No, I would not. And frankly, I would not put it past his wife."

"Holmes, you cannot be serious."

"The most winning woman I ever knew "

"I know about her, Holmes. That was years ago. Surely, you do not think this one could have become so vile."

"A woman's preference in men can change. There is no accounting for taste."

I was not inclined to argue with him and enjoyed the remaining sips of my brandy before rising to return home. I bade Holmes a good day, descended the stairs and stepped out on to Baker Street. In doing so, I very nearly bumped into a young woman who was about to ring our bell.

Chapter Nine
According to the Ex-Wife

"ARE YOU DR. WATSON?" she said, beaming a radiant smile at me. "I do hope you are not leaving, are you? If you can stay just a few minutes longer, I promise it will provide interesting content for your stories."

She did not wait for an answer and breezed past me and up the stairs. I resigned myself to an apology to my dear wife for holding up supper and followed the woman. I must confess, the fact that she was exceptionally attractive might have played a small part in my decision.

I entered the front room immediately behind her. Without waiting for an introduction, she breezed her way into the parlor and took a seat on the sofa and removed her bonnet, displaying a gorgeous countenance and head of perfectly coiffed blonde hair.

"Good evening, Mr. Sherlock Holmes. Did you have a pleasant chat with my husband, Sir Humpty? Oh, please, no need to stand up. Not on my behalf."

Holmes, for once was speechless and stared at her in amazement. He sat up straight and recovered.

"Mrs. Agnes Fallingbrook, I presume."

"The one and only. Sir Humpty said he was coming to see you, so I followed him. I waited in the cab until I saw my husband depart and then came to make sure that England's most famous detective received a true account of events and could act accordingly. Are you interested?"

She was smiling warmly at Holmes and then turned to me.

"Oh, please, Doctor. Do be seated. I am sure you will want to take complete notes on what I have to say. I would not want to miss a chance to appear in one of your wonderful stories. I find them utterly irresistible."

I nodded, sat down, and pulled out my notebook and pencil. Without waiting for either Holmes or me to say anything, she began her story.

"Let me guess, gentlemen. Did my husband tell you that we met at some salon in the Sixth Arrondissement? That's what he tells everyone. It makes the two of us seem so much more *sophistiqué*. The truth is that it was in a café in Montmartre. Lester and I had had a charming little flat and studio there, and I worked as a barmaid over the lunch hour. Humpty walked in demanding lunch, in English, loudly. I recognized him straight away but did not let on, but I did smile at him and chatted in English. He was quite pleased and stayed well past the lunch hour, consuming far too many glasses of French liquor. At three o'clock, he made a very indecent proposition to me. I had no interest in agreeing but, I confess, Mr. Holmes, I did recognize an opportunity.

"I told him to wait for a few minutes whilst I changed my clothes. I quickly donned a more flattering dress and exited the back of the café and ran and found a photographer friend of ours and told him to follow me. For the next two hours, I led the oaf into some of the most degenerate haunts of the *demi-monde*. He was drunk and was having a rollicking good time, and the photographer kept taking pictures of him not only with me but with any number of *madams et mademoiselles*. The photographs were, shall I say, unfortunately compromising. At seven o'clock, I put him in a cab and sent him back to his hotel down in the Fourth. He was quite inebriated, and I am sure remembered very little of our adventure.

"The photographer worked through the night to develop several sets of prints, one of which was delivered to Humpty's hotel first thing in the morning. I put a charming little note in with them telling him how much I enjoyed our intimate time together and thought he would like to have the photos as a reminder of our *rendezvous*. The photographer, I informed him, had offered them for sale for a mere five hundred pounds."

"You blackmailed him?" I said. "Madam, that is a serious felony."

"Oh, no, doctor. I was merely an agent offering to sell several pieces of art. They were truly wonderful photographs, and the price was a bargain. One day they would be worth far more. It was an investment, you could say. Every young artist in Montmartre was using the same line trying to sell paintings to American tourists. It was completely in keeping with how the French do business. Not surprisingly, Humpty purchased them. The photographer took one hundred pounds, and Lester and I lived on the remaining four hundred. Of course, I could not tell Lester. He is a bit of a lovable fool with no head at all for money, but he is honest and would never have let me away with it. But we could not live on the meager allowance his mother was sending. So, I carefully managed the funds until it was time to return to England.

"Our little family had our ups and downs back in our flat in Norwood, and I could see that we would end up in the poorhouse if I did not do something, so I made some inquiries about Sir Humphrey Fallingbrook. I discovered that his wife had divorced him and gone to America. Therefore, I paid him a visit. He was, I dare say, not entirely pleased to see me. I told him that he had the opportunity to become a patron of the arts by being the benefactor of an emerging young English artist. It would only require a donation of thirty pounds every month. Now wasn't that a splendid opportunity, Mr. Holmes?"

"And you included a reminder of the photographs, I assume."

"Why of course. The surprising thing was that when we met each month for him to entrust me with his donation, we started to get along. Any woman knows that when a man feels good about himself when he is with you he is quickly convinced that he is in love with you. And, I confess, I had become reasonably adept at the fine art of flattering rich men. Soon, he was asking to meet more often. We had delightful lunches at Simpsons, and the Langham, and the Dorchester. And my family lived acceptably well. But after a short time, he shocked me and said that he thought I should be his wife. Such a thought was impossible as I was married to Lester.

"Then, Mr. Holmes, he asked a very strange question. He asked me if anything, perhaps a terrible accident, were to happen to Lester, and I were to become a widow, would I accept his proposal of marriage. I gave him an honest answer. My own family is not at all wealthy, and I would be destitute if Lester were gone. I told him that a young widow with two children would have no alternative but to be practical and, of course, I would accept his offer. Frankly, I would accept a proposal of marriage from any rich man who was willing to support me and my children. One does have to be practical, you know.

"Mr. Holmes, that conversation took place whilst we were sitting in Simpsons on the fifteenth day of October 1898. I am sure you know what all took place during the following two weeks."

Holmes gave the woman a long cold stare. "Are you suggesting to me, Mrs. Fallingbrook, that your husband was responsible for the murder of Herman Carter and framing Lester McInerney for the crime."

She dabbed her eyes with her handkerchief. "Forgive me, sir. The reminder of Herman's horrible death is very unsettling. It was many years ago, but he had been a dear friend. I am not making any accusations, sir. I am only telling you what took place, Mr. Holmes. However, there is something that I might add."

"Then add it."

"When I heard that Sherlock Holmes had become involved in Lester's case, I thought again that a miscarriage of justice must have taken place. Lester is a foolish man, but he never had any signs of a criminal temperament. Sir Humphrey is the opposite. In my heart, I knew that he was capable of doing whatever he wanted in order to get his way and getting away with it. I took it upon myself to go searching through his bank records and his diary. On the twentieth of October, 1898, there was a withdrawal from his account of two hundred pounds in cash. On the same day, he put a note in his diary that read, and I quote, 'Arrangements concluded with M. Matrimonial bliss shall finally be mine.' I leave it to you, Mr. Holmes, to draw whatever conclusion you wish from that."

"I shall do that, madam," said Holmes. "Now, let me hear your version of how is was that you were able to become the legal wife of Sir Humphrey Fallingbrook."

"It was not difficult, Mr. Holmes. The date of Lester's execution had been publicly announced and was registered in the court documents. Humpty took a copy of the documents to a friend of his who is a bishop and had him issue an annulment effective the day after Lester's death. I thought that I could be legally married again if I were to become a widow, but Humpty argued that it would be a stain on his reputation if it were to be recorded that his wife had previously been married to a murderer who had been condemned to death. The bishop agreed. No one expected that Lester's execution would be postponed. The annulment would never have been granted, had that been known. But the sentence had not been commuted, only postponed and it was expected that it would be only a matter of time until Lester was dead. Humpty went to a priest over in Limehouse, showed him the annulment document, paid him generously, and he married us."

"That," said Holmes, "is now four years in the past. Would you say that your marriage has been loving?"

"Mr. Holmes, a woman with two children has to do what she has to do. I have been the perfect companion of Sir Humphrey Fallingbrook on countless public occasions. I make sure that men are envious of him when they see me on his arm."

"And in private?"

"Mr. Holmes, a wife to do what she has to do. Dear Humpty has no reason to complain. Now, sir, I must be on my way and get back to Belgravia in time for a bedtime story with my children. I shall end my story here, sir, and leave it in your capable hands."

She rose, as did Holmes and I, and bade us good day.

I was now very late for supper with my wife and so followed her out to Baker Street as soon as her cab had departed.

Chapter Ten
No, Not to Belgravia

AT SIX O'CLOCK the following morning, I was awakened by my dear wife's giving my shoulder a firm shake.

"John, darling. There is someone banging on the door. I am sure it is you-know-who, and he wants you, not me."

Still in my night clothes, I staggered to the door and opened it to a fully dressed and obviously agitated Sherlock Holmes.

"Please, Watson, get dressed and come immediately."

I was about to demand a reason for doing so but shrugged, turned and proceed to splash sufficient soap and water over my torso to keep from offending anyone I sat next to and to pull on a set of informal clothes.

"Are you off to prison again, darling?"

"No, my dear, and I have no idea where Holmes is dragging me off to. Possibly Belgravia to apprehend an oversized captain of industry."

"Your favorite type of adventure. I shall expect you for supper unless I hear from you."

I stumbled out of the house and into the waiting cab in which Holmes was sitting.

"Where to, if I might be so impertinent?"

"Scotland Yard," he said. "Forgive me if I do not engage in conversation. I need to rehearse my appeal to Lestrade."

"Will he be there at this hour?"

"He may lack imagination, but he abounds in dedication. He is invariably at his desk by seven o'clock every morning."

"Then the three of us will go to Belgravia? Do you truly believe there is enough evidence to arrest Sir Humphrey in connection with the murder?"

Holmes gave me a look, one I had gotten used to over the past twenty years, but did not appreciate all the same. The look, if it could have been put into language might have said *Watson, how can you possibly be so stupid?*

"No, my dear doctor," he said with condescension dripping from the words. "We are not going to Belgravia. You appear not to have noticed that those two are both consummate liars and deserve each other."

I had not reached the same conclusion and was not about to have my intellect diminished one more time by Sherlock Holmes.

"Holmes, you shall have to explain your statement. Whatever conclusions you appear to have reached were absolutely not obvious."

"Very well, Watson. Sir Humphrey Fallingbrook may be a very shrewd businessman, but when it comes to the opposite sex, he is a fool. It is not without cause that the proverb says that a fool and his money are soon parted. The woman is brilliant in playing men for her benefit. She was willing to throw over Herman Carter because he entered service. She expected a comfortable life when she married Lester McInerney, and he disappointed her. That she blackmailed, Humpty is most likely true. That she has had a case of nerves each time Lester's execution was postponed is also believable. The obvious reason is that if he were to be declared innocent, then the annulment of her marriage to him would be declared invalid, and her current marriage would be itself be annulled. She would lose her comfortable life in Belgravia and revert being the wife of an art agent."

"But why try now to pin the crime on Humpty?"

"If he is carted off to prison she, as his legal spouse, will take control of all of his assets and will, I am sure, transfer most of them to herself and into a trust for her children. Of such a trust she would be the sole trustee. If Humpty were to be convicted of the murder and sentenced to death, then she would be the merriest of widows in the Empire. She is a monstrous scheming vixen brilliant, mind you, but a monster all the same. Lester will be far better off without her in his life if we can succeed in proving his innocence, which, Lord willing, we are about to do."

"So, where are we going?"

"To Norwood. But I need Lestrade with us."

At a few minutes before seven, Holmes rapped sharply on the door of Inspector Lestrade.

"Come in," was heard.

Lestrade was sitting at his desk, reading the newspaper and enjoying a morning cup of tea and a small pile of biscuits. He looked up at us, and his face sank.

"Oh, no. Not you two. Here I thought I was going to have a decent day and in you walk before it has even started. What is it this time, Holmes?"

Holmes and I sat down opposite Lestrade, who had now leaned back in his chair and crossed his arms over his chest.

"You will recall," began Holmes, "the case several years back in Norwood the one concerning the builder, Jonas Oldacre and the poor young fellow, John McFarlane, who nearly went to the gallows."

"Of course, I remember it. You set the place on fire for dramatic effect, but you did prevent a very grave scandal and saved my reputation. What of it?"

"Five years back, you were involved in another case in Lower Norwood, that of Mr. Lester McInerney, were you not?"

Lestrade did not answer. His whole body descended a notch into his chair and he sighed.

"Oh, no. Not again. Might I guess that at this late date you are coming to tell me that we have the wrong man?"

"I am."

"Very well, Holmes. I have learned the hard way that I have to listen to you even when it is the last thing on earth I want to do. Go ahead. State your case."

Patiently but with clear authority and a complete command of the facts, Sherlock Holmes slowly laid out before Lestrade all the elements of the case that cast strong doubt on the guilt of Lester McInerney. It was a masterful recital and exceptionally convincing. Had poor Mr. McInerney had Holmes as his barrister, he might never have served a day in jail.

Lestrade had listened carefully and made copious notes.

"This case was supposed to be open and shut. Why did all this not come out at trial?"

"Because," said Holmes, "his barrister must have given the case only superficial attention once he knew that his client had insufficient funds to support a long trial, and because the lawyers from Lloyd's were not interested in the murder, only in the recovery of the paintings. Those are only my speculations as I was not present."

"No, but I was," said Lestrade, "and I must admit that you may be right. So, what is it you want from me now, Holmes?"

"I need, Inspector, for you to come with us now to Norwood. We need to carry out another search of the house, and I cannot demand entry. You can."

"Is it so urgent that I cannot finish my tea?" asked Lestrade.

"Your current cup, but I fear not a second one," said Holmes.

"Right. Wait at the front door. I will send a wire off to the station in Norwood and call up one of our carriages."

From the office of New Scotland Yard on the Embankment, we sped off across Westminster Bridge, far too quickly to enjoy the City, *all bright and glittering in the smokeless air.* Soon we were galloping south along the Brixton Road toward Lower Norwood. We stopped at the intersection of Circular Road and picked up a local constable. Five minutes later, we entered the gates of the Fitzguilford manor house on Robson Road.

A knock on the front door brought the young butler, Mr. Richard Tanner, to greet us. He initial look of astonishment subsided into a sly smile when Holmes introduced him to Inspector Lestrade and Constable Lewis.

"Please, gentlemen, enter," said Tanner. "Kindly wait here whilst I notify the Viscount of your arrival."

"Bloody hell!" came the shout from the top of the stairs two minutes later. "Get out of this house this instant or I will set the dogs on you."

The same rude young man in his housecoat and pajamas shouted down at us from the top of the stairs. Lestrade was having none of that.

"Viscount Fitzguilford," he shouted back, "I am Inspector Lestrade of Scotland Yard. We are here to inspect your house in connection with a serious criminal act. You will not hinder us in any way. Any attempt to do so will result in my arresting you on a charge of obstruction of justice. Is that understood, sonny boy?"

"How dare you!" shouted the young lord. He came down the stairs shouting curses at the Inspector. I could have warned the man that this was not a good idea.

"Come on," said Lestrade. "be a good boy and hold out your wrists so the constable can snap a pair of darbies on you. You can continue your tantrum in front of a magistrate."

That stopped the fellow in his tracks. He glared at us and then turned and walked back up the stairs and into a bedroom. He made a point of stomping but gave it up after two steps, having noticed that slippers do not produce the desired effect.

The constable gave a friendly elbow to the inspector. "Mind, sir, if I tell this story down at the station. The lads will get a bit of a chuckle from it."

"Go right ahead. One of the few perks of this job is the freedom to put a loud-mouthed lout in his position."

"Are you not concerned," I asked, "that he might attempt some sort of retribution?"

"Oh, no. The ones who shout and curse and strut are cowards. It is the fellows who say nothing and give you a cool, hard stare that you have to be careful of. They are content to wait until they can take their revenge. But enough of them. Holmes brought us here for a reason, did you not, Holmes?"

"I did. Please follow me into the gallery."

The new wing of the house, which I had only glimpsed briefly in the early light of morning, was now bathed in soft sunlight and was rather impressive. The walls were a full thirty feet in height and were lined with three tiers of paintings and other pieces of art. I am no connoisseur of the fine arts, but even I could recognize the hand of several master painters.

"Constable," said Holmes, "would you please assist me? We need to take down the Titian from the wall. Careful, now. It is worth a fortune."

He led the policeman over to a painting that I assumed must be *The Rape of Europa*. I remembered that it had been on the list given to us by Lester McInerney, but not on the second list of missing paintings. Holmes and the constable gently lifted it off the wall and brought it over to a section of the floor that was covered by a plush carpet. Even so slowly, they laid it face down, with the back of the frame now flat and exposed to us. Holmes was smiling. In truth, he was grinning from ear to ear.

"Gentlemen," he said. "Do you notice anything peculiar about the backside of this famous painting?"

Lestrade dropped down to his knees and leaned over the object in front of him.

"How old is this painting?" he asked.

"I read," said Holmes, "that Titian painted it whilst living in Venice somewhere around the year 1500. That would make it four hundred years old, give or take."

"This dust cover paper is new. It cannot be more than a few years old. The brass tacks that hold it to the frame are only partially tarnished. Is that what I was expected to see, Holmes?"

"Precisely. Now doctor, as you have far greater skill and practice in surgery than I, would you mind taking this scalpel and cutting the paper as close to the line of tacks as you can. But take care not to cut deep. Only sufficient to pierce the paper, if you will."

From his pocket, he took out a small leather case and opened it. He handed me a fine surgical scalpel that I immediately recognized as one of my own that I carried in my medical bag. I took it, dropped to my knees beside Lestrade and began cutting the paper.

"Excellent, doctor," he said when I had completed all four sides. "Now remove the paper, please, and toss it aside."

I did and saw what I assumed was the back of the mounting board of the Titian. But then I looked more closely and noticed that the board I was looking at was flush with the frame only on the lower horizontal side and up the right one. It was affixed to the picture frame by a series of small angle brackets that had been screwed into place.

"You next tool, my dear doctor," said Holmes as he handed me a small, fine screwdriver.

Methodically, I undid all of the screws until the board they held in place was free. I removed it and turned it over.

"Voila," said Holmes. "Mr. Rembrandt's *Storm*."

Lestrade gasped. "Has it been here all along?"

"It has been. Now, it may take us an hour or two, but I believe that if we take down the rest of the paintings from the wall, and set aside those with new dust cover paper, we should find nine more that were missing."

"Good heavens," I said as I rose to my feet. "How in the world did you guess where they were?"

"The size," he said. "The size. It made no sense that five of the paintings, all older and very valuable, would be returned and five more recent ones of much less value be taken. When reviewing the photographs and provenance documents provided to us by Sir Edward, it struck me that all of the substitute paintings, the ones by Degas, and the miniature by Rembrandt were not merely less valuable, they were all considerably smaller. The five large ones could not be hidden behind other paintings. So, they were returned and smaller ones substituted."

"All well and good," said Lestrade, "but who did it?"

"I do not know," said Holmes, "but I am certain it was not Lester McInerney. Whoever it was waited until Lester was distracted and taking his lunch. Then he, or possibly she although that is less likely, removed the paintings from the wagon and took them into the basement. Most likely he was discovered in the act by the butler, Herman Carter, and in panic shot him. He then sought to cover his tracks by taking a chisel out of McInerney's toolbox in the wagon and, being careful not to add any new fingerprints, plunged it into the heart of a man who was already dead. That is the best hypothesis I can offer for the facts as we now have them. Would you agree, Inspector?"

"And the switch in the paintings? Same man?"

"Must have been. Sometime during the following few days, he removed five smaller paintings from the gallery and replaced them with five he had stolen. Now the ten stolen ones had their frames removed and were hidden behind larger paintings still hanging in the gallery. Broken up frames are easy to remove and use as fuel."

"Holmes," said Lestrade. "Why are they still here? They are worth a fortune and whoever it was could have sold them, or ransomed them, or turned them in for the reward. Why would he leave them here and get no money out of this scheme whatsoever? That does not make sense. You are the one who insists on asking *cui bono*."

"A very logical question, Inspector. The only answer I have is that there are times when a villain's motives are not related to ill-gotten gain."

Lestrade made no reply, but turned and began to walk toward the door. "I will be back in half an hour. You can remove the rest of the paintings. I have to send off a wire to the Yard and the Courts and tell them to stay the execution."

"Would you mind," said Holmes, "sending one as well to Dirk Savage at Lloyd's? He will be very interested."

It took us well over an hour to find the paintings on the wall that hid the stolen ones and then to carefully remove those that were hidden behind them. Lestrade returned after a half an hour and got to work helping us with the task at hand. I had just removed the Vermeer painting, *The Concert*, and leaned it up against the wall when Geoffrey Fitzguilford, now no longer in his pajamas and slippers, entered the room.

"Are you miserable blighters still here. Can you not " He stopped in mid-sentence and gasped. Then he rushed over and grabbed the Vermeer in two hands, turned and ran out of the room.

"Mother! Mother!" his shouts could be heard as he ran back into the main part of the house. "Mother! Look!"

"Holmes," I said, "either that twit is an excellent actor, or his surprise and reaction were genuine."

"I suspect," said Holmes, "that it was genuine."

"Then he is off your list," said Lestrade. "Who does that leave, Holmes? All well and good to get these paintings back, but I need to catch a murderer."

"As soon as we complete this job," replied Holmes, "I would like us to take a walk. It may help to answer your question."

Lestrade looked at Holmes, shook his head, and went back to removing the paintings.

Chapter Eleven
According to the Gravestones

"THE ENTRANCE to the cemetery is at the corner of Robson and the Norwood High Street," said Holmes after we departed the manor house. "The keeper of the grounds has a small office there. We are going to pay him a call."

He was already walking quickly in that direction, and the three of us followed him, unsure of what he was up to, but we knew him well enough to suspect that something significant was about to happen.

Holmes knocked on the door of the stone cottage that stood just inside the gate of the cemetery grounds. A smallish, somewhat wizened man in an ill-fitting suit answered the door and bade us enter.

"Sir," said Holmes. "permit me to introduce our little group. My name is Sherlock Holmes. I am accompanied by Inspector Lestrade of Scotland Yard, Constable Lewis, whom I expect you already know, and Dr. Watson. Please forgive our interrupting you but we are in need of your assistance."

The poor fellow seemed quite flabbergasted, and I concluded that a visit from people other than families of the recently deceased making inquiries about burial plots was not something that happened to him.

"Why, yes," he said. "of course, please, I shall be happy to help."

"You have, I am sure," said Holmes, "a map of the cemetery showing the names and precise locations of those who are buried here, do you not?"

"Why, of course, I do, Mr. Holmes. Who are you looking for?"

"The Oldacre family. They are local people. The most recent to be buried here was a Mr. Jonas Oldacre, a builder from the village. Would you mind showing us on the map where his grave may be found."

"Oh, you mean that fellow Dr. Watson wrote about a few months back?"

"That would be him."

"No need for the map, sir. I can tell you where he is."

"Excellent. Has he been a current fixture in your mind as a result of the story?" asked Holmes.

"Oh, not really, sir. No more than any other that's here under the ground. I can tell you where all of them are. No need for the maps. Shall I take you to see Mr. Oldacre."

"That would be most kind of you, sir," said Holmes.

The cemetery keeper led us for some ten minutes along one of the paved paths until we reached a place not far from the back section of the grounds of the Fitzguilford manor house. We stopped in front of a cluster of graves, marked with simple stone gravestones.

"Here they are, gentlemen," said our guide. "over there is the earliest stone. It belongs to the father, Nigel Oldacre and his wife. Two of his brothers, Jesse and Jasper and their wives, are alongside him. None of the brothers' children are here. They all went out to the colonies. But the son of Nigel, Jonas Oldacre, is right here. We put him away about four years back. You can see the date on the stone. He never married, so there is no wife either with him or still living. But we did put Mrs. Lexington here. That was according to her wish as well as his although she was not a member of the family. She passed away just last year. Again, you can see the dates on the stones."

"Indeed, we can," said Holmes. "I thank you, sir. You have been most helpful. A question, sir, if I may?"

"By all means, sir."

"Did you know Mr. Jonas Oldacre?"

"I did, sir. Everyone in the village knows everyone else, sir."

"What sort of man was he?"

The groundskeeper gave Holmes queer look before answering.

"That's an odd question, sir, if you don't mind my saying. I would have thought you knew all about him. He was just as Dr. Watson described him in that story. He was a strange little ferret-like man. Secretive and retiring he was. Not at all friendly. Rather a nasty piece of work. Vengeful, he was. You can ask anyone in the village who had aught to do with him. They will all say the same thing—just as the doctor described him in that story. Frankly, sir, what's on his gravestone rather says it all, sir. Now, if you will excuse me, sir, I must get back to my office. You never know when someone is going to die and his family be needing a plot. Good day, gentlemen."

He departed and left us gazing at the small group of graves. The inscriptions on these stones of both father, Nigel Oldacre, and his son, Jonas Oldacre, were indeed unusual. Most of the other stones we had passed bore some standard words, such as *Rest in Peace,* or *Remembered with love.* However, the final message of Nigel Oldacre read *Vengeance is mine, I will repay.* On the stone of the miserable old builder, Jonas Oldacre, were the words, *Vengeance is mine, I have repaid.*

"Constable Lewis," said Holmes, turning to the local policeman. "This village is your home, is it not?"

"Aye, sir. 'Tis."

"Do the epitaphs on these stone make sense at all to you?"

"Can't say, entirely, sir. I never met the old fellow, Mr. Nigel Oldacre. But the son, Jonas Oldacre was as the keeper here described him. Quite consumed with hate and woe betide any who he thought treated him unkindly, or anyone who said a bad word about any member of his family."

"Might Lester McInerney have been on that list, Constable?"

"Can't rightly say, sir. Mind you, Lester's father and grandfather were both successful builders, and there may have been bad blood between them and Mr. Jonas, sir. No one alive can truly say, sir."

"No," agreed Holmes, "no one can ever know. Mr. Jonas Oldacre is now as silent as the grave."

"Holmes," said Lestrade, "are you saying that Jonas Oldacre was the murderer and framed Lester McInerney out of spite?"

"That would appear to be the most likely conclusion at this time, Inspector. Would it not?"

"Then how do you explain," demanded Lestrade, "the attack on Dr. Watson a few days back? Dead men not only do not tell tales, they do not generally commission ruffians to try to scare folks away. Unless you think this Oldacre chap has some ghostly spirit patrolling the cemetery on the lookout for Sherlock Holmes."

"At the moment, I have no explanation for that one," admitted Holmes. "That does not mean that none exists, only that it has not yet been revealed."

"Right, Holmes. Well, whilst you are sorting things out with the spirits, I am hungry. So, unless you have any more dead men for me to investigate, I say we should return to the High Street and find us some lunch."

Without waiting for an answer, he turned and began walking back to the entrance of the cemetery.

Chapter Twelve
An Annuity Contract

LESTRADE, Constable Lewis, and I chatted amiably as we sat around a table at *The Horns* pub on the High Street. The Constable had quite lively and informed opinions about the local football club and the new one that had just formed a few blocks away—the *Crystal Palace FC*—down in Selhurst. Holmes ignored us and sat back in silence, puffing on his pipe and waiting for the day's special lunch, mincemeat pie, to arrive.

I noticed that Holmes's gaze, for several minutes, was fixed on the bar and the barkeep.

"Is there something going on behind the bar that we should know about?" I asked him.

"Right," said Lestrade, "are you watching the ghost of Mr. Oldacre water down the local lager? "

"I am watching," said Holmes without altering his gaze, "the barkeep doing something quite unusual. During the past few minutes, he has received a lunch pie from the kitchen, placed it in a saucepan, added a little bit of water and proceeded to use first a potato masher and then a whip to turn it into a mushy sauce and then pour it into a quart preserving jar. Now he has filled a pint jar with a strong ale and screwed tops tightly on to both."

The three of us turned and looked at the barkeep. As we did so, he called the barmaid up to the bar.

"Here's his lunch, Bessie. Wrap it up, dearie, and take it around to him."

"Did you put another tube in with it? He says the one he has is too small."

"Ah, yes, said the barkeep. "I have one here." He reached under the bar and pulled out a foot length of copper tubing. The barmaid placed it alongside the jars in a square piece of rag and tied it all together. Holmes pushed back his chair and strode quickly up to the bar.

"Pardon me, miss," he said. "We are in no rush and as you are busy, might I offer to deliver that lunch for you?"

She gave Holmes a surprised look and then looked over to the barkeep as if needing his help.

"Right kind of you," he said to Holmes. "But the chap this is going to gives her a good penny for her service. It would not be fair to deprive her of that, sir."

"Oh, of course not," said Holmes. "then I insist that you allow me to give you two thrupney bits for the privilege of being the delivery man." He extracted coins from his pocket and laid them on the counter.

"Oww, why thank you, sir," the barmaid said with a beaming smile. "That is right generous of you sir. It's not far to take it. Just around on Nettleford Place, it is. Number six. Second floor, room five. Can't miss it, sir. The door will be open, and you can let yourself in. Thank you, sir."

Holmes picked up the bundle and came back to our table.

"Your lunch, gentlemen, will have to wait. We have a delivery to make."

"What in heaven's name ," began Lestrade. But Holmes was already on his way out the door, and we scrambled to catch up with him.

"Come along," he shouted. "We shan't want the chap's lunch to get cold."

We walked north past five houses on Knight's Hill and turned into the narrow confines of Nettleford Place. The door to number six was open, and we followed Holmes up the stairs to the second floor.

"I do not wish to unsettle the man's lunch. Constable, would you mind opening the door for us?"

The policeman did so, and the four of us walked into a small bed-sitting room. Sitting in a chair by the window was a somewhat scruffy working man of about a decade younger than me. His face was unshaven, but his clothes were clean, and his hair combed. His right arm was in a sling. Constable Lewis greeted him.

"Good day to you, Jake Mason. Haven't seen you around her for a bit. How are you?"

"Hello, Lewish," came the muffled reply. "Wha' are you doin' comin' inna my room, shir?"

He was looking directly at the Constable, and I could not help but note that his lips did not move at all as he spoke.

"Brought your lunch," said the Constable. "Or, I should say, Mr. Sherlock Holmes has brought it. And Doctor Watson has come along as has Inspector Lestrade of Scotland Yard. You don't get service like that in Wandsworth, now do you, Mr. Mason?"

"Oww, you mushant make me laugh, Lewish. It only hursh when I laugh," he said. "Pleash, gehulmen. Come in. Shoory I have only the one shair. You'll have to sheet on the bed."

I walked over to the fellow and leaned down to have a close look at him.

"It looks as if your jaw is wired shut and your arm injured," I said. "I wonder how that happened?"

I laughed as I spoke and did not yield to the strong temptation to give the fellow a firm clap on his protected shoulder. His speech in response continued without moving his jaw, and I will leave it to the reader's imagination to hear it that way.

"Well, now, doctor, it seems I had a bit of a run in with some old man who must have been trained by the marines. Not at all bloody fair of him, now was it? That might be all right a way to do in a crazy Afghan, but just not a right thing to do to your fellow Englishman."

Now I laughed.

"Would you mind," said Lestrade, "telling me who this man is and what this is all about?"

"My dear Inspector," said Holmes, "allow me to introduce you to Mr. Jake Mason, assuming that the name by which Constable Lewis addressed him is correct. He is a local ruffian for hire and not long out of prison. A few evenings ago, thinking that Dr. Watson was Sherlock Holmes, he rather foolishly attempted to threaten the good doctor with a knife to the throat but, I dare say, his poor judgment has cost him dearly."

"Has not cost me a farthing," Mason replied. "Thanks to you, Doctor, I have been able to double my fee."

"I beg your pardon," said Holmes.

"Well, sir, in my profession, a man only gets a few pence for putting a threat on any old Tom, Dick, or Mrs. Harry. But when the word goes out that he took on the famous Mr. Sherlock Holmes and was willing to take a broken jaw and a torn shoulder in doing so, well, he's moved up several notches in the profession, sir. You enhanced my reputation, you did, sir. And now I shall be able to charge double what I was doing before. But I must ask you that you don't let on that it was only Doctor Watson that I grabbed. That would never do, even if he did turn out to be the tougher old bird than I had expected."

"Is this," asked Lestrade, "the bloke you said attacked you in the cemetery, doctor?"

"Honestly, Inspector, I cannot say. I did not get to see his face for more than a second as it descended toward my knee. Most of what I saw was his backside and his twisted arm."

"You must show me," said Mason, "how you did that so fast. Mind, I'll mostly be accosting gentlemen and toffs from here on, thanks to the two of you."

"Ah, but perhaps I did see the man who threatened Doctor Watson," said Holmes. "And if you do not want to be sent back to Wandsworth for another stretch, you will tell me who you were hired by."

The man's whole body sank as he sighed. "That is a most unfortunate turn of events. Very well, I guess you will have to send me back. You are asking me to do the impossible, sir. In my profession, if it were to become known that I informed on my client, I would be off of business for the rest of my life. I could survive another year or two in prison, but I can't put my livelihood at risk. I have two wives and my children to think of."

Holmes gave the fellow a hard look for a minute and then inquired, "The constable said you were in Wandsworth?"

"Aye, that I was. Two full years, I was."

"Did you happen to get to know another prisoner by the name of Lester McInerney."

"Aye, a fine fellow. Not a very tough chap, but a decent fellow all the same. Got to know him quite well."

"Was he a friend?"

"As much as a fellow prisoner that is on his way to the gallows can ever be a friend to anyone. Why are you asking me about him, Mr. Holmes?"

"Are you aware that he has exhausted all his appeals and delays and will be hanged in less than a week from today?"

"Aye, I read that in the newspapers and what of it?"

"He is my client, and he is an innocent man. Are you so committed to the code of your profession that you would let a friend and your fellow prisoner hang for something he did not do? The man who is paying you is most likely the one who murdered Mr. Herman Carter five years ago."

The man looked quite discomfited. "Give me a minute to think that one over, sir. It's a hard one, it is."

"Then you might add to your thinking that even if your income should be restricted during your remaining years here on earth, there will be a far harder judgment to face when your life is over, and you will have to answer to the Almighty for the death of your fellow man. Are you willing to face that, Mr. Mason?"

The poor fellow let out a long sigh and, by force of habit shrugged his shoulders, resulting in a wince of pain from the shoulder that should not have been shrugged.

"Very well, Mr. Holmes, if you put it that way. But you have to give me your word as a gentleman, all of you, that you will never let on that I informed on a client. Will you do that?"

He looked up at all of us in turn, and we all nodded in the affirmative.

"All right, then. It was Mr. Jonas Oldacre, the builder. It was him what paid me to threaten Sherlock Holmes."

"Bloody hell!" snapped Lestrade. "Enough of your games. Jonas Oldacre is dead and in his grave. We were standing on top of him no more than an hour ago. Now smarten up and tell the truth or I'll have you down to the police station and twist both of your arms until you talk."

"No, Inspector, no. I am not lying. It was an annuity agreement. It does not matter if the man dies."

"Do you think we are fools? You cannot be under contract to a dead man," said Lestrade.

"Yes, sir, you can. It's part of the code of the profession. If you take the king's shilling, as it were, you are bound for life. I took his money and agreed to work for him. And he said it was an annuity agreement and I agreed. And I let it be known amongst my colleagues that I had such an agreement so they would not be trying to take my client away from me. If I were to cheat on it, it would ruin my profession."

"Even though Jonas Oldacre," said Holmes, "is dead and gone, your professional ethics require you to carry out your agreement. Is that what you are telling me?"

"You have it, sir. That is how it works. A man's word must be his bond or he is nothing."

Holmes stood up, walked over to the window, and lit a cigarette. After several puffs, he put it down in an ashtray and grabbed the bundle he had carried into the room.

"Your lunch, Mr. Mason. Do you need any help in opening the preserving jars?"

"Right thoughtful of you, Mr. Holmes. It's a painful thing when your shoulder is separated. Thank you, sir."

On the pavement outside the house, Holmes turned to Lestrade.

"Do you have enough evidence, Inspector, to have Lester McInerney's conviction overturned?"

"Not by a country mile, Holmes. You know I don't. Unless you know of some way of bringing a fellow up from the grave to stand trial, it is bloody impossible to pin the crime on him."

"But you do know, in your heart, that McInerney is innocent, don't you, my dear Inspector. And you are not about to let an innocent man be hanged, are you?"

Lestrade turned and began walking back out to the main street. "Enjoy your lunch, Holmes. I have lost my appetite. I will do what I can."

Holmes looked at the beefy constable. "Mr. Lewis, I have most indecently delayed your lunch, and you look like the type of man who could enjoy several of those mincemeat pies at *The Horns*. Will you be our guest? Dr. Watson has kindly offered to pay the tab."

Chapter Thirteen
A Sunday School Lesson

TWO WEEKS passed before I heard again from Holmes. Then a note arrived asking if I might join him at Baker Street at the end of the afternoon.

"Ah, good old Watson. How kind of you to join me on such short notice."

"You were not dragging me off to prison this time, so I thought I was safe in doing so."

"Indeed, you are. I need you for the polar opposite of prison. I shall have to take on the role of a Sunday School teacher, and I am woefully unqualified to do so."

"And am I any more so?" I asked.

"You could not possibly be less. Now, please have a brandy and enjoy it in silence whilst I read, and we wait for our visitor."

He picked up a book that was on the side table. It was not a Bible.

At a few minutes before five o'clock, the bell rang, and Mrs. Hudson dutifully attended to it.

"It is that Mr. McInerney to see you, Mr. Holmes."

In walked Lester McInerney. He looked pale and gaunt and was wearing a poorly fitting suit, such as are given by charities to prisoners upon their release.

"Please, sir, be seated," said Holmes. "We have all the time in the world for you."

"A good thing," came the weary reply. "I came directly here after I was released two hours ago. Frankly, Mr. Holmes, I had nowhere else to go."

"Not yet, but you shall. Now, please tell Dr. Watson and me what has taken place during the past two weeks."

"I received a reprieve from my hanging with no explanation. Then, a week ago that inspector from Scotland Yard arrived, the one that arrested me over five years ago. He came into my cell and told me all about what took place in Lower Norwood and what was discovered concerning the murder and the paintings. Then he said that as a result of diligent effort by the Yard with some assistance from Mr. Sherlock Holmes, there have been some meetings with the

Crown prosecutor and the magistrate from my case. He said that he has an agreement from them that should I plead guilty to a lesser charge of manslaughter I can walk free with my sentence reduced to time served."

"And your response?"

"I told him to go to the devil. I am an innocent man who has been framed and wrongly convicted. I have never wavered from saying that and I wasn't about to admit to a crime I did not commit. Well, he called me a few names and left."

"How curious, then what?" asked Holmes.

"First thing this morning, a couple of prison guards came to my cell and told me to come with them. I was put in shackles and shoved into a police wagon. I was pulled out again at the Courts buildings and hauled before a magistrate. I had to sit and wait as he attended to a half-dozen other matters and then he called my name. I went up in front of him, and he said, and I quote, he said, 'Mr. Lester McInerney, the charge against you has been changed to manslaughter. Your sentence has been reduced to five years, six months and three days. As that is the time you have already served, you are now released. Remove the prisoner's shackles. Next!' And he banged his gavel, and I was led out, taken back to Wandsworth, given these clothes, told to pay a visit to the John Howard people, and put out on the street. I walked here as I have not a farthing to my name, but I knew I should pay my first visit to you."

"That is wonderful news," I exulted.

"Is that what you call it, Doctor?" he replied. "Wonderful? I think not. It is news, for certain. But five years of my life have been stolen. My wife and children are gone. I am disgraced in front of my family. I have a criminal record for a crime of which I am innocent and no means of supporting myself. And it was all because that horrible man, Jonas Oldacre, whom I hardly knew, wanted to take revenge for something my grandfather did to his father decades ago. With every step I took walking here from Wandsworth, I imagined him standing before me and my wringing his neck, shooting him, setting him on fire, stabbing him — anything — to repay what he had done to me. But he is dead. He got away with murder, and there is nothing I can do. Nothing."

He slammed his fists on his knees as he spoke. His fists were clenched in anger, and his knuckles had turned white.

"There is something you can do," said Holmes.

The man looked bewildered. "There is? What?"

"You can forgive him," said Holmes.

Mr. McInerney just looked at Holmes for a full minute.

"Forgive him? Are you insane, Mr. Holmes? After what he did? How can you think that possible?"

"It is not only possible, it is imperative. If you do not, if you let the hatred and anger eat your heart and soul, then Jonas Oldacre will have triumphed, and you will be the loser."

"But —"

"No but's, Mr. McInerney. He is in his grave, and you cannot do any further damage to a set of rotted bones. If you are a believer, as I think you are, then you know that the soul of Jonas Oldacre is in hell for eternity and there is nothing you can do to turn up the gas and increase his punishment. All you can do is claim the victory that comes with forgiveness and move on."

"But   "

"No, sir. It is your only salvation. And I am sorry if I must be harsh, but I must demand of you, here and now, that you will swear by all that is holy, that you will do so."

"How? It is impossible. You ask too much of me. I cannot in one fell swoop erase all that has happened."

His voice was now trembling, and tears were falling down his cheeks.

"No, Lester. Forgiveness does not happen all at once. Your anger will well up in your heart many times. At the least reminder, you will be filled again with hatred. But each time it does, you must, I repeat, you must, steel your will and say once again, 'I forgive you.' As the months and the years pass, the anger will then die and you will be a truly free man. Will you swear to me, Lester, that you will do that?"

"I can't. I am not strong enough."

"You endured five years in prison, and you kept your spirit strong, knowing that you were innocent. I will promise you, that if you force yourself to forgive and forgive and do so again and again, within five more years, your spirit will be free."

"Do I have a choice?"

"No."

"I know what you say is right, Mr. Holmes. Very well, I will do as you say."

"Promise me, on the names of your mother and father and your children, that you will do so."

After a long pause, Lest McInerney muttered his reply. "Very well, sir. I promise."

"Excellent. Now, Watson, would you mind pouring three brandies for us. And there is an envelope from Lloyd's on the mantle with Mr. McInerney's name on it. Could you hand it to him, please?"

I poured the brandies and handed over the envelope.

"What is this?" he asked.

"There was a reward offered by Lloyd's for the return of the paintings in good condition. It was made out to me, but I have endorsed it over to you."

"But   but   it was you who found the paintings, not me," said McInerney.

"I was under contract to you at the time. That is that way it works," said Holmes. "You will pay my standard fee, of course."

"What? That is all you want?"

"And the promise you made."

"Mr. Holmes, I do not know what to say."

"Then best to say nothing. However, I have somewhat to say unto thee."

"Yes, sir?"

"Have you kept up your knowledge of the world of artists and collectors whilst in prison?"

"I have. It was one of the few things I could do to distract myself from my hatred."

"Excellent. From one of my contacts in America, Boston to be specific, I have been informed of a woman who possesses obscene amounts of wealth and has decided to acquire a collection of masterpieces to enrich the culturally impoverished citizens of Boston. I have given your name as an excellent agent. They are expecting you in America within a month. Your prison record is irrelevant to Americans as long as you are somewhat wealthy, bathe daily, and do not blow on your soup."

"Mr. Holmes, I do not know what to say."

"Again, then say nothing. I have also learned that the obnoxious young Viscount Fitzguilford wishes to sell his father's entire collection. I have passed the word to him that there is a buyer in America who will purchase the whole lot of them and that you are serving as the agent. You should receive a decent fee for your services."

"And please, Mr. Holmes, may I ask the name of the lady in Boston?"

"Her name is Mrs. Isobel Gardner. She has built a magnificent home to serve as her gallery and hired a full set of guards. The paintings will not be stolen again. Now good day, sir. Pray, enjoy your new life."

Over yet another brandy, I relaxed in my familiar chair in 221B Baker Street.

"Tell me, Holmes. If all the masterpieces collected by the old Viscount are to be sold, what is to become of the gallery?"

"Lady Oldacre wishes to replace the collections with several score of paintings by George Stubbs."

"Stubbs? He never painted anything but horses."

"And the occasional dog," said Holmes.

"Is she going to fill that room with nothing but *horses and dogs*? That is appalling."

"Need I remind you, my friend, that there is no accounting for taste."

A request to all readers:

After reading this story, please help the author and future readers by taking a moment to write a short, constructive review on the site from which you purchased the book. Thank you.   CSC

Historical and Other Notes

On March 18, 1990, two men dressed as police officers were allowed to enter the Isobel Gardner Museum in Boston. They succeeded in stealing thirteen works of art—the most valuable theft of art in history. To this date, these works have never been recovered and a reward of $10 million is still being offered. This extraordinary crime provided the idea for this New Sherlock Holmes Mystery. All of the paintings named in the story are owned by the Gardner Museum. Those named in the story as having been stolen and hidden are the ones that remain that way today.

The Crystal Palace was built in Hyde Park in conjunction with the Great Exhibition of 1851. It was subsequently taken down and rebuilt in Sydenham, just south of the village of Lower (now West) Norwood. It was destroyed by fine in 1936.

The Newgate Prison was first constructed in the twelfth century and used for over 700 years. It was demolished in 1904. The Wandsworth Prison was built in 1851 and was considered then to be a model of enlightened treatment of prisoners. It is still in use today.

The Rembrandt painting, *Storm on the Sea of Galilee*, was one of the paintings stolen from the Gardner Museum. It is the only seascape ever painted by Rembrandt and is considered 'priceless.' There are only thirty-four paintings by Vermeer known to exist. One of them, *The Concert*, is among those stolen from the Gardner. It is invaluable. Sir Edward John Poynter, the uncle of Rudyard Kipling, was the director of the National Gallery in 1904.

The Great North Wood was a large tract of forest in the region south of London. It was slowly deforested and turned into farm and residential property. The Norwood villages now stand where the Great North Wood once did.

During the 1830s and 1840s, seven large cemeteries—The Magnificent Seven—were opened in various suburban areas of London to accommodate the need for final resting places of the growing population. They remain in use today. The West Norwood Cemetery is one of them and occupies forty acres on the south side of Robson Road. Tens of thousands of people are buried there.

The Horns Tavern traces its origins back several hundred years. It is still in business at the north end of the High Street in West Norwood.

The names and locations of places in London are generally accurate for the year 1904.

There is strong debate amongst Sherlockian scholars regarding Dr. Watson's wife or wives. Many argue that he had three wives. Some claim up to six. And there are some of us who stick with one wife, Mary Morstan, the only one to be specifically named in the Canon. We defend our position by noting that the references claimed for multiple marriages—Watson's 'recent bereavement' and Holmes's statement that Watson had 'abandoned me for a wife'—can be easily explained without having to posit addition marriages.

About the Author

In May of 2014 the Sherlock Holmes Society of Canada – better known as The Bootmakers – announced a contest for a new Sherlock Holmes story. Although he had no experience writing fiction, the author submitted a short Sherlock Holmes mystery and was blessed to be declared one of the winners. Thus inspired, he has continued to write new Sherlock Holmes Mysteries since and is on a mission to write a new story as a tribute to each of the sixty stories in the original Canon. He currently writes from Toronto, the Okanagan, and Manhattan. Several readers of New Sherlock Holmes Mysteries have kindly sent him suggestions for future stories. You are welcome to do likewise at craigstephencopland@gmail.com.

More Historical Mysteries
by Craig Stephen Copland
www.SherlockHolmesMystery.com

Studying Scarlet. Starlet O'Halloran, a fabulous mature woman, who reminds the reader of Scarlet O'Hara (but who, for copyright reasons cannot actually be her) has arrived in London looking for her long-lost husband, Brett (who resembles Rhett Butler, but who, for copyright reasons, cannot actually be him). She enlists the help of Sherlock Holmes. This is an unauthorized parody, inspired by Arthur Conan Doyle's *A Study in Scarlet* and Margaret Mitchell's *Gone with the Wind*.

The Sign of the Third. Fifteen hundred years ago the courageous Princess Hemamali smuggled the sacred tooth of the Buddha into Ceylon. Now, for the first time, it is being brought to London to be part of a magnificent exhibit at the British Museum. But what if something were to happen to it? It would be a disaster for the British Empire. Sherlock Holmes, Dr. Watson, and even Mycroft Holmes are called upon to prevent such a crisis. This novella is inspired by the Sherlock Holmes mystery, *The Sign of the Four.*

A Sandal from East Anglia. Archeological excavations at an old abbey unearth an ancient document that has the potential to change the course of the British Empire and all of Christendom. Holmes encounters some evil young men and a strikingly beautiful young Sister, with a curious double life. The mystery is inspired by the original Sherlock Holmes story, *A Scandal in Bohemia.*

The Bald-Headed Trust. Watson insists on taking Sherlock Holmes on a short vacation to the seaside in Plymouth. No sooner has Holmes arrived than he is needed to solve a double murder and prevent a massive fraud diabolically designed by the evil Professor himself. Who knew that a family of devout conservative churchgoers could come to the aid of Sherlock Holmes and bring enormous grief to evil doers? The story is inspired by *The Red-Headed League.*

A Case of Identity Theft. It is the fall of 1888 and Jack the Ripper is terrorizing London. A young married couple is found, minus their heads. Sherlock Holmes, Dr. Watson, the couple's mothers, and Mycroft must join forces to find the murderer before he kills again and makes off with half a million pounds. The novella is a tribute to A Case of Identity. It will appeal both to devoted fans of Sherlock Holmes, as well as to those who love the great game of rugby.

The Hudson Valley Mystery. A young man in New York went mad and murdered his father. His mother believes he is innocent and knows he is not crazy. She appeals to Sherlock Holmes and, together with Dr. and Mrs. Watson, he crosses the Atlantic to help this client in need. This new storymystery was inspired by *The Boscombe Valley Mystery.*

The Mystery of the Five Oranges. A desperate father enters 221B Baker Street. His daughter has been kidnapped and spirited off the North America. The evil network who have taken her has spies everywhere. There is only one hope – Sherlock Holmes. Sherlockians will enjoy this new adventure, inspired by The Five Orange Pips and Anne of Green Gables.

The Man Who Was Twisted But Hip. France is torn apart by The Dreyfus Affair. Westminster needs Sherlock Holmes so that the evil tide of anti-Semitism that has engulfed France will not spread. Sherlock and Watson go to Paris to solve the mystery and thwart Moriarty. This new mystery is inspired by, *The Man with the Twisted Lip*, as well as by *The Hunchback of Notre Dame*.

The Adventure of the Blue Belt Buckle. A young street urchin discovers a man's belt and buckle under a bush in Hyde Park. A body is found in a hotel room in Mayfair. Scotland Yard seeks the help of Sherlock Holmes in solving the murder. The Queen's Jubilee could be ruined. Sherlock Holmes, Dr. Watson, Scotland Yard, and Her Majesty all team up to prevent a crime of unspeakable dimensions. A new mystery inspired by *The Blue Carbuncle*.

The Adventure of the Spectred Bat. A beautiful young woman, just weeks away from giving birth, arrives at Baker Street in the middle of the night. Her sister was attacked by a bat and died, and now it is attacking her. A vampire? The story is a tribute to *The Adventure of the Speckled Band* and like the original, leaves the mind wondering and the heart racing.

The Adventure of the Engineer's Mom. A brilliant young Cambridge University engineer is carrying out secret research for the Admiralty. It will lead to the building of the world's most powerful battleship, The Dreadnaught. His adventuress mother is kidnapped and he seeks the help of Sherlock Holmes. This new mystery is a tribute to *The Engineer's Thumb*.

The Adventure of the Notable Bachelorette. A snobbish nobleman enters 221B Baker Street demanding the help in finding his much younger wife – a beautiful and spirited American from the West. Three days later the wife is accused of a vile crime. Now she comes to Sherlock Holmes seeking to prove her innocence. This new mystery was inspired *The Adventure of the Noble Bachelor*.

The Adventure of the Beryl Anarchists. A deeply distressed banker enters 221B Baker St. His safe has been robbed, and he is certain that his motorcycle-riding sons have betrayed him. Highly incriminating and embarrassing records of the financial and personal affairs of England's nobility are now in the hands of blackmailers. Then a young girl is murdered. A tribute to *The Adventure of the Beryl Coronet*.

The Adventure of the Coiffured Bitches. A beautiful young woman will soon inherit a lot of money. She disappears. Another young woman finds out far too much and, in desperation seeks help. Sherlock Holmes, Dr. Watson and Miss Violet Hunter must solve the mystery of the coiffured bitches, and avoid the massive mastiff that could tear their throats. A tribute to *The Adventure of the Copper Beeches*.

The Silver Horse, Braised. The greatest horse race of the century, will take place at Epsom Downs. Millions have been bet. Owners, jockeys, grooms, and gamblers from across England and America arrive. Jockeys and horses are killed. Holmes fails to solve the crime until… This mystery is a tribute to *Silver Blaze* and the great racetrack stories of Damon Runyon.

The Box of Cards. A brother and a sister from a strict religious family disappear. The parents are alarmed, but Scotland Yard says they are just off sowing their wild oats. A horrific, gruesome package arrives in the post, and it becomes clear that a terrible crime is in process. Sherlock Holmes is called in to help. A tribute to *The Cardboard Box*.

The Yellow Farce. Sherlock Holmes is sent to Japan. The war between Russia and Japan is raging. Alliances between countries in these years before World War I are fragile, and any misstep could plunge the world into Armageddon. The wife of the British ambassador is suspected of being a Russian agent. Join Holmes and Watson as they travel around the world to Japan. Inspired by *The Yellow Face*.

The Stock Market Murders. A young man's friend has gone missing. Two more bodies of young men turn up. All are tied to The City and to one of the greatest frauds ever visited upon the citizens of England. The story is based on the true story of James Whitaker Wright and is inspired by, *The Stock Broker's Clerk*. Any resemblance of the villain to a certain American political figure is entirely coincidental.

The Glorious Yacht. On the night of April 12, 1912, off the coast of Newfoundland, one of the greatest disasters of all time took place – the Unsinkable Titanic struck an iceberg and sank with a horrendous loss of life. The news of the disaster leads Holmes and Watson to reminisce about one of their earliest adventures. It began as a sailing race and ended as a tale of murder, kidnapping, piracy, and survival through a tempest. A tribute to *The Gloria Scott*.

A Most Grave Ritual. In 1649, King Charles I escaped and made a desperate run for Continent. Did he leave behind a vast fortune? The patriarch of an ancient Royalist family dies in the courtyard, and the locals believe that the headless ghost of the king did him in. The police accuse his son of murder. Sherlock Holmes is hired to exonerate the lad. A tribute to *The Musgrave Ritual.*

The Spy Gate Liars. Dr. Watson receives an urgent telegram telling him that Sherlock Holmes is in France and near death. He rushes to aid his dear friend, only to find that what began as a doctor's house call has turned into yet another adventure as Sherlock Holmes races to keep an unknown ruthless murderer from dispatching yet another former German army officer. A tribute to *The Reigate Squires.*

The Cuckold Man Colonel James Barclay needs the help of Sherlock Holmes. His exceptionally beautiful, but much younger, wife has disappeared and foul play is suspected. Has she been kidnapped and held for ransom? Or is she in the clutches of a deviant monster? The story is a tribute not only to the original mystery, *The Crooked Man*, but also to the biblical story of King David and Bathsheba.

The Impatient Dissidents. In March 1881, the Czar of Russia was assassinated by anarchists. That summer, an attempt was made to murder his daughter, Maria, the wife of England's Prince Alfred. A Russian Count is found dead in a hospital in London. Scotland Yard and the Home Office arrive at 221B and enlist the help of Sherlock Holmes to track down the killers and stop them. This new mystery is a tribute to *The Resident Patient.*

The Grecian, Earned. This story picks up where *The Greek Interpreter* left off. The villains of that story were murdered in Budapest, and so Holmes and Watson set off in search of "the Grecian girl" to solve the mystery. What they discover is a massive plot involving the re-birth of the Olympic games in 1896 and a colorful cast of characters at home and on the Continent.

The Three Rhodes Not Taken. Oxford University is famous for its passionate pursuit of learning. The Rhodes Scholarship has been recently established and some men are prepared to lie, steal, slander, and, maybe murder, in the pursuit of it. Sherlock Holmes is called upon to track down a thief who has stolen vital documents pertaining to the winner of the scholarship, but what will he do when the prime suspect is found dead? A tribute to *The Three Students*.

The Naval Knaves. On September 15, 1894, an anarchist attempted to bomb the Greenwich Observatory. He failed, but the attempt led Sherlock Holmes into an intricate web of spies, foreign naval officers, and a beautiful princess. Once again, suspicion landed on poor Percy Phelps, now working in a senior position in the Admiralty, and once again Holmes has to use both his powers of deduction and raw courage to not only rescue Percy, but to prevent an unspeakable disaster. A tribute to *The Naval Treaty*.

A Scandal in Trumplandia. NOT a new mystery but a political. The story is a parody of the much-loved original story, *A Scandal in Bohemia*, with the character of the King of Bohemia replaced by you-know-who. If you enjoy both political satire and Sherlock Holmes, you will get a chuckle out of this new story.

The Binomial Asteroid Problem. The deadly final encounter between Professor Moriarty and Sherlock Holmes took place at Reichenbach Falls on 4 May 1891. But when was their first encounter? This new story answers that question. What began with nothing more than a stolen Gladstone bag on wheels quickly escalates into murder and more. And if Holmes and Watson do not move fast enough, it could become much worse. This new story is a tribute to *The Adventure of the Final Problem*.

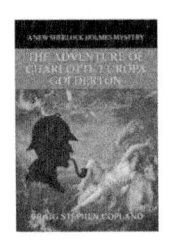

The Adventure of Charlotte Europa Golderton. Charles Augustus Milverton, "the worst man in London," was shot and sent to his just reward. But now another scheme of blackmail has emerged centered in the telegraph offices of the Royal Mail. It is linked to an archeological expedition whose director disappeared one night. Someone is prepared to do murder to protect their ill-gotten gain and possibly steal a priceless treasure. Holmes is hired by three women who need his help.

The Mystery of 222 Baker Street. On the day after Queen Victoria died, the body of a Scotland Yard inspector is found in a locked room in 222 Baker Street. There is no clue as to how he died, but for certain, he was murdered. Then another murder takes place, in the very same room. Holmes and Watson might have to offer themselves as potential victims if the culprits are to be discovered. The story is a tribute to the original Sherlock Holmes story, *The Adventure of the Empty House*.

Sherlock and Barack. This is NOT a new Sherlock Holmes Mystery. It is a Sherlockian research monograph. Why did Barack Obama win in November 2012? Why did Mitt Romney lose? Pundits and political scientists have offered countless reasons. This book reveals the truth - The Sherlock Holmes Factor. Had it not been for Sherlock Holmes, Mitt Romney would be president.

From The Beryl Coronet to Vimy Ridge. This is NOT a New Sherlock Holmes Mystery. It is a monograph of Sherlockian research. This new monograph in the Great Game of Sherlockian scholarship argues that there was a Sherlock Holmes factor in the causes of World War I... and that it is secretly revealed in the *roman a clef* story that we know as *The Adventure of the Beryl Coronet.*

Reverend Ezekiel Black—'The Sherlock Holmes of the American West'—Mystery Stories.

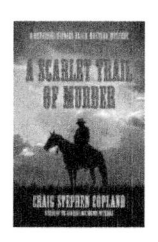

A Scarlet Trail of Murder. At ten o'clock on Sunday morning, the twenty-second of October, 1882, in an abandoned house in the West Bottom of Kansas City, a fellow named Jasper Harrison did not wake up. His inability to do was the result of his having had his throat cut. The Reverend Mr. Ezekiel Black, a part-time Methodist minister and an itinerant US Marshall is called in. This original western mystery was inspired by the great Sherlock Holmes classic, *A Study in Scarlet.*

The Brand of the Flying Four. This case all began one quiet evening in a room in Kansas City. A few weeks later, a gruesome murder, took place in Denver. By the time Rev. Black had solved the mystery, justice, of the frontier variety, not the courtroom, had been meted out. The story is inspired by *The Sign of the Four* by Arthur Conan Doyle, and like that story, it combines murder most foul, and romance most enticing.

www.SherlockHolmesMystery.com

Collection Sets for eBooks and paperback are available at
40% off the price of buying them separately.

Collection One
The Sign of the Third
The Hudson Valley Mystery
A Case of Identity Theft
The Bald-Headed Trust
Studying Scarlet
The Mystery of the Five Oranges

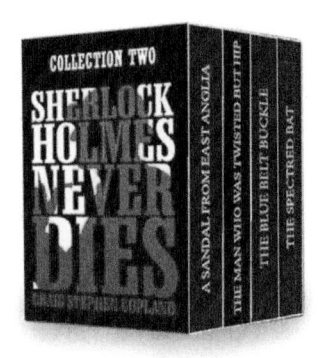

Collection Two
A Sandal from East Anglia
The Man Who Was Twisted
 But Hip
The Blue Belt Buckle
The Spectred Bat

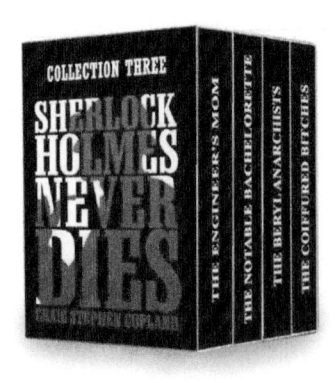

Collection Three
The Engineer's Mom
The Notable Bachelorette
The Beryl Anarchists
The Coiffured Bitches

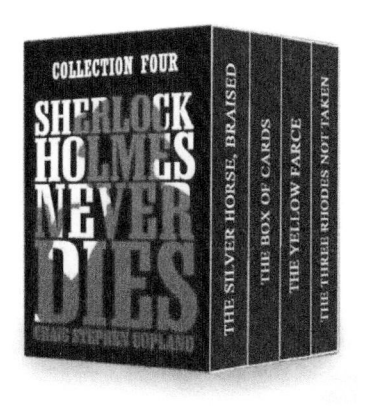

Collection Four
The Silver Horse, Braised
The Box of Cards
The Yellow Farce
The Three Rhodes Not Taken

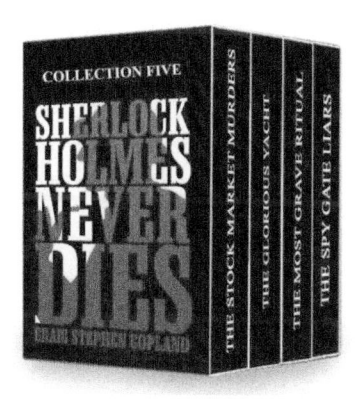

Collection Five
The Stock Market Murders
The Glorious Yacht
The Most Grave Ritual
The Spy Gate Liars

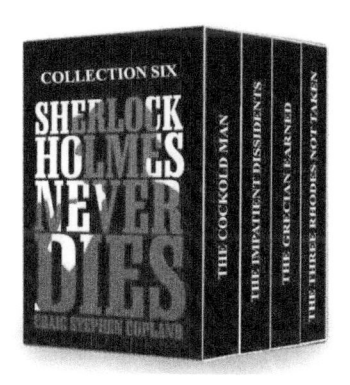

Collection Six
The Cuckold Man
The Impatient Dissidents
The Grecian, Earned
The Three Rhodes Not Taken

Printed in Great Britain
by Amazon